JOE LEDGER
UNSTOPPABLE

ALSO BY JONATHAN MABERRY

NOVELS

Ghost Road Blues

Dead Man's Song

Bad Moon Rising

Dead of Night

Fall of Night

Dark of Night (with Rachael Lavin)

Still of Night (with Rachael Lavin)

The Wolfman

Patient Zero

The Dragon Factory

The King of Plagues

Assassin's Code

Extinction Machine

Code Zero

Predator One

Kill Switch

Dogs of War

Mars One

The Nightsiders: The Orphan Army

The Nightsiders: Vault of Shadows

Ghostwalkers: A Deadlands Novel

Rot & Ruin

Dust & Decay

Flesh & Bone

Fire & Ash

Bits & Pieces

X-Files Origins: Devil's Advocate

NONFICTION BOOKS

Judo and You

Ultimate Jujutsu: Principles and Practices

Ultimate Sparring: Principles and Practices

The Vampire Slayers' Field Guide to the Undead (as Shane MacDougall)

Vampire Universe

The Cryptopedia (with David F. Kramer)

They Bite (with David F. Kramer)

Wanted Undead or Alive (with Janice Gable Bashman)

Zombie CSU: The Forensics of the Living Dead

The Joe Ledger Companion (with Dana Fredsti and Mari Adkins)

COLLECTIONS

Joe Ledger: Special Ops

Darkness on the Edge of Town

Strange Worlds

Tales from the Fire Zone

Hungry Tales

Whistling Past the Graveyard and Other Stories

The Wind Through the Fence and Other Stories

A Little Bronze Book of Cautionary Tales

JOE LEDGER
UNSTOPPABLE

Edited by **JONATHAN MABERRY**
and **BRYAN THOMAS SCHMIDT**

ST. MARTIN'S GRIFFIN
NEW YORK

JOE LEDGER: UNSTOPPABLE. Copyright © 2017 by Jonathan Maberry and Bryan Thomas Schmidt. Foreword copyright © 2017 by Tony Eldridge. All rights reserved. Printed in the United States of America. For information, address St. Martin's Press, 175 Fifth Avenue, New York, N.Y. 10010.

Each contribution copyright belongs to Jonathan Maberry and its respective contribution authors.

www.stmartins.com

The Library of Congress Cataloging-in-Publication Data is available upon request.

ISBN 978-1-250-09080-5 (trade paperback)
ISBN 978-1-250-09081-2 (ebook)

Our books may be purchased in bulk for promotional, educational, or business use. Please contact your local bookseller or the Macmillan Corporate and Premium Sales Department at 1-800-221-7945, extension 5442, or by email at MacmillanSpecialMarkets@macmillan.com.

First Edition: October 2017

10 9 8 7 6 5 4 3 2 1

CONTENTS

ACKNOWLEDGMENTS

The Joe Ledger series has always benefitted from input, advice, information, and suggestions by a host of "friends in the industry." Each volume in the novel series includes special thanks to experts in various fields of science, medicine, technology, the military, law enforcement, and politics. Thanks to all of them (check the novels for names and impressive credentials!) and to other allies, including my coeditor for this project, Bryan Thomas Schmidt; Dana Fredsti; Ray Porter; Robert Allen and his team at Macmillan Audio; my editor (and Joe's favorite uncle), Michael Homler; my film agents, Jon Cassir of CAA and Dana Spector of Paradigm; and the unstoppable force that is my literary agent, Sara Crowe of Pippin Properties. Hooah!

Bryan thanks Jonathan Maberry for letting him play along as not just an editor but an author and for always having his back; the authors for writing great stories and agreeing to be part of it; G. P. Charles for cowriting and sharing dog knowledge; Louie and Amelie for being their silly, charming canine selves; Sara Crowe for setting it up; Michael Homler, Lauren Jablonski, Kevin Sweeney, and Sona, the politest copy editor I ever encountered, and all at St. Martin's for making it look good, and all my fellow fans because this is for you!

FOREWORD

As a movie producer I see a lot of material. I'm sent novels, screen-plays, short stories, comic books, graphic novels, fiction, and nonfic-tion; I speak at writers' conferences all over the country and feel blessed that I'm able to call many bestselling authors my friends.

I love writers and truly admire the courage and discipline it takes to face the blank page day after day and pour one's soul into the abyss, never knowing if those words will see the light of day, let alone find their way to a bookshelf at Barnes & Noble. It's a step-by-step process with its own structural rules. Not unlike the movie business.

Every stage of making a movie is like successfully doing a Rubik's Cube. The development, production, and marketing depend on lining up all the sides in the right colors. It took me eight years to get *The Equalizer* movie made. There were many false starts, big-name actors came and went, as did the directors, screenwriters, studios, and finan-ciers. So close, so many times, but five sides just won't do, because you need all six to make it work. It may look simple, but it takes a special mix of elements to make a movie work.

With *The Equalizer*, it all started with a great character. At one time or another, everybody has wished they had a Robert McCall to help them when no one else would. "Got a problem? Odds against you? Call the Equalizer." The television show ran for five years and resonated with the audience to the extent that many times Edward Woodward the actor was approached by strangers on the street begging for his help. That's why I knew the movie would work. I knew that character would appeal to an actor, but it took years to find the right mix of story and director to fall into place.

I met Jonathan Maberry at a writers' conference in New Orleans. He gave me several of his books and went over the characters and plot points of each. When he told me about the Joe Ledger series I got really excited and could see many of the elements were already there. He gave me a few books and I promised I'd get to them as soon as I was back in L.A. I lied, I actually started reading one on the plane, and by the time I landed at LAX, I was hooked.

I am gleefully grateful to have the chance to bring Joe Ledger to the screen.

He's no martini-sippin' James Bond looking for the baccarat table, and he's no rooftop-jumping Jason Bourne looking to find himself. And if you live your entire life never having run into him, consider yourself very lucky, because if you're in Joe Ledger's path, chances are you're already in deep mind-bending shit of epic proportion.

Drop John McClane from *Die Hard* into an episode of *Fringe* and you've entered the world of Joe Ledger. Ex–Baltimore cop, the enforcer, investigator, facilitator, agitator, expediter, fix-it man, and cleanup guy for the shadowy Department of Military Sciences (DMS) as they defend America from all enemies—foreign, domestic, other-worldly, and unimaginable. Bring on the zombies, aliens, UFOs, cyborgs, robots, replicants, mutants, megalomaniacs wielding weapons of mass destruction, and all manner of evildoers hell-bent on attacking not just America but sometimes the whole human race—Joe Ledger's ready. He's the tip of the spear—Thor's hammer. DMS may be the brains, but Joe is the muscle. Unlike Bourne, Joe knows exactly who he is.

Well, that's not quite true, he knows he's really three people in one body.

Three personalities in constant warfare for control of his mind, heart, and body: the tough ex-Cop, the Civilized Man, and the Warrior. Effective? Oh yeah. Loyal? To a fault. Dangerous? Like cooking nitroglycerin in your kitchen. In other words, the perfect man for the job. Fox Mulder tells us the truth is out there. Joe Ledger knows the truth and it's not out there, it's right here, right now. And it's scary as hell.

I think we all get the feeling there is way more going on in the world than the things we read about in the news. When Edward Snowden lifted the corner of the rug and government secrets skittered out like cockroaches, I doubt many of us were all that surprised. Lift that rug a little more and the world of Joe Ledger is suddenly not only plausible but inevitable. Fiction rooted in reality.

I eagerly await these new Joe Ledger tales as they transport me deeper and deeper into that amazing world of "what if" and . . .

—TONY ELDRIDGE
Producer of *The Equalizer*

INTRODUCTION:
THE WORLD OF JOE LEDGER

Joe Ledger was born in a diner.

That seems somehow very appropriate.

I was sitting at the Red Lion Diner north of Philadelphia having an omelet and (I think) my twentieth cup of coffee while going over notes for a nonfiction book I was writing, *Zombie CSU: The Forensics of the Living Dead*. That book asked the question "What would happen if *Night of the Living Dead* were real?" How would people in various fields—science, medicine, law enforcement, the military, the clergy, the press, etc.—react, research, and respond? While I was editing, a couple of people started talking in my head.

Understand, if you're not a writer, then this is a serious cry for help. You put your shrink on danger pay and get lots of help.

If, however, you *are* a writer, this is another day on the job. You see, for guys like me, there are always conversations going on. There are scenes playing out. It's like standing in the TV showroom at Best Buy when every screen is playing a different channel. That's what a writer's head is like pretty much all the time. The imagination is a multitrack mixing board and sometimes you don't know what random elements are suddenly going to coalesce into a scene, a character, or a story.

Inexperienced writers often try to shut out those voices.

Writers who understand the somewhat eccentric nature of the craft listen for a bit, eavesdropping on the conversation. If it's just background noise—what I often consider "airport waiting room chatter"—then you close it out and go back to work on whatever has a deadline catching fire. If, on the other hand, it has the flavor of importance, then you absolutely must stop and listen closely.

The conversation going on in my head that day was like that. My gut told me that I needed to lean in and pay attention.

I had no idea who these two people were. Not until I started paying attention. It became apparent, though, that it was a cop being interviewed for a job with a covert Special Ops group.

The cop was a smart-ass.

The guy interviewing him was smarter, older, and a little scary.

They were talking about saving the world.

So, I took control of the conversation, as a practiced writer will, and I wrote down everything I could remember of what they said, and then I roughed out the rest of that chat. And I wrote a short follow-up scene, quick and dirty, where the cop is put in a room with a terrorist he killed during a joint police/Homeland raid. The dead guy attacks him.

And that's when I backed up and wrote something that I realized was the opening chapter of a new novel. What I wrote was:

> When you have to kill the same terrorist twice in one week, then there's either something wrong with your skills or something wrong with your world.
> And there's nothing wrong with my skills.

That was Joe Ledger. It was his voice. It was his world. And he'd reached out from some weird place in my writer brain and told me—told, not asked—to write his story.

Details like an actual plot, the names of the characters, the structure of the novel, all came later, but they came very fast. I told my agent, Sara Crowe, about this and she was very excited and told me that it was something she was certain she could sell. Mind you, we had no completed manuscript at the time. She asked for an outline and fifty pages. I slammed that out because I found that once I started writing the book that became known as *Patient Zero*, I could not wait to get back to it every day. It was the most fun I've ever had as a writer.

She sold it very quickly to St. Martin's Griffin and Michael Homler became my editor. He has since become a very good and trusted friend, and together we have worked our way through nine Ledger novels, of which *Dogs of War* is the most recent. By the time *Joe Ledger: Unstoppable* hits stores I will almost certainly have delivered a tenth Ledger novel. I've written a couple of dozen short stories about Ledger, and he's managed to show up in several of my other series, including my teen postapocalyptic zombie series, *Rot & Ruin*; my vampire apocalypse novels and comics for adults, *V-Wars*; short stories involving characters from my *Ghost Road Blues* trilogy; and more. He is ubiquitous in that he is a very difficult person to kill.

Who is he?

Joe is a former Baltimore cop who becomes a senior field agent for the shadowy Department of Military Sciences, run by the enigmatic Mr. Church. Joe leads Echo Team against terrorists who use cutting-edge science weapons to threaten America and the world. Joe is a good guy, but he is not a particularly nice guy. He doesn't play party politics and tends to err on the side of humanism rather than any political agenda.

Joe is, psychologically speaking, a box of hamsters. But his best friend, psychiatrist and trauma specialist Dr. Rudy Sanchez, helps him manage his personal demons.

One thing I've found particularly weird while writing the Ledger stories is that he's funny. He is, in fact, funnier than I am, and I write his dialogue. No, I don't understand that, either, and maybe it's best if we don't take too close a look at it.

Joe has appeared in novels, short stories, graphic novels, and audiobooks and is on his way to feature films. I have no plans to ever stop writing stories about him. I am as excited to write any new Ledger tale as I was the first time.

But I like to share. I was the kid in the playground who liked to let other kids play with my toys as long as we could all have some fun.

Which brings me to *Joe Ledger: Unstoppable.*

When Bryan Thomas Schmidt approached me with the crazy idea of doing an anthology of Ledger stories, I absolutely jumped at it. You see, I love the tradition of shared world stories, and of sharing story elements. I was introduced to the concept through the story cycles of two of my favorite writers from when I was a kid, H. P. Lovecraft and Michael Moorcock.

Lovecraft created his own version of the genre of "cosmic horror" and invited his friends to take elements of it and write their own stories. Since then, thousands of people have jumped aboard the Lovecraft express to write tales of what are variously called "Lovecraftian" or "Cthulhu Mythos" tales, and they include August Derleth, Stephen King, Robert E. Howard, Robert Bloch, and . . . well . . . just the list of names could fill an entire volume! Michael Moorcock invited writers to tell stories of his bizarre Jerry Cornelius, a secret agent, assassin, and adventurer, and writers such as Norman Spinrad, Mœbius, Brian Aldiss, and others took up the challenge.

And so Bryan and I built a wish list of writers we thought would enjoy visiting Joe Ledger's world. A few of the stories are crossovers, in which Joe's world collides with those of other writers who have their own ongoing series. Some stories are set completely in my world, but bring unique perspectives and insights. All of the stories are absolute killers. I couldn't be more pleased.

So, if you're a longtime Joe Ledger fan, you'll no doubt find these stories very satisfying. If you're new to this world and, perhaps, followed one of your favorite writers into new territory, then welcome! In either case, buckle up, because this is going to be a bumpy ride through very dangerous country.

Hooah!

—JONATHAN MABERRY

JOE LEDGER
UNSTOPPABLE

THE HONEY POT

BY STEVE ALTEN

Shadows of movement swam through liquid daylight. Echoes whispered hollow in my brain.

"Where's the car, Cowboy?"

Female . . . European accent. Hot breath in my ear. The stench of expensive vodka and tobacco.

"Come on, big guy. Don't go limp on me now . . . *on me now . . . me now . . .*"

Ceiling spinning, my brain on fire—

Let me die!

Morning greeted me with the abruptness of a sledgehammer. My left temple was pressed flat against a warm ledge of porcelain, its pulse pounding. Pain fought with confusion for my attention—the combatants conceding the contest to my gut.

Straddling the tub—*why was I straddling the tub? why was I naked, straddling the tub?*—I leaned over the toilet and retched. Hot magma christened a bowl dubbed guest-ready by the chambermaid's version of police tape, the damp remains now wrapped around my right wrist.

The minute of hell passed. Having evacuated a lung, I fumbled with my trembling left hand for the flusher, while my right fought to keep my aching skull balanced on the seat.

Throat . . . water—

Squinting, I located the sink and crawled on hands and knees across a thick throw rug. Lunging for the nearest ledge, I pulled myself up off the bathroom floor and fumbled with the faucet, scooping water onto my face and down my seared throat.

A pale, haggard stranger stared at me in the mirror, only I didn't recognize the reflection.

Sledgehammer . . . ledge . . . Ledger. Joe Ledger.

Hey, Cowboy. Go fuck yourself and the horse that kicked you.

Standing on wobbly legs, I popped open the small bottle of hotel mouthwash and gargled—not entirely sure it wasn't shampoo. *Where am I? What the hell happened to me?*

Leaning against the open door frame, I peered out at a hotel suite designed to accommodate a paycheck way beyond my means. High ceilings . . . giant flat-screen television, plush carpet. Through sheer curtains I stared out the private balcony at . . . the Eiffel Tower?

Paris? What the fuck am I doing in Paris?

As I staggered past the king-size trundle bed in my birthday suit, I saw the woman. She was lying on her belly beneath a cream-colored duvet—a mocha-skinned beauty with wavy, raven-colored hair.

I was about to wake her when the thought of being naked in a hotel suite with an exotic woman weighed in. Searching the room, I located a pair of men's boxers, jeans, and a sweater, slightly surprised that everything fit.

"Hey, Sleeping Beauty. Excuse me?"

I shook her and knew, but felt for a pulse anyway. "Shit."

I pulled back the quilt.

She was model-thin, ravishing, and stark naked, save for the silk ties that bound her wrists and ankles to the four bedposts. Her legs were spread-eagle . . . a stream of blood running from the bullet hole in her left scapula where it pooled in the small of her back before seeping down the crack of her perfect derriere.

Before I could render a thought the door opened, revealing the chambermaid. *"Excusez-moi, monsieur—"*

Her hazel eyes darted from me to the dead woman.

The first scream caught in her throat. She managed the second as she fled down the hall, leaving the housekeeping cart wedged in the doorframe.

I dragged it inside and bolted the door.

STEVE ALTEN

You've got three minutes before she reaches the lobby, three more before security questions her, six to ten before the gendarmes arrive.

I searched the room and found the dead woman's clothing . . . a skirt and blouse, silk purple thong and matching bra, along with spiked heels. If she was a hooker, she was an expensive one. Designer purse . . . a valet ticket . . . a wallet!

French driver's license . . . Giselle Rousseau. A wad of euros—

Where was my wallet and passport?

I searched my pockets, locating the stub from an airline ticket dated two days earlier—Dulles into Heathrow. I looked around the room, then under the bed—my head pounding as I found a pair of tennis shoes . . . and a gun. It was a 9mm, a silencer still attached to the barrel.

What to do?

If you offed her, or even if you didn't, you can bet that sweet ass of hers the gun will have your prints on it.

I grabbed the shoes and the weapon. Quickly laced up the sneakers and then checked the gun. No bullets in the chamber . . . one missing from the magazine.

The sound of police sirens rent the late morning air.

Move, douche bag!

I grabbed the woman's ID, cash, and valet ticket and shoved everything in my pants pocket. Using a damp washcloth, I wiped the 9mm free of prints and buried it in the container of soiled towels on the housekeeping cart. Then I opened the door and pushed the device down the hall to the next room . . . Suite 1107, and left it.

Moving on adrenaline and instinct, I headed for the stairwell and descended six flights before exiting on the fifth floor. Smiling, I joined a young couple waiting for the elevator.

"*Bonjour.*"

"*Bonjour.*"

Together we watched the numbers descend from eight to five, my right hand nonchalantly wiping sweat from my brow.

The doors opened, revealing the prototypical American family straight out of a Hollywood script—white-collar dad, homemaker mom, two boys, maybe thirteen and ten, and toddler Jane tucked in a pink stroller.

White-collar dad was wearing a New York Yankees baseball cap.

"Mom, you said we were going to Disney!"

"Disney's tomorrow. Today we're going to tour Paris."

"I don't wanna tour Paris!"

"Paris sucks."

"Easy, guys." Dad shrugged at the French couple.

"My nephews are the same way," I said, squeezing in beside the stroller. "Dan Miller, Brooklyn."

"Herschel Evans, Chesapeake Beach, Maryland. My wife, Suzie."

"Hi."

"Big Yankees fan?"

"Yeah."

"Me too. This is awkward, but would you consider selling me your hat? My one nephew, Gaston, is a huge fan. It's his birthday today and dumb ol' Uncle Dan forgot to buy him a present."

Forty seconds later the elevator released us into the lobby of the prestigious St. James Hotel, the Yankees hat snug on my head, the cap kept low as I made my way across the marble floor with my new best friend.

". . . we were able to get down on the field. I got a selfie with Derek Jeter, want to see it?"

"Absolutely." The peripheral vision in my pounding left eye caught the distraught chambermaid speaking rapidly to hotel security.

We headed outside, the Evans family heading for a colorful lime-green-and-canary-yellow double-decker bus while I waved for the valet, handing him the dead woman's ticket.

"Merci. Une minute, monsieur."

The wail of sirens grew louder, the distraction making it impossible to think. I searched through the wad of euros. Pulled out two tens . . .

Three police cars raced around the private cul-de-sac and screeched to a halt in front of the hotel entrance. The gendarmes dashed inside as the valet pulled up in a candy-apple-red Lamborghini Murciélago.

Great. Why not the Goodyear Blimp. . . .

Every eye turned in my direction as the driver's-side door flipped up. I tipped the valet and slid inside the bucket seat, wondering if I could handle the Italian sports car without looking as if I just got my license. Pulling the winglike door closed, I scanned the cockpit, then put her into gear and flew around the circular exit, hitting the av. Victor-Hugo doing eighty.

The Arc de Triomphe loomed ahead, the monument encircled by a perpetual onslaught of merging traffic. I did three laps on the roundabout before I managed to cut off a bus and exit down the av. de la Grande Armée.

Where was I going? Who could I trust? I was tempted to locate a phone and call Church. But there were questions I needed answered before I was ready to engage the Department of Military Sciences.

Why was I in Paris?

Who was the girl?

Had we been together? If yes . . . was it consensual?

My right hand trembled. I was certainly a man capable of violence, and God knew I had a temper, but rape? No . . . never, not in a million years or a million lifetimes. My high school sweetheart, Helen, had been raped; her suicide was the gasoline that fueled my anger.

No, I couldn't have raped her, but I did wake up in a crime scene.

How did I get there?

Did I shoot the girl?

Would they find my semen in her?

I needed to think!

Grinding the gears, I turned down another major artery, pulled onto a side street, and squeezed the Lamborghini into an alley.

Identify the pieces of the puzzle. You have an airline ticket stub indicating you flew from D.C. into London two days ago. Did the girl pick you up?

My eyes danced across the Lamborghini's cockpit to the GPS. *Check the history.*

After snatching the device off its base, I tracked backward through the programmed stops.

Paris . . . before that London. Shards of memory pierced the brain fog. I remembered landing in Heathrow, exiting baggage claim to find the gorgeous French swimsuit model leaning against her red sports car—a classic honey pot. And now I was covered in it.

It took me nearly an hour to piece together a backstory. . . .

At the age of seventeen, Giselle Rousseau had parlayed a stymied career as a swimsuit model into an all-pass ticket to the inner sanctum of the rich and famous. Sex and drugs, yachts and mansions—the seductive teen was passed around like a joint at a biker rally. By the time she was twenty-seven she had traded in sex and paid companionship from A-list actors and members of their entourage for access into the billionaire boys club—Saudi sheiks who paid lavishly to get their freak on. In the bedroom they preferred young boys; in public—exotic women—eye candy to protect their criminal fetish. Giselle was repulsed by her new Middle Eastern employers, but as long as the mortgage on her condo in the Mediterranean was paid for, she could live with that.

Giselle had met Abdul Hamid bin Rashidi eight months ago at a party in Cannes. The Saudi oil baron had made his billions playing both sides of the Middle East equation, buying Syrian oil at a substantial discount from ISIS, reselling it at submarket prices to oil companies in Turkey and the United States. At one point, he was even selling Assad back his own oil.

As long as everyone was making money, no one seemed to care.

Of course, ISIS was making the biggest share, using the profits to fund their regime. Bin Rashidi knew the men whose faces were cloaked in black scarves; the leaders of Islamic State were all former members of Saddam's Ba'athist army. Back in 2003, Paul Bremer had fired these four hundred thousand trained soldiers from their jobs while signing a decree that prevented the men from being involved in their nation's future.

Four hundred thousand men who could have kept the peace. . . .

Four hundred thousand trained soldiers with access to large caches of weapons.

No potential for chaos there.

With Iraq bogged down in a Sunni-Shiite conflict and Syria's president Assad waging war on his own people, the Ba'athist commandos saw ISIS as the perfect vehicle from which they could retake Iraq and rule the region. As trained soldiers they had no difficulty overrunning Syria's military bases and taking the country's supply of Russian-made tanks and weapons. Within weeks they controlled Assad's oil wells and refineries and were paying workers higher salaries to run things for ISIL. Having organized smuggling networks under Saddam back in the 1990s to avoid UN sanctions, the Ba'athists knew exactly whom to approach to broker the Syrian crude, raking in hundreds of millions of dollars to support their terrorist regime.

Rather than operate in the shadows, bin Rashidi preferred to flaunt his wealth, his stunning Nubian beauty, Giselle, making up for his lack of social graces. By hiding out in the open while extolling Western values, he attracted like-minded Americans and Europeans, creating

STEVE ALTEN

an ISIL/ISIS pipeline from Syria, profiting on everything from stolen museum artifacts to human slaves.

Giselle was living the good life, and with her Arabian sugar daddy preferring young boys in the bedroom, she had more time to feed her own habit—heroin. When bin Rashidi began using her as a mule on his private jets, she had ample opportunity to siphon off some of the product for her own personal use and sale.

She was caught with two ounces entering New York City, a problem that cost bin Rashidi a nine-thousand-year-old Babylonian statue to resolve behind closed doors. When she was caught in her hotel room in Los Angeles with twice that amount, the district attorney wanted cash.

Bin Rashidi warned Giselle that a third arrest would end their relationship. Knowing the Arab would not allow her to become a loose end, she entered a methadone clinic. She stayed clean for six weeks until she attended a Hollywood Oscar party and was arrested at Heathrow Airport.

What Giselle never knew was that the FBI and MI6's antiterrorist division had targeted bin Rashidi and wanted to use the girl to penetrate his organization. They had heard rumors about a major deal set to take place at Le Baron, a private nightclub and discotheque in Paris. The nature of the meeting was unknown, but the involvement of the Russian mafia concerned authorities, who feared it was only a matter of time before Islamic State acquired enough uranium to fashion a nuclear suitcase bomb.

The authorities would drop the drug charges and wipe her slate clean if Giselle wore a wire. She agreed, but only if she had backup. The agent could not be from either British or American intelligence, the girl convinced both sides had been compromised long ago. The FBI and MI6 each submitted facial shots of three members of black ops antiterrorist organizations that serviced North America.

Guess who she selected.

The event had been held last night. Giselle was dead, the French police and, no doubt, MI6 were after me, and I couldn't remember a goddamn thing.

The Lamborghini and its GPS continued to provide clues. After picking me up at Heathrow and entering France via the Chunnel, Giselle had driven us to the town of Annecy, located in the Rhône-Alpes.

The car was not hers; it was registered to an American named Robert Gibbons.

So now I had a name, an address, a full tank of gas, five hundred euros, and a hangover that made me the odds-on favorite to win a pickup game of Russian roulette. Powering up the Lamborghini, I set the GPS and made my way toward the entrance of the A6 highway.

I was two hours into a five-hour journey when nature called. Feeling famished, I turned off the next exit for gas, food, and a bathroom break.

That's when I noticed the fuel gauge was still on full.

Cheap $300,000 sports car . . . the damn float valve must be broken. That's all I need is to run out of gas in a stolen car in the middle of nowhere.

After pulling into an ELF: Les Prix Bas petrol station, I popped the lever to open the tank lid, rolled down the window, and handed the attendant fifty euros. *"Le plein, s'il vous plaît."*

From the side-view mirror, I watched him shove the nozzle in and start the pump. Within seconds gasoline began pouring over the side.

"Le reservoir est plein, l'idiot!" He tossed my money back at me and left to service another customer.

How could I have driven almost two hundred miles without using any gas? Could the engine be a hybrid?

Beyond curious, I parked the car away from nosy civilians and popped the hood.

The device was the size of a hockey puck. It was mounted directly beneath the Lamborghini hood emblem, which had been fashioned with air vents.

I reached for the object, expecting it to be red-hot, yet it was quite cool. It was also vibrating, its internal workings spinning at an incredible velocity.

Leaving the sports car running, I walked to the back of the vehicle and bent down to examine the dual exhausts. No heat . . . and no carbon dioxide!

What the hell had I gotten myself involved in?

With my bladder ready to burst, I shut off the car and headed inside the facility to use the bathroom, grab some food, and call in to one of my guys at DMS. I'd try Rudy first, then Bunny . . . anyone who could report my field status to Church without divulging my whereabouts.

The female former Navy SEAL answered on the third ring. "This is the international operator. I have a collect call from a Mr. Cowboy, will you accept the charges?"

"Yes! Where are you? What's your status?"

"Mobile. Safe at the moment."

"We don't have much time, all our phones are tapped."

My heart raced. "Lydia, I didn't kill her."

"I know that. But they have video of you two leaving the nightclub together before it blew up."

"What?"

"Seventeen dead, including bin Rashidi . . . twenty seconds. Cowboy?"

I hung up the phone as a second police car parked behind the Lamborghini.

I grabbed a container of orange juice from the refrigerator and a pack of cigarettes and handed them to the cashier. *"Avez-vous matches?"*

She handed me a book of matches.

I lit the cancer stick, tossed her ten euros, and exited.

The gendarmes were running the Lamborghini's license plate. Heading straight for the pumps, I casually dropped the lit cigarette onto the pool of gasoline that had spilled out of my tank. Circling behind a truck, I waited.

Seeing the flames, the attendant chased off two cars and ran toward the police.

The first explosion sent the gasoline pump rocketing into the petrol station's roof.

By the time the second pump ignited, I was back inside the car, accelerating onto the A6.

I took the next exit into someplace called Macon and diverted to the A40, heading east toward Annecy. In the distance were picturesque snow-covered Alps, the Geneva border less than fifty miles away.

It was risky hanging onto the Lamborghini, but driving at speeds in excess of 140 miles an hour quickly put a critical distance between myself and the cops, adding far too many route options to organize a roadblock.

It was dusk by the time I arrived at my destination.

The city known as "Little Venice" was built on the northern tip of Lake Annecy. Its streets were picturesque freshwater canals, their presence creating islands that harbored Swiss-style row homes, bed-and-breakfasts, inns, hotels, and shops, all of which serviced a healthy tourist trade.

The address on the GPS turned out to be the Hôtel du Château Annecy—a quaint two-story stone bed-and-breakfast located a block from Annecy Castle.

I took a circuitous route, searching for a place to leave the car. Locating a self-park parking lot, I drove up to the third floor and backed into a narrow space on a crowded row.

Not much of a hiding place for something so valuable. . . .

A minute later, I found myself descending the concrete steps of an empty stairwell. After exiting to the street, I had to cross two pedestrian bridges to get back to the B&B.

Exhausted and hungry, I entered the lobby, registering a strange sensation of déjà vu.

The first floor held an open dining room. The scent of food caused my stomach to growl as I approached the front desk, the diners serenaded by a pianist playing Sinatra on the baby grand.

The owner was gray-haired and in her sixties. She welcomed me like an old friend. "Ah, Monsieur Ledger, we've been expecting you."

"Have you now?"

"We have you staying tonight in your usual room." She handed me the key to Room 4. "Your charges were taken care of this afternoon."

"And which one of my many friends should I thank?"

"I would assume it was your sponsor, Monsieur Clemenza. Your invitation to tonight's big event arrived by messenger. I placed it in your room, along with your luggage."

I stole a quick glance at her nametag. "How thoughtful, Maria."

I headed for the staircase, wondering if I was living a double life.

Room 4 was at the end of an L-shaped hall, the floorboards creaking beneath my weight. Wishing I had kept the 9mm, I pressed my ear to the door and knocked.

Nothing.

I keyed in and entered, greeted by sunshine-orange wallpaper and a queen-size bed with heart-shaped throw pillows decorating a worn

STEVE ALTEN

white bedspread. Wicker chairs, a small wood desk . . . and an envelope leaning against the single-bulb lamp.

The bathroom looked as if it had last been grouted back in World War II.

It wasn't the St. James, but there wasn't a dead girl in the bed, either.

The musk of age greeted me as I pried open the closet door from its warped frame. Hanging from a horizontal pole was a suit bag. I laid it on the bed, then examined the envelope.

It was an engraved invitation, raised white letters on shiny black paper:

> Captain Joseph Ledger:
> Your presence is requested at 9:00 PM at the Castle Annecy.

I unzipped the suit bag. Inside was a black tux, white shirt, belt, shoes, socks, bowtie . . . even a new pair of briefs.

Apparently the honey pot was formal.

I glanced at the alarm clock on the night table: 8:12. "Not much time. I need to shower and shave—"

What the hell was I saying? I needed to think!

From the moment I awoke to worship the porcelain gods, I had been running on a proverbial treadmill, always behind two steps, forced into reaction mode without knowing the rules of the game.

If I had traveled from the United States, then surely I had brought luggage . . . a standard-issue DMS carry-on, the aluminum casing configured to disguise concealed weapons compartments from airport security.

I had a vague recollection of stowing the suitcase in the Lamborghini behind the driver's seat . . . but it wasn't there this morning. And it wasn't in the room.

"The woman downstairs insists I was here. Where would I have hidden my gun?"

I searched every drawer, under and inside the mattress, checked for loose floorboards—

Wait! Who did the woman say had paid for my room?

"Mr. Clemenza."

Clemenza was a character in *The Godfather*, one of my favorite movies. As a prelude to one of the film's major scenes, the fat capo Clemenza had hidden a gun in the men's room of a restaurant where Michael Corleone could later find it and kill the bad guys who were after his father.

I entered the bathroom. Lifted up the lid that covered the tank—

The gun was sealed in a freezer storage bag, held in place at the bottom of the tank by a brick so that it wouldn't interfere with the flush valve.

"Thank you, Mario Puzo."

An hour later I exited the hotel, dressed in a tux that couldn't have fit better if it was custom-made. Looming before me was Annecy Castle, the streets bumper-to-bumper with limousines.

Annecy Castle dates back to the eighth century, when the fortress was erected to guard the roadway linking Geneva to Italy. The structure had been destroyed by fire in 1340 and had been rebuilt several times, eventually becoming the medieval residence of the Dukes of Genevois-Nemours. War surrendered the castle to French garrisons and eventually to the governor of Annecy. The city took charge of the property in 1953, converting it into a museum, observatory, and rental for private galas.

I followed guests along a red carpet to a grand entrance guarded by MPs carrying M16s. Invitations were collected and exchanged for nametags. Female servers dressed in alluring red satin see-through negligees circulated with silver trays of hors d'oeuvres and champagne.

Famished, I filled a plate and ate as I took in the guests, startled to recognize many of their faces.

There were foreign diplomats and heads of state . . . a former CIA director, at least four retired congressmen, three senators, and two members of the Joint Chiefs who were now heavily involved in the military-industrial complex. There were CEOs galore, representing major banks and tech companies, oil oligarchs, and Saudi princes . . . and there was a colonel. White-haired and in his seventies, the scary-looking bastard was staring at me from across the room.

I took three strides in his direction and was intercepted by an American in his sixties, his head cleanly shaven, his gray goatee specked with crumbs.

"What the hell are you doing here?"

I glanced at his nametag: R. Gibbons. "I came to find you."

"Bastard. How much?"

"How much what?"

"Giselle and I trusted you and you sold me out . . . you sold out the planet!"

I grabbed him by the arm and led him down an empty corridor that harbored the restrooms. "Listen, pal, I can't remember anything that happened last night. I woke up in the St. James Hotel in my birthday suit, sporting a typhoon of a headache."

"You can't remember anything?"

"Bits and pieces, but nothing from last night or from two days ago when apparently I was here and we met."

He reached into his pocket and pulled out a set of keys with a small light attached. Aiming it at my left eye, he turned it on and off, checking my pupil's response. "Fucking bastard; he used it on you."

"Who used what on me?"

"Colonel Alexander . . . *Dr. Death.* I told you they possess electronic warfare systems, psychotronic devices that can cause you to submit to any command. You didn't believe me."

"Who is *they*, and what is this all about?"

"*They* is PI-40, formerly SECOR, formerly MAJESTIC-12. I'm a physicist, Dr. Robert Gibbons. Two months ago I completed a zero-point energy prototype."

"Let me guess . . . it's something that can power a car without gasoline."

"Not just a car, Captain. We're talking about a technology that essentially replaces jet engines, steamships, internal-combustion engines, gas, oil, public utilities, rockets, and paved roads—abundant, clean energy that never, ever runs out. In the aggregate, you're talking about replacing several hundred trillion dollars of world activity; by comparison the entire U.S. budget is a mere three to four trillion dollars."

"And you invented the device?"

"Yes and no. I invented the device, but we've had the technology since the mid-1950s. We could have wiped out poverty, hunger, disease, and prevented climate change, only a bunch of rich oil oligarchs, bankers, and warmongers refused to allow us to implement the technology. Giselle provided one of the prototypes to the Jordanian energy minister, Mr. bin Rashidi—"

"Whoa, hold on. I thought bin Rashidi was a Saudi? He was buying Syrian oil from ISIS and selling it to the West."

"That is what you were programmed to think. Giselle works for Mossad, the Israelis and Jordanians were working together to—"

He was cut off by a loud gong, the castle tower clock striking the hour, unleashing the first of nine bells.

Don't ask for whom the bell tolls . . . it tolls for humanity.

A set of massive ancient doors opened, releasing the tide of guests into the courtyard.

"We have to go!" Before I could stop him he darted back to the main room and was swallowed by the crowd.

Pushing my way after him, I followed the throng outside.

The courtyard stage resembled something out of *A Midsummer Night's Dream*. Towering over a wooded clearing was a forty-five-foot-tall statue of an owl. As the ninth gong tolled, a dozen men cloaked in dark brown robes gathered around an unlit ten-foot-tall tepee configuration of sticks, branches, and logs.

For several minutes they pretended to struggle to ignite the bonfire while a voice addressed the crowd over a sound system, alternating every few lines in English, French, and German.

"The opening ceremony begins with the sacrifice of the human symbol known as 'Dull Care,' which represents the burdens and responsibilities of you, our world leaders. Help us to ignite the bonfire by praying to Moloch. Join us now, brothers and sisters!"

"Moloch . . . Moloch . . . Moloch . . . Moloch . . ."

The chanting grew louder as a human effigy was lowered from above.

I glanced over the shoulder of a woman standing in front of me as she Googled Moloch.

MOLOCH: A Canaanite deity worshipped through the sacrifice of children.

Sweet Jesus . . . I'm surrounded by a bunch of Satan worshippers. . . .

Wild applause broke out as an aura of light appeared around the pagan statue's head. With a metallic screech an electrical charge shot out of the giant owl's mouth and down an unseen wire to the gasoline-soaked pile of wood.

With a *whoosh* the pyre ignited, accompanied by the haunting sound of human cries blasting over the PA as the human effigy burned and the sick bastards cheered—

Only it wasn't an effigy . . . it was Robert Gibbons.

"Where's the car, Cowboy?"

Female . . . European accent. Hot breath in my ear. The stench of expensive vodka and tobacco.

"Come on, big guy. Don't go limp on me now . . . *on me now . . . me now . . .*"

The ceiling spun, my brain on fire as I attempted to keep the psychotronic wave of energy from dragging my soul out of my body.

Let me die!

"Shut that damn thing off; it's like an oven in here."

The wave disappeared, my soul easing back into my physicality.

I opened my eyes. I was bare-chested and drenched in sweat, seated on one of the wicker chairs in Room 4 of the bed-and-breakfast. I was neither bound nor gagged—my arms hanging limp by my side. Try as I might, I couldn't move or speak.

The device was situated in a metal attaché on the desk to my left, its disk-shaped antenna aimed at my eye. Even powered down, it was giving off tremendous amounts of heat, turning the bedroom into a sauna.

The white-haired colonel was seated behind me, attaching electrodes to my chest.

Giselle appeared on my right. Her red satin bra and matching thong were moist with sweat. "The colonel is attaching a lie detector. Your voice box should reengage any minute." She moved closer, licking the sweat off my neck. "You wanted me last night . . . I know you did . . . just like you want me now."

Her hand slid up my inner thigh, initiating a primal reflex that caused the tuxedo's pants to rise. "Funny how the first nerve endings to regain their impulses are the sex organs." After reaching into her purse, Giselle removed another 9mm Glock, this one with a silencer attached. She chambered a round and placed the gun on the desktop to my left.

Then she removed her thong and bra and straddled me.

"I'll make you a deal, Cowboy. Tell us where the car is . . . and I'll unzip your pants and fuck you silly before I put a bullet in your brain."

My erection had a will of its own, fighting to free itself while my arms hung limp by my sides. Giselle was intoxicating and I absorbed her with all of my senses, inhaling her pheromones, staring at her womanhood—the sight and scent and touch of the high-priced whore doubling my heart rate, quickening my recovery.

"Agreed," I said, clearing my throat, my mind racing to keep the conversation going, fighting to buy time. "First tell me . . . why? Why keep this energy system from the rest of the world?"

"Why? Because free, clean energy would completely even the global playing field. Big Oil would go belly-up, wiping out the banks. The stock market would collapse . . . there'd be chaos. And for what? So a bunch of Third World countries can have sewage plants? A society where everyone is rich doesn't work, Cowboy. Equality and peace undermine evolution; we are who we are because of the law of the jungle. If you make everyone a predator, society would stagnate."

The trigger finger of my right hand twitched. "Point taken. Who the hell wants peace when we can spend eternity fighting the War on Terror."

"War is profitable, which is why we encourage it."

"Enough!" the colonel barked. "Gibbons is dead; all we need is the car."

I felt pins and needles as sensation slowly returned to my body. "You're right about one thing, Giselle, I do want you. Send grandpa on his way and let's do this."

"First the car."

"Parking lot . . . two canals to the south. Third floor . . . near the east stairwell."

Giselle turned to the colonel. "Well?"

"He's telling the truth." Quickly and methodically, the white-haired sociopath detached the lie detector, then packed it in the metal attaché along with the psychotronic device. "Are you coming?"

"You go. The captain and I have unfinished business."

"You searched him for weapons?"

"The nine-millimeter was found in the laundry cart, along with a clip of blanks. But if it comforts you—" She ran her hands across my bare, sweaty chest, wiping them along the inside of both pant legs. "You may be right; he's definitely packing something."

The old man rolled his eyes and left.

Giselle kissed me on the lips, her flitting tongue tasting of booze and tobacco. "Let's make this interesting, shall we? I know you're stalling, attempting to regain control of your muscles before I kill you. So we'll have a contest—I won't shoot you until you come inside me." She reached between her legs, unzipping my pants. "First one to shoot . . . loses. How long do you think you can hold out, Cowboy?"

I moaned as she reached inside my open fly and beneath my boxer shorts, her left hand working to free me—

—as the fingers of my right hand walked down my right calf muscle to the elastic holster holding the gun strapped around my ankle.

"You ready, Cowboy?" She rose up to guide my traitorous genitals inside her—suddenly noticing the gun quivering in my right hand.

"Shit." She lunged for the 9mm as I blindly squeezed off three shots, the handgun barely a foot off the floor.

The first bullet struck the ceiling, blasting a six-inch divot in the ancient plaster.

The second whizzed past my head.

The third spun her around as it punched a hole in her right scapula.

She looked at me and laughed, the 9mm clutched in her right hand, her arm no longer able to lift it. "You shot first."

"Guess I lose."

She coughed up a wad of blood as we both struggled to raise our weapons, Giselle reaching around with her left hand as I rolled forward off the chair and onto the floor, gaining the critical leverage I needed to get off one quick shot—

It was high and wide, but she spun into its path, the lead missile splattering bone as it jerked her head backward, her shattered skull spitting out gray matter. The Glock flailed wildly in her lifeless left hand, its bullets tearing into the sunshine-orange wall behind the bed.

For several minutes I remained on my back, gathering strength. Finally I crawled to the bathroom on my hands and knees, the effort gradually reducing the molten-lead feeling in my bloodstream. Pulling myself using the sink, I ran the cold water and rinsed Giselle's taste from my mouth. When I was through I staggered to the toilet, lifted the lid off the tank, and flushed, draining the water so I could remove the brick, exposing the plastic freezer bag.

"Assholes . . . you can keep the damn car."

I dressed as quickly as my muscles would allow, making sure I wiped my prints from the revolver before leaving it behind—a lesson Clemenza had taught Michael Corleone on the eve of his battle.

For a long moment, I stared at the zero-point energy device—a precious seed that could alter humanity . . . if it could be nurtured and protected. Until then it was simply a honey pot, its enemies legion, its possession placing a target on my back.

Shoving it in my pants pocket, I gathered my belongings and left.

ABOUT THE AUTHOR

Steve Alten is a *New York Times* and international bestselling author of sixteen thrillers, including the *MEG* series, which was green-lit by Warner Bros. (March 2018 release) starring Jason Statham and Ruby Rose. He is also the founder and director of Adopt-an-Author, a free nationwide reading program for high school teachers. Steve can be reached through his website at www.stevealten.com.

CONFUSION

BY NICHOLAS STEVEN

BELOW PAR
TOP-SECRET RESEARCH FACILITY
CONRAD, MONTANA

"You sure we're in the right place?" Top asked, looking around.

Aside from the ruins of the partially constructed Perimeter Acquisition Radar (PAR) site in the middle of nowhere, Montana, there was nothing but barren fields for miles. Not exactly my first guess for a terrorist target, but at least I wouldn't have to worry about any collateral civilian casualties if things got messy.

The situation reminded me of our recent mission in Pennsylvania. "It's like déjà vu all over again."

"Then it's a good thing we're smarter than the average bear," Bunny said.

"You're mixing up your Yogi quotes there, Staff Sergeant."

"No way, those were both Yogi Bear quotes."

Top rolled his eyes. "You quoted Yogi Bear, Cap quoted *Yogi Berra*."

Bunny shrugged his massive shoulders in a *What's the difference?* gesture. "That just sounded like you said Yogi Bear with a *Super Mario* accent: 'It's a me, Yogi Bear-ah.'" When Top and I didn't humor him with a laugh, he said, "Seriously, there's a real person named Yogi Berra?"

I exercised a lot of self-restraint not to smack him upside his head. A lot. "I'm gonna pretend you didn't say that."

"What?"

"He's one of the greatest catchers in baseball history. How can you not have heard of him?"

"It's un-American is what it is," Top chimed in. I couldn't have agreed more.

"When'd he play?"

"From 1946 to '65."

"Dude's almost as ancient as Top—no wonder I never heard of him."

I chuckled at that. Being the oldest field operative in the Department of Military Sciences at forty-one, First Sergeant Bradley Sims was often the recipient of old-man taunts, just as Staff Sergeant Harvey Rabbit had to put up with little-kid jests and carrot jokes.

My momentary good mood soured when I saw who was waiting to greet us at the entrance to the top-secret underground government facility. The whole reason this felt like déjà vu was that just a few weeks ago we'd been called out to a suspected terrorist infiltration of an ultra-high-security biological research facility in the Poconos. Only this time we were at the supposedly abandoned PAR site. From a quick scan of the mission brief, I'd gathered that the Perimeter Acquisition Radar was intended to detect incoming ballistic missile warheads as they crossed the North Pole region, then the info would've been sent off to the Aerospace Defense Command. At only 10 percent complete, construction was halted because of the ratification of the SALT I Anti-Ballistic Missile Treaty in 1972. Either that, or they figured Santa's sleigh runs would set off too many false alarms.

Or perhaps the whole thing had just been a smoke screen for building the underground base that now apparently had a terrorist problem. And by "apparently" I mean "that's the lie we were fed to get us out here," because the reason the security guard smiling and waving at us like an idiot intensified the disquieting feeling of déjà vu cooling my blood was that he'd been there in Pennsylvania.

I had a very bad feeling about this.

Yeah, I came here to face an unknown force of terrorists and only now was I getting a bad feeling in my gut. That's because last time I saw Lars Halverson, we came up against something much worse than terrorists. Welcome to my world.

"Man, am I glad to see you guys," the security guard said.

"Hey, aren't you the head of security from the Vault?" Bunny asked.

Halverson grinned. "Guilty as charged. 'I do one thing at a time, I do it very well, and then I move on.'"

Bunny just stared at him blankly. Too damn young to get the quote. *M*A*S*H* should be required viewing for all military personnel, if you ask me.

Feeling irrationally old and irritable, I unzipped my windbreaker and whipped out my Heckler & Koch Mark 23 .45 ACP pistol from my shoulder rig and pointed it at Halverson's head. "Tell me we're not here to clean up more mutant cockroach soldiers."

Beads of sweat popped out on his forehead. "No, of course not. You destroyed all the research on those things."

He was holding something back, but I couldn't tell what. Nothing good, that's for sure. "Then what do we have?"

"Better if I just show you."

I stared him down for a moment, but after a nervous glance at my weapon, he turned and stepped into an open elevator. The metal elevator car looked oddly out of place among the graffiti-covered concrete skeleton of the unfinished PAR site, but I had no doubt its existence would somehow be concealed the moment we dropped belowground. I holstered my gun, then followed him, Top and Bunny joining us without a word.

As we descended, I opened the equipment bag I had slung over my shoulder and indicated for Top and Bunny to do the same. "Might as well get our helmets on now," I said. "I have a feeling we'll need our night vision before long."

Halverson shook his head confidently. "Don't bother, Captain Ledger. After what happened at the Vault, one of my first priorities here was beefing up the security on the power grid. *Nothing* will be able to get to it, I guarantee it. And we've got video cameras everywhere, so you won't need your helmet-mounted ones."

I refrained from saying what I felt his guarantee was worth. Not because I cared about hurting his feelings, but because I was distracted by his choice of words. He'd said "nothing" rather than "no one" and I didn't like that slipup one bit.

Nope, not one bit.

"What's this place used for?" I asked.

Even with the hard edge my voice had taken on, I expected Halverson to repeat his claim that it'd be better if he just showed us, so I was surprised when he answered right away. "The egghead in charge has a Ph.D. in psychology and he designed a labyrinth—"

"A maze?"

"Yeah. A big-ass one. The doc's studying the psychological effects of being trapped in a seemingly endless maze, as a potential way to break down a prisoner's will. It's actually proven to be quite a useful interrogation technique."

"Sounds more like psychological torture," Bunny said. He sounded genuinely disturbed that our government would do such a thing. After the things we'd encountered running black ops for the DMS, particularly after discovering American soldiers were being turned into human-cockroach hybrids, I doubted anything would surprise me anymore.

"How is the maze 'seemingly' endless?" I asked.

"You'll see," Halverson said.

I'll be damned if his voice didn't sound ominous as all get-out.

Before I could ask him what the hell he meant by that, the elevator reached the bottom with a jolt and the doors opened.

"Now if that isn't déjà vu all over again, I don't know what is," Top muttered as his gun appeared in his hand.

Just as in our first time exiting an elevator with Halverson, we encountered a steel tunnel splattered with bright red blood. That time there were five bodies, this time only two. Not that that made it any better. Both victims were male, one dressed in a security uniform, the other wearing khaki prison scrubs. The bodies each had twin sets of beer can–sized holes in their torsos.

Top stepped out of the cart first, sighting down the tunnel, while Bunny checked to the left and I moved to the right. The elevator was at the end of the tunnel, so it took Bunny and me all of half a second to clear our corners. We turned back to Top as he called out, "Clear!"

"They're not supposed to be out of the maze," Halverson said as he stepped tentatively out of the elevator, Glock in hand. Fortunately for him, he wasn't pointing his gun at any of us this time.

"Who's not?" I said sharply. Halverson didn't reply fast enough for my liking, so I got right in his face. "Who did this? There are no damn terrorists, are there?"

"No, but I needed to get you here."

"Me specifically? Or just someone like me and my team?"

Halverson stepped back, looking skittish. My instinct was to keep crowding him until he gave me a straight answer, but he held up his hand and said, "Wait! I heard something. Listen."

I did. He was right. I heard a soft scuffing sound. Then immediately another.

Footsteps. Two sets.

Top and I looked down the hall at the same time, the red dots on our laser sights each finding an approaching man's chest.

No, that wasn't quite right. The chest I'd targeted, though not particularly large, was definitely female. Like the man beside her, she wore a security uniform and carried a Glock pointing downward. They were both wise enough not to raise their guns.

"It's okay, they work for me," Halverson said. He started to reach out, as if he'd intended to push my gun arm down, but then thought better of it. Smart choice. He turned his attention to the guards. "Sanders, Gale, what the hell happened here?"

The pair stopped just a few feet short of us. I don't know if they even realized Top and I had a bead on them. That's when I noticed they only had eyes for the corpses and their superior. They kept looking back and forth from the bodies to Halverson, as if silently imploring him to explain what was going on.

He didn't.

That made me want to point my gun at him again. Instead, I just lowered it, motioning for Top to do the same.

"Your orders were clear, Sanders," Halverson said to the man. "I told you to stay in the cell block with the prisoner. None of you were supposed to be in this wing at all. You most definitely were not authorized to go into the maze."

"It was all Johnson's doing," Gale said, pointing at their dead coworker. Convenient. "He was frustrated that the prisoner wouldn't confess. Turned out the bastard killed a bunch of tourists in Mexico that included Johnson's cousin. Small world, huh?" When her weak grin didn't garner any return smiles or head nods, she added, "Johnson wanted to personally throw him into the maze and leave him there without any food or water. We refused to help him, but . . . we didn't stop him, either."

"Not long after he led the prisoner away at gunpoint, we heard shots," Sanders said, picking up the story. "We thought Johnson had executed him. Instead, we found a blood trail leading from the maze entrance to here. When we realized that whatever had killed them had gone back to the maze, we raced back and closed the door. Then we heard the elevator and here we are."

Gale glared at Halverson. "What's in the maze, boss?"

"You wouldn't believe me if I told you," Halverson said.

"Maybe they wouldn't," I said, "but you know I would."

"Still, it's better if I just show you all." Then, as if afraid I'd force him to change his mind, Halverson strode forward.

I immediately followed him, Top and Bunny falling in behind me. I glanced back and saw Sanders and Gale reluctantly bringing up the rear. "Stay alert," I said, mostly for their sake.

A few hundred yards down the hall, we came to a T-junction. A long corridor with several closed doors branched off to the right. To the left, a short, dead-end hallway greeted us. Yet Halverson turned that way. He swiped his personnel badge on a scanner on the back wall near the corner. With a low hum similar to the elevator engine, the wall at the end of the hall slid to the right, creating an entryway into the maze.

He motioned for us to go in. Aside from the blood trail that disappeared a few feet in, there was no sign of whoever—or *whatever*—had killed the men, but I followed my own advice to stay alert. The murderer could be lurking beyond any of the maze's twists and turns.

The labyrinth was brightly lit, with steel walls reaching up a good twenty feet to a concrete ceiling. There were jagged spikes of dried cement hanging down—like a popcorn ceiling on steroids. It was probably done to give the illusion of stalactites in a giant cave, but it also gave the unsettling feeling that the stone spikes could drop on us at any moment, crushing our skulls.

"The psychologist who came up with this place has a disturbing mind," I said, turning back toward Halverson, who'd yet to enter the maze. "What did you say his name was?"

"I didn't say, actually." A disconcerting smirk flickered across Halverson's face. "It's Dr. Goldman."

"Son of a bitch." That was the name of the madman who created the cockroach soldiers. "You somehow working for a ghost now?" I said. With the things I'd come up against at the DMS, I didn't completely rule that out.

Halverson chuckled. "Not quite. But like Gale said earlier, it really is a small world. This"—he indicated the maze—"is the creation of Goldman's twin brother. Interestingly, this Dr. Goldman also studied bioengineering, psychology just being more of a hobby for him."

I had a very sick feeling in my stomach, and I had to suppress the urge both to vomit and to shoot Halverson in his smug face. "How much did Goldman pay you to lure us here?" I asked. Clearly, this was about revenge for my killing the scientist's twin.

Halverson wiped a hand across his forehead, as if trying to remove the red dot my gun's laser had placed there. "Look," he said, no longer appearing so smug, "I had no idea he'd lure you here. Really. I just thought he wanted his brother's research as a memento of sorts. I didn't know what else to do with the files I smuggled out of the Vault— I'm no traitor, so selling them was never my goal. Although, the doc did insist on rewarding my resourcefulness. Plus, I'd just started here, so I didn't know the medical wing was equipped for genetic experiments from a previously failed project—"

Halverson clamped his mouth shut, as if realizing he'd said too much.

"I destroyed everything," I said, though my voice didn't have much conviction to it. *Son of a bitch.*

Halverson raised his left hand in a *calm down* gesture, wisely leaving his right hand with the Glock pointing at the floor. "You did destroy all the cockroach research," he said. "But that was far from *everything.* . . ."

A loud thump from down the corridor almost made me turn away, but I trusted Top or Bunny would alert me if a threat presented itself. Halverson, however, must have expected the sound to distract me, as he immediately sprang into action, swiping his badge across the scanner and pivoting away from the already shrinking doorway.

Shooting him wouldn't keep the wall from sliding closed; instead, I unslung my equipment bag and hurled it toward the gap. It landed perfectly, half in and half out of the entryway. An instant before the wall hit the obstruction, the bag was yanked away from the other side. I never would've expected Halverson to have such quick reflexes, but I guess you didn't get to be head of security for a top-secret base without having some skills.

In the same motion as I'd thrown my bag, I launched myself toward the entryway. With no propped-open gap to force my way through, I considered putting on the brakes, but instead channeled my anger at Halverson into a bone-rattling shoulder slam. The thick, sliding steel wall didn't budge.

I let out an impotent growl of frustration, then turned to face the others.

Top was unzipping his own equipment bag, and as he reached into it, a quick procession of confusion, realization, and frustration crossed his features.

"The C4 . . . ," he said.

"Gone," I responded with a nod.

Normally we'd each have a couple bricks of C4, blasting caps, and det cord in our packs, but I'd been the only one who brought along explosives this time because the Warehouse's armory had been low on stock. DMS missions often involve blowing shit up, so it's no surprise that we'd run out. Still, I'd planned on giving the responsible pencil pusher a piece of my mind when I got back to headquarters, but seeing as how I'd literally just thrown away the only explosives we had, I decided it'd be best to just call it even on the fuckups.

We couldn't blast our way through the wall, but maybe we didn't need to. We did, after all, have two members of the base's finest with us. I looked at Gale and Sanders expectantly. "Please tell me you know the way out of here."

"There aren't any scanners on the inside of the maze," Sanders said, waving his personnel badge, "so this thing is useless. We're just as stuck as you are."

"How do you normally get out?" Bunny asked.

He pointed at a video camera mounted near the sliding door. "We usually just wave at the camera and the person in the control room lets us out. If for some reason the door doesn't open right away, we use our radio." As if just realizing he had a way of communicating, he unclipped his radio from his belt and spoke into it, looking hopefully up at the camera. "Halverson, you piece of shit, let us out of here!"

No response.

Gale lifted up her radio, but took a considerably more conciliatory tone. "Come on, Halverson. Someone killed Johnson. We don't know what we're up against. You gotta let us out."

Surprisingly, Halverson replied. "I'm sorry you and Sanders got caught up in this, Gale. I really am. I'm just following Goldman's orders. You should've followed *my* orders and stayed put in the prison wing. But, hey, at least you got laid one last time before—"

"You bastard!" She threw her radio at the video camera, shattering the lens. She had a good arm on her. She turned away from the camera to find the rest of us staring at her. "What?"

"You slept with the boss?" Sanders said.

Gale shrugged. "I was bored. But if I get out of here alive, I'm going to shoot him in the balls."

"Speaking of getting out of here, is there like a back door or some-thing?" I asked.

Both guards shook their heads miserably. "Not that we know of, anyway," Sanders said.

"I could take Farm Boy and do some recon," Top offered.

"This place is a maze, literally," I said. "We should stick together."

We heard another loud thump from somewhere in the maze. We had bigger problems than just finding a way out.

"We need to find out what we're up against," I said. "Move out."

Top took point and I motioned for the guards to follow him so I could watch their backs, while Bunny brought up the rear. All of us had our necks on a swivel, our gun barrels moving in sync with our eyes. I got the feeling the place was massive, but with my view being contained to one corridor a time, I couldn't be sure.

I stepped up beside Sanders. "Halverson said the maze is 'seem-ingly' endless. What'd he mean?"

"It's the walls, they—"

The elevator engine sound returned and Bunny let out a startled cry.

I spun around to see a wall sliding across the corridor behind me as the big staff sergeant dove forward into a roll, just barely squeezing through the diminishing gap.

As the moving wall connected with the opposite side of the corri-dor, it locked in with a thump—the same sound that we'd heard ear-lier. One mystery solved.

"Yep," Sanders said, "the walls move. I don't know if there really are an endless number of configurations, but to the prisoners it probably feels that way." He looked around hopelessly. "And to us, too, now, I guess."

I studied the walls and noticed there were barely visible seams every fifty yards. "Okay," I said, "stay close and keep alert for moving walls."

We walked on for several minutes with nothing happening and my mind wandered to what Halverson said about selling research files to Goldman's evil twin. I was thankful that we wouldn't have to deal with soldiers mutated with cockroach genes again, but I had a bad feeling this would be something worse.

I mean, we were in a labyrinth after all. . . .

As if to confirm my fears, I heard a loud exhale of breath, like a horse would make . . . or a bull.

Gale looked back over her shoulder. "Don't worry," she said, "that's just a recording the doc uses to freak out the prisoners."

The animal sound came again, louder. Closer.

"Well, it's working," I said, feeling pretty damned freaked out.

Gale smiled reassuringly. "Just wait until he switches to the—" Her expression instantly changed to abject terror as she saw something behind me.

"Bunny!" I shouted as I turned. "Watch your back!"

Bunny instinctively sidestepped before turning to look behind him. "You've got to be shitting me," he grumbled.

The bastard had actually done it. Dr. Goldman had created a human-bull hybrid.

A freaking Minotaur. In a maze. Barreling at me, head down, horns first.

Bunny didn't shoot. I didn't shoot. Mostly because the last time we encountered mutants like this, they were our brothers in arms, misled into believing they'd be turned into supersoldiers, not monsters.

I also didn't shoot because the thing was damn fast.

I was faster. Gale wasn't.

A split second after I pivoted out of the way, Gale screamed as the Minotaur's horns impaled her. The creature was tall, so even hunched over with his head down, his horns hit her chest, puncturing her heart and lungs in unison.

The Minotaur shook his head and flung her away. She was already dead. For a brief moment, the Minotaur stared at her with a look of sadness. Grief. He had horns sticking out of his forehead and his nose looked all bull, but his eyes were still human.

He hadn't wanted to kill her. He hadn't even glanced at Bunny. He'd been aiming for me.

Confirming my suspicion, the man-bull turned toward me, his nostrils flaring as his breaths came quickly. He looked agitated, confused. It seemed clear I was his target, yet his heart wasn't in it.

A red dot appeared over his heart, on the thick brown hair that covered his shirtless chest.

"Should I take the shot, Cap'n?" Top asked.

"Wait," I said, once again getting a feeling of déjà vu. I looked into the mutant's human eyes and said, "U.S. Army. We're the good guys. And I think you're a good guy, too." I glanced down at the tattered remains of medical scrub pants on his powerful, hairy legs. He hadn't been a prisoner, he wasn't a terrorist. "I don't think you meant to kill Gale, or the other two, either." He nodded emphatically; I was on the right track. "And you don't want to kill me, either."

He shook his head slowly, with a level of indecision that I didn't like. Then his eyes narrowed, as though he'd made a difficult decision and he was about to do something risky.

Something dangerous.

He charged.

Top would've taken him out before he reached me. Well, assuming his bull hide wasn't thick enough to stop a bullet. Hell, I would've put at least two bullets in him myself. Bunny, too, if he'd had the right angle. But there was something I'd forgotten and two things I hadn't counted on: the Minotaur was damn fast; it wasn't actually charging at me; and Sanders rushed toward it, causing me to yell for Top and Bunny to hold their fire.

Sanders evidently thought I was shouting at him, because he replied, "Screw you and screw that thing! It killed Gale and Johnson and I'm taking it down."

He fired his Glock, but he got only one shot off before the fleeing Minotaur rounded a corner.

I thought I heard a grunt of pain, but I couldn't be sure because the wall engine fired up at the same time. I rounded the corner to see Sanders's second shot ricochet off a closing wall.

The Minotaur was gone.

No doubt Goldman didn't want Sanders killing the Minotaur before it killed me.

Something was nagging at me, as though I weren't getting the full picture. Then Top put his finger on it for me. "Something I don't get, Cap," he said. "Goldman knows we're an elite black ops team, yet he traps us with just one monster?"

"Budget cuts?" Bunny offered.

"You think he's got a whole herd in here?" I asked.

"We got a big influx of prisoners a couple weeks ago," Sanders said.

"How many we talking about?"

"A dozen." He no longer looked hell-bent on vengeance; he looked suddenly petrified. To put it bluntly, he looked ready to piss his pants.

To lighten the mood, I said, "I've always wondered what it'd be like to do that running of the bulls thing. Now I don't have to go to Spain to find out."

"I'd rather do the one in New Orleans," Bunny said. I raised a quizzical eyebrow, so he explained. "Instead of bulls, you run with Roller Derby girls wearing bull-horn hats. They won't gore you, but they'll whack you with plastic baseball bats."

"Dewey Beach, Delaware, has the best one," Top said. "No bats, just some dude in a bull costume and a lot of girls running in bikinis."

The mood suitably lightened, I suggested we move on. I should've known better than to relax, even a little—I was just taunting Murphy's Law.

So, obviously, it was right at that moment that a strange wheezing sound started up. It could've just been that one of the Minotaurs had asthma, but something about it seemed wrong. As the sound grew closer, my mouth went dry and my ass cheeks clenched.

I blamed Goldman. And since I couldn't shoot him, I chose the closest camera. I got a childish pleasure out of watching my bullet smash through it.

I also distracted the others at the exact wrong moment, just as that bastard Murphy would've wanted.

Sanders shrieked, dropping his Glock as he was yanked off his feet by something that most definitely was not a mutant man-bull.

More like—

"The Fly!" Top shouted.

"Fruit fly," I said distractedly as I tried to get a clear shot, which was near impossible with the way the man-fly was jerking around, apparently having difficulty staying aloft with the added weight.

"How can you tell?" Bunny asked, agitated.

He had a point.

While the shape and translucence of the mutant's wings could have been from a housefly or a fruit fly, the chitinous scales that blotted out most of his skin were a yellow brown rather than black. And his eyes were a bright red. "Isn't it obvious?" I said. "Actually, I remember the original Goldman mentioning something about fruit flies."

"I dunno," Top said. "This guy kinda looks like Jeff Goldblum if you ask me."

Sanders struggled to get free, but the attacker held on to his prey tenaciously. As I jogged along after them, I tried to recall what I knew about fruit flies. Did they just eat rotting fruit or would they eat meat?

The security guard flailed around and managed to grab hold of the creature's left wing. He threw his whole body into a strong tug and yanked the wing right off the man-fly's body.

The monster let out a very human shriek of pain. Although his right wing kept flapping ineffectively, he instantly lost the ability to fly, dropping straight down. Still gripping the severed wing, Sanders hit the floor first and I lost sight of him when the giant fruit fly landed on top of him.

Before I could check to see if they were alive, the wheezing noise—which I now realized was a messed-up human-fly *buzzing* sound—returned.

Even as I called out a warning, they were on us.

They flew in from behind us. I thought I heard words beneath the incessant buzzing—two repeated words, like a chant—but I couldn't wrap my mind around what they were saying before the inquisitive Cop part of me was overtaken by the Warrior.

Two of them lifted Bunny off the ground. Each gripping a shoulder, they struggled to carry the big man, but then a third grabbed him by the neck.

I shot that one first. An instant later, Top hit the one on the left and I hit the right. All head shots. Those bulging red eyes were the perfect bull's-eyes.

All three of the creatures dropped dead onto Bunny, knocking him down. His knees hit the concrete floor hard, causing him to let out a cry of discomfort, which was immediately muffled as one of the men-flies' bodies forced his face down, smothering him.

I didn't have time to dig him out from the pileup as four more mutant fruit flies swarmed down on me and Top.

Top screamed, or maybe I did—probably we both did—as we swept our guns across their bodies. We didn't call out our targets, we didn't aim for the bull's-eye eyes, we just sprayed them with industrial-strength bug spray. For monster-sized pests, forget DEET, lead is much more effective.

Bunny shoved his way out from under the bodies covering him just as the remaining men-flies dropped dead onto him, knocking him back down. He groaned, though out of pain or irritation, I couldn't tell.

"You okay under there?" I asked, doing a poor job of suppressing a morbid chuckle.

Bunny shoved a single hand up between two bodies, his middle finger extended.

"Pretty fly for a white guy," Top said just loud enough for me to hear. I groaned.

"I'm okay!" Sanders suddenly called out, apparently thinking my question to Bunny had been for him.

Then suddenly he was not okay.

"Ah!" he screamed. "It's alive!"

The fruit fly creature that had tried to abduct him moved feebly, trying to stand up. He repeated the same words the swarm had been chanting, only this time I made them out: "Kill me."

I don't know if Sanders heard and understood the mutant's plea or if he was just scared out of his wits, but he moved with unexpected speed. He dove for his fallen gun, snatched it up, and spun around, grouping three bullets into where I assumed the man-thing's heart still resided. I was impressed.

"Now that's how you swat a fly!" he said. "Booyah!" He got to his feet and surveyed the gore on the walls around us. It looked exactly as if we'd swatted seven very large flies. Sanders's puffed chest deflated. "Well, I guess you guys know how to take care of monster pests, too."

Throwing the guy a bone, I said, "Hey, smart thinking yanking that thing's wing off."

He perked up. "Thanks. When I was a kid, I, er, a friend of mine used to pull the wings off flies."

"I heard one of the early signs of serial killers was that they pulled the wings off butterflies as kids," Top mused.

"Butterflies are beautiful and graceful, flies are ugly and annoying," Sanders said defensively.

"You're starting to look ugly and annoying," Top said.

"Cool it, First Sergeant," I said.

Top scowled at Sanders. "I bet the guy was the type to put firecrackers in frogs' asses and blow them up."

Sanders looked as if he were going to deny it, instead he blurted out, "George W. Bush did that, too!"

"Yeah, and he probably shot them with BB guns, as well," I said. "For all we know, there could be mutant man-frogs waiting around the next bend that *we'll* have to shoot, so let's reload and move out."

Farther into the maze, a loud buzzing heralded the approach of a new threat. The sound was similar to the droning of the fruit fly monsters, yet distinctly different. Angrier.

I racked my brain for any other flying insects the Vault's Goldman had been working on. Then I remembered.

Wasps.

Why couldn't it have been bullfrogs?

I've been stung by a regular-sized wasp. It hurt like hell. And damn, did it itch. I was certain the poison from a man-sized wasp sting would do more than just itch. It'd kill.

"I'm allergic to bees!" Sanders screamed. He took off at a run.

"Wait!" I shouted. Besides the fact that we needed to stay together because of the shifting passages, the buzzing sound wasn't coming from behind us like last time . . .

He was running straight toward them.

Sanders rounded a corner and let out a blood-curdling scream. I gave chase, expecting to find him impaled on a giant stinger.

I found the guard holding a bloody hand to his neck, but he appeared relatively okay.

The lone man-wasp standing a few feet away from him looked more predatory than the men-flies had. He had jagged, enlarged teeth, his wings were thicker and slender, and antennae jutted out of his ears. Where a tail would be on a monkey, a big-ass needle stuck out of him.

Whether because he'd already written Sanders off as dead or because he saw me as a bigger threat, the man-wasp faced off against me. "Kill," he said. He repeated it in a low, hoarse voice. Over and over.

Probably the creepiest damn thing I'd ever heard.

He spread his wings. I thought it was a macho thing, showing me how big he was.

Nope. It was the start of a lightning-fast attack.

Before I could get a shot off, he launched himself up over me. My barrel followed him, but he immediately plunged down stinger-first toward my upturned face.

I barely had time to pivot out of the way, but even as I turned, I was planning my counterattack. He adjusted his plunge to land on his feet, his knees bending on impact, his stinger nearly touching the ground. I raised my booted right foot and stomped hard at the base of his stinger. With more of a crunch than the snap I'd expected, his unnatural appendage broke off, splattering my leg with black blood and yellow poison.

Shrieking with pain and rage, he spun toward me, mouth wide-open. His teeth reminded me of shark teeth. The original Goldman had been trying to create new strains of humans that could withstand global warming or a nuclear apocalypse or whatever other damage we might do to our planet, so it made sense that he'd have shark genes in the mix since those beasts have survived four hundred million years of climate changes.

This beast didn't survive another four hundred milliseconds.

I got my gun up just in time to shoot him in the mouth. The bullet sent shards of teeth that didn't belong in a human mouth into a brain that was no longer human.

"Get down!" Sanders shouted.

I instinctively dropped to the ground as two more man-wasps buzzed over me. They got close enough for me to feel a breeze. And I swear I smelled pollen on them.

"Kill. Kill. Kill," they chanted with creepy, raspy voices.

"Die, die, die," Bunny shouted in response as he came around the corner. He collided with one and inadvertently drove it back toward me.

I didn't have a safe shot with it tangled up with Bunny, but when I reflexively crab-walked backward out of the way, my left hand fell on the first mutant's separated stinger. I snatched it up and used it to deflect the second mutant's stinger, which Bunny was unknowingly shoving toward my face.

Weirdest sword fight ever.

Bunny had his hands full trying to keep the monster's teeth away from his neck, so I needed to end this. The man-wasp wore a hospital gown. Yeah, the kind that flaps open at the back. I stuck that stinger deep into a place where nothing sharp and pointy should ever go.

Not my finest moment. Made even less so by my shouting out, "Tooshie!" the way a fencer yells, "Touché!"

I don't think anyone heard me, though, because at the same time Top emptied an entire mag into the third man-wasp. The creature dropped to the ground, his torso resembling a giant, blood-streaked slab of honeycomb.

"A little overkill, don't you think?" Bunny said, shoving away from the man-wasp I'd killed.

"I did *not* want to get stung by that thing," Top said, looking around at us. His eyes landed on Sanders, who had an angry red bump the size of a golf ball on his neck. "Oh. Uh, how are you feeling, Sanders?"

The base guard managed a weak smile. "I think I'll be okay, actually," he said. "Maybe I'm not allergic to mutant human wasp venom."

We continued on, but while I knew I should stay alert for more threats, I found myself constantly glancing at the big bug bite, until it got to the point where I couldn't take my eyes off it.

It was growing.

It was the size of a baseball now.

I put my hand on the rapid-release folding knife clipped to the edge of my pocket. "Hey, Sanders," I said. "That bump looks uncomfortable. You want me to poke a hole in it? See if some monster puss drains out?"

Sanders turned and opened his mouth to speak, but only a gasping sound came out.

Forget pricking the bump, I was ready to amputate it. That wouldn't help him, though, if what he really needed was a giant EpiPen.

As if reading my thoughts, Top said, "He's not going into anaphylactic shock, that thing's grown so big it's crushing his throat!"

He was right and there was not a damn thing we could do about it.

Sanders gurgled out some words that sounded eerily close to the fruit fly men's "Kill me," but I didn't have to make that hard decision. Sanders's eyes rolled up in their sockets, then he collapsed, his chest no longer moving.

Guess he really was allergic. Poor bastard.

I looked toward Bunny and Top, who were both staring at Sanders's neck, and it took my mind a moment to process what I was seeing behind them.

A tall naked woman—the term *Amazon* came to mind—appeared to be twerking, of all things. I thought she was trying to mesmerize me with her booty shake. As a battle tactic, I have to admit it almost worked.

Until I noticed what was above the full moon.

Just in time, I realized she was actually winding up to do a giant swing toward my teammates . . . using her massive *stinger* like a sword to slice them both in half.

"Down!" I shouted.

Top and Bunny obeyed without question.

As the queen bee completed her swing, she continued the motion so that she stood facing me. The chitinous scales that covered her naked body reminded me of a girl with freckles I'd once dated. "You must be Captain Ledger," she said in a surprisingly normal voice. Deeper, raspier, sure, but very feminine and seductive. "I'm going to eat you alive," she said.

I almost considered letting her.

The Warrior overruled the Horn Dog and I aimed my pistol at her. Blood and gore exploded from her chest.

Weird thing was, I hadn't pulled the trigger.

She lifted off the ground, yet her wings weren't moving. She flew sideways, crashing into the wall. She fell dead to the ground.

She'd been impaled and flung away by the maze's alpha predator. The Minotaur.

"Thanks?" I said.

He glared at me, nostrils flaring. "Don't thank me," he said, his voice labored, as if it were a struggle to speak properly through his mutated mouth. "Dr. Goldman promised to reverse my mutation if *I* kill you. I just didn't want her to get the credit."

He looked ready to charge me. Bunny and Top already had their laser sights on him and I could get off several shots before he reached me, but his leathery hide looked tough. Would our bullets even slow him down? I wore light body armor, but I didn't think it'd be any match for those powerful horns.

The Minotaur's eyes widened when I raised my gun and fired toward his head.

"That's not going to stop me," he said when he realized I'd been aiming at the video camera on the wall behind his head. "I don't need Goldman to see me kill you. I'll just drag your body to the next camera."

"That's what I was planning on," I said.

The Minotaur looked just as confused as Top and Bunny.

I holstered my gun and used my knife to cut two horn-sized holes in my jacket. I rubbed some of the wasp woman's blood onto my chest to complete the disguise. I was a dead man.

"What about us?" Top asked.

"What about the other two?" Halverson echoed a moment later, when the Minotaur used Sanders's radio to inform him of my death.

"They said they were with you when Goldman's brother died. They said you should let them go."

To my surprise and relief, Halverson replied, "Okay. You can bring them, but they have to leave their weapons. Remove Captain Ledger's weapons as well."

Well, damn.

As the Minotaur dragged me roughly along by my left arm, the walls rearranged themselves to give us direct passage to the entryway.

"Have his friends bring him out," Halverson said when the door opened. "You stay there." He pointed his gun at the Minotaur.

Top and Bunny each grabbed an arm and dragged me out next to Halverson. They weren't any gentler than the Minotaur. Payback for all the times I'd kicked their asses sparring.

I left my eyes open. It was a calculated risk since it was going to be hard not to blink, but I wanted to be fully aware of my surroundings. And right now I could see that Dr. Goldman had joined Halverson. Like his twin brother, he wore thick glasses and had the nervous habit of running his tongue along his lips.

"You don't need to point that gun at me," the Minotaur said, struggling to control his anger. "I just want what was promised to me: the cure."

The doctor sighed, actually looking apologetic. "Do you remember Nurse Joy?" he asked. I couldn't move my gaze off Goldman, but I assume the Minotaur nodded an affirmation, because the evil scientist continued. "I turned Nurse Joy into a Minotaur as well. I did it so I could test the cure on her. I figured if it didn't work, you would at least have some companionship in the maze." He shook his head with fatherly sorrow. "Unfortunately, not only did the cure not work, it killed her."

"You lied to me!" the Minotaur screamed. Goldman might as well have waved a red flag at him. But the beast didn't move. Halverson's weapon kept him in check.

The head of base security took a nervous step backward nonetheless. That was enough of a distraction for Top to make his move. He had the man disarmed before he even realized what had happened.

Goldman blindsided us by whipping out his own gun and pointing it at Bunny. "Don't move," he said to Top.

I didn't recognize the gun, but I could tell it shot sedative darts.

"I'm a trained soldier, you're a mad scientist," Top said, steel in his voice. "I could shoot your man, then you, faster than you could get off a single shot with that tranq gun."

"Tranquilizer? No. The dart in here will pump a special cocktail into your friend. Then the maze will have two Minotaurs. Remember, there is no cure."

Top cursed and returned the Glock to Halverson.

The only upside to the confrontation was that no one was paying any attention to me. I inched along the floor, getting closer to Goldman.

The doc suddenly let out a nasally laugh. "You didn't really believe I'd let you two leave here, did you? I made these darts especially for you. I needed more test subjects. . . ."

Son of a bitch!

In one smooth move, I rolled onto my chest, brought my knees up under me, and leaped up, grabbing the dart gun with my left hand while my right punched the little weasel in the gut.

At the same time, Top relieved Halverson of his weapon once again.

With the tables suitably turned, I shoved Goldman toward the Minotaur. "You owe him a cure," I said. "Maybe he'll let you live if you promise to get back to work."

"There really is no cure," he said, shaking.

"Maybe he needs more motivation," the Minotaur said. He reached a hand out to me and understanding dawned as I passed him the dart gun.

Goldman immediately figured out what the Minotaur intended to do as well. He bolted. Into the maze.

There was enough time for the man-bull to shoot the doctor in the back, but he didn't. Instead, he snarled at Halverson, "I heard what you did. You caused all this. This is your fault."

"No," Halverson said. "No."

The mutant bull grabbed him by the neck, but then let him go. He shoved him into the maze.

Halverson turned back. "Please," he said. The Minotaur pointed the gun at him and he ran.

This time, the Minotaur pulled the trigger. Halverson cried out in pain and terror. He turned back toward us, but the man-bull waved his hand and the wall slid closed. The Minotaur had torn off the lanyard that Halverson had been wearing with his personnel badge.

"I wanted the doctor to be chased through his own maze by one of his own creations," the Minotaur said, "just not by me. I'm never going back in there."

"I can't make any promises," I said, "but I'll do whatever I can to find someone capable of creating a cure for you."

"No," he said. "If more scientists study me, they might try to duplicate Goldman's experiments. This has to end here."

I looked sadly at him. "What do you have in mind?"

"I used to work here," the Minotaur said. "I confided in Goldman that I had a gambling debt and he offered to pay it off for me if I let him test a new type of supersoldier steroid on me. I know how to lock the place down, hard." He slid open a panel under the scanner, revealing a number pad and an ominous red button. He tapped in a long sequence of numbers, then pressed the button. "I've triggered the bio-hazard emergency protocols."

I knew what that meant. A different kind of sliding steel wall would drop in front of the elevator and thermite charges would seal it permanently in place. No one that knew about this place would ever give the order to dig us out.

A courteous female voice emanated from speakers somewhere down the hall. She informed us that the fail-safe had been initiated. "Countdown is commencing. One hundred, ninety-nine, ninety-eight . . ."

"You better run," the Minotaur said.

". . . ninety-five, ninety-four . . ."

We ran as though the hounds of hell were chasing us. And after everything the Goldman brothers had thrown at us, I doubt giant demon dogs would have even surprised me.

But there were no surprises. We made it out in time. I just hope to God Mama Goldman didn't have triplets.

ABOUT THE AUTHOR
Nicholas Steven is the new action-adventure pen name of a bestselling ghostwriter. If you ask him his real name, he'll give you the old "I could tell you, but then I'd have to kill you" line, and he'll say it just ominously enough that you won't ask again. He'll then give you a charming smile that's at odds with the unnerving hold his steely eyes have on you, and he'll strongly suggest you take note of his alias so you don't miss any of his future publications, which he promises will be killer reads.

TARGET ACQUIRED

BY CHRISTOPHER GOLDEN AND TIM LEBBON

Miranda had always thought one of the beauties of Venice was its anonymity. A city of magic and elegance, so unmistakably Italian—so iconic—it was nevertheless a place where one could vanish completely. In the crush of tourists in St. Mark's Square, disappearing was simple, but it was only a tiny bit more difficult in the city's less traveled alleys. Tourists were everywhere, clothing and faces and styles from all around the world. Almost from birth, Venetians learned not to see them, to let all of those unfamiliar faces blur together until they became, for all intents and purposes, invisible.

Invisibility made a killer's job much simpler.

She carried a large coffee in a travel cup from a busy café, both part of her masquerade and a caffeine junkie's necessity. This mission would have been so much simpler a few weeks earlier, in the middle of Carnival season, when meandering the bridges and alleys of Venice wearing an actual mask would not have seemed at all out of place. But mid-March worked just as well for Miranda, really. She had spent a lifetime mastering the art of the true masquerade, disguising herself without any mask at all. Changing her walk and her bearing, her body language and demeanor, her hair and her style, her tone and her language.

In a beige wool coat, gray leggings, and high black boots, with a burgundy-and-white-checked scarf that set off nicely against her dark features, she bore the look of just another British tourist. The badly folded map in her left hand completed the picture, and she made sure to pause to glance at it now and again for a sense of verisimilitude. The day's high temperature would barely reach forty-five Fahrenheit, so the stylish hooded coat would seem sensible and not at all out of place, and it would hide a variety of weapons.

Weapons she did not expect to need.

The cobblestones beneath her feet were damp from rain, but as she emerged from an alley onto the Fondamenta Orseolo, a narrow walkway that ran beside a canal, she saw the way the water lapped up onto the steps at a gondola station, and she knew that some months it was not rain that dampened those cobblestones. The sea was rising and the city was sinking, both slowly, both surely. In time, the whole city would be underwater, washing away the evidence of a great civilization, and centuries of crimes. The city flooded so regularly now that in many buildings the ground floor had been filled with concrete, surrendered to the future. The last time Miranda had visited Venice she had hidden two corpses in one of those ground floors, the night before the concrete had been poured.

Venice hid a multitude of sins.

But none of those sins were as black as Joe Ledger's.

From behind thousand-dollar Dita Cascais sunglasses, she caught sight of him crossing Ponte della Piavola fifty feet ahead. Precisely where she'd expected him to be. Miranda had measured her pace, timed every pause, so that the two of them would be in this very position. For eight days she had arrived before dawn to take up her position behind the construction fence of an eleventh-century church whose renovation had been abandoned for more than a year. A forgotten place, nearly as invisible as the face of a tourist. From behind the fence, she had watched the façade of the neglected apartment building where Ledger had been laying his head, emerging after he emerged, every morning a different persona for her, a different masquerade.

Miranda had followed him, timed his walk from the apartment building to the crumbling, abandoned villa where he'd been convening daily with members of a European antiterror task force. Each day she appeared to be meandering instead of stalking. Morning after morning she had scanned the architecture and the canals for ambush points. Nothing had satisfied her.

Last night, she had run out of patience. The desire to see Joe Ledger dead outweighed all else.

Now she reached the bridge and paused to sip her coffee and consult her map, glancing both directions along the canal. A gondolier called happily to another passing by, then disappeared beneath the bridge. A young couple—American by the look of them—ate pastries and drank coffee in the gondola, gazing around with wide eyes at the dying beauty of the place. Miranda had been on a gondola tour once, but so many of the narrow canals stank of piss that her stomach churned at the idea of eating or drinking anything as a gondolier poled his narrow vessel around those tight dank corners.

But she didn't care about the gondola. She counted seconds, let a dozen people pass over the bridge before her, and then continued on. For several seconds she lost sight of Ledger, something not easy to do with a man as large and formidable as he appeared to be, but then she saw the back of his head, spotted the freshly clipped hair that he'd had buzzed three afternoons before, and she felt reassured.

Seven minutes and two bridges later, she paused in front of the immaculately clean plate-glass window of a shop that sold marionettes. Saints and Pinocchios and Carnival puppets were on display, including a Bauta and a jester who seemed to be sparring. Someone had rearranged the display in the three days since she'd stopped in the same spot to study them.

When she turned and glanced down at her map, eyes flicking back up to track Ledger, she saw him entering the dilapidated villa. Once the place had no doubt been full of light and color and music and art. Now the stonework had begun to crack and crumble and crude graffiti had been painted onto the foundation, just at the waterline. Another forgotten piece of the great history of the city. Time and neglect would swallow it before the sea ever could.

Miranda had no idea what the task force might be working on, or why they were meeting in secret here in Venice. She had identified agents of Interpol, Italian military, and OSCE operatives. The grouping suggested an imminent terrorist attack in Venice, or at least the suspicion of one, but it was Joe Ledger's presence she did not understand. Most of the world remained unaware that the U.S. government had added yet another covert agency, the Department of Military Sciences, to handle the continually evolving dangers created by scientific advancement. More than likely, the Americans had insinuated themselves into a European operation both uninvited and unwelcome.

She wondered what the rest of the task force might say if they knew they had a traitor among them. A murderer. A terrorist. A man who would take whatever he learned of their activities, twist it, and use it against them. Who would kill hundreds of innocents, soak the cobblestones of Venice with their blood, just to make a point.

As he had done with the Royal London Hospital, orchestrating the explosion that had killed hundreds of people. Including Tess.

Just the thought of her name sent a fresh wave of pain rippling through Miranda. No one on the street would see it. Not while she was in the midst of a hunt, not while she needed to keep up the masquerade. But one reel of their years together kept playing over and over in Miranda's head, the joyful grin and the laughing gleam in Tess's eyes as she tucked a lock of red hair behind an ear and stared at the engagement ring on her finger. They'd climbed all the way to the top of St. Paul's Cathedral and stood in the Whispering Gallery, just inside the dome. If you whispered from one side of the dome, anyone standing directly opposite on the far side could hear every word with perfect, almost sensual clarity.

She'd asked Tess to marry her.

Later they'd walked among the roses in Queen Mary's Gardens in Regent's Park and Tess had kept shaking her head and stifling a laugh behind her hand. Then had come that joyful grin and the tuck of hair behind her ear, and those nine words—the words that played on a continuous loop in the back of Miranda's mind.

"I can't believe I'm going to be your wife," Tess had said.

But she never would be.

The next morning she followed Ledger along a similar route, though not identical. Close to the old villa once again, she veered off and entered a run-down hotel. This was the day. After much thought, Miranda had decided to take him out in the open.

Her main intention here was Ledger's death, but she was equally concerned with her own escape. Ledger had been the main triggerman for the London hospital bombing, but Miranda knew there must have been others involved whom she'd need to mop up. She'd discover their names, track them down, and kill them, and every time it would be Tess's smile urging her on.

She'd only briefly considered trying to glean these names from Ledger. One look at him had convinced her that this would be a bad idea. The man was a killer, just like her, though more brutal and indiscriminate. He was calm and detached and, for a big man, almost as invisible as she was among the crowds, and just as alert to danger. That was what made this such a challenge. Although she was confident of her skills, she also prided herself on her sense of self-preservation.

She had no intention of getting close enough to Ledger to ask him any questions. Two shots to the chest, one to the head, less than a second between the first and last shot. That would be her justice. She'd snipe him when he went for lunch, put him down, and make her escape in the panic and chaos. That was what made the hotel rooftop a perfect location for the ambush.

She'd checked into a second-floor room under a false name the day before, and passing reception now, she offered the old hotelier a small nod and smile. He barely acknowledged her. Only when she was out of sight around the first landing on the narrow staircase did she increase her speed, passing the second floor without a pause. On the third floor she moved swiftly along a hallway smelling of cleaning products and the ingrained must of ages, pausing outside a locked wooden door that bore no number or spy hole. The sign read STAFF ONLY in Italian. She had already been inside.

She picked the lock and entered again, cautious as ever.

Tess grinned at her from inside. A shadow, a memory, the two combined to flash her a fleeting, startling image of the dead woman she loved. It happened from time to time, and on every occasion Miranda found herself momentarily thrown. She was a woman in complete control—always aware of her surroundings, conscious of who was around her, cognizant of escape routes and angles of fire. She'd spent most of her adult life never sitting with her back to open doorways, yet the doors that these memories of Tess crept through were in shadowy places she did not know. Her own mind surprised her. It made her feel less in control, yet she welcomed these interludes. It was as if Tess were still with her, just for those few brief, beautiful moments.

She'd discovered from the coroner's report that Tess had been one of thirty people crushed to death when a ward ceiling came down. A nurse, she'd most likely been trying to save her patients.

"Not now," she whispered, breathing deeply. Shadows and sunlight formed more mundane shapes, and Miranda headed past the window and toward the small wooden staircase, heading up.

The rooftop was unchanged from yesterday. Two telltales she'd left across the access door remained in place, as did the heavy canvas bag she'd hidden hooked into an air-conditioning exhaust duct. The AC in the hotel probably hadn't worked in years, and the duct was spattered with pigeon shit and caked dust.

Ensuring she was out of sight behind the low-rooftop greenhouse, Miranda opened the bag and went about constructing the rifle.

"You're so good with your hands," she remembered Tess saying. That had been one evening in Paris, when Miranda had to fix a broken balcony door in their hotel room. Tess's playful smile had made Miranda weak, and she'd felt a momentary pang of guilt—her hands had slit throats, punched, and killed, as well as bestowing intimacies.

Tess had never known. Miranda was pleased, because her fiancée had been a good person and would never have understood.

Assembling the weapon without conscious thought, Miranda spent those few seconds drifting back to the explosion's aftermath. She had become a machine focused on information, accessing countless police, MI5 and Anti-Terrorist Squad transmissions. She'd even hacked into a series of electronic COBRA meeting minutes, gleaning as much information as she could about the perpetrators as quickly as possible.

Grief had driven her on. Revenge had burned bright, fueling her, feeding her. Never once had she allowed herself time to pause and breathe. To do that would be to crumple. Perhaps when this was done she would allow herself that brief loss of control.

But probably not.

With the rifle assembled, Miranda crawled across the filthy rooftop to the parapet. She'd planned and memorized the route to minimize any chance of being seen from surrounding buildings. There were only a few buildings higher in this neighborhood, and most of them were far enough away to lessen the angle of sight.

The time was close. Lying behind the rooftop parapet, she stared up into a clear blue sky and felt the sun on her skin. Tess had loved the sun. She could spend hours sitting in sunlight, reading, listening to music, or simply relaxing, letting her thoughts fly. Miranda was the opposite. Her mind was always working, even though often she did not betray that externally. For her, relaxing was akin to letting down her guard.

"You'll be able to relax soon," she whispered, not entirely certain if she was speaking to herself or to Tess.

Down in the street, she heard the bustle of tourists and the peeping of moped horns. She would soon silence that street. The gunshots would be loud, reverberating between the buildings. The sight of the big man falling, his brains splashed across the window of the café where he went for lunch, would stun everyone silent.

When the screaming and chaos began, Miranda would make her escape.

Anger seethed within her, eager for the kill. "You see?" the tall man with nine fingers had said to her. "There? And there?" He'd shown her photographs of Ledger at the hospital the day before the explosion. Documents. Mobile phone data. Every shred of evidence had confirmed his assertion that Ledger was responsible for the explosion.

She'd asked the nine-fingered man what his motive was in revealing this to her.

"My nephew was in that hospital. I know the kind of man Ledger is, and I can't do it myself."

It seemed the man had known the kind of woman she was, too.

As she waited to kill the man who'd murdered her beloved, it was the moment of Tess's death that played over and over in Miranda's mind. The terror she must have felt. The shock. The awful realization when the building collapsed around and onto her, and the pressure, the pressure, the unrelenting crushing pressure as . . .

Miranda had seen enough people die to know what her fiancée must have looked like when they scooped her up.

She glanced at her watch. She was expert enough to not shift position, however uncomfortable she became. Any movement could give her away. The drainage hole afforded a good view down along the street, and she'd already run through events the previous evening. Now, all she had to do was wait.

The rifle lay propped before her, barrel contained within the hole's shadow, nothing protruding beyond. She viewed along its sights. This was close-in work, no scope required. She could put a hole in a tin can at two hundred yards, and this would be less than fifty.

"Come on, you bastard," she muttered, berating herself for talking. But no one would hear her up here, other than the pigeons that cooed and shit around her. Even they'd become used to her. One had even pecked at the grip on her right boot.

The lunch crowds passed by below. A few people stepped into and out of the café, but none of them was Ledger. She looked at her watch again. It was past 1:00 PM, usually he'd have been and gone by now.

Miranda breathed deeply and calmed herself. Tess smiled in her memory.

"Come on. Come on." The whispers were little more than breaths, and when she heard another breathlike sound behind her, for a second she thought it was a pigeon flapping its wings.

A second was all he needed.

"Nice and steady," a voice said.

Miranda held her breath, hands squeezed around the rifle. She could roll, bring the weapon up out of the drainage hole, finger squeezing as it came, and fire.

"I've got about three pounds of pressure on a four-pound grip," he said. "Don't even think about it. Drop the rifle. Crawl back on your belly."

For a crazy second Miranda thought about making her move, but then she came to her senses. His voice was so assured and in control. And she hadn't even heard the pigeons move.

No one was that quiet and smooth.

She let go of the rifle and pushed herself back, just a little.

"Now roll over and sit up, hands where I can see them."

As she rolled and sat, several pigeons fluttered and took flight as if only just surprised. Ledger crouched ten feet across the rooftop. The access door was still closed behind him. She saw scuffs on his knees and the toes of his boots, a smear of dirt on his left elbow. He'd climbed the fucking wall.

He held a pistol in one hand, the other hand cupping the grip. He was a big man, hard, but he exuded grace and control.

"Now then, we're going to—"

"I'm going to kill you," Miranda said, surprising herself with the venom in her voice. It must have surprised him, too, just for a second—his eyes went slightly wider, his head lifted a little.

"Not any more," he said. "Maybe if I hadn't seen you following me two days ago. Maybe if you hadn't given yourself away like the amateur you are."

"So shoot me if you think I'm an amateur."

"I don't go around killing people for no reason."

"Bullshit."

CHRISTOPHER GOLDEN AND TIM LEBBON

Ledger shrugged slightly, never taking his eyes from her. "I've taken pieces off the board, sure, but there's always been a reason. So don't give me one."

"I'll give you hundreds, but only one of them matters to me. Royal London Hospital. You killed the woman I love." She pressed her lips tight, trying not to betray her frustration. She shouldn't be talking with him. Making this feel personal might strip away her edge, and until now she'd kept the grief and burning need for revenge buried under a veil of professionalism. She couldn't let that change.

She had to make her move.

"I got the bastards who did that," he said, and she could hear the uncertainty. Fear at being found out, no doubt.

"I've seen enough evidence to nail you to the cross, Ledger. I'm here to do just that."

She sensed his confusion. His eyes flickered past her to the rifle she'd left lying beside the parapet. That was all she needed.

Miranda *flowed*. Every shred of her power, every ounce of grace, went into rolling to her right and powering toward Ledger. He fired his gun and the bullet whispered past her ear and over her back, so close that her clothing flicked and her belt tugged. Then she was on him, one hand batting his gun hand aside, the other driving up into his chin in a palm slap that cracked his teeth together.

She drove one foot between his and turned, still grasping his right arm at the wrist, tripping him and using his own weight to drop him to the rooftop. She went with him, drawing up her knee to land on his balls with all her weight.

He switched to the side, grunting as her knee crushed into his thigh.

Miranda head-butted him in the nose. She felt a warm splash of blood. Driving a fist into his left ear, hard, she rolled to her left.

Ledger had recovered from his surprise. Spitting blood, he followed her movement, twisting hard to free his shooting hand. He still grasped the gun, and Miranda knew she had to force him to let go or this was over.

She focused all her strength and attention on that hand, twisting, trying to haul it across her leg so she could break his wrist. Ledger did everything he could to prevent her from doing so.

Which was exactly what she wanted.

He didn't see her right hand swing around, the blade glinting in the hot Venetian sunlight, its razor sharpness kissing against his neck.

Now, she thought, and one flick would open his carotid artery. She'd watch him bleed out on this dirty rooftop, and it might be days before anyone found his body. Blinking Ledger's blood from her eye, she saw Tess tucking her hair behind her ear, saw her beautiful smile.

Ledger grasped the moment, writhed and flowed in her grip, releasing his gun and plucking the knife from her hand, smacking her down onto her back, pressing the knife against her throat.

Blood smeared his face. He breathed hard, but not panicked. He was totally in control.

"Fuck you," Miranda hissed, and she so wished she believed in any sort of God. If she did, then perhaps now she'd be looking forward to seeing Tess again.

It felt like a minute, but must have been only seconds.

"Whatever you think I did, you're wrong," Ledger said. He sat up, left hand raised in a gesture of truce, right hand still pressing the knife hard against her throat. Fighting her for less than a minute, he'd already grown to know her well.

Then he did the thing that shocked her even more than his stealth. He cast the knife aside and backed off her, both hands raised as if in surrender. The blade skittered and skidded along the rooftop, but Ledger remained on his knees, hands in the air, gaze locked on hers. Still on her back, Miranda was so stunned that at first she couldn't think to move.

"The hospital bombing—I was one of the investigators, not one of the evil pricks behind it," he said. "I made them pay. They're not going to hurt anyone again."

Heart pounding, breath shallow, Miranda scrambled to her feet, crouched and ready for a fight. Ledger still didn't move. He'd had her, could have slit her throat, but he'd tossed the knife away. He was on his knees now, there would be no way for him to catch her if she ran for the knife or her rifle. All she had wanted was his death. She could feel it now, a tangible thing, could see in her mind's eye what his face would look like when he breathed his last. Her hands opened and closed as she studied him. But while she was picturing Ledger's death, she couldn't see Tess's face in her mind's eye.

"Go on," Ledger said. "Grab a weapon if it makes you feel safer."

Miranda felt the hatred and grief rush up inside her. She took a step toward him. "I don't need a weapon to kill you."

"The way you fight, maybe you don't," Ledger said.

Nothing more. No explanation for throwing the blade away, no wheedling plea for his life, no further defense. Just letting his words sink in.

"I'm just supposed to believe you?"

"Up to you," he said. "I guess in your situation, I'd want to backtrack to whoever put the wrong guy in my crosshairs, figure out their motives."

Miranda felt the Italian sun on her back. From somewhere far off, two men began to shout amiably to each other—something about an upcoming wedding. She could smell peppers roasting on a grill in a patio restaurant someplace close by. Tess had never been to Venice, but she would have loved the people here. Loved the sounds and the smells and the ancient magic of this place.

She ignored Ledger now, walked back over to the edge of the roof, and picked up her rifle, began to break it down and pack it away. Her back remained to him for long seconds, so she wasn't surprised when she stood with the gun case and turned to see that he'd risen to his feet. His hands were at his sides, but he'd kept a respectful distance.

Still, his eyes were hard. "Seems like we've got mutual enemies now."

Miranda inhaled slowly. Exhaled. She believed him, of course. How could she not, when he'd given up an opportunity to kill her and put his life in her hands instead? It gave her some comfort to know the people responsible for the hospital bombing had been dealt with, but it was cold comfort indeed. She had wanted to get vengeance for Tess herself.

She carried the gun case at her side and headed across the long roof. This time she heard Ledger's footfalls as he followed her. Pigeons scattered in an irritated shush of wings.

"You're not just walking away after that," Ledger said.

Hatred had distracted her before, too much noise in her head. Now she listened to the rhythm of his footfalls and the shifting of his weight on the roof as he caught up behind her.

"Look, whatever your deal is, I need to know what you know," he went on. "I get it, you want to take out the people who pointed you at me, tried to get you to pull the trigger for them, but I was the target. So we need to talk. I don't know you well enough to just assume you're gonna get the job done. Damn it, are you even listening to—"

She sensed it the moment before his hand landed on her shoulder. Her fingers wrapped around his wrist and she drove her other elbow into his gut. Still holding that wrist, she twisted out to one side, wrenched his arm back, and swung the gun case with perfectly calculated force. It struck Ledger's skull with the sound of a cricket bat connecting with a ball. He staggered, but the son of a bitch was so strong, so determined, that he stayed on his feet. He'd been staggering to his left, trying to stay upright and keep her from dislocating his shoulder, and now she released her grip on his wrist.

As he righted himself, turned to face her, shooting her a pissed-off look that said all of his patience was at an end, Miranda snapped a high kick at the center of his chest. Ledger stumbled back a foot—but the roof had only six inches left to give. His arms pinwheeled as he went over the edge. Knowing there might be eyes on her, Miranda didn't stay to watch him hit the water, but she heard the splash in the canal as she bolted back toward the stairs.

A trace of guilt flickered through her mind as she fled, gun case in hand, but it was gone as swiftly as it had arrived. Ledger could have killed her. If the tables had been turned, she doubted she'd have been so understanding. But he'd taken the vengeance that should have been hers. The killing wasn't over, but the important killing—the killing that would have given her a sense of balance—had already been done, and Miranda knew that would haunt her for the rest of her life. That, and images of Tess that would continue to flicker into view, continue to linger in her thoughts, the ghost who walked the corridors of her heart. She couldn't escape the feeling that the two most important moments of her life had been stolen from her before she'd even lived them.

A wedding and a killing.

In a narrow back alley, passing over a canal in a dilapidated part of Venice that the tourists never saw, Miranda pitched the gun case into the water and walked on without watching it sink into the murk.

There would be other guns.

ABOUT THE AUTHORS
Christopher Golden is the New York Times **number one bestselling author of** Snowblind, Tin Men, Of Saints and Shadows, **and many other novels. With Mike Mignola, he co-created two cult-favorite comics series,** Baltimore **and** Joe Golem: Occult Detective. **As editor, his books include the anthologies** Seize the Night, The New Dead, **and** Dark Cities. **Golden is a co-host of**

the pop-culture podcast *Three Guys with Beards*, co-founder of the writing workshop and literary event company River City Writers, and frequent conference, school, and library speaker. His works have been published in various languages around the world. Please visit him at www.christophergolden .com.

Tim Lebbon is a *New York Times* bestselling writer with more than thirty novels published to date, as well as dozens of novellas and hundreds of short stories. Recent releases include *The Silence*, *The Hunt*, *The Family Man*, and *The Rage War* trilogy (licensed *Alien* and *Predator* novels). Forthcoming novels include the *Relics* trilogy and *Blood of the Four* (with Christopher Golden). He has won four British Fantasy Awards, a Bram Stoker Award, and a Scribe Award and has been short-listed for World Fantasy and Shirley Jackson Awards. A movie of his novel *Pay the Ghost*, starring Nicolas Cage, was released in 2015, and other projects in development include *My Haunted House*, *Playtime* (with Stephen Volk), and *Exorcising Angels* (with Simon Clark). To find out more, please visit www.timlebbon.net.

EDITORS' NOTE: This story is a crossover between the *Joe Ledger* series and Scott Sigler's novel *Nocturnal*. In that novel, San Francisco homicide inspectors Bryan Clauser and Pookie Chang follow a trail of brutal serial killings tied to a secret, subterranean war that has raged through the city for more than a century.

VACATION

BY SCOTT SIGLER

A spectacular sunset over the Golden Gate Bridge, turning the few wisps of fog below it a reddish orange. A view of Alcatraz Island, old and solid and full of legends. And me—just some guy sitting on a park bench at Marina Green with his dog lying down next to him, big white head in my lap.

A perfect moment. I shouldn't have answered the phone, but old habits die hard. And then there was the fact that calls to *this* phone were not to be ignored—especially when those calls came from *that* man.

I had to jostle Ghost a bit to pull the phone out of my pocket. The white German shepherd glanced at me, just to check that everything was okay, then put his head back down on my lap.

I answered.

"Know what, Church? I'm buying you a dictionary."

"So I can look up what the word *vacation* means, I assume."

I hate it when he does that.

"The least you could have done was let me have the fucking punch line."

"If you want the punch line, Joe, tell better jokes. Don't worry, this probably won't take long."

That's the thing with Mr. Church. His *probably* has a completely different definition from what you'd expect. Yes, a dictionary would be the ideal Christmas present.

In my life, perfect moments are rare. Church had interrupted that moment. I breathed deep, slow, petting Ghost's head. A big head, because he's a big dog. As in *almost fifty kilos* big. I'd had him only a few weeks, and we were already bound by blood. He'd taken a bullet that would have killed me. He'd also torn the hand off a human being who'd murdered the love of my life. I'd never been a dog person, but in my mind Ghost wasn't really a *dog*—he was a fellow soldier. He was my pack member.

That bullet hurt him, though. An inch-wide streak of shaved fur on his left shoulder surrounded eight stitches dotting a line of pursed flesh. While he recovered, I'd decided to reward his performance with a "sniff all the things you can" tour of San Francisco.

Of course, this trip wasn't just for Ghost. I needed recovery time, and not the physical kind. The wounds of Grace's loss were too fresh. Too raw. I wasn't ready to deal with people. I sure as hell wasn't ready to go back to work.

"You promised me time off after Veder," I said.

"Veder. Curious how everyone in the world has lost track of him."

"Yeah," I said. "Quite curious."

I'd buried that assassin on a beach. I pissed on his grave. So did Ghost. The only creatures who would ever see him again were crabs that dug deep to feast on his rotting flesh.

"I need you to track down a lead," Church said. "Kraken Team was running an op in El Paso. The Mexican cartel seems to be working with some new muscle."

"And we care, why? The drug business isn't our business."

"It is when multiple sightings of that *muscle* describes them as *orcs*."

Most people would have laughed at that. Most people don't work for the DMS. With the shit I've seen, I didn't second-guess Church, even for an instant.

"Orcs," I said. "That's new."

"Three of them. In gangland circles, they've come to be known as *Tres Hermanos Orco*."

"The Three *Orc Brothers*? Fantastic."

"There are no pictures," Church said. "No video, just a sketch. The DEA lost two undercover agents to these guys. A survivor of that incident described them, and that filtered back to me. We sent Kraken

Team to help out. Found them pretty quickly. There was a firefight. Imura says he landed three shots with an M110 SASS, all center-mass, from a distance of fifty meters. When Kraken Team closed in, there was blood, but no body."

"Could the other two brothers have carried the dead one out?"

"Spotters saw three big bodies leaving, leaving *fast*."

Sam "Ronin" Imura is the best sniper I've ever met. If he says he landed three shots center-mass, then that's a fact. The M110 fired 7.62 × 51 mm rounds—*número uno orco* should have been hamburger.

"Body armor?"

"Imura didn't see any, but these were big guys. Easy to assume body armor was involved."

"So how does this involve me?"

"Blood analysis turned up something funny—a third sex chromosome."

"Klinefelter syndrome?"

"No, not XXY," Church said. "Something I've never seen before. It's more like a Z. Here's where it gets strange. Hu processed the genome. MindReader ran that info through every database you can imagine. It got a hit, but a hit that was erased years ago."

It wasn't surprising MindReader could find something that wasn't supposed to be there anymore. That computer was Church's creation, a silicon god that seemed to move in and out of the world's databases like an all-powerful tech phantom.

"MindReader found a mitochondrial DNA match with a Jebediah Erickson, resident of San Francisco. Whatever the Orc Brothers are, their mother is Erickson's mother."

"So it's Quatro Hermanos?"

"Maybe, but Erickson is old. He was in an insane asylum for vigilante murders back in the eighties. That information, too, had been wiped out of multiple databases. If it wasn't for MindReader, Erickson's crimes and his time in the asylum wouldn't exist."

With the foes the DMS had faced, I knew age was a relative thing.

"You want me to bring Erickson in."

"Just talk to him," Church said. "I'd leave this to the locals entirely, but if Erickson *is* involved, the last thing we want is more good cops dead. See if the guy knows anything about his brothers. Our assets are stretched thin right now. You taking care of this lead saves me the headache of pulling someone off an assignment."

Were we that maxed out? Maybe. Or maybe Church was giving me a guilt trip for being on vacation. Well, fuck him—I'd earned a few days off. Still, though . . . a new chromosome, dead DEA agents . . .

"You think Erickson is dangerous?"

"He's seventy-three. Although he did win a gold medal in archery in the Pan Am Games, so if he pulls a bow on you . . .'"

That was Church's idea of a joke.

"And you made fun of *my* punch lines?"

"Touché. So, can you do this for me?"

I slowly petted Ghost's head.

"Fine," I said. "Happy to be a team player, as always."

"Good. An Inspector Chang is on his way to pick you up at Marina Green."

"What, *here*? You called the SFPD and told them I was in before you called to ask me?"

"I had a hunch," Church said. "If there's weird shit going down in San Francisco, the mayor said Chang is our guy. Chang is aware of Ghost. I'm getting DMS people out there for this. Gather what info you can and hand it over when they arrive. Let me know if you find anything."

He hung up.

I sat there, taking in the amazing view, gently petting Ghost. Ghost was loving it, his eyes narrowed both from the light breeze off the bay and from the attention.

"Well, pal, looks like we have to put in some work. You mind?"

Ghost's eyes widened to their normal, thousand-yard-stare width. He *whuffed* once and stood, slowly, favoring his wounded leg.

Marina Green was once a landing strip, I'd learned. Long, rectangular, and—obviously—*green*, it had a parking lot along one side and a footpath on the other, separating it from the water. No more than thirty or forty seconds after the call with Church, I heard the honk of a car horn.

An Asian man wearing a brown sport coat stepped out of a shit-brown Buick. He waved at me. Heavy black hair, about thirty pounds too many.

I walked across the grass to the car, Ghost at my side.

"Howdy do," the man said in a Chicago accent so thick I wouldn't have been surprised to find a bratwurst stuffed in his coat pocket. "One giant-sized white canine, *check*. One badass-looking mofo with all the charm of someone who just had a homeless guy drop a corned-up chocolate dragon in his Cheerios, *check*. Agent Ledger and Ghost, I assume?"

"And you must be Inspector Chang," I said, shaking his offered hand.

"Call me Pookie. Everyone does."

"I'm Joe."

"Joe, what the fuck happened to your face?"

I'd forgotten about that. Before I killed Veder, he'd done a number on me: blackened left eye, purple bruises on my chin and throat, a knot on my forehead that looked like half a golf ball surgically implanted beneath yellow-purple skin.

"It was just a scuffle."

"Let me guess," Chang said. "I should see the other guy."

I shrugged. "Sure. If anyone ever finds him."

Chang nodded slowly. "I think I'm done asking questions. Let's go."

He opened the passenger door—not to let me in, but to clean up a stack of overstuffed manila folders so old and reused they shed tan dander all over the place. He moved the folders to the floor of the rear seat, then cleared off more of the same to make room in the back for Ghost. Chang held the door open.

"Hop in, pup."

Ghost didn't move.

I flicked a finger to the car. Ghost leaped in.

"Nice," Chang said. "My buddy has a dog. Not quite as well behaved."

"Yeah, Ghost is a real cream puff. Just do me a favor and keep your hands away from his mouth."

Chang half laughed, as if I were joking, then realized I wasn't.

"How about I just avoid getting anywhere near the cuddly little feller?"

I nodded. "That's probably for the best."

We drove out of Marina Green, then through tree-lined streets full of three-story buildings, most of which sported San Francisco's famous three-sided bay window architecture. I'd walked these same streets in the past few days, assuming most apartments held tech rich kids paying at least twice as much for seven hundred square feet as I did for my entire house.

"Chief Robertson told me to help you out," Chang said. "He said in no uncertain terms that you were some VIP big shot or what have you. I speak politician, so allow me to paraphrase what he said: 'Chang, if Ledger wants a Flint Crankshaft with a complimentary Rhode Island Reach-Around, then you give him a Flint Crankshaft with a complimentary Rhode Island Reach-Around.'"

Chang talked too much. Every police force has at least a few of him, though. Law enforcement is a difficult, often thankless gig, which means morale is just as important as target practice. Guys like Chang make a shitty job a little less shitty.

"Do I even want to know what a Flint Crankshaft is?"

"Depends," he said. "You the kind of guy who frequents swinger parties and has a lifetime subscription to *Naughty America*?"

"No."

"Then you don't want to know. On the serious tip—mind telling me why I'm taking you to see Erickson?"

"He's a person of interest in a case my department is working on."

"Yeah, about that *department*. This alphabet soup gets so confusing. PMS? PBS? Say yes to the dress? What was it again?"

I don't mind a little lightheartedness, but Chang's flippancy was starting to annoy me.

"*DMS*," I said.

"And why interrupt your doggie vacay instead of having one of us follow up on this for you? I'd be happy to take it off your plate. It is my town and all."

He seemed a little too eager for that solution. Territorial pissing? All too common in police work. Maybe he smelled involvement in a federal case, something that would look good on his annual review.

"Two undercover DEA agents were murdered," I said. "Erickson might be related to the killers. Listen, I was a cop once. I know playing taxi driver is annoying as hell, so I suggest we get this over with as quickly as possible. Then we'll all go on our merry way."

Chang changed lanes for no reason, cutting off a silver Mercedes that honked angrily.

"Asshole," Chang said. "Roads are full of 'em."

"Apparently."

"Listen, Joe-Joe, I can save you some trouble. I've talked to Erickson before. He's nobody. Not worth your time."

Yes, I had been a cop once, and now those cop instincts rose up like lava under high pressure. The very guy sent to escort me around town was hiding something. My bullshit alarm jumped straight to DEFCON 2.

"Let's cut to the chase," I said. "Take me to Erickson's house, or I go by myself and inform my boss—who apparently knows *your* boss—that you were less than helpful. Your choice."

Chang let out a low whistle.

"Well, that adds up, doesn't it? And you can fuck your math teacher, but you can't fuck math."

We drove in silence for the next ten minutes. Maybe that was a mistake on my part, because silence gave me time to think.

Grace was gone. I knew that, accepted it, yet the realization kept hitting me over and over, the pain fresh and abrasive each time. I'd killed the man who had killed her. That hadn't brought her back, just added one more body to the endless train of death that was my life.

San Francisco is a city with amazing architecture. Ghost and I had spent two days walking the streets and hills, seeing the sights, taking in the views. More Victorian homes than you could shake a stick at. Most of them were long since converted to bed-and-breakfasts or divided up for apartments.

Not so with Jebediah Erickson's place.

The onetime Pan Am Games gold medalist and institutionalized vigilante killer lived at 2007 Franklin Street, a gray Victorian that sat so close to the three-lane one-way it almost leaned over the road the way a cat leans over a wounded mouse.

Chang pulled into the driveway, parked next to a black Dodge Magnum station wagon. It had gotten dark quickly, but there was enough light for me to see a black-and-white German shorthaired pointer run down the house's marble steps and put its paws on the Buick's back door—the dog's nose was separated from Ghost's only by the window glass. Both tails wagged furiously.

"Goddammit, Emma, get off my car," Chang said in the voice of one who knows the dog isn't going to listen.

"She lives here, Pooks," said a man walking down the same steps. "She can do what she wants."

"She doesn't live in *my car*, all right?"

The man had pale skin, but everything else was black—hair, work boots, jeans, a black sweatshirt that barely hid the telltale bulge of a handgun. Everything black, save for a three-day growth of red beard. The man had a vibe: the kind of guy who could handle himself in any situation. He instantly reminded me of my DMS squad mates.

"Agent Ledger?" he said.

I nodded. "And you are?"

"Jebediah Erickson."

Mid-thirties, max, unless I'd somehow stumbled into *another* Nazi genetics experiment.

"I assume you mean Jebediah Erickson *Junior*? Or perhaps *the third*?"

He shook his head.

Make that DEFCON 1.

"You're in good shape for a seventy-three-year-old man," I said, shaking the offered hand.

"Benefits of clean living," Erickson said. "Come in. Bring your dog with if you like."

Two things dominated my thoughts: one, this was not the real Jebediah Erickson, and two, this guy—like me—was once a cop. When you wear the badge as long as I did, it's something you just know.

Right off the bat, there was something about him I liked. I had to remind myself he might be involved with the Orc Brothers and the death of DEA agents. Still, there was a calmness about Erickson, the kind you sense only in people who've performed well in intense combat.

I leashed Ghost and let him out. Emma immediately went in for the butt sniff, so fast and sudden that Ghost actually scooted away before turning to sniff her. I swear, it's the first time I've ever seen my dog look *worried*.

"Emma's overly friendly," Erickson said. "Come on inside."

Dogs have a powerful sense of smell, but in a way I do, too—I can smell my own. This "Erickson" was a killer. I just hoped he was one of the good guys.

The house's interior was just as spectacular as the exterior. Everything looked antique, as if the furniture had been made from a mixture of old money and social status poured into a mold built by long-dead lumber barons. But there were strange things, too: muddy dog prints on couches that cost more than my car; a huge flat-screen TV that looked completely out of place among the decor; textbooks and *Seventeen* magazines scattered all over. The place smelled faintly of gun oil.

He was clearly rich as hell, and also clearly didn't give a crap about the stuff in this house.

"Got kids, Mr. Erickson?"

"It's *Jeb*," he said, gesturing to a chair that should have been in a museum. "And no, I don't. A woman and her two teenage daughters live here. They've been through some hard times."

At this, Chang laughed, a huff of agreement that screamed *You can say that again*. Another part of this strange story?

I sat. Ghost sat at my feet. Emma rushed in for another butt sniff. I started to warn Ghost to behave, assuming he'd growl, but he just wagged his tail.

"Ghost and Emma sitting in a tree," Chang said. "Your dog fixed, Joe?"

Honestly, at that time, I didn't know.

"Emma, *come*," Erickson said.

The pointer wasn't as stoic as Ghost, but when Erickson called her she ran to him and sat, mouth open, tongue lolling, looking up at the man as if he were the greatest thing that had ever lived.

"Agent Ledger, I'm friends with the mayor," Erickson said. "He called and told me to help you out if I could, but I'm a busy guy. Can we get to the point?"

I gave him the rundown that Church gave me. When I got to the part about the Z chromosome, Chang and Erickson exchanged a glance—they not only knew about it, they thought they were the only ones who did.

I showed Erickson the sketch Church had texted me. An Orc Brother: cammo raincoat over shoulders that could have belonged to an NFL lineman or a gorilla; hunched back; flat, wide nose; beady eyes beneath a heavy brow. Whatever hair it might have had was hidden beneath the raincoat hood. And, yeah, two actual *fangs*, jutting up from the lower jaw.

"That's not good," Erickson said.

Not *Oh, give me a break*, or *Stop wasting my time*, just *That's not good*. My BS alarm continued to scream—this guy had no problem accepting this as real. Outside of the DMS and the people we'd fought against, I didn't know *anyone* who wouldn't instantly question that sketch.

"So, uh," Erickson said, "my mom is their mom?"

I nodded. "That's what I'm told. Of course, I now have my doubts that you were even *born* by the time the real Jebediah Erickson was institutionalized. Where is he?"

Not-Erickson thought for a moment, then plowed forward, not bothering to lie.

"He's dead. And no, I didn't kill him. Agent Ledger, if you—"

"Call me *Joe*," I said. "Because that's my actual name. What's yours?"

The world narrowed to our locked stare: half battle of wills, half evaluation of the soul. My instincts told me he was good people, but then again, I'd thought the same thing of the man pretending to be an FBI agent who turned out to be the very assassin who'd killed Grace, almost killed Ghost, almost killed me.

Maybe my instincts were on vacation, too.

"Bryan," the man said.

Chang stood up, instantly agitated. "Bry—Bry . . . I mean, *Jeb*, aren't we going a little fast here?"

Erickson's—*Bryan's*—eyes never left mine.

"Joe, the mayor said your DMS was a big deal. I understand you have a job to do, but there's more going on in this city than you could know. This is San Francisco—things are different here."

I couldn't stop myself from laughing.

"Bryan, you have no idea of what we do at the DMS."

He raised an eyebrow. "Whatever it is, trust me, we've seen shit that would make your head spin."

Like this identity thief had ever seen hybrid gorilla soldiers, wasp-dogs, fucking zombies, and a dragon? I'd faced actual, honest-to-God *monsters*.

My cell phone rang. More good news from Church. I answered it.

"Ledger here."

"The Orc Brothers are in San Francisco. MindReader analyzed the combat footage from Kraken Team and nailed an algorithm for the way they walk. The Brothers were spotted in the Presidio—based on your GPS, you're maybe fifteen blocks from where they are. I'm sending Kraken Team, but their earliest ETA is four hours from now."

MindReader could identify people from the way they *walked* now? That machine got spookier every day.

"Send me the GPS location." With the phone still to my ear, I held out my hand to Chang. "Give me your car keys."

"Don't fucking think so," Chang said.

"Church, say hello to Inspector Chang and tell him it's in his best interest to give me his car, right now."

I offered the phone to Chang. He hesitated, then took it.

"This is Inspector Chang."

To this day, I don't know what Church said to him. I knew my boss, though, and knew MindReader would instantly cough up every little sin this guy had done, both on the clock and off.

"No shit," Chang said into the phone. "Um . . . what if I told you I didn't know she was married, and that wasn't even my wheelbarrow?"

A moment of silence, then he hung up. He handed me both the phone and his car keys.

"That guy can fuck your math teacher, then fuck math, then give physics a reach-around *and* a Chang Bang while he's at it," Pookie said. "Try not to wreck my ride."

His car drove like shit. My cell phone and the map had me to the Presidio in minutes—the wonders of modern technology. The lights of San Francisco quickly faded away, vanishing as I drove into the Presidio. Houses gave way to trees, to a surprising level of darkness. Cloud cover hid stars and moon alike. And, of course, there was fog and plenty of it. I felt more as though I were in the hills of Pennsylvania than in the midst of one of the world's great cities.

The cell's GPS took me far up a winding road to a parking lot that overlooked the city. Ghost and I got out. I drew my SIG Sauer and scanned the area. Darkness on all sides save for straight ahead, which was a sprawling view of house lights, car lights, and streetlights struggling to be seen through the fog.

Just one light pole here: and on it, a small closed-circuit camera. That was how MindReader had seen the Orc Brothers. Two immediate thoughts: one, MindReader was some seriously frightening Big Brother stuff; and, two, if this one little camera could spot the Orc Brothers and we had no other MindReader-based sightings of them in El Paso or anywhere else, Tres Hermanos Orco were very, *very* good at not being seen.

Ghost began to growl. The hairs on the back of my neck stood up. Ghost took a few steps from the car, body low, hackles raised—he was on point, nose aiming toward the dense shadows on the side of the parking lot.

I'd made a mistake: I had my SIG Sauer, I had my Wilson Rapid Response knife, but no body armor, no night vision, and no backup.

Ghost's growl changed to a bark of challenge just as something—something *big*, too big to be a normal person—burst out of the woods.

I didn't bother with questions: I started shooting. Seven rounds in less than a second, then the shadow turned and fled back into the woods.

Ghost went after it. I'd just started to give the *stay* command when I heard a horrible crunch of metal and breaking glass, and something hit me so hard it threw me through the air.

Half-stunned, I slid across the pavement, shredding both my shirt and the skin below it before I managed to roll to my knees. The Buick's passenger side was caved in, a crater like a wrecking ball—an Orc Brother had hit the car so hard it smashed into me. And leaping over the Buick's rear, lit up in the single streetlight, that same Hermano Orco—a big-ass, hunchbacked man wearing a camouflage raincoat.

Flat nose flaring, mouth open, two lower teeth sticking up like spikes of bone, he rushed me. I emptied my magazine. I capped off the last round from not even a foot away. It should have blown his heart straight out his back, dropped him like a bag of concrete—the fact that he didn't even slow scrambled my thoughts for a moment, long enough for his huge fist to deliver a crushing body blow.

I felt ribs snap. The blow lifted me off my feet, threw me back, sent me tumbling across the pavement. I rolled to my feet for the second time, trying to brace for the pain, compensate for it, but no matter how tough you are broken ribs jam up the way you move.

The Orc Brother came straight in—hunchbacked, shoulders wide as a door, a steamroller with a raincoat trailing like a supervillain's cape.

Knowing how bad the move would hurt, I feinted right, then stepped wide left. Orc matched the feint, but when he corrected, it was too late—I was already outside his right shoulder, my right hand driving my knife up into his chest. The point slid home just below his sternum; I had a flash of satisfaction that I'd pierced his heart just before his momentum slammed into my arm and shoulder, spinning me around, tearing the knife from my grasp.

I landed on my broken ribs. What air I had left in my lungs took a fast exit. I couldn't tell if one of those lungs was punctured. If so, I still had a good chance of living longer than the asshole I'd just stabbed.

My enemy was down. Still rolling around a bit—it might take him a few minutes to die.

"Fuck you," I said through clenched teeth.

And then, the asshole got up.

He stood slowly, but he *stood*. The knife was still sticking out of his chest. With one gray hand, he gripped the handle and pulled it free. Blood spurted once, twice . . . then stopped.

"No," the Orc Brother said in a voice that—like his body, like his face—wasn't quite human. "Fuck *you*."

He smiled, staggered toward me, his balance becoming more sure with each step.

I had shot this prick at least five times at close range.

I had stabbed him in the goddamn *heart*.

And he was still coming.

A flash of white: Ghost jumping between me and the Orc Brother, fur raised, lip curled back to show wet teeth, a low growl gurgling in his throat.

A second flash of white—white with black spots. It was Emma, Erickson's dog, at Ghost's side, the two of them barking madly. Smaller than Ghost, but equal in projected ferocity.

The combined canine warning made the Orc Brother stop. Maybe he'd have come right at Ghost, but the pair gave him pause.

"I hate dogs," he said. "Gonna kill your dogs. Gonna eat 'em while you watch, then gonna eat you."

Fantastic.

I struggled to my feet, one hand holding my ribs. No weapon—I had to find a way to stop this bastard.

A hiss of air slipping past my right ear.

A *thunk*.

The Orc Brother looked down at the arrow shaft sticking out of his chest. He seemed confused.

"Burns," he said. "Never burned before."

A voice from behind me: "Welcome back to San Francisco, shitbird."

The Orc Brother fell to his ass, still staring at the arrow shaft.

I recognized that voice: Jebediah "Bryan" Erickson. Whoever the hell he really was. I turned, expecting to see that pale face with the red stubble, the same black hair. Instead, I saw a man wearing a black navy pea coat, black jeans, black gloves, black skullcap with a black mask dangling from it—eyeholes and death grin poorly stitched in white. He held a black carbon fiber compound bow.

This circus sideshow had just jumped up to a full-on freak exhibit. What the hell was all this?

"You've got good moves, but the wrong weapon," he said. "If the other two assholes come, use this. Stick it where it counts, leave it in."

He handed me a sheathed KA-BAR. I took it.

"Watch my dog for me," he said. "I'll be right back."

He stepped between Ghost and Emma. Bryan/Jeb pulled an identical KA-BAR from inside his pea coat. Black anodized blade. Only the edge caught the glow of the single streetlight.

The Orc Brother saw him coming. For the first time, I saw fear in the monster's eyes.

"No," the monster said in that inhuman voice. "No, not *you*!"

The man in black closed the distance. He kicked out a booted foot so fast I didn't see it move, just saw the Orc's head snap back, one long tooth spinning into the night.

Bryan/Erickson grabbed the Orc by the throat. He stabbed the long blade into the Orc's left eye, so deep I heard the tip hit the inside of the skull.

The dark wood rang with a sudden howl of anguish, a pair of inhuman voices combined into one. The trees at the edge of the parking lot erupted—the other two Orc Brothers came at us.

One rushed the man in black, one rushed me. Both screamed nonsensical words of hate, or revenge.

Ten meters from me. Broken ribs. A bulletproof foe, or at least one that bullets didn't bother. I'd already stabbed his brother in the heart, to no effect.

Seven meters.

Stick it where it counts, leave it in.

Five.

I gave Ghost a hand signal: *hamstring*.

Ghost sprinted wide of the oncoming enemy, then turned sharply and bit at the back of his ankle. Canine fangs punctured cloth and leather.

At two meters, the Orc Brother turned to swipe at Ghost, but his forward momentum brought him stumbling straight at me.

Putting the KA-BAR in his throat was almost too easy.

I felt the blade scrape cervical vertebrae, and then the huge man— what, maybe 140 kilos?—fell past me. I let the knife go.

The Orc Brother hit the pavement. Blood sprayed everywhere, blackish red in the single light, but unlike when I'd stabbed his brother's heart this blood didn't stop spurting.

Not for another ten or fifteen seconds. Not until there wasn't enough blood left *to* spurt.

I heard the sound of fists smashing into flesh, the cracking of bone. I turned to see the man in black straddling a prone Orc Brother, raining down blow after blow. Each time he pulled back a fist, it trailed an arc of blood.

I thought of the movie *Rocky*, of Sly Stallone hitting that side of beef over and over again. Finally, Bryan/Erickson stood. Emma ran to him, tail wagging, tongue lolling as if this were nothing more than a walk at the beach.

The man in black looked at me. "Ledger, you all right?"

I nodded toward my fallen foe. "Better than him."

Bryan/Erickson pulled a rag—black, of course—from an inside pocket. He wiped blood, bits of bone, and, probably, chunks of brain from his leather gloves.

"Why didn't my bullets kill the first one?" I asked. "Or my knife? Why did *your* knife work?"

"Ancient Chinese secret."

He came closer.

"You owe me," he said. "Let me hear you say it."

I glanced around at the carnage, but didn't need to—he was right. If he hadn't shown up, I'd be dead. Probably Ghost as well.

"I owe you," I said.

"Give me your word," he said. "You don't talk about this, to anyone. Do that and we're even."

I thought about what he'd told me at the big Victorian house: "This is San Francisco—things are different here." A quiet little war, but this guy, this man in a psycho mask . . . we were on the same side.

"You have my word," I said. "You look like the kind of guy who doesn't appreciate publicity. Want me to make these bodies go away?"

He shook his head. The skull smile mask swayed slightly.

"The bodies are mine," he said.

He moved quickly, carrying each Orc Brother body into the dark woods. The way he picked them up, as though they weighed little more than a bag of flour . . . this guy had serious strength.

Inhuman strength.

Enough to make me wonder if he had that Z chromosome, and what it meant.

He walked back to me.

"What, exactly, are you doing with those bodies?"

"Bringing a truck, taking them to my basement."

His basement. Of course. I wanted the hell out of San Francisco.

"Need a ride?" he asked. "Hospital, maybe?"

"I've got it covered. Did you walk here?"

I'd almost said, *Did you fly here*, as if he were some kind of *X-Men* mutant, but caught myself at the last second.

He pointed to the edge of the parking lot, close to the winding road. There sat what looked like a sci-fi version of a Harley.

"That an electric motorcycle?"

The masked man nodded. "Yup."

"With a sidecar, for your dog?"

"Yup."

"Might have to get me one of those."

"You owe Pookie a car first."

True enough.

His eyes narrowed with anger, but not directed at me.

"*Emma!* Stop sniffing that poor dog's ass!"

Sure enough, the dog had her nose jammed into Ghost's butt. Ghost had that worried look on his face again.

"*Emma!*"

The pointer reluctantly ran to the sidecar and hopped in.

"Listen," I said, "I have resources. Whatever is happening here, if it gets out of hand, you can call me."

He thought about it for a moment, then nodded.

"Fair enough. And if you have targets in SF again, I'm your huckleberry."

I offered my hand. He shook, and that was that. Two warriors, blindly trusting each other based on nothing more than a two-minute skirmish that had left three enemy combatants dead.

In my world? Sometimes, that's enough.

He drove off in his motorcycle, which didn't make a sound. No wonder I hadn't heard him come in. I watched the man in black, whoever he was, fade into the night.

A wet nose nudged my hand. Ghost, asking to be petted. As I scratched his big head, I called Mr. Church.

"Joe, you okay?"

"Call off Kraken Team," I said. "The Orc Brothers are neutralized."

"Excellent news."

"Get an ambulance to my location, stat. Keep it quiet."

"You going to tell me what happened?"

"Can't," I said. "I gave my word. And don't call me until I return—I'm on fucking vacation."

This time, I got to hang up on him.

Ghost and I walked to the edge of the overlook. Together, just a man and his dog, we stared out at the foggy night and waited for the ambulance.

ABOUT THE AUTHOR

Number one *New York Times* bestselling author Scott Sigler is the creator of fifteen novels, six novellas, and dozens of short stories. His works are available from Crown Publishing and Del Rey Books. In 2005, Scott built a large online following by releasing his audiobooks as serialized podcasts. A decade later, he still gives his stories away—for free—every Sunday at www.scottsigler.com. His loyal fans, who named themselves "Junkies," have downloaded more than forty million individual episodes. He has been covered in *Time*, *Entertainment Weekly*, *Publishers Weekly*, *The New York Times*, *The Washington Post*, the *San Francisco Chronicle*, the *Chicago Tribune*, *Io9*, *Wired*, the *Huffington Post*, *BusinessWeek*, and *Fangoria*. Scott is the co-founder of Empty Set Entertainment, which publishes his *Galactic Football League* YA series. He lives in San Diego, California, with his wee little dog, Reesie.

BANSHEE

BY JAMES A. MOORE

Bug and MindReader did all the heavy lifting. I can't clarify that enough. Without their work we would have never even had a case. The situations might have come across as natural circumstances or death by misadventure. Hell, there wasn't even going to be an autopsy on a couple of the victims until MindReader suggested it.

I was catching up on paperwork, which is to say, wishing I could find a way to blind myself or at least shatter all of my fingers so some-one else could do the boring stuff, when Bug told me what was going on.

"So, there are three confirmed cases and two maybes here, Joe, but MindReader thinks we've got an assassin on the loose."

"Bug?" I thought long and hard about a beer, but decided water would do the job. The weather was hot and it was only getting hotter. Summer in D.C. is like a special kind of roulette wheel where sometimes you win a perfect day and other times you win clouds, humidity, disgusting heat, and more of the same. Now and then, though, you get a quick rain that drops the temperature down by thirty degrees and makes you feel human again.

That wasn't why I was drinking water. Beer probably wouldn't go well on a mission and I had a feeling we were revving up for one.

"Yeah, Joe?"

"You want to fill me in on some details? It sounds like we're dealing with three-fifths of an assassination." Now and then I liked pulling Bug's leg a little. He got so serious when he was working.

"What? No. No, Joe. We're dealing with at least three deaths and I think maybe two more that need confirmation. And if MindReader is right, we have at least five more diplomats who could be dead by the end of the week."

All the jest went out of me that quickly. No one likes the idea of that sort of national crisis. "Talk. Tell me why this is Department of Military Sciences, so I can convince Mr. Church."

We don't get to pick and choose our cases. They are picked for us, but when something comes along and Bug tells me we should be interested, I do what I can. That means I need to be able to prove my point to the boss.

"So, here's the thing. A week ago, Hiro Tanaka, attaché to the Japanese ambassador, was found dead in a hotel room in New York. He was there for a business meeting with Walker Financial. Typical business. The same sort of thing he does all the time. He's found in his hotel room, alone, the doors locked, the room high enough up that the windows don't open.

"Two days later, in Boston, Alejandro Humbre, a bigwig in the Spanish ambassador's security detail, was also found dead in his room. Doors locked, windows closed, no signs of forced entry. No explanation as to why he was there, but the ambassador was supposed to be visiting so it's a safe bet he was there just to do his job.

"Next day in Philadelphia we have the same sort of situation with the personal secretary to Belgium's ambassador.

"Same day in D.C. we get the exact same scenario with the aide to the personal attaché to South Africa's ambassador, only this time there's a difference."

"Wait. All of these are supposed to be natural causes?"

"Joe, most of these aren't even supposed to get autopsied. I only have information about the cause of death because of MindReader. In three of the cases, the description comes down to internal organs that have been liquefied. As in several ribs not shattered but turned into powder, and the organs in the abdomen and chest turned into a meat frappé."

That sort of visual is how Bug gets his revenge for paperwork. I'm convinced of it.

"But in one case, Joe, we got something different. We got a scale stuck in the fabric of the victim's robe. The robe he was wearing when he died."

"A scale? What kind of scale?"

"Not the kind you weigh stuff with. More like a snake scale, only in this case, it's completely synthetic. I pulled a few strings and got a schematic of the thing. It's not organic, but it's also not standard plastic. This thing is designed to do something; I'm just not sure what without more of the big picture."

"So we have a plastic doohickey in the shape of a scale. That might not be enough to get Church all kinds of excited."

"That was in Philadelphia, Joe. Here in D.C. there are ten more of those scales, three of them found embedded in the victim's chest and flesh. Currently they're on their way to DCPD Forensics. You think Mr. Church might be able to get a couple of them sent my way?"

I smiled. That was the sort of information that made Church a happy man. It was the kind of information he could sink his teeth into.

"So why does MindReader think all of these are connected? What was the red flag here?"

"Joe, all of these guys move in the same circles, right? But none of them really have a reason to be hanging out together. It could be coincidence if all of their bosses were hanging around together and doing their political dances, but each and every one of these people has been together every other month on the fifteenth in places where their employers were not hanging around together. MindReader caught on to that. MindReader also caught on to the weird cause of death."

Bug was sounding like a proud papa again. He should have been. He was the one who built MindReader from the code up, and his creation was capable of pulling together algorithms that no one else knew existed, because MindReader could get into programs that no one knew were out there in the first place while completely hiding its trails. Believe me when I say this: MindReader made everyone who knew it existed a little nervous, and the list of people who knew about it was very small.

"Let me talk to Mr. Church. We'll find out what's going on from there."

Three things about that case made me happy. First, Bug had just proven the value of MindReader beyond a reasonable doubt. Second, there was a chance we could stop a burgeoning international incident from exploding all over the faces of the right people. Third, I got a good reason to hold off on finishing my paperwork.

I talked to Church.

He agreed. We had to get on it.

The problem with multiple possible targets is that there are multiple possible targets. All we had was a list of five names that *might* be targeted for assassination by someone who had successfully avoided every security tape and file in places known for their overzealous use of security cameras, apparently crept into rooms that were secure (and in two cases had chains or slide locks across the doors), and then left again with no obvious cause of death to the victims. Aside from the synthetic scales that Bug was going crazy over, there was no proof beyond the state of the corpses that any kind of attack had happened. And whatever the cause of those deaths, it wasn't chemical, electrical, or connected to any known firearm.

Piece of cake, right?

Without the right information, without any real understanding of how the assassin was working, there was nothing we could do.

Once again, Bug is the real hero here. Well, with a little help from Circe.

When he got back to me, he was babbling like a kid for three minutes. After that, I told him to calm down and explain.

"Okay, so, with just a little bit of current running through one of the scales two things happened. First, they're photosensitive in a way that is crazy. I mean cray-cray crazy. They don't actually disappear, but they take on the closest colors to them. They're a little bit like the skin of a chameleon."

"So, invisible?"

"No, just super well camouflaged. You can find them, but you have to look. After we figured that out, we checked the footage from the previous victims' hotels from around an hour before their deaths and for about an hour after. In two cases there's a definite distortion. It moves slowly. Very slowly. I'm not saying whoever it is couldn't be seen, but you seriously have to be on the lookout for something to spot."

"Yeah, that's not gonna be a problem."

"Actually, it won't. It only works in the regular spectrum. IR and UV are loud and proud. So there's that. You're gonna have to run with goggles, but it's not going to be impossible to see the target."

"That's a plus. What else?"

"They vibrate."

"Excuse me?"

"The scales vibrate, Joe. I mean they seriously run hard-core, at a speed that is insane. We activated one and it was like watching an ice cube in a hot pan, floating on a field of boiling oil. That sort of vibrate. The damn thing bounced halfway across the room the first time. Took me five minutes to find it again. I've never in my life seen technology like this. I can't completely tell if it's synthetic or organic or maybe even a blend. It's the sort of thing that makes me believe in intelligent life on other planets."

"You're babbling again, Bug."

"Sorry. Okay. So near as we can figure these scales move fast enough to actually change the molecular frequency of the person wearing them."

"In English?"

"Okay. This is why I'm freaking out. These scales? Enough of them on the right sort of suit would make a person nearly invisible and allow them to walk through walls."

"Bullshit."

"No, seriously. The scales they found on the victim and in the victim? They weren't shaken loose. They were left behind. They were pulled out of the suit, and we think that happened when the assassin shoved a hand into a living body and let it vibrate there for a few seconds."

You ever hear the term *my blood ran cold*? I had a serious case of the shivers at that notion.

The last bit of research was as vital as the first. We had an idea of how it happened. We knew where it had happened. Now all we had to do was safely predict the next target and neutralize the threat.

Mr. Church didn't say there had been ripples from the previous murders, but he didn't have to. No one was admitting to anything, but everyone involved was tense.

The U.S. didn't seem to be involved and that made them tense, too. All we had to go on was a series of meetings that took place in different parts of the country and even in other nations, between people with plausible deniability. No one could point a finger and prove anything. MindReader didn't need to prove anything. It just needed to guess the next target.

Two of the possible targets were actually out of the country. One was in California getting ready to watch the premiere of the latest superhero extravaganza with his wife and three kids. That left two possible targets in D.C., and we had no reason at all to contact them and warn them of the possible dangers, except for the fact that we needed to alert them in order to save their lives.

That was where Mr. Church came in. Have I mentioned that he gives us the best toys to play with?

Instead of dealing with the massive NV goggles we used in the field, we got slightly clunky-looking eyeglasses that allowed for a "full spectrum" of visibility. Let me translate the way I made Bug translate. The glasses weren't as good as NV goggles or UV goggles, but they altered the spectrum we could see enough that we could sort of see through walls. Not actual X-ray vision, but a modified ability to see body heat.

We could look through a wall that was nearby and see heat signatures for about fifteen feet. More important, they'd theoretically let us see the chameleon armor of our assassin. Why did Church have these things lying around? Apparently they were a failed experiment. I had my doubts. He never struck me as the sort to leave extra junk around to clutter his closet, if you see my point.

At any rate, it was me and Bunny at the Madison Hotel.

The Madison and the Dolley Madison are the sorts of hotels no one goes to, unless they're diplomats. There are a lot of political figures who use the hotels for rendezvous or just to drop into town overnight. The security is good and the discretion of the employees is better. Somebody wants to hang out and play poker with some buddies? No one hears about it. Somebody else wants to call in a high-level escort? The press never knows. Allegedly there are tunnels under the buildings. I've never been able to find them.

What we did find, thanks to Mr. Church, was a vacant room on the left of Maurice M'Gombe's suite. M'Gombe was in town for only one night. He seemed the most likely target.

I sent Top and Warbride to the Dolley Madison, where the other target was staying for a few days. It was always possible the next attempt would be at the other target or that the assassin would go for a twofer.

Dr. Hu—not the one from the BBC—called me on the comm-link with a final warning or two, just to make sure I was properly paranoid.

He said, "Cowboy, we have examined the hotel rooms involved in the previous assassinations and seen a disturbing pattern."

"How so?"

"The walls of the hotels are structurally sound enough, but there are microfractures running through what we believe were the access and egress points for your assassin." Sometimes I longed for the simplicity of a conversation with Bug.

"The walls were damaged when the assassin came and went?"

"Exactly so." Lucky guess.

"What does that mean?"

"By itself it would mean nothing, but the actuality is that the structural damage to the walls actually gets worse if we visit the sites chronologically." There was a pause while I was trying to translate that, and then Hu had a little mercy on me. "We believe the suit might be damaged. The scales are an indicator. Each wall has been more destabilized by the vibration frequencies used to ghost through them. Unless the creator of that suit makes adjustments or builds another suit, it's very likely that the phasing issues will only get worse."

"Worse how?"

"From a practical standpoint, we think the suit could cause serious damage to the wall and to the wearer if too many more attempts are made. We also believe that the scales that fell off are very likely having a destabilizing effect. Who can say how many scales have actually been lost? The suit doesn't use very much power, but it definitely generates serious vibrations. If the suit were to malfunction or be seriously damaged, there's a chance the vibrations could create the equivalent of a localized earthquake."

"A localized earthquake?"

Bunny looked at me and shook his head. He wasn't any fonder of that notion than I was.

"How big are we talking here?"

"Impossible to know, but certainly enough to level a story or two of a building."

From our perspective that would only mean about ten additional stories of structure falling down on our heads.

"How do we avoid damaging the suit any further?"

"To be perfectly honest, I can't be certain. I'd suggest a head shot or making certain that if there is a noticeable battery pack, or anything that looks like one, you avoid shooting it."

The sound came down the hallway a few minutes after I'd finished my conversation with Hu. I was about to check in with Top when I heard it.

Have you ever placed a tuning fork near your ear? There's a sound, of course, but it's not really just a sound. It's also a sensation. That's the vibrations from the sound waves hitting your body. I mean, we've all been to a concert where the bass pounded through us, but this was different. This almost tickled.

There had been no reports of sounds before. Not at any of the previous crime scenes. Rather than open the door, Bunny activated his glasses and then nodded. Someone was coming down the hall and they were heading directly for M'Gombe's suite.

The idea was never to let the assassin reach the target, so Bunny signaled and then moved into the hallway, his Glock tucked into the small of his back, and I followed after him.

The sound was clearer out in the hall. The air was distorted by vibration and our glasses saw something in the center of that distortion that fluctuated and shimmered. It was a form, but it was either a teenager or a woman if I had to guess. The figure seemed too small to be a man of even average size, but I couldn't bank on that. The distortion was too much.

That shape reached for the door, not even bothering to look in our direction. Maybe it couldn't see us clearly. Maybe it didn't care.

Bunny drew, sighted, and fired one round. That should have been the end of the situation.

The bullet passed right through the ghostly shape and the air around it screamed at a nearly deafening volume. That wave of vibrations changed right then and there. Whatever Bunny had hit, it seemed to have caused damage of some kind. The ghost didn't fall down and die, didn't seem to be bleeding, but something had changed.

Subtlety was out the window and the ghost looked right at Bunny and changed course.

"Fuck." Bunny has always had a way with words.

I backed up and he backed up as the ghost came at us. Bullets went right through. Hadn't really counted on that. I'd been hoping that the vibration thing happened only when going through walls, and maybe that was supposed to be the case. It just never crossed my mind on the bullets part.

I hoped to live and learn.

We backed into our hotel room. That was intentional. We weren't limiting our access to anything. We were drawing the ghost away from a target. Bunny took a chance and tried firing again with the same result. There was that high-pitched scream as the bullet moved through without actually touching the target. What came out the other side didn't look like a bullet. A missile went in and black dust came out the other side. Near as I could figure, the vibrations shredded the bullet as it passed through. That hadn't happened to the walls before and it hadn't happened to the people the ghost killed.

I tried warning Bunny, but I don't think he could hear me over the noise, so instead I pulled on his shoulder and urged him backward. He nodded and retreated.

The ghost's hand touched the air where Bunny had been a second before. Looking at that blur was disorienting.

At the same time, he tried for another head shot and the scream came again. Not a ghost, a banshee. It was screaming and I was beginning to think we were dead.

The ghost's hand bumped into the wall and instead of phasing through anything, it disintegrated the drywall and the wooden studs behind it. A trench exploded along the wall where the hand touched. The ghost paused long enough to look at the damage and then came at us even faster.

Bunny retreated and I grabbed the mattress on the bed and hurled it as hard as I could toward the approaching killing machine.

There were bits and pieces of mattress exploding all over the place and the scream came back again. Bunny fired three more head shots and this time around our resident spook stumbled backward.

I couldn't tell if it was the weight of the mattress or if it was the bullets.

I screamed, "Shoot it again!" and whether or not he heard me, Bunny cut loose. The screams came loud and fast, like high-pitched thunder cutting loose from two feet away. I felt the vibrations in my fillings and my vision distorted even more as my eyes shook in my skull.

Still, the ghost fell back again and again, until it struck the wall. The wall screamed and so did the ghost.

The wall shook and shuddered and started to crumble. I didn't have another mattress to try my luck with, but I had to try something. Bunny's shots had caused some sort of damage, but it was impossible to say how much. What was certain was that the suit was still functioning enough to be a serious problem. The wall was fracturing and neither of us could grab the ghost and try to pull the assassin away without being vaporized.

"Screw this!" I ran past Bunny and headed for the bathroom. I'd call it instinct more than anything else. The suit ran on electricity and maybe there were a few holes in the wiring. If so, there was a chance to short the thing out, but better than nothing. I grabbed two tools. The first was the fire extinguisher under the bathroom sink. The second was the ice bucket. I put the bucket in the tub and opened the tap. Cold water sloshed into the bucket and the tub.

I didn't wait for it to fill, but instead pulled the ring that prevents accidental discharges on fire extinguishers and ran back to the main room. The ghost was half-buried in the wall. The wall was vibrating and Bunny was looking a little desperate for something he could do about it.

I gave him the fire extinguisher and went back for the water. When I got back into the bedroom, Bunny was covering the ghost in foam that vibrated itself all over the place. Nothing ventured, nothing gained.

My bucket of water, maybe a liter all told, splashed all over the ghost and the suit.

There was another scream, but this one was more human and less terrifying. Several very large sparks arced from the ghost and then the screaming stopped.

My ears were ringing. My body ached from the levels of sound that tore through me and I could see Bunny wincing even as he looked over our ghost.

The entire suit was gray now, the sort of gray that settles on dead flesh, though I could clearly see scorch marks and circuitry in places. I now understood what Bug had meant about scales. They were all over the place, buried in the mattress ticking and the walls, and now that the fun was over, I could see where two of them had hit me and, thankfully, bounced. The red marks showed me where the bruises would be.

Bunny got the worst of it. He had about a dozen spots where the scales had hit him like high-velocity guitar picks. They weighed almost nothing. If they'd been heavier, we likely would have been dead or at least punctured in places I don't want to think about.

I still couldn't hear much, but I called it in to Bug and the other team.

The cleanup team wasn't going to like us very much. I knew that.

The wall was ruined. More important, our ghost had stopped vibrating at the wrong time. She and the wall had become one.

I can't call this one a victory. I mean, partial, yes, we stopped the execution of several foreign dignitaries. Top and Warbride never saw a sign of any sort of ghostly assassin, so we decided there was only the one. It could have gone either way, I think. Their diplomat could have been first on the list or Maurice M'Gombe could have been first. Bunny and I just got lucky. The entire thing was over before they could make the distance from the Dolley Madison to the Madison, and the two hotels are less than a block apart.

But back at the offices I discussed the entire thing with Mr. Church.

After we were done with the formalities, we got down to business. I like that about my boss. He doesn't usually dance around the subject.

"Bug got back to me on the suit."

"Yeah? What did he have to say?"

"The sort of thing that makes him happy. Point of origin unknown. There is some very common electronics at work, but only some. The scales and the fabric they were woven into are both puzzlingly organic."

"Come again?"

"They're artificial, but they show signs of having been grown, not manufactured." Church reached for one of his vanilla wafers and contemplated it before speaking again. "There are at least four separate elements that no one in our department can identify."

"Let me guess, extraterrestrial?"

"We can't identify them. That means the possibility is real, no matter how improbable."

"What about our banshee?"

"Is that what you're calling her now?" He offered the smallest hint of a smile and then took a bite of his wafer before answering. "She's a complete unknown. The damage to her body was very nearly on a cellular level. No teeth for dental records. No fingerprints, as her flesh was liquefied. If she has her DNA on file anywhere, we haven't been able to locate it. Red hair, pale skin. That's all we have."

"Got to wonder what our foreign dignitaries were up to."

Mr. Church nodded. "I was thinking the exact same thing. Interestingly enough, three of the survivors have been pulled from duty in the United States. Either their home countries are afraid we'll start watching them or they're potentially embarrassed by what was going on behind doors."

He finished his wafer. "Either way, it'll be interesting to discover more information."

"Not a closed case?"

"Not remotely."

Have I mentioned how much I hate unsolved riddles? Not as much as Mr. Church, but then again, that's one of the things I like about my boss.

ABOUT THE AUTHOR

James A. Moore is the bestselling and award-winning author of more than forty novels, thrillers, dark fantasy, and horror alike, including the critically acclaimed *Fireworks*, *Under the Overtree*, *Blood Red*, *Serenity Falls* trilogy (featuring his recurring antihero, Jonathan Crowley), and *Seven Forges* series. His most recent novels include *The Silent Army* and the forthcoming *The Last Sacrifice*. In addition to writing multiple short stories, he has edited, with Christopher Golden and Tim Lebbon, the *British Invasion* anthology for Cemetery Dance Publications.

RED DIRT

BY MIRA GRANT

Pallets of bottled water sat stacked against the wall of a storage container, waiting to be shipped on to their next destination. They were a new brand, something hoity-toity that claimed to come from the purest sources on Earth. As if that weren't what they all said; as if it weren't pure bullshit, designed to strip-mine the wallets of the rich and indolent. This stuff cost pennies to make, and probably drained some poor community that couldn't afford to lose its groundwater in the process.

Matthew O'Neil had been a night watchman for seven years. He knew where the cameras were. He knew when the other watchmen came through. Most of all, he knew what was safe to steal—or to allow to be stolen. He never took a damn thing for himself. That would have been a crime and a sin, and his mama didn't raise no sinners. She'd raised three good, God-fearing boys who just wanted to give back to their communities in whatever way they could.

The men who stood before him now, looking at the water, were practically drooling in their excitement. Clean water was always a good thing, and too often, it cost too dear for the people who needed it the most. The shelters and the hospitals would benefit like nothing going from having this, and the people who'd shipped it here? Who'd abandoned it here? They wouldn't even notice that it was gone.

"You're sure?" one of them asked, for the fifth time.

"Bill says it was supposed to ship out months ago," said Matthew. "I don't know whether a wire got crossed or whether their original buyer got cold feet, but it don't bother me none. No one's watching this stuff. Take it away, and if anyone ever comes looking—which I doubt—I'll play dumb. Get it where it's needed."

"You're a good guy," said one of the men, clapping Matthew on the shoulder. He drank in the praise, and watched as the three of them began hoisting water onto their shoulders and toting it away.

God might help those who helped themselves, but there was nothing wrong with giving His hand a little nudge in the right direction every now and then.

TROY, ALABAMA, SIX MONTHS LATER

Sick people had a smell.

Kathleen had known that since she was a little girl, when her Gram had gone down ill with the cancer, and taken to her bed to sweat the sick out as much as she could. "No hospitals for me, muffin," she'd said when she caught her granddaughter and dearest love looking at her with concern. "Doctors can't cut out what ails me, and they'll just take all we've got left to us in the world and not leave you with a penny to call your own. Let me sleep. I'll get better, if I can sleep."

Kathleen had known even then that cancer wasn't like the flu. You couldn't just sleep the cancer away. Cancer would have its due, and cancer had *had* its due, putting her Gram into the ground not six months after she'd been diagnosed. Half the town had come out for her funeral. Kathleen had spent the entire thing hiding her face in her mother's skirts, and all those people had called her shy and delicate and sad, and not one of them had realized that she was furious. Rage was eating her alive the way cancer had eaten her Gram, because where had all these people been when Gram was dying? A dollar from every one of them would have paid for doctors, and tests, and time. Money bought time.

Rich people could afford to get better. Poor people couldn't afford anything but sleep, and when sleep didn't cure what ailed them, they'd get a six-foot hole and a good pine box, and someone else would get their feather pillows.

Kathleen had gotten her grandmother's feather pillows, and then, when the will had been read, her grandmother's life savings, kept in the bank and hidden from everyone else in the family. Her mother had been the one to take her down to the bank, to hear the number, and to tell her daughter, in a voice Kathleen had never heard before, "You need to pretend this never happened. You don't have that money. You can't loan it to me for the grocery bill, or use it to buy yourself a new pair of shoes. That money isn't real until it's time for college. Do you understand?"

And Kathleen, who never wanted to see another person sleep the cancer away, had nodded. Had told her "Yes," even though she hadn't fully understood—not then, and not for another ten years, not until that money had been the seed that she planted to carry herself all the way to college, and then to medical school after that. No one else in her family was ever going to worry about a doctor taking them for everything they had. Never again.

Now, as she walked the halls of Troy Memorial, heading for her office, she wanted nothing more in the world than to sink into her bed—still loaded down with feather pillows, even if they didn't smell like Gram anymore—and sleep something else away: exhaustion. Being the head of Oncology for a hospital this small and this strapped really meant being the head of Whatever Damn Well Needs Doing. Over the course of the day she had set two broken bones, talked a pair of children into getting their shots, given prenatal vitamins to Susie from down the block, and helped a young woman get her brother, who was obviously suffering from some sort of overdose, into the exam room. It wasn't just that she was young, and pretty, and still new enough to be enthusiastic about her work. It was that she *came* from here.

Every other doctor in this hospital came from Away, that wide and nebulous place outside of Alabama, where people who didn't understand their way of life tried to make laws defining it. There were people who didn't want to be seen by anyone but her. She'd come from Here. She understood them in a way that no doctor from Away could ever hope to. So when emergencies came in, even if she wasn't on call, she was more likely to be called in than anyone else in the building.

Because of all this, and more, it was no surprise when she heard running footsteps behind her. "Kat! Wait up!"

"Phil, no, and no, Phil, and every other variation on that sentence that you can come up with." She turned, making no effort to hide her weariness. Maybe if he realized how tired she was, he would have mercy for the first time in his benighted life. "I've been on shift for twenty-four hours. I'm not a resident anymore! This shit is supposed to stop!"

"I know, I know, and you know I wouldn't do this unless it was an emergency." Phil slowed to a stop, shoving his glasses back into place. They had slipped halfway down his nose, giving him the appearance of a genially absentminded professor.

The impression wasn't too far wrong. Dr. Phil Clines was a general practitioner, and was actually responsible for the sorts of things that Kathleen spent half her time doing. She wasn't picking up his slack, either—if there was anyone at the hospital who worked as hard as she did, it was Phil. It was just a matter of too many patients and not nearly enough funding keeping them perpetually scrambling for solid ground.

He really *did* look worried. Kathleen took pity. "What is it?"

"I've had three cases in the last week that don't match up with anything I'd expect to be seeing. You had one of them, actually. Winston Black?"

"Presented with difficulty speaking and tracking conversation, mild motor impairment, and difficulty breathing," said Kathleen without hesitation. "All signs pointed to a mild stroke. We kept him overnight for observation, and then his family took him home."

"He died."

Kathleen froze. "What?" she finally managed to squeak. Apart from his stroke symptoms, which had been reasonably mild, Winston Black was a man in the pink of health. He didn't smoke, didn't eat red meat, and ran two miles every morning. She had actually been worried about how healthy he was—paradoxically, the people who had the fewest problems *before* a stroke could have some of the worst problems after, when they had to adjust to their new limitations. Physical therapy and rehabilitation could restore the bulk of their lost function, but not always. There was no magic bullet where brain damage was concerned.

"This morning," said Phil. "He was also presenting with early-stage cataracts."

"Yes, I noted that on my report."

"Kat, he had galactosemia, and we didn't catch it, and he died. His heart stopped."

Kathleen stared.

Phil continued: "I only caught it because something looked off on his blood work, so I dug deeper. There was a child in the family fifteen years ago who died of the same thing."

"I remember." Little Suzie Black, less than a year old, and dead because her family hadn't trusted the doctors who tried to convince them to cut all dairy from her diet—even her mother's own milk. They'd heard galactosemia as lactose intolerance, and thought the doctors insisting that it was something different were just busybodies, looking to interfere with the way they'd always done things.

Kathleen had been in college when Suzie Black died. It had been in all the papers, and she remembered thinking that it was a death that she could have prevented, if she'd been there to talk to the family, to explain to them what was happening to their daughter. They had needed the local touch. That was one of the cases that had sealed her determination to come home after she had her degree, to work at a local hospital and make sure that things like this would become the anomalies they should have been all along. But Winston . . .

"That's not possible," she said, finding her voice again. "Galactosemia appears in children, *infant* children, not in adult men. It must have been something else."

"There's a family history. He shows the blood markers."

"I've seen him eating pizza with his family! He wasn't even lactose intolerant!"

"I know how this sounds, but I'm telling you, it was galactosemia, and that's not the real problem."

"What is?"

Phil looked at her wearily. "We have two more cases presenting exactly like his."

BALTIMORE, MARYLAND, THREE HOURS LATER

Rudy Sanchez was considering the merits of a cold beer, a warm bath, and a bed that split the difference between the two when his phone rang.

His first impulse was to ignore it. He wasn't on duty, and the number wasn't Joe's: for Joe, he would have answered even if the world had been on fire. There were other people who could do everything he could do for the office, and many things he *couldn't* do: everyone who worked for the DMS had their own area of specialization. Let someone else mop up the mess for a change. He'd earned the time to himself.

Guilt followed hot on the heels of the idea that he had earned *anything*. He was still standing, wasn't he? So many others weren't. They deserved his full attention to duty, the willingness to serve when he was called upon, no matter what. He grabbed for the phone.

The ringing stopped.

Rudy blinked for a moment, nonplussed. Then he chuckled, half-wry, half-relieved. "That settles that, I suppose," he said.

Someone knocked on the door.

He was on his feet before he'd consciously decided to move, heading for the sound with long, ground-eating strides. Not fast enough; the knock came again, harder this time, until the entire door shook in its frame.

"I'm coming!" he shouted as he reached the door, unlocked it, and swung it open to reveal two of the last people he'd been expecting to see on his doorstep. He blinked.

Bunny, standing with his massive hand raised for a third round of knocking, looked abashed. "Evenin', Dr. Sanchez," he said. "I wasn't sure you were home."

"The lights are on, my car is in the driveway, and when I left, I said I was going home," said Rudy. "Where else would I be? Mars?"

"I hear the weather's good there," rumbled the mountain standing behind Bunny. Top was one of the only men Rudy could think of who could make the hulking Farm Boy seem to have been built according to normal human scale.

Just my luck, he thought. *I wanted to help the world, and wound up playing the Lilliputian in an action remake of* Gulliver's Travels. Aloud, he asked, "To what do I owe the honor?"

"We have a bit of a problem," said Bunny.

Nothing about this was normal. Had he been looking for normal, Rudy wasn't sure he would have been able to find this moment on the adjoining maps. He took a step back, making space for the two to enter. He did not, however, invite them in. If they wanted that particular pleasantry, they were going to need to explain what they were doing there after hours.

Rudy would never have done this if Joe had been on his doorstep. But Joe was his friend, even outside of work, and more important, if Joe had been involved, the world would already have been on the brink of ending.

They came in. "One of the analysts flagged a report from a hospital in rural Alabama," said Top. "Lots of medical jargon, but one bit that really stood out: they're seeing a sudden cluster of adult-onset cases of a rare genetic disorder called 'galactosemia.'"

Any thoughts Rudy had about his disrupted evening dissolved like sugar in water. "That's not possible," he said. "Galactosemia is diagnosed in childhood. It's diagnosed, or you die."

"Well, we've got five cases at a hospital in Troy, Alabama. Started at three a few hours ago. Four of the people involved are related."

The Dragon Factory. The diseases they'd designed to kill the people whose genetic backgrounds they hadn't approved of. People like him. "That's not *possible*," Rudy repeated, even though experience told him that it was bitterly, brutally possible. Things like this happened every day, whether he wanted them to or not. "All the agents were caught before they could deploy the viruses. We stopped the release of the bottled water that would prime populations for contamination. We stopped it."

"Nice 'we' there," said Top with dark amusement. "Doesn't change the report we intercepted."

"Joe—"

"Joe's busy," said Top in a tone that brooked no argument.

Rudy wondered sometimes whether Joe was aware of how many of his men—of his friends—would gladly die to protect him, even when he didn't need protecting. He didn't think so.

"I'll get my coat," he said. "You call Dr. O'Tree. If we're doing this, I'm not going to be the only medical authority on hand. I'm not that kind of doctor."

"So we're doing this?" asked Bunny.

Rudy paused long enough to look at him wearily. "Was there ever any question?"

TROY, ALABAMA

"Kat, we're up to fifteen cases, and we've lost three more." There was a weary helplessness in Phil's tone that Kathleen had never heard before, not once. He sounded beaten.

That frightened her.

"What did the CDC say?" she asked.

"They're sending a team, but they don't expect to be here before morning. The fact that it's clustering in families makes them think it's something environmental, and that moves it down on the priority list. Government funding isn't what it used to be."

A chuckle crawled up Kathleen's throat and escaped before she could bite it back. "Oh, is that what they call leaving the poor to die in their own filth these days? 'Government funding'? Maybe I should go tell everyone in the waiting room to go home and sleep it off."

"I wish you wouldn't."

The voice was female, and unfamiliar. Kathleen and Phil turned.

The woman behind them was stunningly beautiful, enough so as to appear to have wandered out of Central Casting and into a medical drama. Her long black hair was pulled into a ponytail, and she was dressed practically, not calling any attention to her curves. She didn't need to. Even if she hadn't been the kind of lovely that launched a thousand ships, the fact that she was flanked by a pair of men large enough to have been professional wrestlers would have commanded a certain amount of attention from anyone who saw her.

The third man was of slightly less imposing build, being roughly the height of a normal human being, with dark, tousled hair and a blazer over his button-down shirt. He produced an ID wallet from inside his jacket, snapping it open to show them the badge and snapping it closed again before Kathleen could get more than a glimpse of the credentials inside.

She was about to protest when the man said, "We're from the government, and our funding is just fine. Please, will you show us your patients?"

Kathleen knew these people were more likely to be from a tabloid looking for a scoop or from a company that thought its products might be somehow responsible for the situation than from the government, but in that moment, she didn't care. She had people sick, and she knew them: if she didn't do something, they would go home to "sleep it off," just like her Gram. They'd all die. Just like her Gram. If trusting these people—if risking them betraying her—meant even a sliver of a chance, then she'd take it.

"This way," she said, and turned on her heel, motioning for them to follow.

Phil fell into step beside her. "You know they're probably not with the government. Last time I checked, the American government didn't base its hiring decisions on 'could they break kneecaps for the Mob.'"

"I know," said Kathleen. She felt oddly serene, as if a weight were being lifted from her shoulders. These people wanted her problems? They could have them. Let *them* pore over the charts and data, let *them* scowl at lab results that couldn't possibly exist. She'd go back to the patients. She'd hold their hands and keep them breathing calmly until a treatment was found. "I just don't care. If there's a chance that they can help, we're going to let them try."

"Excuse me." It was the woman. Kathleen turned. The woman smiled. "I'm Dr. Circe O'Tree, and this is my associate Dr. Rudy Sanchez. Whether or not you believe we're with the government, I'm afraid we're definitely not deaf. I read the report you sent to the CDC while we were on the plane. Can you please walk me through this?"

The shorter man was close behind her, where he would be able to listen as well. Kathleen swallowed a sigh.

"First thing you need to know is that this could be a lot more widespread than we're seeing," she said. "People around here don't think much of doctors, and the symptoms come on vaguely enough that we may have a lot of folks staying home and waiting to feel better until it's too late."

Dr. O'Tree frowned. "I heard you say the CDC suspected an environmental cause, due to the family clustering. Have you contacted the police, asked them to check the homes inside the infection zone?"

This time, Kathleen actually laughed. "Oh, because people who don't like it when they have to go to the doctor are going to react so well when they find the police on their doorsteps. I start sending the cops around, I might as well buy a bulk lot of plots down at the boneyard. No one else will die from this disease, because they'll all be too busy shooting each other."

"My apologies, Doctor . . . ?"

Kathleen flushed red. "Dr. Kathleen Abrams. This is my colleague, Dr. Phillip Clines."

"You're the head oncologist, aren't you?" asked Circe. "I saw your name on the directory near the front desk."

"Yes, but I'm also our . . . call it 'cultural ambassador' to the locals. I grew up here. I know how people think."

"That's more important than a lot of people realize, especially when you're dealing with an isolated population," said Dr. Sanchez. He sounded almost admiring.

Kathleen relaxed a little. Maybe these people weren't just here digging for a story after all. "It can be hard to get people who've never had the government on their side to understand that doctors aren't all here to hurt them," she admitted. "But we've made great strides—or at least, we had, before all this. Honestly, I'm hoping the CDC is right and it's something environmental that just happens to perfectly mimic adult-onset galactosemia."

"What *is* galactosemia?" asked Bunny. He put on his best expression of profound puzzlement. "I don't have a medical background. Use small words."

"I know someone playing stupid when I see it," said Kathleen. "But in the simplest of terms, galactosemia is a genetic disorder which stops the body from properly processing galactose."

"What's that?" asked Bunny.

"You've heard of lactose intolerance?"

"Yeah. I had a buddy in the service who'd get the worst gas you'd ever smelt if he had so much as a piece of cheese. We all used to say that his ass should have been banned as a weapon of mass destruction."

"Well, lactose intolerance stops the body from properly breaking down lactose. Galactosemia doesn't do that. Lactose breaks down normally, into glucose and galactose. That's where the body gets confused. It can't break down the galactose. It doesn't know what to do with the stuff, and so it builds up, leading to all sorts of complications. Renal failure, cataracts, cognitive impairment, neurological impairment—"

"You just said that," said Bunny.

"No," said Kathleen. "Cognitive impairment impacts the mind. There can be massive learning disabilities and delays as a consequence of this condition. Neurological impairment tends to manifest itself as tremors, seizures, other issues involving the interface between body and brain. It's hard to say which kills more quickly. Infants with galactosemia have very poor survival statistics, especially when it goes undiagnosed or is not immediately taken seriously by the family. If they attempt to treat it like lactose intolerance, and continue breast-feeding or otherwise exposing the children to lactose, they can and will die."

"But it doesn't manifest in adults," said Phil, jumping into the silence that followed her explanation. "There's just no way. This *can't* be galactosemia, because if it were, all these people would have died years ago. Decades ago."

"All right," said Dr. Sanchez. "I think that's enough background to bring us all up to speed. Can we see the patients now?"

Kathleen and Phil exchanged an uneasy glance before nodding.

"This way," said Kathleen.

Sick people had a smell. The smell of the sick people packed into their makeshift isolation ward was sweet and cloying, almost sugary. Twelve of the beds were occupied. Four more waited, empty, for their occupants to come.

"I thought there were fifteen cases?" Rudy made the question mild, looking around as if he expected three more patients to simply appear.

"The others are under three years old," said Phil. "They're in a sterile ward, intubated. They've all stopped breathing on their own. That's part of why we think this must be something else that mimics galactosemia— it doesn't move this quickly. Even in children with the condition, we'd expect to have several months between presentation of symptoms and a total system collapse."

"Thank you," said Rudy, and produced a pair of gloves from his pocket, moving forward into the room. Circe and Bunny followed, leaving Top standing next to the two doctors.

The team moved from patient to patient with ruthless efficiency, reading charts, checking pulses, doing everything short of drawing more blood. When they had reached the far side of the room, Rudy looked up and nodded, once.

"These families," said Top. "What do they all have in common?"

Kathleen jumped. She couldn't help herself. She'd been so wrapped up in watching the rest of them that she'd managed to virtually forget Top was there.

"They've all been living here in town for generations. They're proud of their self-sufficiency. Don't like asking for help."

"Do they attend the same church? You mentioned that they don't like asking for help. Do they visit a local food bank?" Sensing Kathleen's reluctance, Top lowered his voice and said, "Help us help you. If there's an environmental factor, we need to know how to find it. Even if you don't want to trust us, we're your best chance at finding a solution for these people."

"They . . . don't go to a food bank, no," Kathleen said reluctantly. "But there's a church group that distributes supplies. Things that they say would go to waste, so it's really a charity to take them."

"The hospital doesn't accept any of their donations," Phil added. "They mean well. They're also a little fast and loose about the legality of the things they pass around, and we've never wanted to risk getting caught in a lawsuit."

"Understandable," said Top. "Tell me, does either of you have close contact with the families who receive those donations? Outside of the hospital, I mean?"

"Vince Taylor works at the coffee shop where I stop most mornings," said Kathleen. "Nice kid. Smart. He's going places. I know his family gets donations from the church."

"All right. This may seem like an odd question, but have you seen him drinking bottled water recently?"

"Bottled water? Please. No one around here would waste money on—" Kathleen stopped. There had been that nasty business with the water filters downtown, hadn't there? They'd stopped cleaning the water properly, and some people had gotten sick. Not *bad* sick, no, just some minor bacterial infections, but it had been enough to scare a few households into drinking bottled water, at least until the matter was resolved.

"Oh, God," she said. "I saw Vince with a bottle of water last week. I didn't even think about it."

"Was it a brand you recognized? Had you ever seen that kind of water before?"

"I don't think so, no. I wasn't really paying attention."

Top nodded grimly. "People generally don't. It's interesting. A man switches from Coke to Pepsi, people will notice. Switch brands of bottled water, and it's just so much background noise."

"Was the water poisoned? Was there some sort of federal recall?"

Top and Bunny exchanged a look. "Is Vince Taylor one of your patients?"

"No," said Kathleen. "And don't think I didn't notice you changing the subject. I noticed."

"That's fine, ma'am, but right now, I think we need to find Vince and see if he can tell us where he got that water. Preferably before there's some sort of a public panic." Top folded his arms. "Can you do that?"

Kathleen was suddenly, terribly reminded of how large these two men were. If they wanted to break her, they could.

But her people needed her. The people she'd grown up beside, the people who believed she could take care of them, they needed her. If these men were government goons sent to make this whole thing disappear, she could work with that. First, she needed to know what "this whole thing" actually was.

"Dr. Clines, please stay here with our guests," she said, offering Phil a short, tight nod. She wanted him to know that she understood what she was doing. She wanted him to know that she'd be fine.

To her great relief, he nodded back and said, "I'll notify you if anything here changes."

"Thank you," she said. "Gentlemen? Please follow me."

Rudy glanced up as Top and Bunny filed out of the room. Then he went back to reviewing the chart he was holding, while Circe made notes.

This was bad. This was very bad.

The coffee shop where Vince worked was only a few blocks from the hospital—close enough that it wasn't unusual to see doctors in their white coats and nurses in their scrubs passing their lunch breaks packed around the tiny tables, desperately trying to consume enough caffeine to stay standing for the rest of their shifts. The place kept hospital hours, staying open late into the night, and profiting accordingly.

The two men behind Kathleen drew considerably more glances than she did, some appreciative, others wary. She looked toward the counter.

Vince wasn't there.

Kathleen frowned as she walked up to the register and waved for the attention of the woman on duty. "Sandy, when was the last time you saw Vince?" she asked.

"He called in sick Monday and Tuesday, and today, he just didn't show." Sandy frowned. "It's not like him. Anyone else, they'd already be fired, but Vince . . . You know something I don't?"

"We have a few of his relatives at the hospital. Looks like it might be food poisoning. He's probably exhausted and trying to sleep it off, but I'll go and check on him." Kathleen forced herself to smile. "I'll stop by on my way back."

Sandy brightened, a look of pleased surprise on her face. "You'd do that?"

"It's no trouble." Kathleen kept smiling as she turned and walked out of the coffee shop, with Top and Bunny behind her.

The smile died as soon as she was outside.

"The Taylors live about a mile from here," she said. "I'll need to get my car."

"No, you won't, ma'am," said Bunny. "We parked on the street." He pointed to a black SUV that all but screamed *government agents,* and smirked. "Seemed like the right car for the job."

"Of course it did," said Kathleen.

She was now not just leaving with two strange men who might or might not be who they claimed: she was getting into a car with them. If her body was never found, well, that would just about serve her right. But if there was anything she could do to save the people who were filling her hospital, she had to do it. She had to try. That was what she had promised to do when she'd gone away to medical school, and that was a promise she intended to keep.

As if sensing her discomfort, Bunny smiled and said, "We're pretty good drivers. We almost never get into Vin Diesel–style car chases. And when we do, we always win."

"Encouraging," said Kathleen, and followed them to the car.

It was a new model, kitted out with all the bells and whistles that people seemed to expect these days. The seats adjusted themselves automatically when Top started the engine, and the air-conditioning was better than anything Kathleen had experienced as a child. She watched out the window as Top followed her directions to the Taylor house, wondering what her hometown looked like to these strangers, these men who could afford new suits and fancy rental cars and last-minute plane fares.

Growing up poor in Alabama meant hands stained red from the dirt and scabby knees stained the same color by eating pavement. It meant making do and making repairs and making a dollar do the work of ten. It meant pride, because pride might not fill a belly, but it could sure make the sting of hunger seem righteous, like something that had been honestly earned. Kathleen had always hated the rich, happy-looking kids she'd seen on television, because they were nothing like anyone she'd ever met. Where was the red dirt under their fingernails, the stains that could have been earth and could have been blood and were really both at the same time? Where was the hunger, big enough to eat the world? Where was the *need*?

It was here. It was ever and always here.

They pulled up in front of the Taylor house. It was small, and clean, with a well-weeded vegetable garden out front. Kathleen frowned when she saw Top eyeing it speculatively.

"Sorry there isn't a truck on cinder blocks out front, to tell you you've got the right place."

He turned his gaze on her. "You've got a lot of mad in you. That can be a good thing. But please don't aim it at me. I've never said a thing to make you think I'd be that judgmental."

Kathleen flushed red. "I'm sorry. It's been a long week."

"I'm sure it has."

They got out of the car, Kathleen leading the way up the narrow path to the front door. She rang the bell, stepping back and waiting. And waiting.

And waiting.

"Let me try," said Bunny. He stepped past her and twisted the doorknob hard to the side. There was a clicking noise as something inside the lock broke. He pushed the door open, offering Kathleen an apologetic smile. "Looks like it was open."

"I hope you're ready to pay for that," said Kathleen, and stepped past him into the hall.

The smell of sickness stopped her in her tracks.

Sick people had a smell, and that smell hung heavy in this house, sinking into the walls. She took a breath and started forward, Top and Bunny close enough behind her that it should have felt claustrophobic. Instead, she found their presence oddly reassuring, as if by having them there, she could prepare for whatever she might find.

She was not prepared.

The back room—formerly the TV room—had been transformed into a makeshift medical ward, presumably because the family couldn't afford to send anyone to the hospital, if they even trusted it after the number of people they'd seen admitted over the past week. Four of them were lying there, two on the couch and two on the floor. All four were dead. Kathleen recognized Vince and his sister, Angie; the process of elimination said that the other two must be their parents.

Something scrabbled at the back door. They had locked the dogs out at some point, maybe when they realized how sick they were. That was all that had saved them from being eaten by their own pets, whose domesticated behaviors would eventually have given way in the face of hunger. Kathleen's stomach did a slow roll. This was so much worse than she could have dreamed. So much worse.

"Look." The voice was Bunny's. She turned to see him holding up a bottle of water. The label was something bright and geometric, with no clear brand. He was looking at Top, expression grim. "We missed one."

"Fuck," Top said tonelessly. He sounded resigned, as though he had never expected anything better from the world.

"Does someone want to tell me what's going on?" asked Kathleen.

The two men exchanged a look.

Kathleen sat behind her own desk, fuming silently. These people—these strangers—came to her town and refused to answer questions, refused to provide solutions; refused to do anything beyond going through the Taylor house and confiscating half a flat of bottled water. It didn't make any *sense*.

"We're not from the CDC," said Dr. Sanchez.

Her head snapped around. "You said—"

"We said we were from the government: that was true," he said. "We belong to a bioterrorism task force, responsible for preventing and intercepting scientific threats to life as we know it. What I am about to tell you is confidential."

"People are dying," she said.

"You have my profound sympathies, but those people are already dead," said Dr. O'Tree. "They have been exposed to a biological agent which has caused a normally genetic disorder to become communicable over short distances. The good news is, it can only activate when the exposed person is already a carrier for the gene in question."

"The bad news is, there is no cure," said Dr. Sanchez.

Kathleen stared at them. Phil spoke first.

"This is bullshit," he said. "What is this, a chemical spill? There was something in that water, something that wasn't supposed to get out, and now you're making up stories to cover your own asses? You may think we're hicks here, that you can say whatever you want and we'll just believe you, but we're American citizens. We have rights. You can't just use us for your experiments and expect to get away with it."

Dr. Sanchez looked briefly, profoundly, weary. Kathleen found herself wondering how old he really was, how many rooms like this he had sat in, how many suspicious local medical experts had called him a liar because he'd given them information that they didn't want and didn't know what to do with.

She believed him.

It was a small, terrible realization. Small because it came so easily, at the end of so many other, impossible things; terrible because it meant that she now lived in a world where this sort of thing could be believable, where this sort of thing could be *real*. This could be her reality. It was not a comfortable thought to have. She would have rejected it, if she thought that she could.

"What can we do?" she asked.

Dr. O'Tree looked to her. "You can make them comfortable," she said. "The normal treatments for galactosemia should slow the progression of the more ordinary aspects of the disease, while the rest continue unabated. You're going to lose them all. You should accept that now. It will make everything else easier."

"If this is in bottled water, there should have been some sort of public notice," said Phil. "A recall. A health and safety alert."

"It's not *only* in bottled water," said Dr. Sanchez. "There are two aspects to this attack. Bottled water, to provide the activation sequences; in this case, they activated the carrier gene for galactosemia. And the groundwater."

"What?" Kathleen half stood, alarmed. "It's in the water?"

"Without the bottled water, what's in the groundwater is harmless," said Dr. Sanchez. "My people will sweep the town and recover all remaining bottled water. We think the biological agent was released accidentally. A storm, a crack in a containment tank—or this town was meant to be one of their testing grounds, and was canceled before it could be activated. Whatever the reason, this is a terrible accident. You have our full sympathies. The CDC is already en route, and they will be able to help you with the care these people need."

"How many more cases can we expect?"

"It all depends on the water."

There had been six flats of water.

Top and Bunny had been able to recover five, and the three remaining bottles from the sixth. They had been stored in garages and under the stairs at the church soup kitchen. Top stacked them in the back of the SUV while Bunny looked on.

"There's one good thing about all this," he said.

"You found something good?" Top asked. "What's that?"

"It's not summer yet."

It took a moment for him to catch Bunny's meaning. He grimaced. "Hell."

"Yeah."

Summer would bring soaring temperatures and increased water consumption. Many more families would have been exposed, if it had been summer. This was a tragedy, but in July? It would have been a disaster.

Top put the last of the water into the back and slammed the hatch. "All done," he said. "We'll get this home and hand it off to the techies, and then I'm going to take a long damn shower."

"Do you think this was the only place?" Bunny asked. "No other leaks?"

Top looked toward the hospital, where even now Rudy and Circe were trying to make the locals understand that there would be no coming back from this. No miracle, no cure; no chance of survival. The bastards at the Dragon Factory had been too damn good at their jobs.

"I hope so," he said. "I really fucking do."

The Alabama sun shone down on a red-dirt town, and there was nothing else to say, and nothing else that could be done. Not for the living; not for the dying; not for the dead.

ABOUT THE AUTHOR

Mira Grant lives and writes in the Pacific Northwest, where her home overlooks a large swamp filled with frogs. Truly the best of all possible worlds. When not writing as herself, Mira writes under the name "Seanan McGuire" and releases a truly daunting number of books and stories during the average year. She regularly claims to be the vanguard of an invading race of alien plant people; any time spent with her will make this surprisingly credible. Mira shares her home with two enormous blue cats, a lizard, some very odd bugs, and an unnerving number of books about dead things. She loves horrible diseases and is not always a good dinner companion. Keep up with Mira at www.seananmcguire.com, or on Twitter @seananmcguire. Mira would very much like to show you what lurks behind the corn, but for some reason, the editors won't let her.

BLACK WATER

BY WESTON OCHSE

"That could be you," Wheatie said in my ear. "Joe Ledger. Teen heart-throb."

"I don't think so," I said.

Yet here I stood at Patton's Pond, designated make-out spot for Baltimore high schoolers near and far. The only problem was I didn't have a date. It was just me and Wheatie on stakeout.

"You know she's hot," Wheatie said.

And she absolutely was. But me being here had nothing to do with Susan Fraily. Instead, me being here had everything to do with Greg Monger—high school star quarterback and professional scumbag. Rumor had it that Greg liked to bring girls to this spot and force himself on them. I hated bullies, and rapists were the ultimate bullies, taking from someone something that they could never return. So when I'd heard Greg was bringing Susan here, I'd decided that maybe this time there should be some chaperoning. Problem was, they were just sitting in the front seat talking.

"Do you smell that?" Wheatie asked.

I did smell something . . . something chemical that tickled my nose. But I didn't want to be distracted. Any second and the scheming rapist might make his move. I wanted to be ready when it happened. Still, I couldn't help but ask, "What is it?"

"Whatever it is, it shouldn't be here." Wheatie went over to the water's edge. "Look here. See the foam? It looks like the water is black."

"I can't look. I'm busy."

"No, Joe, I'm serious. You need to see this. Someone's been messing with the water."

I sighed. Wheatie just didn't understand the concept of surveillance. "It's a stakeout, Wheatie. I can't look now."

"Okay, Magnum, P.I. Just don't come running to Wheatie when you drink this shit and your pecker falls off."

I couldn't stop my lips from curling into a smile. That was actually funny, so I glanced over at the water. "What do you think it is?"

"How am I supposed to know? I look like Mr. Wizard to you?"

The sound of a car engine turning over made me return to my vigil, but it was short-lived. Monger put his Trans Am in reverse, then pulled away, the crunch of gravel receding until he hit the main road. He hadn't tried anything tonight, but that didn't mean he wasn't going to try tomorrow night. And when he did I'd be ready.

The next morning was Saturday, so no school. The weather was still cold, but April was promising to be warmer than March. I spent three hours at the dojo working up a sweat, then went to Luskin's and unloaded trucks for a few more hours. It didn't pay much and the hours sucked, but it gave me enough cash to be free from my father.

After slamming a burger and fries, I met up with Wheatie. His discovery intrigued me. The Pond had always been an idyllic spot. When we were younger I'd fished from its banks. I never caught anything impressive, but it was the fishing that was important. Then when I was older and when Helen was still in my life, we'd swim there. Once we even went skinny-dipping, but I was too embarrassed to look at her and she was too embarrassed to look at me. Now, it was where we brought dates . . . scratch that . . . where other people my age brought dates. And it was cyclic. The young get older and go from fishing to kissing. I bet there were some eight- and nine-year-olds who wanted to fish there but couldn't because of the pollution, and that pissed me off. So the question was, where did the pollution come from?

It was a chemistry lesson that gave me the idea to go to a swimming pool store and get a water test kit. During daylight, the water looked far worse than at night. Not only did it have a black color in places, but in others it had the telltale rainbow of gasoline, especially near the cattails. I decided to ignore the gasoline and go for the mysterious black water. I was forced to wade knee-deep out into the pond. I'd capped the plastic tube and was about to turn around to leave when I heard a voice.

"There he is, boys," came a voice I knew and hated.

I spun. Where the hell was Wheatie when I needed him? He was supposed to be watching my back and now he was gone, leaving me to confront Monger, the right side of the offensive line, and the running back, Eric Mattis. The size of the two linemen with them was impressive. Each of them was at least two people. For all I knew, they probably ate their way out of their mothers, then ate their fathers. I supposed if I cared about football I'd know their names, but for now, I referred to them in my mind as Thing 1 and Thing 2.

"The Peeping Tom returned to the scene of the crime," said Mattis, his voice girlish despite his twenty-one-inch neck—sort of like Mike Tyson on helium.

They'd arranged themselves in an arc at the edge of the water. I played out five different scenarios, in each one knocking them all down. I wasn't scared because I knew I could take them, despite Thing 1 and Thing 2.

"I see you brought your sisters, Monger," I said.

This turned all four of their faces red—the quarterback, the running back, and the two linemen.

I looked past them, hoping to see Wheatie, but no joy.

Thing 1 and Thing 2 had balled fists the size of softballs.

"Who you calling a sister?" Mattis asked in his girl's voice.

That made me smile, which pissed him off royally. He lunged toward me, but Monger put a hand on his chest.

"He's just trying to goad you into something." Monger eyed the water. "You actually swimming in there? That shit will make your pecker fall off."

"Since when did you care about my pecker?" I asked, remembering Wheatie had said much the same thing. I stepped forward and kept walking until I was at the water's edge. As I approached, they backed away, allowing me to step onto the bank. My sneakers were wet and muddy and didn't promise a lot of traction. I'd have to be careful.

"I saw you trying to sneak up on me last night," Monger said. "I want to know why."

I raised my eyebrows and shook my head slightly. "So you wouldn't rape Susan Fraily," I said.

I saw Mattis whip a fist in my direction. I leaned back, grabbed his wrist, and used his momentum to pull him past me, releasing him face-first into the water. The move was perfect, but I felt my feet slipping. In an effort to correct my balance, I brought my head forward—a terribly bad move. One of the Thing 2's softball hands, which was anything but soft, connected with the back of my head. I dropped like a bag of cement, my face planting in the mud.

I moved to get up, but felt a boot connect with my ribs. Then another and another. They began singing the high school fight song as they kicked me over and over. All I could do was squirm enough to avoid a kick to the head or groin area.

Galaxies of pain were born and died every microsecond of their attack. I felt a rib crack. The bones in my left hand snapped. The toe of a boot found my kidney and I knew I'd be peeing blood for days.

There was a lull in their kicking, as if they wanted to examine the newly pulped being they were creating. I used the opportunity to slide back into the water by twisting to my knees and launching myself. I hit the water on my left side. They ran to the water's edge, but I pulled myself deeper into the pond, grabbing mud from the bottom as purchase. As polluted as the water was, it soothed my body, reducing the pain to mere explosions instead of the never-ending avalanche it had become.

"Who you calling a sister?" Mattis howled, dripping black water on the edge of the pond.

Then they patted themselves on their backs and retreated. Eventually, I heard two cars start and roar away.

"Hey, you okay?"

"Where the hell were you?" I asked, each word a jolt of pain.

"I'm here now, aren't I?" Wheatie splashed into the water next to me.

I held up my broken hand.

"Damn, they got you good."

It was two hours before I managed to limp home. I emptied the ice container in the bathtub and got in, turning the cold water on. The ice melted right away, but the cold remained. I stayed that way a long time, then went straight to bed.

When I woke the next morning, I felt as if I'd been steamrolled by a ten-thousand-pound Zamboni. My father cracked open the door a little after eight. It was Sunday, so he was off and he usually spent the day down at the races, betting on horses. When he saw me, his face fell into something akin to Roosevelt on Mount Rushmore.

"You were in a fight again."

If you call being jumped by four football players getting into a fight, then yes, but I didn't answer.

He made no move to come in the room. "Your mom isn't going to be happy about this."

I wouldn't expect her to be.

A few more seconds ticked by, then he asked in a monotone, "Do you need a doctor?"

If I asked for one, he'd get pissed. It's not as though we could afford one. Then he'd be ragging on me for days, if not weeks.

"No, Dad. I got it covered."

"You sure?" he asked.

I nodded, gritting my teeth at the pain.

He began to close the door.

"Uh, Dad?"

He stuck his head back in the room. "Yeah?"

"Did Wheatie stop by?"

He stared at me for a long moment, as if he were contemplating saying something, but then just shook his head and closed the door.

I listened through the walls as he began to talk to my mom, probably telling her not to worry.

The next time I woke the clock said 1:00 and Wheatie was at my side.

"Brother, you are one messed-up dude."

Wheatie helped me out over the next four days. My hand swelled up like a purple pumpkin, but by day four, it was back to regular size and discolored. I kept it wrapped, applying ice when I could. My ribs were okay, just bruised . . . as was the rest of my body. I ate by grabbing whatever was available in the fridge. By Friday I was ready to return to the real world, but I wasn't ready to go back to school.

My water sample was unbroken. Because it was in my pocket by my groin, it had been protected. So the first place we went after I left the house was the swimming pool shop to have the water analyzed.

When the nice man behind the counter got the results later in the day, he frowned. "If you're swimming in this your pecker's going to fall off."

"So I heard," I said, remembering having to scramble in the water to save myself. I was lucky it hadn't already plopped to the ground. "What's in it?"

"Mostly sodium and turpentine," he said, eyeing me speculatively.

"Sodium like salt?"

He hesitated before responding. "There are different kinds of sodium. My machine can't tell the difference." He looked around the swimming pool showroom, then added, "If you want a definitive answer, I'd recommend going to the University of Maryland's Science Department."

I wondered what sodium and turpentine were doing in the water.

"There were also trace amounts of lead, mercury, and argon."

"What could be doing this?"

The man leaned over the counter and whispered, "Listen, you didn't get this from a pool. I know. I'm not sure where this is from, but I don't want any part of this. I recommend you just leave this alone."

"Why? What's the matter?" I asked.

He gestured toward the readout. "I looked this up. You've tied into some black liquor." Seeing the expression on my face, he explained. "It's the substance that's created when wood is pulped in the process for making paper. I made a few calls, including Patton's Paper Plant, and was told to shut up."

"Or else what?" I asked.

"Or else I might wake up one night to find my store a pile of ashes."

"The paper plant told you that?"

"No. Someone else. Someone . . . how do I put this . . . connected. He didn't say his name; he just said to lay off. He called and that's all I'm saying."

This was a turn of events I hadn't anticipated. I was keen on getting to the bottom of the pollution and eventually stopping it. But if the Mob was somehow involved, I wasn't sure what I'd do. Then I smiled. Truth be told, I didn't know what I'd do even without the Mob. But I trusted my mind and body to figure it out.

I nodded. "Don't worry about this. As far as we're concerned, I was never here."

He nodded. Then he paused. "We?" he asked nervously. "Who else have you told about this?"

"Just me and Wheatie," I said. "No one else."

I turned and left, Wheatie beside me. When we hit the street, we walked for a time so I could figure things out. Even I knew I couldn't go against the Mob. Heck, I couldn't go against four football players. No, that wasn't what I was going to do. One day I'd be in a position to do something dramatic, be Spider-Man. But for now I'd have to settle for being Peter Parker. I'd gather evidence and find a way to report it. If not for me, for the memory of Helen, because the more that I walked, the more the memories of the two of us morphed until we were swimming together in a cauldron of black water, pieces of our skin smoking and then falling away.

Just as she began to scream, Wheatie brought me back to the present.

"What now, boss?"

"Now I go and find a camera."

"What's the camera for?"

"Another stakeout."

Wheatie groaned.

"Except this time we're not hanging out just to see if an asshole is going to rape some girl. This time we're there for that and to see who's dumping in the pond."

I went around to Luskin's to apologize to Mr. Howison, but that didn't go well. I really should have called and he let me know just that.

"Plus, I can't have any fighters working for me. I mean look at you. What would the customers say if they saw you?"

I wanted to say, *That I was jumped by four of your high school football heroes*, but I didn't. Mr. Howison was a nice guy and was also a football booster. Assholes like Monger and his crew came and went. I wasn't the sort to paint everyone with the same brush. And I understood where Mr. Howison was coming from, even if I was always in back on the loading docks and never saw any customers. He needed to count on me and my head wasn't in the right place. Hell, it hadn't been in the right place for years.

He gave me sixty bucks and we shook hands. No hard feelings. I took that sixty to a pawnshop. Their 35 mm cameras were out of my price range, but there were some Instamatics I could buy. Problem was, it was going to be in low light, or even no light, so I'd need a flash. Then I spied a Polaroid. The instantaneousness grabbed me. The audacity of stepping out of the bushes and taking a picture of them in the act of polluting was a powerful pull. So $30 later, I purchased a Polaroid OneStep Flash. Then, after I hunted down some batteries and film, I was ready to save the planet . . . or at least the place where my memories of Helen were perhaps the best.

I spent that Friday night hiding in the weeds near Patton's Pond, waiting on a truck to show up. The spot had the usual traffic of guys with girls, steaming up the back windows of cars. Once I heard a scream come from the rear of an Impala, but it was followed by a giggle. With all the boy-girl action, it wasn't long before my thoughts drifted into the dismal memories surrounding Helen. Part of me couldn't help wondering what it would have been like with us had she not been attacked . . . had I been able to save her. There was a hole inside me a mile deep where what-ifs and what-could-have-beens fought Texas cage death matches, possibilities plowing into each other with barbed-wire fists and razor-blade feet, only to be reborn to fight again. The images were never-ending and tended to blend into reality until I believed I was seeing things that couldn't possibly be there. For a year after the rape I'd see her, only not as she'd been before, but after, standing by a bus stop, bruised, bloody face cracked open or standing in line, her face purple, eyes accusing.

I'd tried to be with her at first, hoping I could be part of the recovery process. But it wasn't long before I realized she wanted nothing to do with me, so I stopped trying to see her. She'd become such a recluse, all I could do was wonder if she spent her time blaming me. The attack was the very reason I'd found martial arts. I vowed that I'd never be in such a helpless position again.

Not that I hadn't utterly failed in that plan the other day. I knew how I'd let them get the best of me. I knew it and hated myself for it. Overconfidence belonged nowhere near a fight. Neither did hesitation. I should have taken it to them the moment they'd confronted me, but instead I'd posed like a character out of a Bruce Lee movie who was reluctant to fight, but who everyone knew would eventually unload a can of kung fu whoop ass and be the hero.

Yeah, that's me.

Stupid.

A station wagon pulled up and parked. Thing 1 sat in the front. Thing 2 sat in the back. Their dates sat beside them and looked like children. The size difference was so improbable that I almost laughed. They drank a few beers and groped the girls. Just as I was thinking they'd leave, Thing 1 spilled out of the front seat and began walking toward me, unzipping his fly. I eased myself deeper into the bushes. Yet still he came. I doubt he saw me, but I sure saw him. I watched with more than a little disgust as he relieved himself, the sickly stream landing just in front of me, splattering my knees. As if things couldn't get any worse. I heard a car door slam and then Thing 2 was beside Thing 1, adding a new stream. I couldn't look away. If they saw me, I needed to be ready. So here I was, kneeling in the bushes, forced to watch two gigantic offensive linemen holding their rods, inches away from me, giving me a golden shower.

I held my breath until they left, packing, zipping, turning, wiping their hands on their pants as they returned to their dates.

The rest of the evening was uneventful. I stayed until morning, but no dumping.

I made it back by nine, in time to see my father leave. We nodded to each other as we passed, our only connection. I slept for ten hours and woke at seven. My father still wasn't back. Probably at the track.

Wheatie showed up as I was wolfing down a can of pork and beans. "How're you feeling?" he asked.

"Fine," I said around a mouthful. "Where'd you get to last night?"

"Was busy." He glanced around. "Your dad around?"

I shook my head.

"Good," he said. Then he asked, "What do you think of your dad?"

"What kind of question is that?"

"Simple question formed from a leading interrogative, followed by a subject and a verb and an object . . . the object of the question being your dad, with me asking what you think of him."

I sighed. I forgot sometimes that Wheatie was a smart-assed genius. "I try not to think of him."

"You know he doesn't like me, right?"

"He just doesn't understand."

"I think he does. And you know what else? I think he loves you."

"You don't know anything I don't tell you to know."

"That's sort of harsh."

"Well, I'm feeling fucking harsh." I tossed the can in the trash and the spoon in the sink. "You ready to go, or what?"

We were in place by nine, watching the steady flow of hormone-fueled teenagers come and go.

About eleven, Wheatie asked, "You're hoping you see them, aren't you?"

Some questions you can answer with a nod or a word, but this wasn't one of those. The answer ran back years to those hideous moments when Helen was on the ground and four older teens were doing to her what no man should ever do to a woman. Despite the sketch artists and police promises, they were never identified, although I swore to myself I'd know them if I ever saw them again. Was I out here looking for them? I never stopped looking for them. I looked for them in every store, on every street, and in every place I went. Instead of answering, I continued my vigil. Whether it be Monger, the polluters, or one of them, I was on the lookout, and by God, I'd find one of them.

Wheatie bugged out at three in the morning, but I stayed until dawn. No sign of Monger. No sign of anything. I was halfway back to my house when I heard the rumble of an engine. I looked over and saw a station wagon. Thing 1 and Thing 2 filled up the front. They were in sweats and it looked as if they'd just worked out as they pulled up next to me.

"What's going on, ground stain?" Thing 1 asked, prodding Thing 2 in the rib with an elbow.

"What's in your purse?" Thing 2 asked, all grins and steroid acne.

I had a small pack with a water bottle and my camera. It wasn't a purse, but they didn't need to know that. Instead of answering, I cut across a lawn, leaving them in the street. They'd either drive away or—

I was gratified to hear the sound of two doors opening, then slamming shut.

"Don't you walk away from me when I'm talking to you," Thing 1 growled.

I turned and watched him stomp across the grass, hands working around invisible necks. Instead of running, I took three quick steps and got into his guard. He reached out and I hip-chucked him ten feet. Before he landed, I was on Thing 2, firing two punches to his kidney, then raking my foot down his shin and into his instep. He fell to the ground, grabbing at his foot.

Thing 1 started to get up and I kicked him in the face.

Thing 2 saw it happen and stayed in place.

"What's wrong? No one to sucker punch me?"

Just then a cop car pulled to the curb. Its lights began to flash and I could see the cop talking into the radio and eyeing me as if I were an escaped convict. Then he got out of the car, his hand on his pistol.

"What's going on here?" he asked.

Neither Thing 1 nor Thing 2 said a word.

"You and you, on your feet. What's going on?" he asked, looking at me.

"Fellas tripped is all."

Thing 1 wiped blood from his broken nose with the sleeve of his sweat suit.

"I know you guys. You're on the football team."

They both nodded but said nothing. Thing 2 glared at me, but Thing 1 wouldn't meet my gaze. The cop shook his head. "I don't know what really happened here, but let's not do this again." He pointed back to the station wagon. "This belong to you two guys?"

They nodded.

"Get it moving. And you," he said, pointing at me. "Where should you be?"

"Home, Officer."

"Then get there."

I nodded and left.

Half an hour later I was home and in bed and I fell asleep with a grin on my face.

Sunday night as I was about to leave, my dad came in the kitchen.

"Where you going?" he asked.

"Out."

"Where out?"

I glanced at him from where I was eating a microwaved burrito, leaning against the counter. Why was he suddenly wanting to be the good father? I guess I took too long to answer, because he rolled his eyes and lowered his voice.

"Listen, Joe, I just want to make sure you're safe."

"I'm safe."

"Seriously. You're out at all hours of the night doing God knows what. Your mother is worried and I just need to make sure you aren't breaking any laws."

"I'm not breaking any laws," I said, finishing the burrito.

"Then where are you going?" he asked.

I turned to him. "Out," I said, daring him to ask me again, act as though he cared, maybe even be a father and stop me from being rude.

For one solid moment, I thought he would. But then he sighed, turned, and walked out of the room.

I left the room, too, leaving it as empty and sterile as it had been before. Thirty minutes later I was in the weeds on stakeout.

At 10:53 a flatbed truck pulled up at the far edge of the pond. Wheatie had gone out for some Cokes, so I was alone. I began to edge my way around. As I was navigating the bushes, I heard Monger's Trans Am pull up as well. I took a long look and saw that Susan was with him. Her head moved funny, as if it wouldn't stay up. Then it hit me. Fucker had rufied her, or maybe gotten her drunk. This was the night for certain.

I stared at the flatbed. Six metal drums were on the back of it. I had no doubt that the two men in front were going to dump them in the pond.

Caught between two competing decisions, I wasn't sure what to do.

The two men got out and began to wrestle a barrel onto the ground.

I decided that concealment was overrated. I stood my full height and ran toward them, pulling the camera from my bag as I went. They heard me when I was ten feet away.

"Get out of here, kid."

"I know what you're doing." I pulled out the camera, pressed the on button, and snapped a picture. The flash blinded them and me both. Then the camera whirred and spit out a picture. I grabbed it and shoved it in my back pocket.

"Hey!"

"You can't do that." The driver reached out his hand. "Give me that now."

I backed away and took another picture. Then another. "You don't get out of here now these pictures will be in the *Baltimore Sun* tomorrow." I took a picture of the side of the truck where it said CANELLI BROTHERS, then a picture of the front license plate.

"You can't do that!"

"I can and did. Take your barrels somewhere else."

I backed away and took one last picture.

They cursed as they loaded the barrel back on the truck.

"If I see you, you're dead," the passenger growled.

I held up the camera and grinned.

Then they drove away.

I turned and sprinted back around the edge of the pond. I could see movement in the Trans Am. The passenger seat was lying flat. Monger was on top of Susan. When I arrived at the car, I began taking pictures.

One. Monger on top of Susan. Her eyes closed. His hands up her shirt, groping her breasts.

Two. Monger's face surprised. Susan's eyes still closed, his hands pulling free of her shirt.

Three. Now Angry Monger. Susan's eyes still closed.

Four. Monger launching himself out the window.

I ditched the camera and put all the pictures in my back pocket with the others.

Wheatie appeared behind Monger, and behind him came the station wagon.

"The others are here, Joe. Be careful."

Monger got to his feet. At six five, he towered over me, but that didn't matter.

I planted a boot in his crotch and watched with satisfaction as he fell to his knees. Then I brought my own knee into his face and was pleased to hear the crunch of his nose.

The others bailed out of the station wagon and gathered in front of the headlights.

"Leave him alone," Mattis howled.

I stalked toward them, every step, every movement, with dire intention. For however long it took the police to come and arrest me, my targets were no longer Monger, Mattis, Thing 1, and Thing 2. Instead, they were the four strange boys who'd brutally raped Helen, shattering her life and bruising her soul.

It was because of them we were no longer friends.

It was because of them I couldn't look into her eyes.

It was because of them she couldn't participate in the world.

Wheatie and I sat in the holding cell for three hours. Two drunks and a perplexed-looking man in a suit and tie sat on the metal benches. Twice Wheatie tried to engage me in conversation, but each time I ignored him.

I remember that they had to bring two ambulances.

From the back of the police cruiser where I sat handcuffed, I watched Monger leave in one of them.

Thing 2 left in the other. I'd broken his arms and shattered his knee.

Thing 1 would be peeing blood for a few weeks.

Likewise, Mattis would be doing the same. If he ever held a football again with that right hand, I'd be surprised.

"Come on, Joe. It was four against one. They can't hold you."

I glanced over at Wheatie. He was a good friend and I was lucky to have him.

"But I attacked them," I said.

"The cops don't know that."

Just then my father appeared, his face a crimson ball of anger. As a cop, he knew it looked bad to have his oldest son in jail.

"What did you do?"

I stopped a man from raping a girl and stopped two men from polluting the pond.

He shook his head. "You've gone too far."

"I had to do something."

"Do something? You almost killed those boys."

"They had it coming."

"Do you hear yourself? 'They had it coming'?" He shook his head again. "You have got to stop this, Joe." He turned to look behind him. "There's only so much I can do."

Now I shook my head. "As long as there are bad men out there, I won't be stopped."

He pointed to his chest. "I'm your father and you will do as I say."

"Better listen to him," Wheatie said.

My father lowered his voice. "I spoke to the other parents. They were going to press charges, but the police found your photos."

"What did they show?"

"Two men with a barrel by the pond and what looks like the boy you hurt on top of an unconscious girl. Care to explain the pictures?"

"I think they're self-explanatory."

He stared at me for a long moment. "Listen," he said, "I know I haven't been the best dad. I know I can be better. You have a few more months before you can leave on your own. Let's make those months good ones. If not for our sake, for your mother's. Okay?"

I felt a powerful emotion grow in my chest. For the first time in forever, he was acting like a father. He was doing everything I'd wanted him to do. I opened my mouth to speak, but found I couldn't.

"Let me sign some paperwork, then you and I can be on our way," he said as he turned.

"Hey, Dad?"

He turned back.

"Can you get Wheatie out of here, too?"

My father's smile fell and his face contorted into a mask of tortured anger.

"What is it?" I asked. "What's wrong?"

"Wheatie."

"What about him?"

"You keep talking about him as if he's still alive."

"What are you talking about?" I turned to where Wheatie sat. Gone was his usual smile. He frowned and his face looked different.

"Wheatie drowned in that pond the same day you and Helen were attacked."

I watched as Wheatie's skin began to flake away and his hair began to fall out. A spider crawled out of his mouth and found a home in his now empty eye socket.

"The doctors said that I shouldn't press it, that I should let you realize his death on your own."

"Wheatie's dead?" I asked, the words whining from my mouth. I went to repeat it, but only my mouth moved. No sound came out.

"Yes, son."

Where Wheatie had been, there was nothing but a pile of dust and bone. Wheatie had disappeared into that black water the same night four strangers had left permanent bruises on our souls.

I remembered.

I remembered it all.

"They pulled him from the water the next morning," I said.

My father nodded.

"No one knows why he was in the pond. He didn't even know how to swim."

He nodded again.

"Why didn't you tell me? Why'd you let me go on like that?"

"I have told you. I tell you every year and then you just sort of forget. The worse things get, the more you seem to need Wheatie."

I felt a pressurized balloon blow inside me and emotion rushed to my face. I couldn't help it as I cried over the loss of a friend who'd died a few moments ago and four years ago.

Wheatie.

Helen.

The Black Water.

"Oh, Dad, it's just too much," I managed to say between sobs.

Then the ghost of Wheatie whispered into my ear, "Joe Ledger. Teen heartthrob."

And I completely lost it.

ABOUT THE AUTHOR

Weston Ochse is a former intelligence officer and Special Operations soldier who has engaged enemy combatants, terrorists, narco smugglers, and human traffickers. His personal war stories include performing humanitarian operations over Bangladesh, being deployed to Afghanistan, and a near miss being cannibalized in Papua New Guinea. His fiction and nonfiction have been praised by *USA Today*, *The Atlantic*, the *New York Post*, the *Financial Times of London*, and *Publishers Weekly*. The American Library Association labeled him one of the Major Horror Authors of the Twenty-first Century. His work has also won the Bram Stoker Award, been nominated for the Pushcart Prize, and won multiple New Mexico–Arizona Book Awards. He has written more than twenty-six books in multiple genres, and his military supernatural series *SEAL Team 666* has been optioned to be a movie starring Dwayne Johnson. His military sci-fi series, which starts with *Grunt Life*, has been praised for its PTSD-positive depiction of soldiers at peace and at war.

INSTINCT (A GHOST STORY)

BY BRYAN THOMAS SCHMIDT AND G. P. CHARLES

A nuclear bomb.

My master and I had just fought our way past armed thugs into the bowels of the Aghajari Oil Refinery near Tehran, Iran, and now this. Hidden in a cavern carved out deep underground. Walls chiseled out of stone, lined with stacked wooden crates, surrounded us on all sides. The chamber itself was massive. Water dripped from the ceiling high above and pooled around broken rock and clay, and at least two dozen human corpses. The air smelled of mold, moss, sweat, dust, oil . . . and death. So much death. I shivered involuntarily, unnerved. And my master gave me a concerned look.

I was trained for all kinds of situations. Especially dead bodies. I should not have been afraid. But I was. I couldn't help it. The fear in the air crushed around me like a human embrace.

"Easy, boy," he said. "It's okay, Ghost . . . it'll all be okay."

My master shone his light around the cavern, turning back, and found a dozen sets of clothes, folded neatly atop a nearby crate. "Oh shit," he muttered. He dropped his balaclava and began winding through the stacks, examining the crates, illuminating them with his flashlight as he went. Then he froze. And I sensed his tension rising. Heard his heart pound faster.

I moved cautiously up beside him to peer at what he was seeing: a real, live nuclear bomb.

As my master would say: What the fuck were we doing here?

Even in danger, my master's a smart-ass.

With one sniff, I could tell my master found it just as unsettling as I did, despite our expectations. I sensed he wanted to run, but instead we both just stared at it.

Joe Ledger, that's my master. Kind of a badass to most people. Of course, I can hold my own, too. In fact, he may get most of the credit, but I like to think he couldn't do it without me. Ghost, that's my name, and with a name like that, I suppose a lower profile is only natural. That, plus the fact I walk on four legs and am a lot shorter.

We'd come here for this. That had been the assignment. Terrorists threatening to set off multiple nukes—our job was to find them. That didn't make it any more pleasant realizing you actually had and were standing right next to it, a few feet away. It lay in the center of the cavern floor with thick, snakelike power cords coiling off from it toward a nearby wall.

It didn't help that the whole place had the overwhelming odor of rot and death, either. Rotting meat was just part of it. My nose crinkled as I digested this. There was one more smell, too—adrenaline, hot breaths, warm blood—fear.

My master tapped his ear—no doubt hoping for the signal he needed to communicate with the team. His shoulders sank again, and I knew it wasn't working. He stood there for the longest time, examining the bomb. It was at least twice my height and several times longer and wider than me. There was no ticking sound, but I didn't know if that was good or bad, and from the way my master looked at it, I could tell he wasn't quite sure, either.

"Okay," he said, and moved around it, going for a closer look, his flashlight's beam leading the way.

With a clink, he removed his tool kit from his pack, unrolled it, then took a screwdriver in one hand and the flashlight in the other and went to work. My master is smart and he knows lots of stuff, but I had to fight the urge to shrink back as I thought, *I hope he knows what he's doing*.

I sniffed again, listening to the air around us as my master removed a metal shield. Sweat poured down his face to sting his eyes and he winced before taking a metal plate and several screws and setting them gently aside. I locked my eyes on his face, watching for any signs as he examined the interior of the bomb. What was it? I wished he'd tell me, but instead he took the screwdriver and began unfastening something else I couldn't see.

As his hand came away again, the plate he pulled back was the same metal but smaller. He was seeing something. And I sensed him relax, even as tension left his body and his eyebrows raised in question. "What the fuck?" he muttered.

Still no ticking. Even the scent of his adrenaline faded a bit. Was that good or bad? I wagged my tail, hoping he'd tell me.

"Ghost, old buddy," he said as he continued staring at the bomb, "I think we got lucky."

Then my ears popped up at a soft scuffing behind me and we both spun around. A growl rose in my throat as the smells of fear and death grew stronger again.

There were two of them. One a major my master had fought earlier, who'd lost his teeth. The other in orange coveralls of refinery staff. The major smiled, showing fangs, his real teeth. Long fangs. Red Knights!

Though both were armed, neither they nor my master had drawn their weapons. But their eyes glowed at us: red, haunting.

My body started shaking and I let out a whimper as my bladder let go. I had no control. Now the urge to run was almost overwhelming, but I couldn't move.

The two men's smiles widened.

And I was torn between the shame at my own fear and immobility, sensing the disappointment of my master. He was counting on me and yet I couldn't do a thing. A thousand blips of memories, of things Joe and I had been through, flooded my mind, taking over all my thoughts. Desperate for something to ground the world around me, I focused on one, the earliest. The day I met my master.

He was broken, I could sense it. Not physically—though he bore the evidence of that as well. Damaged in a way I couldn't see. And I didn't like it. I didn't like him. He reminded me of the Man, the ex-Marine who caged my mum and me and my siblings in filth. Whose voice was as harsh and cruel as the wire we slept on each night. The Man and this Joe Ledger had the same hair color, the same . . . hardness . . . to their eyes. From experience, I knew that hardness changed only when it came with pain. My pain. My mum's pain. The pups around us who I could smell and hear but never saw. If I was too eager for my food, a steel-toed boot would thump into my ribs. And those eyes glinted like glass.

I couldn't possibly be safe here.

I narrowed my gaze on Joe and lowered my ears.

My trainer, Zan Rosin, smiled at Joe. "He's a very nice dog," she said. "He's exceptionally smart and has already passed through standard and advanced training in search and rescue, bomb detection, bark and hold, high-speed disarm, cover and concealment . . ." Her words trickled down and stopped.

Joe scowled at me. He didn't like me much, either. Fine. I'd put an end to this and go back with the woman who'd spent so much time teaching me. The woman who'd rescued me and taught me kindness. I curled my lip and bared my teeth.

I tried to pull myself out of the cycling memories, back into the cavern of rot and death. But the fear . . . I was back in that horrible puppy mill again, terrified to poke even my nose out of my cage when Zan rescued me, certain the pain would come again. That maybe this time, like my youngest littermate, I wouldn't survive it.

Memories cycled again. Another took over, an echoing laugh that was warm, friendly, and accompanied belly rubs. *Rudy.* Rudy was always safe.

"How long's it going to be, Joe, before you acknowledge the pain instead of trying to drown it? Grace is gone, and I miss her, too, but she'd roll over in her grave if she could see you right now," Rudy said, his usually kind voice harsher than what I'd become accustomed to.

Joe instantly turned cold, his words sharp and intense, though not a shout. "Fuck you."

"Nothing changes no matter how often you say that. I get the message— I'll let you wallow. You do that damn well." He snatched his keys off the table and stalked to the door.

Joe made no move to get up. Confused, I glanced between the closed front door and my master. I'd only known him a couple of weeks, but I'd not seen him this way. As if Rudy's words stole something from him.

Joe lifted his beer bottle at me and cracked a sardonic smile. "Cold, hard honesty." He took a long slug, frowned at the bottle, then set it aside and stared out the window.

Something was different. I didn't know what, but I sensed it in my bones. And I was Joe's companion now, so I did what seemed right. I rested my nose on his thigh. His hand fell on my head, fingers barely shifting through my hair.

"He's right, you know," he murmured quietly. "I am wallowing. Because

nothing's the same without her. You'd have liked her, Ghost." He shook his head. "You'd have loved her." His fingers gripped tighter—not painfully—and then relaxed completely.

"I'm going to bed. You coming?" He pushed out of the chair.

I wagged my tail hesitantly. My dog bed was evidence of my new freedom—no kennel at night. Run of the house. Soft bed to curl up on while I guarded him and the house. Only Joe had never invited me. I followed as I ought to. Something had definitely changed.

The following morning Rudy interrupted our training session—something completely out of the ordinary. "Joe, they found him," he said urgently.

Joe froze in place. He radiated an intensity I only ever felt when Rudy brought up his lost mate. In moments, we were running, meeting with the man Joe called Church, and what seemed even seconds later, boarding a giant winged bird, heading someplace called Amsterdam. I asked no questions. It was my duty. I was working . . . and I sensed Joe was, too.

We met another man—one I'd end up never forgetting—after the long air ride. Spurlock, Joe called him. During the taxi ride to what would be our destination, they talked about Joe's mate, Grace. Joe didn't like what Spurlock said. And strangely, I found myself not liking him for upsetting Joe. We hadn't been together long, but I liked him. He treated me like a friend. A partner in all he did.

"Well," Spurlock said, "at least we have the bastard cornered. Time for a little bit of payback."

Silence filled the car. Outside the windows, the island rolled by, green and pretty. I watched Joe, though. His energy was all over the place. I didn't know how to communicate with him, not in the way he talked with me, at least. I didn't have words. But I did have a voice.

I whined, telling him I understood.

Joe reached back and ran a hand over my head.

I've got this. I'm right here, I wanted to say. But he'd never understand my limited language. I couldn't rumple his fur, but I could lick his fingers. And so I did.

"Fetch dog," someone said as my eyes focused again. The two knights kept staring at me. The major laughed and sneered as he touched his chest and drew a line with his fingers above his eyes. What did that mean? Some sort of crazy human ritual?

"If you kill that piece-of-shit dog, we will make it easy for you," said the other knight, the one in the maintenance uniform, smiling.

And I shrank back involuntarily, afraid, even as my master's eyes went from fear to fury.

"Here's an idea," my master said, and instantly threw a screwdriver at the maintenance knight with his left hand while drawing his pistol with his right. The shiny, well-oiled black metal glinted in the low light.

The knight in overalls caught the screwdriver.

Then a red dot opened in his forehead as my master fired the pistol right at the knight's nose and he flew back. Blood and brains splattered out the back of his head as his neck snapped with a crack and he landed hard against a stony wall, sinking into a heap on the floor.

The major didn't even react. Instead, like a blur he rushed my master and me. I barked and lunged as my master fired again, but then stopped myself. I was trained not to jump in when my master was shooting.

The bullet hit the major sideways, passing through his elbow and sinking into his hip. He seemed to lose footing then, falling to the side and screaming.

"Hit!" my master ordered.

I was on the major like lightning, as fast as I could, tearing at his flesh, as the Red Knight's screams rose in pitch and desperation. I smelled garlic and gunpowder mixed with his warm, dead blood as it soaked into my fur, and I tore out his throat, then ripped his arm to shreds as he tried to deflect me. Nothing entered my mind but *kill*. End him as fast as I could.

And it was over quickly.

As my master turned, contemplating his next move, I caught the scent of more death, more Red Knights—they were coming closer. I growled and barked in warning, staring down the hallway in the direction of the scent.

My master turned and spun his gun up as we saw movement in the shadows. Thirty or forty this time—indistinct forms in the darkness, so many forms.

One of them stepped forward as the others parted. His skin was white as snow, his eyes redder than blood, and he seemed taller and more muscular than the rest. Over his black clothes, a necklace with a silver teardrop glinted through the shadows.

My master aimed his gun at him, but then there were footsteps behind and around us. I turned quickly, taking in the targets. More knights. We were surrounded.

"White dog . . . ," they whispered, and it spread through their numbers. "White dog!" Then they all touched their chests and drew lines over their eyes. Were they afraid of me? It was hard to sense it over my own terror.

The leader half turned and growled, silencing them, then turned back to my master. "I know who you are. You are Captain Ledger." His voice was icy as winter wind, and I shivered hearing it.

"Oh shit," my master mumbled beside me, shifting with uncertainty.

"You are a traitor to your own people," the lead knight continued, "and an enemy of mine."

Damn right. Kill you all.

But instead my master said, "What the fuck are you talking about?"

The lead knight smiled. "Our friend told us." His teeth shone. They were sharp, sharper than mine, menacing. My heart thumped harder as I felt the fear again.

"He said that you conspired with Rasouli and the Red Order to keep us in chains," the leader continued.

My master's face didn't change as he replied, "I don't have a clue what you're talking about, pal. I'm here to keep this bomb from going boom. When I'm done with that, we can sit down with a latte and talk about it."

I sniffed the air, listening for Echo Team, but got no hint of them. We were still alone. Trapped.

"Do you know who we are?" the lead knight taunted as the others moved in, surrounding us.

I whimpered beside my master, shivering. We were in trouble. I trusted my master, but what could he possibly do? We'd waited too long. We should have run at the first sign of them.

"At a guess?" my master replied. "Grigor, chief bloodsucker of the Upierczi."

The leader only nodded with approval, his face frozen in that terrifying smile. He told my master it would be an honor to die by his hand, as if the Red Knight knew it with certainty. I didn't doubt him at the moment, but my master just stared.

"That's actually not on my day planner," he said.

The lead knight's eyes cut left and right as the others moved closer. "Bring him to me!" he ordered.

"Ghost—hit!" my master yelled.

But I couldn't move. I was trembling too much, drool dripping from my mouth. I wanted to respond. I always obeyed my master, but then my bladder released again and warm fluid ran down my legs onto the floor.

The knights stared at us a moment, then burst out laughing.

"Oh shit," my master breathed again.

I looked to him, ashamed, but then the nearest Red Knight was on me, kicking my side. Pain swelled and filled my entire body as I rose into the air and flew against the side of the metal case that held the bomb. I yelped as I slid down, my feet scrambling for purchase, then landed in a heap, whimpering and wincing from the pain.

The knights laughed and laughed, red eyes staring at my master.

He pivoted suddenly and shot the knight who'd kicked me. The bullet sliced clean through him and into a companion behind him, slicing into his thigh. Both emitted high-pitched screams as they fell, smiles disappearing from the others' faces. And then my master let loose with his pistol, firing again and again. My mind clouded over with pain as I tried to recover, calm myself, rise and go to his aid.

What was wrong with me? I'd give my life for him, and I had no doubt he would for me. My master needed me. Right now. If I could just catch my breath.

Instead, my thoughts wandered again to when I'd been hurt before. Before Zan found me. At the puppy mill. I hated Red Knights as much as I feared them. I hated anyone who would abuse the innocent. . . .

The sun beat down—Arizona in the throes of midsummer. Joe and I had been working since dawn, out in this miserable weather, closing in on the last link in a chain of domestic terror strikes. I'd learned over the short time we'd worked together it was impossible to follow the names. There were too many, and in some cases, there was only one threat known by multiple names. Names didn't matter anyway. Just the "solution," as the humans around me often called it.

We carefully navigated around a thick tree line that bordered a sprawling estate: several small adobe cottages spread out around a large, central manor, all with red tile roofs baking in the heat. We'd run out of shade soon and be back in that miserable sunshine. Joe looked as worn out as I was. Sweat trickled down his temples and his shirt was plastered to his back. Air-conditioning would be our reward, if this guy hadn't ditched us again.

Joe pushed aside a branch on a small sapling and ducked under. I followed on his heels, ears pricked to catch any hint of voices or other unnatural sounds. Like, maybe, the click of a gun's hammer. Only I heard nothing. Nothing at all. Which only made me more uneasy. Silence was never a good thing, I'd come to discover. It usually preceded total chaos, or, as Joe liked to say, all hell breaking loose.

Before us stood an imposing iron fence. A few feet to Joe's left, an old gate hung cockeyed on its hinges, evidently unused for some time. A gate only those who knew to look for would ever find amid these thick trees. Forgotten, maybe, though I doubted it. That would be too easy.

A breeze stirred, rustling the overhead leaves. I put my nose to the sky, aching for just a bit of relief, a tickle of the fur, anything to cool the heat.

Then I smelled it.

A scent I'd thought never to encounter again. A stink of cruelty and evil that went beyond torture. Beyond even death. Feces. Urine.

And dog.

Not the kind of dog that prowled the ground, a vigilant sentry to all within. Not the kind of dog I'd become—a warrior and protector that could kill a man in seconds flat for the right reason.

Multiple dogs. Washed in misery.

My puppyhood slammed into my memories, and I couldn't stop a growl. Joe glanced down at me, his face full of concern. I spared him only a glance, then stared at that rusty gate. I didn't want to go in there; I knew what we'd find. Would Joe care? Or would the human threat be more important?

He approached cautiously. I lagged behind. We'd become good friends. I liked him a great deal. I didn't want all that to change . . . and I knew, somehow, that what happened when we breached this fence would alter us forever.

Joe scowled, motioning me forward. I had no choice in this. Duty demanded I obey. I took a step closer, and caught a faint, nearby whine.

Joe must have heard it, too. His head snapped up, his focus beyond the gate, where the backside of a long garage-type adobe building sprawled across the brown lawn. Small windows tucked against the eaves, interspersed with metal vents. I sniffed. Those vents funneled the stench.

Something distracted him, and he pressed a finger to his ear. Then his shoulders slumped. "Copy that. Damn it." He turned to me, his frown deep and dark. "He got the drop on us again, buddy. Looks like we came out here for nothing. Team's reporting the main house is empty and there's no sign of activity on the grounds."

He pressed his finger to his ear once more, listening to the voice in the tiny device as dread welled inside me.

"Roger. We'll regroup for morning." He turned his back to me.

No! He wasn't going to walk away. He couldn't. He'd heard that whine, I was certain of it. My lip curled, disgust rising before I could control it.

"Hold position, Tevares. I've got something here I want to check out."

Check out? I blinked.

Joe strode through the gate, his stride long and confident, though I knew he kept a watchful eye on his surroundings. He walked straight for that building.

He wasn't . . . I darted forward with a sharp yelp and bounded to his heels. He dropped a hand to the nape of my neck and ran his fingers through my hair. Another whine came from within the building.

We turned the corner, and Joe stopped in his tracks. Not much of ordinary life startled him, and given what we encountered daily, I understood why. I'd never seen him freeze as if fear possessed him, as he did now. Only fear wasn't the emotion rolling off him. I couldn't put a name to it, and looked from him to the open lawn.

Heavy-duty wire panels formed a circular ring in the middle of the yard. The grass around it had been stamped to hard-packed dirt. Blood spatters stained the ground inside the large cage, fresh crimson with a pungent scent. On the other side, against a small, gray shack, two motionless canine bodies lay in the scant shade. No scent of decay drifted from them. Only a few flies gathered on their mottled, bloodied fur.

What had they done here? This wasn't what I'd expected at all. My muscles tensed as apprehension and anger brewed inside me.

Joe's gaze cut to the long building at our left. He drew in a long, audible breath and started for the door. Glancing between him and that ring, I followed, uncertain what I should do. What I should prepare for.

He pushed the door open. The stench rushed out. "Stay here," he commanded as he pointed at the ground by the door.

I sat. Joe ducked his head into the shadows.

"Damn it!"

Anger drove him forward, and he burst inside as if he were hot on the trail once again. Any minute I half expected him to draw his gun and fire. But the only bullets that exploded were his exclamations of profanity that tripled in volume. As they grew, concern overtook me. I couldn't sit here and wait for something to happen to him.

So I charged inside.

I skidded to a halt on the concrete floor, nose to nose with a six-foot-tall, narrow kennel. In the far corner lay a dog. She lacked the strength to lift her head, and a large, festering wound covered her right shoulder.

I knew wounds like that. I made wounds like that.

Her eyes met mine, full of sorrow and lost hope. I looked away, helpless for the first time since I'd been a puppy. I sought Joe, and found him five kennels down, jimmying the lock on another cage. It popped with another of his exclamations, and he flung the door open, tearing at his shirt even as he surged inside.

I trotted cautiously closer. A warning growl from the cage to my immediate right gave me momentary pause, but as I looked, I found a dark black dog locked safely behind bars. Convinced there was no immediate threat, I followed Joe inside the kennel. He knelt beside a fawn-and-white dog and wrapped his shirt around its neck. It let out a soulful whine—the same whine we'd heard outside.

"It's okay, girl," Joe murmured. "You're going to be okay."

The dog rolled its gaze to him, but didn't otherwise move. This poor female dog was harmless now. Too wounded to hurt me, or Joe. I reassured him in the only way I could. I dropped my nose to his.

Joe pressed his earpiece again. "Tevares, get your ass down here. I've got a fresh dogfight—we must have interrupted them. Call Animal Control. There's twenty dogs in here. Some healthy, some in terrible condition."

I stood close enough to Joe that I could hear the voice crackle in response. "Copy. Already on it. I must have the winners over here. Found four chained to barrels covered in blood but otherwise healthy."

"Yeah," Joe muttered. "I've found the bait."

I glanced at the dog before us, then slowly around us. Bait. I didn't need human intelligence to understand the role these dogs played.

"Back, Ghost," Joe murmured.

Dutifully, I backed off ten steps. Joe stepped over the dog, moving behind it, then carefully slid his hands beneath. When she offered no sign of protest, he eased her into his arms. Another whine slid free. Blood seeped beneath his makeshift bandage to stain the patch of white fur around her throat.

As he stood, three men tromped into the building.

"Joe, that dog could turn on you," one of them cautioned.

Joe shook his head. "Don't really care. She's not going to make it if we wait for help. Lock this place down. Get these dogs out of here. Find the cats. Or rabbits. Or whatever else they're using for training bait. I'm taking this girl to the closest vet. Call me if you run into any problems."

As Joe started for the sun-baked outdoors, I stared after him, caught momentarily by surprise. He hadn't turned away. Man. Dog. Cats. Rabbits. He cared.

And I was part of his world. He was part of mine. I had never thought to respect a human this much. In that moment, he wasn't just Joe, he wasn't just my partner. He was my master, and I would willingly give my life for him. I bounded after, more proud than I'd ever been.

My master's screams jarred me from the memory.

The smell of rot and death surrounded me again as I heard laughter, cackling knight laughter, and my eyes focused. My master was pinned inside a pile of splintered crates, jagged edges cutting into his flesh, his clothing torn. Blood seeped from various wounds, and I spotted his knife lying out of reach on the cavern floor, his pistol clasped limply in one pinned hand as he struggled to free himself.

And the knights were sneering, laughing, their snow-white leader leaning over him with a look of triumph. I sensed it then: a predator preparing for the kill. My master needed me. Strength surged as blood and adrenaline poured through my body. My legs stiffed, a growl rising inside me.

I've got this. I'm right here! my mind shouted even as I pushed to my feet and launched myself at the pale, undead leader. My growl became a howling, primal declaration for all the world that they were hurting my master and I was going to hurt them, make them pay for it with all I had.

I leaped into the air and struck the lead knight like a bolt from the sky, turning his laughter into a terrified shriek as I tore at him again and I bore him back into the darkness with all I had. My howling mixed with his shrieking into a mournful serenade that only energized me further. My master had screamed, so this one would scream worse.

The knight slapped and punched at me, hands and feet flailing in vain attempts to dislodge me from atop him. My teeth sank into flesh and ripped chunks free—a finger—I shook my head, sending it flying in a trail of blood. Then another.

He screamed for his companions, begging for help, pure desperation.

I ripped at him again, tearing flesh from his arm, spitting it out, and going for more. The fear that had consumed me had been replaced by fury and focused determination. You. Don't. Hurt. My master.

The knights around us moved then, rushing to assist him, and my master's hand clamped around his pistol as he cocked it and aimed, then thunder exploded around us.

A whole line of Red Knights closest to my master shuddered and fell in heaps. Others spun, eyes seeking the threat, and then many of them died, too, bullets ripping into their faces, chests, arms, limbs.

More shrieks joined those of my target as I continued tearing at him.

My master joined the firing as a deep, leathery droning sound filled my ears—fuzzy at first, then becoming clearer: "Echo! Echo! Echo!"

And I smelled the scent now: Khalid, Lydia, Bunny, Top, Violin—our team had arrived. I knew then we could do it. We would kill them all. Destroy them as they'd tried to destroy us. I howled in welcome, then went back to tearing at my victim. Any dwindling trace of fear was gone now, replaced by hunger, instinct, an unquestioned focus on killing every target in reach.

Then our team joined the fight, filling the cavern with echoing bullets, the smell of sweat, powder, adrenaline, and knights' blood. More dead. More dying. Rotted dead flesh. Bodies. I looked over to see my master pulling free of the crate, shooting back, fighting alongside me.

I was right where I belonged.

ABOUT THE AUTHORS

Bryan Thomas Schmidt is an author and Hugo Award–nominated editor of adult and children's speculative fiction. His debut novel, *The Worker Prince*, received Honorable Mention on Barnes & Noble Book Club's Year's Best Science Fiction Releases of 2011. His short stories have appeared in magazines, in anthologies, and online and include entries in *The X-Files*, *Predator*, Larry Correia's *Monster Hunter International*, and *Decipher's WARS*, among others. As book editor for Kevin J. Anderson and Rebecca Moesta's WordFire Press, he has edited books by such luminaries as Alan Dean Foster, Tracy Hickman, Frank Herbert, Mike Resnick, Jean Rabe, and more. He was also the first editor on Andy Weir's bestseller *The Martian*. His anthologies as editor include *Shattered Shields* with co-editor Jennifer Brozek, *Mission: Tomorrow*, *Galactic Games*, and *Little Green Men—Attack!, and Monster Hunter Files* with Larry Correia (all for Baen); *Infinite Stars* and *Predator: If It Bleeds* (for Titan Books); *Beyond the Sun*, and *Raygun Chronicles: Space Opera for a New Age*. Find him on Twitter @BryanThomasS or via his website at www.bryanthomasschmidt.net.

After years of working in fantasy game design and Web development, G. P. Charles traded in computer programming for fiction writing and escaped the nightmare of missing semicolons and infinite loops. Now, instead of daydreaming about throwing the computer out the window, G.P. finds every day an exciting adventure. When not writing, downtime is spent at home on the farm, raising horses, chickens, and two boys who are too intelligent for their own good but a constant source of joy. To learn more, check out www .gpcharles.com.

NO GUNS AT THE BAR

BY AARON ROSENBERG

"On my mark," Bradley "Top" Sims declared over the comms. He stood to one side of the front door, pistol out and at the ready. Beside him, Lydia "Warbride" Ruiz nodded, her own gun also out.

"This is Bunny, copy that," Harvey "Bunny" Rabbit acknowledged. He and Montana "Stretch" Parker were stationed by the back door, while the team sniper, Sam "Ronin" Imura, covered them from the neighboring rooftop. Ronin checked in as well, and Top nodded.

"Echo Team, let's do this," he called out. "Go!"

With that he aimed a heavy kick at the front door, splintering the flimsy lock and sending the cheap wooden barricade smashing inward with a cloud of sawdust that filled the air around them. On the house's opposite end, Bunny did the same. The four team members barreled into the small dwelling, scanning the rooms they'd entered but finding nobody.

"Clear!" Top shouted. Bunny responded with the same, and both pairs moved on to the next rooms. In under a minute they'd covered the entire one-story building and found it empty.

"Well," Bunny commented as they regrouped in the living room, "that was a bust. And not the kind we figured."

Stretch rolled her eyes at the bad pun. Warbride snorted. Top just ignored it. "Cowboy, this is Top," he called in. "Nothing here. Looks like a wash."

"Roger that, Top," their boss, Captain Joe "Cowboy" Ledger, replied. "Head on back in."

"Copy that." Top reholstered his pistol. "Pack it up," he told his team, and they all nodded.

"Feels weird, not shooting anybody," Bunny remarked as they all made for the front door. He brushed some sawdust from his sandy-blond hair, scattering it all around him.

Walking just ahead of him, Warbride swiveled around to eye him warily. "Don't get any bright ideas," she warned. "Friendly fire or not, you draw and I'll put you down."

"Would I do that?" Bunny asked, plastering what was probably supposed to be a wide-eyed look of innocence on his broad face. The two of them laughed as they exited the building. Top didn't. The DMS had been in plenty of ugly scrapes, and he should have been relieved to have something turn out completely innocuous for a change.

Instead, it had him worried.

"Must have been bad intel," Ledger commented. Echo Team had returned to the Pier, their DMS base, and Top had just been debriefed. "Not sure how I feel about that."

Top nodded. He and Ledger had been working together for a while now—Ledger had been the original head of Echo Team, and Top and Bunny had both been in it with him since the beginning—and they often thought alike, so he knew his superior was feeling the same unease he was. The DMS didn't always have all the details, and sometimes they missed stuff just like anybody else. But to be completely wrong like this? That'd never happened before.

"Tip was plausible," Top remarked. And it had been. They'd heard that a terrorist cell had taken up residence in that nondescript little house on the outskirts of Dallas and had been working to fashion a bioweapon of some kind. And that they'd been close to activation. The DMS had dealt with plenty of bioweapons in the past and knew just how deadly those things could be, so they'd immediately jumped all over this. Only to find an empty house with no signs of activity at all, much less the marks of a terrorist group.

"It was," Ledger agreed. He rubbed at the stubble on his chin. "That's what worries me. It's not like a neighbor called in about loud music or somebody rifling through the trash. And the house was completely empty?"

Top nodded. "There was a FOR SALE sign out front," he reminded Ledger. "And the place was furnished, but all bland, no personality. Like you do when you're looking to sell."

The two of them sat there frowning for a minute before Ledger threw up his hands. "Well, whatever. We checked it out, and that's that. There isn't anything else to be done—and no other missions on hand." He grinned at Top. "Which means you and the rest of Echo Team can take the night off."

"Yeah?" Top peered at him warily. "What's the catch?"

That got a bark of laughter from the boss. "No catch," he answered. "Go on, get out of here. Relax a little. Let your hair down." He eyed Top's buzz cut, which was just starting to show hints of gray amid the black. "Metaphorically, anyway. Unless you want to help me with all this paperwork?" Ledger cast a sideways glance at the pile stacked on his desk.

"No, sir!" Top snapped to attention, popped off a quick salute, and reached for the door, all in one breath. "Thank you, sir! Good night!"

He could hear Ledger laughing behind him as he hotfooted it down the hall.

"For reals?" Bunny asked, eyes wide. "No night ops, no field prep, no training, no nothing?"

"You want I should change my mind?" Top suggested, arching an eyebrow.

"Nah, man," Bunny replied quickly. "I'm good." He grinned. "So, bar?"

Top laughed. "Bar," he agreed. What the hell, it wasn't as if he had a wife to go home to anymore anyway. He scanned the rest of the team. "Any of you in?"

Ronin shook his head, gave a short half bow, and walked away, all without a sound. "You talk too much, man!" Bunny shouted after him, earning a dismissive wave from the departing sniper.

"I'm out, too," Stretch said, grinning wickedly. "Got a hot date." She turned and sashayed off, to catcalls and whistles from both Bunny and Warbride.

"Well, those guys are wet blankets, but I'm in," Warbride declared. "Let's go get drunk and tear it up, yeah?"

"Right on!" Bunny held up a hand—though not too high, since at six feet six inches he towered over Warbride and even Top—and she high-fived him. Top rolled his eyes.

"Why do I feel like I'm about to be on chaperone duty," he muttered as the three of them strolled toward the Pier's main exit. Still, it was nothing a good stiff drink couldn't fix.

"Why here?" he asked twenty minutes later, squinting up at the weather-beaten sign dangling above them. DRINKS DRINKS DRINKS, it declared, as if one time were not enough. Then again, considering that the building looked as battered as the sign, maybe they really did need to advertise as much as possible.

"Why not?" Bunny answered with a shrug. "Besides, look at it." He pointed at the sign in question. "Drinks, drinks, drinks—it's an echo." He grinned. "Get it?"

"Yeah, we got it," Warbride acknowledged. She shoved him toward the door. "Let's hope they have at least that many, 'cause with dumb lines like that we're gonna need it."

The inside was no prettier than the place's outsides, with a long, scarred wooden bar taking up most of the right side, worn booths along the left, a few tables scattered in between up front, and a pair of old pool tables near the back. The place was maybe a third full and at least half of those were wearing black leather, which made Top sigh.

Not just a dive bar but a biker dive bar, he thought, shaking his head. *Perfect.*

Still, the bartender wasn't a hipster, which was a plus. And he didn't bat an eye when Top ordered Jameson, neat.

"Whatever ale you've got on tap," Bunny instructed, then glanced at Warbride. She nodded. "Make that two."

"Lightweights," Top teased as the three of them took adjoining stools.

"Hey, we're working up to it," Warbride replied with a grin. Which was probably true. She'd been a SEAL before joining DMS—one of the first women in that elite unit—so Top had no doubt she could hold her own at the bar. He knew she could in a fight. And he and Bunny had been out drinking plenty of times in the past. Which didn't stop him from teasing the younger man about his drinking choice, or much of anything else.

The bartender set their drinks in front of them, and Top handed him a credit card. "Run a tab," he said, and the guy nodded.

"Want to check out the pool table?" Bunny suggested with a gleam in his eye. He'd been a champion volleyball player before he signed on, and still went in for any kind of sports he could.

Top was game, though. He liked the tactics and calculation of pool. Besides, it beat just sitting around. "Sure," he agreed, taking a sip of his drink as he swiveled on the stool and rose to his feet.

A guy was just stomping past as they rose, and brushed past Bunny. "Watch it, pretty boy," he growled.

"You watch it, ZZ Top," Bunny snapped back, which made the man stop and turn, backing up to get in Bunny's face.

"What was that, punk?" the guy snarled. He was big, not as tall as Bunny and not as built, but still beefy, and he really did have the long, pointed beard of an old country gent—or an old rocker.

"You heard me, grandpa," Bunny replied, not backing down. "I said—" By then Top was slipping between them, using his own bulk to force both of them back a step.

"All right, simmer down, the pair of you," he instructed. Bunny was fuming but did as he was told, which left Top to face off against the belligerent bar-goer. "We wouldn't want anybody getting hurt here."

"What's it to you—," the man started, but bit back the last word when he saw the glare in Top's eyes. Given his attitude, and Top's ethnicity, it seemed pretty clear where he'd been heading, but Top chose to ignore it.

"Listen, friend," he said instead, twisting and wrapping an arm around the man's shoulders. "I get it, I do. You've probably had a crap day, you're pissed off, and you're looking to blow off some steam and make yourself feel big again by picking on somebody. Am I right? And you're not dumb enough or drunk enough to take on a whole biker gang, which only leaves you a few targets." He tightened his grip enough to make the man wince, though subtly enough that no one else would notice. "Here's the thing, though." Top leaned in and lowered his voice. "My friends and I, we've had a rough day, too. See, we thought we were gonna get to kill somebody, and then we didn't. So we're also a little pent-up. But hey, the night's still young, and you're right here." He locked eyes with the man. "So just say the word," he warned.

The other man flinched and pulled away. "Y'all are all crazy!" he stammered, backpedaling so fast he almost tripped over his own feet. The next minute he was out the door and gone, still looking back from time to time.

"What'd you say to him?" Warbride asked, laughing.

Top shrugged. "Just told it like it is. Now let's go shoot some pool."

They were each on their second drinks (same ones as before, which had earned Warbride a knowing sneer from Top) and their second game—Warbride having beaten the two of them handily on the first go-round—when Top spotted someone off to the side, watching. He straightened up from his shot—he'd had nothing open so he'd settled for burying the cue ball in a pileup, earning groans and curses from his two teammates—and glanced over. Three guys were watching them play, and at the sight of them Top's hackles immediately went up. The trio were all big, burly, and fit, but it was more than that. The way they stood, balanced on the balls of their feet, and the way they stayed just far enough apart to not get in each other's way, turned slightly from each other so they could cover more of the room—they were clearly military, and clearly combat vets.

And good ones.

Finding three of them here, in this out-of-the-way little bar that Echo Team had just happened to pick, felt like too big of a coincidence.

Top looked back toward Bunny and Warbride, but neither of them had noticed—he was too busy lining up his shot, and she was too busy trash-talking to make him mess up. With a sigh Top turned, figuring he'd go brace the trio on his own—and stared.

They were gone.

But he'd glanced away for only a second. There was no way they could've left that quickly, and they'd been near the back corner, not the front, which meant they'd have had to cross his path in order to reach the front door or even the small side door by the bar that he guessed led back to the place's kitchen.

So where had they gone?

"Damn!" Bunny shouted, banging his fist on the table. "Girl, you cheat!" he accused Warbride, but he grinned as he said it.

"Just using what the good Lord gave me," she replied with a saucy wink and twist of her hips. "Yo, Top, you're up, man."

He nodded, forcing himself back to the game at hand. "Yeah, all right."

He still scanned the area before and after his shot, searching for that trio. Something told him that whoever they were, he'd be seeing them again.

Twenty minutes later, Bunny declared that he needed to see a man about a horse.

"What, you want me to hold it for you, Farm Boy?" Top asked, gathering pool balls to rack the next game.

"Hold this," his best friend replied, giving him the finger as he turned and made for the bathroom. When he came back, he looked puzzled.

"What, things not where you expected?" Top inquired, raising an eyebrow. "Need me to explain them to you? Your daddy really should've covered that, you know."

But Bunny ignored the dig. "There was a guy in the bathroom," he started. "Didn't get a look at him, but your height and build, I'd say. And armed, if I had to put money on it."

Neither Top nor Warbride mocked him for being able to give such details despite "not getting a look" at the guy—in their line of work you learned to gauge such things by footfall, shadow, breathing, and other measures, and you did it on a subconscious level all the time, with everyone.

"He was over in the corner, I figured he was just taking a leak like me, but then he said, 'Nice night for an echo, huh?'" The frown marking Bunny's face deepened. "When I glanced over, he was gone. And I don't mean ducked out the door, 'cause it was on my other side. He just wasn't there anymore."

An hour ago, Top might've joked that his partner was losing his marbles. But not after his own experience. "Something funny's going on," he said instead. "And I don't mean ha ha." He told Bunny and Warbride about the trio he'd seen—and about how they'd vanished as well.

"What're we looking at here, Top?" Bunny asked, rubbing at his face. "An ambush?"

Top shook his head. "You picked this bar at random, right? 'Cause of the sign?"

"Yeah, I saw it one time and thought it'd be a kick," his partner agreed. "No way anybody knew we were headed here."

"We should call it in," Warbride suggested.

But Top didn't agree. "And say what?" he asked. "That we've seen some shady characters who pop in and out? Nah. Besides," he added, "we're off duty."

She didn't seem entirely happy with that, but Top was team leader and it was his call. So instead they ordered more drinks and started the next game.

But all three of them were wary now, and Top noticed that the other two had both automatically checked the smalls of their backs, where their shirts covered their holstered Mark 23s. He'd done the same, and was reassured to feel the pistol there, as always.

It never hurt to be prepared.

They were nearly done with the game—with Warbride beating the pants off them yet again, proving that the former SEAL was a serious pool shark—when she announced that it was her turn to use the facilities.

Top pretended not to notice Bunny watching her go. Lydia Ruiz was a fine-looking woman, no question about it—she had the perfect combination of curves and muscle, and the deadly grace of a panther, coupled with dusky skin and dark, wavy hair. And although in any normal military unit fraternization within the ranks was frowned upon, the DMS was hardly normal, and didn't have to play by the standard rules. Top figured as long as those two kept their relationship from interfering with the work, he was fine with ignoring it. Hell, Ledger'd had a thing with Major Grace Courtland, who'd headed Alpha Team and been Church's second back at the Warehouse, where Echo Team had begun. It hadn't ended well, but that was because she'd given her life to save the world, not because the relationship itself had gotten ugly. Nor had anyone seen any evidence that their relationship had jeopardized either of them, or either of their teams. So there was precedent.

Still, he felt better acting as though it weren't happening in his own team. At least, as long as they were keeping it on the down-low. This way, if anyone did ask, Top could claim he had no idea what they were talking about.

But when Warbride returned she didn't just look confused, she looked downright pissed. "How long was I gone?" she demanded.

"Maybe three minutes," Bunny answered. He glanced at Top for confirmation, and he nodded. He hadn't checked his watch, but most soldiers had a decent time sense and it had been about that.

"Motherfuckers!" Warbride slammed a hand down on the pool table, making both the balls and their drinks jump. "Must've been fast-acting, then." She looked ready to kill someone.

"What was?" Top went from puzzled to concerned. "You think somebody drugged you?"

"Must have," she replied, still scowling fiercely. She lifted her shirt to show off a tanned, toned stomach. "Because it's gone."

Top didn't know what she meant at first, but Bunny obviously did, because he started. "What the hell?" the big guy blurted out.

"My belly-button ring," Warbride explained. "It's an anchor—I got it after leaving the SEALs."

Now that he looked more closely, Top could see the puncture marks. "You had it earlier?" he asked, even though he already knew the answer to that.

Sure enough, she nodded. "It was there when we changed out of our gear," she replied. "Most of the time I don't really notice it anymore, you know? But when I went to do my business, it was gone."

Top hated to ask, but knew he had to. "Did they—?"

"No!" she almost shouted, then visibly forced herself to lower her voice. "No, nothing like that." Top breathed a sigh of relief, as did Bunny, but Warbride was still clearly pissed off. She banged the pool table again. "Somebody's just screwing with me, and they're gonna pay for it!"

Bunny looked as if he were ready to take the whole place apart with his bare hands, and Top didn't blame him, but he put a hand on the younger man's shoulder anyway. "Slow your roll, Farm Boy," he warned, but gently. "We don't know the lay of the land yet, so no sense going off half-cocked, am I right?"

It took a second, but his friend nodded. "Yeah, I hear you," he answered. "But promise me when we do find out who's behind this . . ."

"Oh, they'll pay," Top assured him.

Just then, Warbride let loose a string of curses.

"They got my piece, too," she declared in between profanities. "And my keys."

"Anything else missing?" Top asked. He did a quick double check, just leaning away from them so his back brushed the edge of the pool table, and relaxed a tiny bit as he felt the reassuring bulk of his pistol pressing up against him.

Warbride was doing a quick personal inventory. "ID's still here," she reported after a second. "Phone's fine. Cash and cards, too. Change is gone, though." That was odd. Keys and weapon Top could understand. And taking her belly-button ring, that was just a personal dig. But why take loose change, especially if you didn't touch the cash or her credit card? Weird.

"And you didn't see anybody, hear anything, notice anything? Nothing at all?"

She frowned. "A shadow, maybe," she answered after a second. "Like somebody was standing there, just outside the bathroom when I went in. That's it. And I'm not even sure about that much." She glared up at him. "Now can we call it in?"

Top shook his head.

"You really want to explain all this to the captain?" he asked. "How somebody jumped you in a dive-bar bathroom, got your piece, took your body jewelry, and made off without a sound? Besides, the minute we call in it's an active case, and we're on the job again." He lifted his glass and took a slow, deliberate sip, letting the Irish whiskey burn its way down. "I say we hold off as long as we can, make sure this is really worth all that hassle."

Warbride grumbled but grabbed her beer and downed it, setting the empty glass back on the table with a bang. "Fine, but next round's on you," she stated. "And if I see somebody waving my ring or my gun around, they'd better watch out."

Top nodded and signaled the barman for another round. Inside, however, he started to wonder. Both about what was really going on here and about whether he was right to keep the DMS out of it.

Still, for now it all just amounted to some harassment and some petty theft. Not worth calling in the big guns. Yet.

But he was definitely keeping his options open.

Top was just leaning over to take aim at the eight ball—for the first time he'd tied with Warbride, and if he sank this he'd actually win one—when a shadow fell across the table. He glanced up, not allowing the cue to shift.

"Good game," the man standing there said. "Any chance of getting in on the next one? We could play teams."

On the face of it, the comment was harmless enough. But the speaker wasn't. He was one of the three Top had spotted earlier; he recognized the blond brush cut and the strong, stubbled jaw. The guy wore black BDUs and a gray shirt with black combat boots, nondescript enough to pass for regular clothes, but to Top's seasoned eye clearly fighting gear. And judging by the way the man stood—feet apart, shoulders back, hands loose at his sides—he was ready for a fight, too.

Top took the shot. The cue smacked the cue ball right in its sweet spot, sending the white ball careening across the table—to tap the eight ball ever so gently on its left edge.

Just hard enough to spin it into the side pocket it had rested beside.

"Nice!" Bunny shouted, crowding in close for a high five. Still, he and Top had worked together too long for Top not to notice how the younger man's jaw had set, and how he'd positioned himself just a bit farther away than you'd expect for a buddy congratulating you on a good shot.

But the perfect distance if you were both about to throw down on someone.

So yeah, Bunny had made the newcomer, too.

And his crew. Because the other two members of the trio loomed right behind the speaker. And again they had spaced themselves professionally. These guys weren't about to get caught unawares.

"Good shot," the first man said. "So, about that game?"

Top straightened and studied the guy, leaning on his cue as he did. "I didn't catch your name, friend," he said slowly.

"Call me Mac," the man replied. He didn't offer his hand. "And you're Top, Bunny, and Warbride. Echo Team."

Beside him, Bunny stiffened. Warbride, who'd come around to flank Top's other side, tensed as well. But Top schooled himself not to react. "Seems you know more about us than we do about you," was all he commented. Inside, though, he gauged distances, angles, kill spots. It was just like pool, really. Only deadlier.

"Oh, we do," Mac agreed. "We know all about you." He made a show of turning and looking around the bar. "Nice place. Clever, too. Who'd think to look for you guys here? What, you've got the main base down below, is that it?" Top had a top-notch poker face, but Bunny and Warbride were more expressive, and Mac laughed at their reactions. "Whoops, sorry, was that a big secret? My bad. Oh, hey, and—surprise!"

He stepped suddenly to one side, and the man to his left already had something aimed at Top, something that looked more like a small video camera than a gun. Top stiffened, unable to dodge as a red beam played across him. But it didn't hurt. It didn't even tickle. In fact, it didn't feel like anything at all. What the hell?

The one on Mac's right had played a similar beam across Bunny, who also looked angry, surprised—and both relieved and confused when he realized he wasn't hurt.

Somewhere behind him, Top heard shouts of panic. The other bar patrons, he guessed. They'd seen Mac and his friend pull what looked like guns, and that was enough to send any normal person running for the door. Good. It meant fewer civilians to worry about.

"Okay," Top said slowly. "This has gone far enough." He straightened, and released the cue with his right hand to reach around behind him. "I suggest you three get the hell out of here before—" But he faltered as his fingers grasped empty air.

His gun was gone!

Mac grinned. "I know, right?" he said conversationally, his two buddies smiling with him. "Crazy stuff. There's a whole scientific explanation for it—something about isotopes and ions and ores and breaking atomic bonds and whatever—but the dummy version is, we aim it at you, all your metal goes away. Poof." His grin sharpened, like a wolf's. Or a shark's. "Which leaves you totally unarmed. You were saying?"

Top frowned. Something about that tickled his memory—making him think back to a previous encounter with high-end combat vets decked out with beyond-cutting-edge gear. "You're Closers," he guessed, and knew he'd gotten it right when Mac stiffened, his grin curdling just a little.

Beside him, he could practically feel Warbride's fury. They'd faced the Closers before, shortly after she'd joined the team. Top-notch mercs whose gear all came from Majestic Three, a crazy think tank that specialized in next-gen military gear. The Closers were tough as they came, and often augmented themselves. Their gear presented as practically science fiction, it was so advanced.

And now they'd tracked down the three of them, and taken away their weapons.

Swell.

That didn't mean Echo Team was going down without a fight.

Top forced his shoulders to slump a little, his whole body to droop. "Crap," he muttered, ducking his head.

Then he slammed the cue forward with his left hand.

It banged hard against the pool table, not damaging anyone or anything. The sudden impact brought renewed screams from the few bar patrons still left, however—and made Mac and his men jump.

Which gave Top the half second he needed to grab the nearest pool ball—the fifteen—and hurl it like a fastball right at Mac's head.

He tried to dodge, and almost made it, but he was too close to evade it completely. The ball, which had been aimed square at the center of his forehead, instead smacked the Closer in the right temple, hard enough that Top thought he heard it crack bone. Mac dropped like a sack of potatoes. His two men grabbed for their guns.

Which was when Bunny gripped the side of the pool table with his massive hands, gave a mighty heave, and flipped the entire thing over on its side. The other two Closers both danced back, narrowly avoiding losing their toes. The fallen Mac wasn't so lucky, and a heavy, ominous snap and a wet squish arose as the table landed on some part of his anatomy.

Top didn't waste time standing around feeling sorry for the guy. He dropped into a crouch behind the table, joined by Bunny and Warbride. They immediately cast about for anything they could use as a weapon.

Unfortunately, they didn't have a whole lot on hand.

"*Now* can we call it in?" Warbride demanded, phone already in her grip. She'd hit the rapid-call for the Pier even before Top had finished nodding, but a second later she scowled. "No signal—they're jamming us," she reported.

Of course they were. Top sighed. It was, after all, exactly what he'd do.

"Okay," Bunny said, ducking a little lower as the two remaining Closers opened fire, their bullets alternately slamming into the heavy slate of the pool table and shooting past above their heads. "So we've got two Closers on us, both heavily armed, and we've got no weapons and no way to call for backup. That about cover it?"

Top started to answer, but stopped as something to the side caught his attention. "No," he answered, fighting the urge to rub at his eyes. He knew what he'd just seen. "*Five* Closers, all heavily armed, and us with no weapons." He gestured, and his two teammates both looked in that direction, to where three more Closers approached from the bar's rear corner.

"Crap," Bunny muttered. "Where did they come from?"

"I don't know," Top answered, "but they weren't there a second ago. Literally—I looked up and suddenly there they were."

"Teleporters?" Warbride shook her head. "Yeah, that fits." It did, too—it explained why all night they'd been seeing the Closers for just a second, or hearing them, and then nothing. "Which means they could call in as many as they want. We're hosed."

"We would be," Top said slowly, "except for one thing." He waited a second to make sure he had his teammates' attention. Then he grinned. It was his slow, nasty grin, the one he reserved for right before delivering a serious ass-kicking. "These fuckers are messing with Echo Team. Which means they're about to find out what being hosed is all about."

"Hooah," Bunny replied, matching his grin, and Warbride echoed him. "You got a plan, boss?"

Top nodded, his mind already ticking elements into place. "I do, yeah," he replied. "You ain't gonna like it—but I guarantee those Closers'll like it even less."

Warbride laughed. "Then let's do it," she said. "Those fuckers owe me a belly-ring."

A lull settled around the place. Top guessed that the Closers had exhausted their first volley. Now they waited to see what Echo Team did next. None of the shots had penetrated the heavy pool table, but that didn't mean a ricochet couldn't have gotten lucky, even if there weren't any groans or cries to confirm a hit. So they waited.

Quiet hung over the bar. Any remaining patrons had fled as soon as the shooting had started. If any of them had called the cops, they were still a ways out. Not a hint of sirens.

Top pointed a finger at Bunny, who nodded back. The big man tensed his muscles, gave a mighty heave—and, with a terrible screech, the pool table practically jumped across the room, slamming into the wall on the other side with a resounding crash.

The Closers had been spaced out facing it, with three right in front and one to either side. Of the three, one managed to get clear completely. Another had the heavy table slam into his ankle as he fled, hard enough to crush the bone there and to spin him around.

The third one, the man in the center, was still fully behind the table when it hit the wall. A wet sound erupted as the two heavy surfaces smushed him between them like jelly on a sandwich.

The remaining Closers all darted forward, ignoring their wounded and fallen comrades for the moment to go after the now exposed and presumably defenseless Echo Team.

The first one to get a clear shot fell backward before he could fire, his forehead caved in by an expertly thrown pool ball.

The second one slipped on a pool of liquid from a tossed pint glass—before he could clamber back to his feet Warbride leaped on top of him, impaling him through the eye with a broken pool cue.

The third found himself staring down the barrel of a gun—an all-too-familiar gun, because it was one of their own. Before he could figure out how that had happened Top shot him twice, once in the chest and once in the head.

Warbride had grabbed her target's gun from his hands and rolled to the side, clearing the body and coming up shooting. Bunny made the long reach and wrested the gun from his victim, and now Echo Team was properly armed again.

"Head shots!" Top reminded his teammates. "They've got body armor!"

Echo Team had discovered the hard way in their previous encounters that the Closers wore some kind of fancy micromesh that stopped not only the bullets themselves but also their impact. They'd been cocky tonight, though, and weren't wearing helmets.

Only two Closers remained, but they were too experienced to panic at the sudden reversal of fortune. Both ducked down behind tables for cover, and returned fire with Echo Team. In the reflection from a bar mirror Top could see one of them speaking rapidly into a throat-mic. Probably calling in a sit rep and asking for reinforcements.

Apparently the call didn't go the way they'd hoped, but it did yield results. Because suddenly the bar fell quiet again, as the two remaining Closers disappeared.

"Hold your fire!" Top ordered, and all shooting stopped. He scanned the bar quickly. Not only had their last two foes vanished but so had the others' bodies. "Damn. Clear."

Bunny and Warbride nodded. Now that the fighting had stopped, they could hear sirens in the distance. "Stay or go, boss?" Bunny asked.

Top considered. "Go," he finally decided. "I'm not in the mood to stand around answering questions." He looked at the other two. "Let's clean it up."

They both nodded. Warbride grabbed the pint glasses she and Bunny had used, Top's whiskey glass, and their pool cues. Bunny went behind the bar and found the surveillance system, yanking out the drive. He also retrieved Top's credit card, which he handed back to him as he returned. Top had collected the fifteen ball he'd thrown at Mac and the ball—the eight, amusingly enough—that Bunny had used on the other Closer. He surveyed the rest of the room, but other than incidental contacts or places where there'd be too many fingerprints to distinguish, they were clean. All that had remained of the Closers were the guns Echo Team had taken off them, and they'd bring those along as souvenirs.

"Time to move," he ordered once they had everything. The sirens blared closer now. The three of them headed out the door double time, and were safely around the corner and a block or two away, walking as though nothing strange were going on, by the time the first cop cars arrived.

Top was already thinking about how he would explain all of this to Ledger.

"So they had some kind of teleporters, and a ray gun that could target and destroy anything metal, and they tracked you to this bar and jumped you two to one, and you handed them their asses?" Ledger asked, leaning back in his chair.

Top, who stood at ease across from him, nodded. "Yes, sir. No idea how they found us, either. They seemed to think the bar was our base, or at least a cover for it."

Ledger nodded and lifted a piece of paper off his desk. "I can answer that." He waved the paper at Top. "Analysis from Bug and Hu," he explained, meaning their computer expert and their science director. "You'd mentioned something about sawdust at that site yesterday, the one that was a bust? It wasn't all sawdust. Some of that was nanites, designed to form a networked tracking signal."

"So it was a setup," Top guessed.

"Looks that way. They tipped us off, we sent you in, and they basically bugged you so you'd lead them back here." Ledger grinned. "But I gave you the night off. Maybe it took them some time to lock down the signal, or maybe they were just basing it on the highest concentration, but they saw you three at the bar and figured that had to be our base."

"Especially given its name." Top was glad now that Bunny had picked the place he had.

"Right. Then they decided to mess around before picking you off." Ledger actually chuckled at that. "Stupid."

Top nodded. "So what happens now?"

His boss shrugged, though he didn't look happy about it. "Nothing. It's not like we know where the Closers operate, or where Majestic Three is right now, or we'd shut them down regardless. They tried for you, you beat them down, that's that." He shook his head.

"Well, all right, then." Top turned toward the door. "Guess I'll head home."

"Ah, not so fast." Ledger gave him a sharp not-smile. "You're going to need to file a report on all this."

Top groaned. "Come on, Cap. It's my night off!"

"It was," Ledger agreed. He glanced up at the clock, which read 12:03. "But now it's morning. Welcome back. Hope you enjoyed yourself."

Top grumbled something under his breath that, in most agencies or units, could have gotten him brought up on charges. Ledger just laughed some more.

But, Top thought as he left the office and trudged down the hall, he had to admit something, even if he never gave Ledger the satisfaction:

He *had* enjoyed himself.

And what amounted to a simple bar fight, albeit one with guns and fatalities?

For Echo Team, that *was* a night off!

Was it worth the paperwork, though? That was the real question.

ABOUT THE AUTHOR

Aaron Rosenberg is the author of the bestselling *DuckBob* SF comedy series, the *Dread Remora* space-opera series, and, with David Niall Wilson, the *O.C.L.T.* occult thriller series. His tie-in work contains novels for *Star Trek*, *Warhammer*, *World of WarCraft*, *Stargate: Atlantis*, and *Eureka*. He has written

children's books (including the award-winning *Bandslam: The Novel* and the number one bestselling *42: The Jackie Robinson Story*), educational books, role-playing games (including the Origins Award–winning *Gamemastering Secrets*), and short stories. He is a founding member of Crazy 8 Press. You can follow him online at www.gryphonrose.com, on Facebook at www.facebook.com/gryphonrose, and on Twitter @gryphonrose.

EDITORS' NOTE: In Jon McGoran's thrillers *Drift*, *Deadout*, *Down to Zero*, and *Dust Up*, Philadelphia detective Doyle Carrick confronts frighteningly plausible crimes at the cutting edge of today's biotechnology. In "Strange Harvest," he teams up with Joe Ledger to take on a mystery more bizarre than anything he's ever encountered.

STRANGE HARVEST

BY JON McGORAN

The hotel carpet muffled my footsteps so completely that for a moment I wondered if it wasn't just blindingly hideous but somehow deafening as well. Then I saw the door to Room 517 ajar and heard drawers and cabinets opening and closing inside. Easing the door open, I saw a broad-shouldered man who was not Melissa Brant searching her room.

I was supposed to be on vacation, a few quiet days in the Poconos catching up on some much-needed rest while Junie was doing her UFO conference thing, and then eating, drinking, and fooling around with her while she wasn't.

The first night had been great. Junie's friend Melissa, a charming if tightly wound young astrobiologist, was supposed to join us for dinner, but she called to cancel, saying she was on to something really big that she'd be announcing at her presentation in the morning. Junie had put down the phone, climbed on top of me in bed, and whispered that she was on to something big, too, but she'd be keeping it to herself.

Things had gone great until the following morning, thirty minutes ago, when Junie woke me up saying Melissa had missed her big presentation and apparently disappeared.

Junie wasn't one for melodrama, but I had thought she was overreacting. Until now.

I'm never completely on vacation, completely at ease, but so far that weekend I had been close, content to be "Joe Ledger, Civilized Man," leaving my darker selves in the background. That was the point of the getaway. The work I do, the things I see, sometimes the Civilized Man at my core gets edged out of the way.

Like right now. I took out my badge, the one that said I worked for Homeland Security. I didn't. I worked for the Department of Military Sciences, or DMS. There was no badge for that.

As I entered the room with my gun out and my badge held high, the Cop inside me told the Civilized Man, *I'll take it from here*.

Before I could yell, "Freeze!" the guy turned around. And he had a gun, too. Before I could think about it, I kicked it out of his hand. My badge dropped to the floor as my hand clenched tight and rocketed toward his face. I didn't put everything behind it, just enough to eliminate any disagreement about how things would be going from there.

He was quicker than I expected, bobbing his head out of the way. Rage flared deep down inside me and burned closer to the surface when the guy backhanded my gun out of the way. The Warrior inside me reveled in that rage, tried to elbow Joe the Cop out of the way. *You don't win a fight pulling punches*, said the Warrior's voice.

I ignored it, or tried to, slamming my elbow into the guy's face. But he landed a solid left under my ribs that weakened my resolve not to go full Warrior. I landed a left of my own, and felt the exhilaration of the other man folding. The Warrior wanted off the leash, to press this momentary advantage into triumph, beat this guy down, and ask questions later.

As I paused, conflicted for a nanosecond, an uppercut clipped my chin, and in my head, I heard the Warrior in me telling the Cop, *You might not want to watch this*.

I could feel air on my teeth as I launched myself, grinning, at my enemy. The guy was bringing something up in his hand—a knife, a gun, I didn't care. He wouldn't have it for long. The right-left combination that was going to shatter his nose and close off his larynx became a right-left-right that would disarm him first. My right hand chopped the bundle of veins and nerves and tendons on the underside of the guy's wrist, and whatever was in his hand went tumbling through the air. As my left fist tore through the air with everything behind it, from the corner of my eye I saw the object tumbling through the air: leather, gold, leather, gold, leather, gold.

A badge. Then the guy said, "Police!"

My shoulder locked, the muscles in my back and arm twisting and seizing as I applied the brakes to the ball of knuckles rocketing through the air. My fist stopped three inches from his face.

"Police?" I said, looking down at him.

"Police," the guy said, looking down even farther.

I followed his gaze and saw he had a second gun, and it was pointed at my midsection.

That's why you don't pull your punches, the Warrior growled in my head as it returned to the depths where it spent most of its days.

That's why I do, I thought to myself.

"Me too," I said out loud, stepping back, giving the guy some space.

He kept the gun on me as he retrieved his badge from the corner of the room. "Really?"

"More or less." I picked up my own badge.

The guy looked it over. "Joseph Ledger," he said, then handed it back, "Homeland Security, huh? I know some people there." He rattled off a few names.

I shook my head. "And who are you?"

He held up his badge. "Doyle Carrick. Philly PD."

"And what are you doing here?"

"I might ask you the same thing."

"You might, after you answer me."

Carrick's mouth formed a tight smile. "A friend of mine has gone missing. Bruce Scott. Goes by Moose. The girl staying in this room, Melissa Brant, was the last person who saw him."

"Missing?" I could feel the situation getting more serious around me. I thought back to Melissa's call, saying she was on to something big.

"How'd you get into the room?"

"The lock was busted. Fried. Moose's room, too." He raised an eyebrow at me, reminding me it was my turn to explain.

"Brant's gone missing, too."

His eyes darkened. "Since when?"

"She was supposed to give a big presentation this morning. She didn't show. No one can find her." I looked around the room. "Did you find anything here?"

"Her computer's gone, but the case is here. Handbag's next to the bed. These were inside it." He handed over a prescription bottle, Tapazole, and an iPhone.

The phone was locked, but the display showed two medication reminders: YOU HAVE MISSED ONE DOSE OF TAPAZOLE and YOU HAVE MISSED TWO DOSES OF TAPAZOLE.

There were also five missed calls.

"Two of those calls are from Oscar Tubbs, a mutual friend of theirs. The rest are from me," Carrick said, holding up a different phone. "Calling from Moose's phone. I could hear her phone buzzing from out in the hall."

"Not quite probable cause, is it?"

He shrugged. "I'm out of my jurisdiction anyway. We're twenty hours away from the local police starting a search. I'll worry about probable cause later. Right now, I'm worried about my friend."

Fair enough. "How'd you get into his phone?"

"It wasn't locked."

I nodded. "So, they're friends, Melissa and Moose?"

He shook his head. "They met last night, through Tubbs. How do you know Brant?"

"She's friends with my girlfriend. They're here at the conference together."

"The foraging conference?"

"No, the UFO conference."

Carrick snorted and looked away.

My face darkened as I fondly thought back to three minutes earlier when I'd been kicking his ass. Junie had long since stopped being bothered by people's reactions to her field of expertise. I wasn't quite there yet.

Carrick straightened out his face. "Okay, then."

"You said Melissa was the last person to talk to Moose but they weren't friends," I said as I started looking through Melissa's things. Carrick had searched the place, but I hadn't. "What's the deal with that?"

Carrick sat on the bed and watched me. "Moose is here for the foraging conference. I drove up yesterday from Philly to see him. I figured we'd have a few beers at the hotel bar, maybe grab breakfast the next day, but instead he wanted to take me foraging."

"What do you mean by foraging?"

"Apparently, he hunts for wild delicacies out in the woods, mushrooms and stuff, and sells them to restaurants."

"Really?" I said, moving from the desk to the bathroom.

Carrick shrugged. "Says he makes decent money at it. Anyway, so he wants to show me this secret, hidden spot he found a couple summers ago, where there's something called tiger cress growing. A half-hour drive and a twenty-minute hike later, we climb up this steep little hill and down into this tiny valley, and it's carpeted with these plants. I was actually a tiny bit impressed, but then Moose says, 'It's not right.' I ask him what he means, and he says, 'It's the wrong color and it shouldn't be growing so thick.' Then he steps on it and it stinks like hell, like sulfur mixed with menthol."

I was done searching, but I would have stopped at that point anyway. Carrick smiled. "I know, right? I'm thinking maybe it's like cheese, like the stinkiness is why it's so expensive. But he says it shouldn't smell like that at all."

"So what was it?"

Carrick shook his head. "He said it was the tiger cress, all right, but different. He bagged some up and took it to Tubbs, who's a botanist at Gareth University, not far from here. Tubbs checked it out and contacted Brant. He thought she might be interested, for some reason."

"Tubbs thought Melissa would be interested?"

"Yeah. Why?"

I shrugged. "Just weird. Melissa's an astrobiologist."

"Meaning . . ."

"Her specialty is extraterrestrial life."

Carrick smiled but then saw how much I wasn't and straightened out his face.

He clearly didn't believe, but I'd seen stuff that I was pretty sure he hadn't. I didn't need him to believe, but I wanted him to take it seriously.

"Do you think you could find your way back to this place where you found the plants?" I asked.

"No. But I'd recognize it if I saw it."

"Where was Tubbs when you called him this morning?"

"His lab at the university."

"I'd like to talk to him in person."

Carrick nodded. "I was thinking the same thing."

We dropped in unannounced. Carrick didn't suspect Tubbs of anything nefarious, but he was the only connection between Moose and

Melissa and we couldn't rule anything out. If he had something to hide, a surprise could make him slip up.

During the twenty-minute drive, Carrick and I talked a little about our backgrounds. We both had our secrets. We both told some lies. We both seemed comfortable with that.

Mostly, we talked about Melissa and Moose, found photos of them online, and compared notes on what we knew about them. We needed more information to begin forming legitimate theories. The illegitimate theories—the connections between Moose's bizarre weed patch and Melissa's bizarro specialty of extraterrestrial life—we kept to ourselves.

We found Tubbs in his third-floor biophysics lab surrounded by clicking and whirring machines and the vague smell that could have been the sulfur and menthol Carrick had described. Tubbs's head, shaved clean where it wasn't already bald, was bent over a microscope.

Carrick knocked gently on the door frame, trying not to startle him. It didn't work.

Tubbs jumped as if the microscope had bitten him. "Who are you?" he demanded.

Carrick put up his hands reassuringly. "I'm Moose's friend Doyle. The one who called earlier."

Tubbs's eyes shifted to me. "Who's he?"

I held up my badge. "Joe Ledger. Homeland Security," I said. "I'm a friend of Melissa Brant. She's gone missing, too."

Tubbs's eyes filled with dread and he looked down at the floor. "I've been trying to call her."

"We're trying to find them both," Carrick said. "So you need to tell us what's going on."

He gestured at his microscope. "That stuff Moose found is very, very strange."

"Strange how?" I asked.

"All these weird compounds, some highly toxic. The arsenic content is off the charts. That's why I called Melissa. That's her thing, you know? Searching for life forms that use arsenic instead of phosphorus. But she's been focusing on microbes so she didn't believe it at first. But the more we looked at it, the more convinced she was that there was something important here."

Carrick held up his hand. "Wait, why is she looking for life forms based on arsenic instead of phosphorus?"

Tubbs shrugged. "There's a theory that some of the life on this planet might not have originated here, a 'shadow biosphere.' And if it originated somewhere else, one theory is that its metabolism might use arsenic instead of phosphorus, which this stuff seems to do."

"So what are you saying?"

Tubbs put up his hands. "Well, *she* was saying it might be of extraterrestrial origin. *I'm* not saying that. In fact, now I'm pretty sure she's wrong."

Carrick snorted. "Yeah, I'm pretty sure, too."

I ignored him. "Why's that?"

"After they left, I compared the DNA to regular tiger cress DNA. It's identical except for three chunks that are totally different."

"You mean like, mutations?" I asked.

"Or do you mean like splices?" Carrick said.

Tubbs pointed at Carrick and said, "Bingo. There's a company called Xenexgen, maybe ten minutes from here, that specializes in bioremediation using engineered microbes to pull contaminants out of polluted soil. One of the biggest sequences spliced into the tiger cress genome is almost identical to one they use for their arsenic remediation products. The weird thing is, most bioremediation products sequester the arsenic so it is less bioavailable. Melissa specifically said this arsenic is highly bioavailable."

I shook my head. "It's genetically engineered? Who would engineer a toxic version of a wild plant?"

Tubbs bit his lip. "Melissa's theory is that it might not be toxic to everyone, or everything."

Carrick snorted. "So, what, you think it's genetically modified Purina Alien Chow?"

Tubbs didn't smile. "Sounds crazy when you say it out loud, but I'd love to take another look at it."

"What happened to your samples?" I asked.

"Moose and Melissa only left me a little bit. It turned into green goo overnight."

As soon as we got outside, Carrick said, "You don't believe that stuff, do you? The extraterrestrial stuff?"

I shrugged. "I'm just trying to find Moose and Melissa."

"Right." He rolled his eyes and shook his head. "So, next stop Xenexgen?"

I nodded and called Junie to see if she'd heard from Melissa.

"No." Her voice sounded tight. "No one has seen her since last night. That presentation was a big deal for her. She wouldn't have blown it off. Have you found out anything?"

"The last person she talked to was a guy named Moose Scott, a friend of a friend who found some weird plants out in the forest. He gave samples to Melissa to look at. Does that mean anything to you?"

"She's an astrobiologist. Weird plants are kind of her thing."

I told her what Tubbs had said.

"Arsenic? Hmm. Maybe that was her big thing she was on to. Did you talk to this Moose person?"

I paused. I didn't want her to freak out, but I didn't like keeping things from her—especially not things I knew she'd find out later. "Moose is missing, too."

She gasped. "Joe, are you serious?"

"It doesn't mean anything. They could have hit it off and gone somewhere together." Although they wouldn't have left their phones behind. "But I'm comparing notes with a friend of Scott's, a Philly cop named Carrick. We'll find them."

I could hear her voice getting thick and wet. "Okay. Keep me posted."

As I put down the phone, Carrick looked at me. "She's worried?"

I nodded.

"You too?"

I shrugged. If I wasn't worried, I wouldn't be looking for her. "I don't know Melissa well, but she didn't seem the type to flake off."

We drove in silence for a minute or two, then Carrick asked, "So what do we know about Xenexgen?"

It was a good question. I picked up my phone and called my pal Bug.

"Hey, Joe. How's it going?" he said. "You and Junie having fun with all the saucer heads?"

I smiled. "Having fun being away from you guys, that's for sure."

Bug laughed. "I'd be deeply hurt if I didn't know that was a lie. I know you miss me—why else would you be calling me?"

The conversation chilled the tiniest bit. I wouldn't be calling him without a good reason, and good reasons were never good news. I was calling him because he ran MindReader, the DMS's supersecret, superpowerful computer system.

"What can I do for you?"

"I'm here with a new friend," I said, letting Bug know I was not speaking freely. "Philadelphia detective Doyle Carrick and I are looking into a couple of missing friends."

Bug typed for a second. "Carrick looks legit . . . a bit of a loose cannon, makes some enemies, but he's a righteous dude who makes a lot of busts and has been on the right side of some nasty fights."

"Great. We're looking for a Bruce 'Moose' Scott and a Melissa Brant, both went missing sometime last night."

"Want me to track 'em? Credit cards, cell phones, the usual?"

"They left their phones and wallets behind, but see if anything pops up. Also, Brand left behind a prescription drug called Tapazole. She's missed a couple doses, so anything you can find on that would be great. First, though, I need you to look into a company called Xenexgen." I spelled it.

Bug typed some more, then said, "Headquarters in Oslo, Norway, and Monroe County, Pennsylvania."

"What the hell are they doing out here?"

"Looks like the company was originally involved in coal. Acquired three years ago by current CEO Cecil Bortman. Very closely held, very quiet. . . . There's some very heavy-duty encryption protecting their systems."

"Apparently they have a line of bioengineered products used for hazardous waste remediation?"

"Let's see . . . yes, Clean Sweep, a line of microbial products that sequesters heavy metals and other pollutants in soil. It seems to be one of their main product lines. I don't see much in the way of sales, but they seem sound financially."

"What's their communications like?"

"Not as secure as their servers, but they're pretty quiet."

"Okay. Keep an eye on that. We're about to visit their Monroe County location."

"You thinking they might get chatty after you leave?"

"Exactly."

"You got it."

We drove through fields and farms and wooded hills, rounded a bend, and there was Xenexgen. The front was all high-tech global HQ office chic with the chrome double-helix X logo. As we pulled into the vast and almost empty parking lot, we could see production facilities in the back. Along one side, there was a long row of shipping containers with the blue Xenexgen logo being loaded with pallets of blue-and-white sacks.

Carrick parked in front of the main entrance, a curved overhang of mirrored glass sheltering a row of green glass doors. Inside, the lobby was more mirrored glass and chrome, a very modern impression that was seriously undermined by the cardboard boxes stacked two deep, at least three or four high, against the marble walls. The old guy at the desk eyed us for employee badges, then sat up straighter, surprised that we didn't have any.

"Can I help you?"

I held up my badge. "We're looking into a possible link between a couple of missing persons and one of your products."

He stared at us for a second, then picked up a phone, spoke quietly into it, and told us, "Someone will be with you shortly."

Half a minute later, a short, odd-looking man in an expensive suit appeared behind us. His face was pale and disconcertingly placid, his eyes drooped, and his skin was smooth but saggy, like bad cosmetic work.

"How may I help you gentlemen?" he said. He had an odd hitch in his voice, like a faint but unfamiliar accent. He extended his hand. Shaking it felt like grasping a wisp of smoke.

"How do you do, Mr. . . . ?"

"Bortman," he said. "I'm the CEO here at Xenexgen."

I looked over Bortman's shoulder at the security guy behind the desk. He shrugged and nodded.

"Unusual for a CEO to respond in person to a request for information," I said.

Bortman smiled again, weirdly. "We take our support for law enforcement very seriously. So what can we do for you?"

"We're looking into the disappearance of a young woman named Melissa Brant and a young man named Moose Scott."

He paused, as if thinking about it, then shook his head. "I'm afraid I don't know them. Are they employees here?"

"No, but they recently discovered a plant growing in this area that seemed to match some of the genetic characteristics of your Clean Sweep soil remediation microbes."

Bortman let out a hiccup that was probably intended to be a laugh. "As you said, Clean Sweep is a microbe, not a plant."

Carrick said, "So you're not developing green plants with similar characteristics?"

Bortman shook his head.

"Any chance the gene splice could have jumped species?" Carrick said.

Bortman hiccuped again. "No, but we'd be happy to look at a sample, if you have one."

"We don't, unfortunately," I said, handing him a card. "If you have any other thoughts, please let us know."

Bortman did his smilelike thing and said, "Certainly." He palmed the card and slipped it into his pocket, reminding me of one of those old-fashioned toy banks with the hand that comes out and swipes the coin.

As we turned to go, Carrick pointed at the stacks against the wall. "What's with the boxes? Are you moving?"

"Minor restructuring."

Back in the car, Carrick said, "That was one strange little man."

I nodded. "Seriously strange."

My phone buzzed. It was Bug. I put him on speaker. "What have you got for us?"

"First, that Tapazole is heavy-duty stuff, used to treat hyperthyroidism. Missing a dose can be extremely dangerous. Second, we just monitored two bursts of transmissions from Xenexgen, both seriously encrypted, one routed back to Oslo, and one to a cell phone a few miles away from you. The coordinates don't match anything on file, but I'll send them to you."

Carrick watched as I opened the coordinates in my GPS. The map revealed a solid expanse of green.

"Zoom out," he said, and when I did, Schoolhouse Road appeared to the south.

"That's it," Carrick said. "That's where Moose found the tiger cress."

I pressed the navigate button and Carrick turned the car around.

Twenty minutes later, we were stumbling through the woods, holding out our phones. Me with my GPS, Carrick with a compass app.

"This looks familiar," he said.

"GPS says we should be almost there."

He pointed at a rocky incline twenty feet high. "Right over there."

As we climbed up, I smelled something different from the rest of the woods, but it wasn't weird or chemical or alien. It smelled natural. When we reached the top, I recognized the smell of soil. Exposed earth.

Below us, the entire valley was stripped clean, scoured of vegetation. It wasn't level, as if it were ready for builders, it was just a raw, open wound.

Carrick said, "Huh," as he tramped down into the middle of the glen and turned in a slow circle.

"Not how you remembered?" I called down to him.

He shook his head. "Weird. There's no sign of heavy equipment."

"You're sure it's the same place?"

He nodded, then something caught his eye, a little scrap of white and blue in the middle of all that brown. He picked it up and looked at it, recoiling as he sniffed it.

"What is it?" I asked, coming over to where he was.

He held up a scrap of white plastic with the blue Xenexgen logo. "Clean Sweep," he said, holding it up in front of my face.

I caught a faint whiff of that strange mixture of sulfur and menthol. Just then my phone buzzed. "Bug. What have you got?"

"Shit's going down."

"Talk to us," I said, putting him on speaker.

"I'm breaking into Xenexgen's files and they're being wiped clean even as I'm doing it. The place is bustling, too. Lots of data coming in and out, ever since you guys left. We got satellite thermal scans. I'll send you one. But here's the thing, people are scrambling all over the place, all except for two figures lying horizontal in a room on the third floor and two other figures standing outside the room, like they're guarding it. I think your friends might be in there, and it looks like whoever is keeping them there is packing up and getting ready to go."

By the time the scan came through, we were already crashing through the woods so fast, I was worried one of us would break a leg or get impaled on a broken branch. Miraculously, we burst out of the woods right next to the car, unharmed.

Carrick pulled the car in a tight, loud circle, and we sped back toward Xenexgen.

Almost immediately, Bug called back. I put him on speaker.

"Xenexgen just closed down their operations in Oslo," he said.

"Today. Announced the sale of their assets to a German chemical company, and the transfer of their patents to a trust in the Cayman Islands."

Carrick whistled.

"Anything else?" I said.

"I'm working on it. I'll call you when I get anything."

"If I don't answer, text."

"Got it."

"Do we have anyone in a fifty-mile radius?"

"I'm in Trenton."

I was quiet. Bug was a badass with a computer, but not so much in the conventional sense.

"Okay, okay," he said. "I hear you. I can assemble a team, but they won't be our guys."

"Do it."

"Probably take them a half hour."

"Then tell them to bring bail money and Band-Aids."

I thumbed off the phone and Carrick said, "Jesus, big day at Xenexgen. What's that about?"

"Let's find out."

Even in the bright sunshine the Xenexgen compound looked dark. Armed guards patrolled the lawn, and Carrick eased up on the accelerator so we could get a look at them. The place disappeared behind a bend in the road and Carrick pulled off the road, rumbling thirty feet down a slight incline.

As we came to a stop, I turned to him. "You're armed, right?"

He nodded. "One on my hip and one on my ankle. Are we here to ask questions or are we just going in to get our friends?"

I shrugged. "What did you think of the answers we got last time?"

"Point taken." He rubbed his chin, an expression on his face as if he were chewing something awful that was going to be even worse to swallow. "We sure we don't want to involve local law enforcement?"

"Do you even know what jurisdiction we're in?" I could have asked Bug and found out in three seconds, but that wasn't the point. I did not want to involve local law enforcement. "Technically, Melissa and Moose are still hours away from being officially designated missing persons."

He nodded, looking relieved. "No, I hear you. I'm trying to make it a habit to at least ask. Nice to hear someone else saying it."

"You want to wait for backup?"

Carrick shook his head. "I hate waiting." He paused. "I'm not really crazy about backup, either, but . . ."

My phone buzzed again with an updated thermal scan, recent enough that it showed our car parked off the road. "There's seven guards out front plus two in the back," I said, counting. "Another dozen inside the main building."

Carrick pointed at one of the two horizontal figures. "This one's suddenly brighter than the others."

He was right.

Melissa's phone buzzed in my pocket and I took it out. Another medication reminder, only this one said, URGENT WARNING: FAILURE TO TAKE TAPAZOLE AS DIRECTED MAY RESULT IN SERIOUS COMPLICATIONS INCLUDING DEATH.

"Jesus," Carrick said, squinting over at the Xenexgen complex, as if he were trying to see if they were in there.

I called Dr. Rudy Sanchez, chief medical officer at DMS and my best friend.

"Hey, Joe—"

I cut him off. "Sorry, Rudy. Urgent medical question: What are the symptoms if someone taking Tapazole misses a couple of doses?"

"Um . . ." He thought for a second. "Let's see, that's hyperthyroidism, very dangerous. There's a high fever—"

"Great. Thanks. Gotta go." I ended the call and pointed at the bright figure on the thermal scan. "That's Melissa Brand," I told Carrick. "She's lighting up because of a fever. She's in danger and we need to get her out."

He nodded. "Let's go."

We checked our weapons, then got out and slipped through the woods.

From the tree line, the glass façade lay to our right, across forty yards of rolling lawn. To our left was a sprawl of industrial buildings, warehouses, and cargo containers. As we watched, a door at the rear of the main building opened and two guards with rifles emerged. They walked around to the front while the heavy, reinforced door closed slowly behind them. It took forever, especially the last six inches.

When it finally clicked shut, Carrick said, "Nine seconds."

"Are you fast?" I asked him.

He shrugged. "If I'm motivated. You're thinking next time we try to catch it before it closes?"

"Without getting shot, yeah."

"Right. Without getting shot." He eyed the door, then the two guards disappearing around the front of the complex. "Yeah, I'm fast."

We hunkered down, waiting.

Thirty seconds later, Carrick tapped my arm and pointed to two guards approaching from the left.

We watched as they opened the door and slipped inside, then we dashed across the grass. I was reaching for the edge of the slowly closing door when it swung out toward us. Two new guards were coming toward us, speaking in Swedish or Norwegian. They had the same saggy skin and drooping eyes as Bortman. I didn't have time to think about it because they raised their guns and we went in punching. They were bigger up close, but surprisingly fragile. I planted a right on my guy's chin and he dropped before I could follow up.

Same thing with Carrick—a thunderous right to the other guy's nose and he was down.

We exchanged a shrug, then dragged them inside, catching our breath as the door slowly closed. The latest scan showed the room next to us empty. We dragged the guards inside, cuffed them to a radiator, and took their ID cards and rifles.

As we headed to the stairway thirty feet away, we heard voices approaching, that same lilting Norswitzdenavian or whatever. We slipped through the door and into the stairwell, hugging the wall behind the door, in case they were headed our way.

They were. The door swung open and two huge Norswitzdenavians came through, looking just like the others. They raised their rifles, but we were already on them: one to shut them up, one to knock them back, then they were crumpled on the floor, leaving us with that weird feeling that we should still be fighting.

A flicker of doubt ran through my mind. They had big guns and they were quick to point them, but maybe they were glorified suburban office park security staff instead of paramilitary goons. Maybe Moose and Melissa weren't here and nothing nefarious was going on.

That's what was going through my mind as we rounded the steps and another one entered the stairwell.

"Police!" I said, holding up my DMS badge.

For an instant we all froze, Carrick behind me, the guard six steps up from us, staring down with a blank expression. In a flash, he raised his rifle in an arc headed right up my middle.

I heard two explosions, almost simultaneous, one behind me and one in front, excruciatingly loud in the cinder-block stairway.

Firing around my head, Carrick managed to clip the guard's shoulder. The rifle went off as he fell, peppering us with hot concrete chips as the bullet slammed into the steps.

I grabbed the rifle before he hit the ground and Carrick patted him down for other weapons, then he stopped and put a hand on the guard's neck. He looked up at me, bewildered. "He's dead. . . ."

I felt the guy's wrist. Nothing.

It didn't make sense. Not in the "killing is senseless" way, although maybe that was true. But shooting around me, Carrick had barely tagged the guy. He should be rolling around in pain and calling us assholes.

Carrick shook his head. "He shouldn't be dead."

He was right. But we didn't have time to discuss it. I clapped my hand on Carrick's shoulder. "Maybe he hit his head or had a heart attack. Who knows? But he was pointing that thing at me, so thanks. Now, we've got to get Moose and Melinda and get out of here."

He nodded and we continued up the steps, pausing at the top while I peered through the door. The scan showed Moose and Melissa—if that's who it was—in a room with two guards down the corridor to the left of the one I was looking out onto.

As we crept toward the next corridor, Carrick tapped my elbow and motioned that he would go low. I nodded, and took out my badge and held it with my gun. Carrick counted down with his fingers—three, two, one—then I stepped out from behind the wall as Carrick slid across the floor with his gun two-handed in front of him.

"Police!" I said. "Don't move!"

For an awkward moment, they didn't. There were two of them in front of the door, staring at us out of faces remarkably similar to the others. I felt bad for Carrick, down on the floor, ready for action that it seemed wasn't going to happen.

Then, without a word or a glance at each other, they raised their guns at us. *"Don't Move!"* I thundered, but they did. And we shot them.

When someone's ready to shoot a clearly identified cop, you don't mess around.

Carrick rolled to his feet and we approached them fast but cautious. They were already dead.

"What the hell?" Carrick asked. "Are they even human?"

I was thinking the same thing. It gave me the creeps, but there wasn't time to discuss it.

The door was unlocked. We burst through it, Carrick first, me covering, ready to shoot the first easy-to-kill whatever-they-were that made a move. But the room was empty except for two sofas, Melissa on one, Moose on the other, just waking up.

Moose looked disoriented but otherwise fine. Melissa was flushed red and shivering, her hair plastered to her face with sweat.

"Joe . . . ?" she said. "What's going on?"

"Doyle?" Moose said. "What the hell?"

They seemed relieved to see us, but increasingly alarmed, especially when they saw our weapons.

"We're not sure," I told them. "Are you okay?"

"Where are we?" Melissa asked. She seemed about to swoon, then her eyes went wide and she hugged herself. "What time is it?"

"It's two in the afternoon," Carrick told them. "You're at Xenexgen headquarters. How did you get here?"

Moose shook his head and said, "I have no idea."

At the same time, Melissa said, "Two PM?! No wonder I feel like crap. I need my medicine."

"We have it right here," I told her, and shook a pill out of the bottle. She dry swallowed it and said, "I think I need a doctor."

"Sure thing," I said. "But first we need to get you out of here." I squeezed her shoulder reassuringly. "There's been some violence outside. People have been killed." Her eyes went wide. So did Moose's. "We had to fight our way to get you, and we're probably going to have to fight our way out. So you've got to keep it together and try to keep up, okay?"

Carrick tried to give Moose his backup piece, but he didn't try too hard, as though maybe they'd had this conversation before. Melissa was in no shape to handle one, even if she wanted to.

"Okay," I said, "you two just stay behind us." I told them the route we'd be taking. "Stay close and be ready to run like hell when we do."

Moose put his arm under Melissa's to steady her. But when I opened the door, there was no sign of the two dead guards, no blood on the floor, nothing. Carrick and I stopped so abruptly that Moose and Melissa stumbled into us from behind.

"What is it?" Moose whispered loudly.

Carrick and I looked at each other, but I didn't have any answers and apparently neither did he.

He turned to Moose and put a finger to his lips. As good a response as any.

We walked around the spot where the two dead guards had been, then crept along the opposite side. Carrick took the lead. He didn't bother taking out his badge. We were done with that for now.

The next hallway was clear and so was the stairway. No bodies, no blood, just a divot in one of the steps and a sprinkling of concrete chips that ground under our feet.

Melissa seemed oblivious, just trying to keep up, but Moose studied the looks passing between Carrick and me. We kept moving because we had to, but frankly I would have liked to stop right there and talk it out.

The first floor was empty, too. I was mostly relieved, but something weird was going on and it was getting weirder. Carrick slowed, so I took the lead. The exit was twenty feet away. The car sixty yards farther. I just wanted to get us the hell out of there. But as I was about to open the door, I heard another door open behind me. I looked back to see Carrick checking the room where we had cuffed the first two guards.

He shook his head—it was empty—then joined us at the exit.

Just then my phone let out a long buzz, startling me, a string of texts from Bug, as if service had been cut off and now it was back. The texts asked what was going on, then were we okay, then said backup was on its way. The last one was another thermal scan, showing just four figures—us—approaching the back door. No one else was in the building. No one was patrolling the lawn. The accompanying text said, *Is that you? What's going on in there?*

"What is it?" Melissa whispered.

"Yeah," Moose said. "What's going on?"

"We'll talk about it later." Carrick shook his head. "Let's get out of here."

Stepping outside, I would have known even without the scan that no one was out there. It was absolutely quiet except for a soft breeze. As we crossed the lawn toward the tree line, I heard the distant thump of rotor blades approaching.

Moose and Melissa looked to the sky as the helicopter appeared over the trees. Carrick tensed, still holding his gun.

Another text came in saying, *We have your visual.*

"They're with me," I said.

He relaxed slightly and Moose stepped up next to him, raising his voice over the throb of the helicopter blades.

"Thanks for getting us out of there," he said. "Now, can you tell us what the hell's going on?"

As we waited for the chopper, Carrick filled them in on most of what had happened, and what little we knew about why. By the time he was finished, they both looked dazed again. Then he looked over Moose's head and said, "The containers are gone."

I turned and saw he was right. In the ten minutes we'd been inside, the entire row of containers had disappeared. After that it was too loud to hear any of us speak, and I was relieved. The chopper dropped fast but landed softly. Four SEALs in tactical gear hit the ground just before the chopper did, followed closely by a pair of medics.

I held up my badge and three of the SEALs fanned out past us, alert, lethal, ready for anything, and surprised to find nothing. The leader came up to me, looking around as he did. "Ledger?"

I nodded. "Pretty sure the place is deserted. Just secure it until my team can evaluate it. And don't touch anything."

He nodded and trotted off, speaking into his throat-mic. I grabbed one of the medics and pointed toward Moose and Melissa. "She's missed two or three doses of this. We just gave her one, but she's in bad shape. And they both seem like they were doped, so check them for signs of chloroform, Rohypnol, anything like that, okay?"

The medics nodded and then guided Moose and Melissa over to the chopper. The blades had stopped spinning. As they passed, Moose leaned toward Carrick and said, "Might be a while before I go foraging again."

Carrick slapped him on the shoulder. "You'll be fine."

That's when Bug jumped out of the chopper and ran over, looking around to see if things were hot.

"They're gone," he said just as Carrick came up beside me and said: "We need to figure out what the hell that was all about."

I introduced them and they shook hands, then Carrick continued. "Seriously. Apart from whatever happened out in the woods, they kidnapped two people, drugged them, did who-knows-what," earning an alarmed look from Moose. "We need to find them and arrest them. Get to the bottom of all this."

Bug shook his head. "They're gone," he repeated. He held up a tablet computer with a thermal scan showing the entire complex empty except for the four of us crossing the grass.

"Then we need to find out where they went," Carrick said.

I nodded and turned to Bug. "We'll find Bortman. And we'll send a team to their offices in Oslo."

Bug shook his head again. "Joe, you don't understand, they're *all* gone. According to Mind—" He glanced at Carrick and caught himself. "According to our electronic surveillance, Xenexgen's computers don't even exist anymore. The company has been dissolved. As of an hour ago. The assets were liquidated. Everything. The leases on Bortman's penthouse apartment in Oslo and his mansion in Waverly expired today. Even this whole complex," he said, waving his arm. "Some holding company bought it at a steal. I don't know how long the deal's been in the works, but it's done."

"That's crazy," Carrick said. "You can't make an entire multinational corporation disappear in a matter of hours."

Bug shook his head. "I wouldn't have thought so, either, but apparently these guys did. They're gone completely."

Melissa broke away from the medics and came over. "They can't be gone," she said. "Why would they go to the trouble of engineering a terrestrial plant with a totally alien nutritional profile if they weren't planning on staying?"

"An alien nutritional profile?" Carrick said, laughing. He rolled his eyes and opened his mouth as if he were about to say something sarcastic. But then he stopped, as if suddenly things made sense. His face turned pale as he looked to the sky.

"Melissa's right," I said. "We need to scour this place for clues. Their Oslo facilities, too. And the spot out in the woods. We need to find out as much as we can about these guys. They might be gone for now, but I'm pretty sure they're coming back."

ABOUT THE AUTHOR

Jon McGoran is the author of the Doyle Carrick thrillers *Drift*, *Deadout*, *Down to Zero*, and most recently *Dust Up*, from Tor/Forge Books. His YA science fiction thriller *Spliced* will be published November 2017 by Holiday House Books. Writing as D. H. Dublin, he is the author of the forensic thrillers *Body Trace*, *Blood Poison*, and *Freezer Burn*. His short fiction includes the novella *After Effects*, from Amazon StoryFront; the short story "Bad Debt," which received an honorable mention in *The Best American Mystery Stories 2014*; and stories in a variety of anthologies and publications in multiple genres, including the *X-Files* anthology *The Truth Is Out There* and the *Zombies vs Robots* anthology *No Man's Land*, from IDW. When not writing fiction, he works as a freelance writer, editor, and story consultant. He is a member of the International Thriller Writers and the Mystery Writers of America and a founding member of the Philadelphia Liars Club. Find him on Twitter @JonMcGoran, on Facebook at www.facebook.com/jonmcgoran, or at www.jonmcgoran.com.

NO BUSINESS AT ALL

BY JAVIER GRILLO-MARXUACH

The fuckwits had the temerity to call it *Department Zero*.

Mr. Church didn't like to put me out there solo. Said it was for my protection. I often wondered whose protection he really had in mind. Truth is, without the blessed stabilizing influence of a Top, Bunny, Ghost—or Rudy—it was a fifty/fifty that I'd corkscrew the head off of any maroon who tried my patience.

And the guy in front of me was doing the merengue on the wrong side of that border.

His name was J. D. Goldfarb, and, to my very great credit, I cowboyed the fuck up the first twenty minutes of his thrilling description of the hidden meanings, and the expense, of his yakuza sleeve tattoos before my homicidal Lorelei started singing her song.

Because God is Love, that was as much time as J. D. needed to figure out I didn't instinctively recognize him as the writer of the Big Time Studios production of *Department Zero*, and that I was most likely "below the line." That's a fancy Hollywood term for "the folks who do all the real work on a movie set."

Unaware that he was saving his own life, J. D. Goldfarb quickly pushed up his chunky Prada glasses and shuffled his John Varvatos leather boots and black Thomas Pink shirt away from the craft services table, and the hell out of my sight. "Craft services," for those keeping score at home, is another fancy Hollywood term. This time for "snack bar." It's where actors go to "eat their feelings."

The craft services table is also the unofficial center of "base camp." That's where all the trucks, tents, trailers, and cars supporting the $150 million production of *Department Zero* parked while on location.

Even I can't deny that there was an exciting zip to the place, what I imagine people must have meant when they fantasized about running away to join the circus, and there I was: watching a clown scamper back to his car while I waited for my mark to arrive.

The mission should have been simple. When MindReader intercepted an email from a Big Time Studios server with a "log line" for their upcoming production *Department Zero*, Mr. Church did something he seldom deigned to do. He paid attention to the movies.

On the surface, the screenplay for *Department Zero* did bear some resemblance to our august organization: telling as it did the story of the eponymous top-secret government unit. Headed by one mysterious "Mr. Chapel." Department Zero also counted among its operatives a former Special Forces man named "Jack Counter." A tough-as-nails-and-take-no-shit leader of the heavily armed and state-of-the-art "Mirror Team," Counter stood at the bleeding edge of the fight against criminal abuses of science-fictional technology.

Of course, Jack Counter kept his personal demons—which were legion, by the way—at bay with the help of his long-suffering Mexican-American psychotherapist, named "Ryan Vazquez." That she was Jack Counter's love interest, in a breathtaking abdication of professional ethics, didn't seem to set off Mr. Church's bullshit meter in the least.

As you might imagine, it took all of one day undercover as "Special Covert Ops Technical Adviser" to the star of *Department Zero* to figure out that this was a case of "parallel development." That's a fancy Hollywood term for "someone had the same idea we did around the same time we did."

Hell, I could have told Mr. Church that without leaving the cold one I was nursing on the lanai when I got the call. . . .

But being as my boss's paranoia is a self-sustaining ecosystem with its own predatory megafauna, and that he was probably spending nights awake wondering if some sinister power was using the billion-dollar machinery of the entertainment-industrial complex to get the word out about our operation to their allies, I took pity on the guy. I figured a few days in La-La Land investigating this bunch of posers to make sure none of them had unauthorized access to government secrets would be cake.

Now, I don't want to give away any "spoilers," but here's the entirety of the written report I turned in to Mr. Chapel—er, Church—on that score:

> The producers of *Department Zero* know about as much
> about our operation as their screenwriter knows the yakuza
> from his own asshole.

But that didn't mean everything was hunky-dory on the set of *Department Zero*.

First of all, *Department Zero*? Excuse me, I work for a living. Contrary to popular belief—and popular culture—government agents don't sit around coming up with snappy, eye-catching names for their black-bag outfits.

Think it through: some dime-store Snowden downloads the wrong d-base, the first thing they are going to do is click on the sleek and sexy code names. On the other hand, "Department of Military Sciences"? Now there's a designation guaranteed to cure the insomnia of even the most obsessive-compulsive spreadsheet sniffer.

Second, even though the movie's leading man (and, according to Dr. Hu, it was shocking I'd never heard of the guy before), international superstar Cole McAdams, was pushing sixty, he played the role of Jack Counter with all the brio of a man a third that age. I'm talking Navy SEAL endurance.

Cole McAdams legendarily did his own stunts, threw his own punches, piloted his own helicopter to remote locations, never forgot his lines, and always hit his marks with spit-polish and devil dog precision.

Normally, that wouldn't have given me any pause. A star like that? His entire life centers on his "instrument"—a fancy Hollywood term for "his body." And what's a guy like that got to do with his day other than keep his abs up?

With every aspect of his existence taken care of by assistants, secretaries, housekeepers, stylists, and personal trainers, Cole McAdams's racehorselike reality consisted of two activities: staying chiseled and handsome at all costs, and collecting a portfolio of skills every bit as ridiculous as those of the characters he played.

Having earned between $5 million and $20 million, with gross-profit participation, in every one of his projects almost all the way back to his breakthrough starring role as "John Hawk" in the early eighties action extravaganza *Relentless* and its seven sequels, prequels, and equals, Cole McAdams had amassed not just enough wealth to own his own lavishly restored 747-100 (one of the first off the Boeing assembly line in '67, he informed anyone who would listen) but also the free time to earn his pilot's certification. He also designed a small private airport in the style of Eero Saarinen behind his third and largest home, located in the Arizona desert.

After spending three minutes with the guy, you'd learn not only that he knew how to pilot a jumbo jet as well as a P-51 Mustang and a Mikoyan-Gurevitch Foxbat (yeah, he called it that instead of "a MiG-25," just to be sure I "got it") . . . but that he could also scale mountains, rocks, and buildings with and without ropes and carabiners . . . and that he had ranking in multiple martial arts, including Brazilian jujitsu, Wing Chun, Krav Maga, and Systema.

Longest three minutes of my life.

Wanna hear about the next three minutes? They're the reason I know that Cole McAdams owned an extensive collection of guns from his films—including such exotic gear as the fully functional "hero prop" rocket-powered grenade launcher from *Relentless 2* ("hero prop" is a fancy Hollywood term for "the real deal that looks good on camera and might even be fully functional")—that he could free dive to a depth of a hundred feet for more than eight minutes, and that he had learned parkour from the Yamakasi, precision stunt driving from Rémy Julienne, and black-and-white war photography from James Nachtwey.

Then there were the singing and guitar lessons from Eddie Vedder that he took in preparation for his role as an ostensibly aging rocker in his 2014 relationship comedy, *Tour Bus Blues*.

Yeah. That one hurt.

Anyway, I knew something was wrong with Cole McAdams the first time I laid eyes on him. It had nothing to do with his fame, fortune, or hobbies.

It was the road rash.

Whenever Cole McAdams left his large, midcentury modern compound in the Hollywood Hills, assuming he wanted to drive himself that day, he decided among the dozen cars, and twice as many motorcycles, in his air-conditioned garage. Then, his assistant, a driver, and a bodyguard piled into a lumped-out Cadillac Escalade, which followed Cole McAdams and whatever conveyance he had selected for himself to his destination.

No matter where Cole McAdams went—an exclusive sushi joint in the foothills over the Sunset Strip or the private home of a fellow mogul—the Escalade and his vehicle du jour would wait for him at the entrance. Both with the engine idling. Whenever Cole McAdams was done doing whatever it was that Cole McAdams did, wherever it was that Cole McAdams did it, Cole McAdams would choose whether to get back in his private car, or bike, or the Escalade. If Cole McAdams got in the Escalade, then the assistant drove his car or motorcycle back home for him. If Cole McAdams got back in his car or bike, the Escalade, once again, followed at a close distance to ensure his privacy and safety.

In short: It's good to be Cole McAdams.

On my first day visiting the production of *Department Zero*, filming on location in downtown Los Angeles on a Friday morning, Cole McAdams had chosen to ride to work on his custom-painted orange-and-gray Suzuki Hayabusa. In spite of his toned musculature and complete control over his mental and physical faculties, Cole McAdams somehow missed a pool of oil-based paint spilled near the prop master's truck.

I had been instructed to show up first thing in the morning, while most of the crew were getting breakfast at the catering tent, and then further instructed by an assistant director to wait for Cole McAdams's arrival at the door to his triple-wide motor home/trailer/dressing room/porta-mansion, parked near the props fabrication truck. So I alone saw him hit that puddle in 1080p hi-res.

I may be a grown-ass man, but I'm not above admitting a measure of envy over another guy's sweet gear, which I could never afford . . . which is why the resulting wipeout was so uniquely satisfying.

Cole McAdams's Suzuki Hayabusa screamed around the corner to the deserted midway between the parked production vehicles, mobile offices, and dressing room trailers. As if that weren't enough, he then popped a wheelie on the last leg of the journey to his triple-wide. His face, visible through the transparent visor on his matte black helmet, was a study in steel-eyed intensity. Until his rear wheel went into a skid.

Then it became a study in wide-eyed hilarity. There are few things funnier than watching this cruel world show some poser just how little mastery he truly has over all he surveys.

The Escalade lumbered around the corner as I took a few steps toward the conflagration. Within seconds, Cole McAdams's retinue surrounded him in a flurry of iPhones, loudly voiced concern for the meal ticket, and removal of witnesses.

By the time Cole McAdams's Blond Mountain of a bodyguard shooed me away from the scene, well before any further onlookers could have twigged to the crash, my offer of assistance had been soundly rejected. I had also been asked to relinquish any cell phone video of the incident (I had none) and reminded that should word of this get out to something called "TMZ," I would be held personally responsible for violating the ironclad terms of the nondisclosure agreement that made it possible for me to visit this location in the first place.

That's when I noticed the compound fracture.

When 550 pounds of rice rocket lands on a man's wrist, it's gonna leave a mark. This one was a beautiful specimen, even viewed in passing as Cole McAdams's assistant and driver under-the-shouldered him past me, three inches of pearly white in a foot-long lake of gore, road rash, and shredded motorcycle leather.

Now, I've seen some shit. And when you've seen shit like I've seen shit, you don't go looking for shit. And you don't go starting shit unless you're ready to end some shit. But you sure as shit know some shit when you see it . . . and what I saw next was some shit.

I whiled away the hour after the incident on a folding plastic chair over at "extras holding" (a fancy Hollywood term for "the fucking ghetto of the untouchables"), and was then summoned by a production assistant (one of an army of young people in cargo pants, T-shirts, and headsets who beavered over every facet of the operation like some unholy mating of worker bees and Santa's elves) and instructed to wait for Cole McAdams at the craft services table. Twenty minutes and one tedious exchange with a tattooed screenwriter later, my time in "the Presence" was afoot.

It wasn't hard to spot McAdams coming toward me. Everywhere he went, he strode with purpose, and the world parted around him. Struggling to keep up with him was a young woman—couldn't have been more than twenty-five—in cargo shorts, T-shirt, and headset.

Her name was Amy Garfunkel. She was the dictionary definition of "cute" and "eager"—bustling, unadorned, and wide-eyed—with a palpable brio that made it clear to all that she had come to work as hard as humanly possible in the hopes of making it in the circus. Unlike the sleek and tall actors running in packs around the makeup and wardrobe trailers, Amy had a beauty that came from a compact and practical place. It wasn't looks that made her sparkle, but rather an enthusiastic work ethic that time wouldn't mar nearly as easily.

As I watched them, I wondered when the last time was I had been that young. I also made note of Amy's beaming smile as she listened to Cole McAdams.

She'd been given the gift to stare at the sun without injury.

As Cole McAdams ended his conversation with Amy, I felt the approach of the Blond Mountain behind me. I chose not to acknowledge it. Just as I chose not to snap his wrist when he put his hand on my shoulder.

"Cell phone, please," he demanded.

"Excuse me?"

"Cole McAdams can't speak to you unless you surrender your cell phone. People like to record what he says and sell it."

"Lemme guess, TMZ?"

Blond Mountain let out a rumbling grunt.

I handed over my cell phone. He then exchanged a subtle nod with Cole McAdams, who gave Amy a warm and sincere hug and seamlessly made his way to me. Blond Mountain turned his back on us as Cole McAdams closed the distance, taking off his leather jacket, a pristine duplicate of the one he wore in the crash, to reveal a clean arm.

You got that right. Clean. No protruding bone. No trace of blood.

Not even a spot of road rash.

Eighty minutes ago, I saw an injury on this guy that should have taken a team of orthopedic and vascular surgeons eight hours in scrubs to sort out just enough for a lifetime of rehabilitation and phantom pain. That injury should have shut down production on *Department Zero* for weeks and made the studio's insurance company call the fire department.

Now Cole McAdams was stopping on a dime in front of me in his brand-new leathers, and though his viridescent eyes made it clear he wanted me to feel like the center of the universe, what he clearly wanted even more was for me to walk away from this meeting knowing in no uncertain terms that he was fine.

The charm offensive continued with a warm, firm handshake. It then proceeded with Cole McAdams inviting me into his circle of masculinity by looking back at the receding Amy Garfunkel and letting his gaze rest subtly but discernibly on her ass.

"She's a sweetheart," volunteered Cole McAdams. "Works as a painter in the props department."

"Didn't think they'd be your favorite people right around now," I said, taking the bait. I figured the next step in his charm offensive, being as I did not accept the invitation into Cole McAdams's circle of masculinity (I like women my own damn age and wasn't about to validate his ogling a girl who could have been his granddaughter), was to let me know that he was a nice fellow and had forgiven all her trespasses.

"Oh, everyone makes mistakes," he said with a *what the hell* grin I can only describe as "weaponized." Cole McAdams then turned to Blond Mountain. "Hey, Lemmy, get her on the guest list for that thing tonight."

Now I knew four things about Cole McAdams.

1. If I wanted to be aggressively heterosexual around him, he was fine with that as an exercise in male bonding.
2. He had a "thing" tonight and—while it was clearly something very exclusive—an invitation was on the table if I was willing to discern, and then perform, the necessary forms of fellatio.
3. His arm was fine.

Number four?

That one I figured out for myself. Everything about this encounter had been engineered to make sure I understood the first three things.

Yes. Technically, I also knew that Blond Mountain's name was "Lemmy," but fuck that shit.

Anyway, I introduced myself to Cole McAdams, but I couldn't get more than fifteen seconds into the carefully crafted layers of my manufactured identity as "former CIA agent turned movie set consultant Hank McClaine." Cole McAdams grabbed on to the first conversational handle I threw at him and launched into a monologue about his many skills and accomplishments.

As I said, those were the longest six minutes of my life.

I nodded and smiled, denying him the pleasure of seeing me impressed, and definitely not trying to match his list of accomplishments with some of my own. You know parkour? That's nice: I killed an army of transgenic cockroach men in the Poconos. You own a jet? That's nice: I stopped zombie terrorists from blowing up the Liberty Bell. You have a big gun collection? That's nice: I helped space aliens stop a nuclear holocaust.

No. Sometimes, you just gotta shut up and take the hit.

Finishing up, Cole McAdams flashed me his best *good talk* expression. He then clapped me on the shoulder, let me know he'd be consulting me when he found some piece of operational jargon in the script that he didn't understand, and was halfway down the midway with an iris closing over him like the end of a *Looney Tunes* cartoon before I realized my audience with the king was over.

The thought *How do people fall for this horseshit?* had barely coalesced in my brain before Blond Mountain put the phone back in my hand and fucked off to wherever it is that people with necks that big fuck off to.

Apparently, everyone was now duly convinced that I was duly convinced that I had not seen what I knew I had seen.

Of course, I knew what I had seen. And I was about to start some shit.

I found a relatively quiet spot near the "honey wagons" (that's a fancy Hollywood term for "chemical toilets"). I lifted the phone and dialed.

A familiar voice said hello on the other end and I launched into it:

"Hey. Dr. Hwang. It's Hank McClaine. I know it's been a long time since the farm, but I got a lead on something I think you might find interesting. Could be our ticket back in."

"Hang on a minute, I gotta put my earbuds in . . . ," acknowledged the voice on the other end of the line.

"I'm made of time," I replied.

"Okay, do tell."

"You remember that advanced Lin28a research we caught the Chinks doing back in '08?"

"Oh yeah, crazy-ass shit."

"They ever deploy that? Black market, maybe, party favors for the superrich?"

"Never cracked it far as I know. You want me to look into it?"

"Nah, I'll get back to you." I clicked off.

Here's what actually happened in that call:

I found a relatively quiet spot near the "honey wagons" (that's a fancy Hollywood term for "chemical toilets"). I lifted the phone and dialed.

A familiar voice said hello on the other end and I launched into it:

"Hey, Bug"—yeah, "Dr. Hwang" was our little joke—"I'm using my cover because I suspect my phone is being monitored. If it is, I want to make sure they think I am sort of on to what they are doing and I need for you to play along and maybe improvise a bit."

"Please clarify whether you're under duress," acknowledged the voice on the other end of the line.

"I'm not under duress," I replied.

"Your phone is bugged, confirmed. Run your sting."

"I am making up a bullshit case and throwing in a technical term which anyone monitoring could easily figure out has to do with regeneration of limbs and other living tissue."

"Oh yeah, crazy-ass shit." (Okay, that wasn't code—it was in fact some crazy-ass shit.)

"I'm gonna throw out some more vague suspicions as bait."

"I'm helping you make that bait tantalizingly tasty, but letting you perpetuate the idea that you're acting alone."

"I definitely want them to think I'm acting alone." I clicked off.

For a man with such massive hands, Blond Mountain had slipped the paper-thin DxO 9 monitoring chip in my phone with great ease. The thing was a masterpiece: something I would have been surprised to see in the hands of a fellow operator. I left it in there, knowing that whoever was working with Cole McAdams (if this was indeed something more than a very rich wannabe getting his hands on some top gear) was tracking my movements along with my calls, and that red flags would go up if I dropped the surveillance.

Also, I didn't want to risk tampering with my phone. Why? Because I knew damn well—unless something was way off with my operational radar—that Cole McAdams's "people" would be calling any minute.

The call came less than an hour later, as I waited patiently, sipping cold coffee from a white foam cup in the folding plastic chair ghetto. It was Cole McAdams's "appointment desk assistant," and she wanted to know if I would join Mr. McAdams and a few of his friends at the after-hours VIP set he was hosting with DJ Takakura at the Garbo on Selma.

I pretended to know what the hell she meant, and was told that a

Town Car would pick me up at my hotel (the production had arranged for lodging during my consultancy).

My gambit had worked.

I figured their next step would be to put a gun in my face right after I got in the Town Car . . . take me somewhere remote, rough me up a little bit, ask how much I knew, and then, realizing I knew nothing, release me and have me discreetly fired from the production . . . perhaps after giving up some useful clue about the real reason why Cole McAdams had the healing ability of an axolotl on meth.

What I did not expect was that Cole McAdams would call me in to consult on the scene being shot, and that he would listen intently to my advice on handling a supersonic fléchette gun with honeycomb rounds, and then keep me on the set and ask me spycraft questions between takes for the next ten hours. What I also didn't see coming was that while this was going on, Blond Mountain not only ran the dossiers on my manufactured identity but also ascertained my threat level, and then left the set, snuck into my hotel room, and injected every one of the bottles in my minibar.

So basically, the party invitation and Town Car had been an elaborate ruse to keep me from being suspicious when I opened the bottle of Starbucks Iced Coffee in the back of my minibar (the production was paying my expenses, so I figured why not live a little?) and guzzled down enough gamma hydroxybutyrate to drop a water buffalo.

There's a lot of shit that pissed me off about this mission, but fucking with a man's minibar? That's just mean-spirited.

I don't always get drugged and abducted, but when I do, I tend to wake up duct-taped to a chair and naked. So tonight was a definite improvement.

I came to on a chair, no duct tape, in a midcentury modern office in a large house in the Hollywood Hills. The view alone—on a clear day it must have gone all the way to Long Beach—must have set Cole McAdams back well into the eight figures. Cole McAdams looked fabulous, etched against the setting sun in gray trousers and a tight, long-sleeved black oxford with the top three buttons undone.

Behind me, I noticed three things. First, Blond Mountain, in his bodyguard-black suit with a black T-shirt underneath. Second, another man, shorter, with close-cropped steel-gray hair, wearing a navy three-piece suit that would not have looked out of place in a board meeting in a London bank in the early 1960s. The third thing I noticed was a wall festooned with trophies on shelves.

Even I, with my meager knowledge of popular culture, could discern the conspicuous absence of an Oscar. That made me chuckle.

"We don't want to hurt you, Hank," declared Cole McAdams with a probing smile, "and we don't want there to be any trouble, but we got trade secrets of our own around here, and we just need to know that you're cool."

"What do you want from me?"

"Silence . . . ," Cole said, letting it hang there with a charming shrug, then adding, "And no more phone calls to your cronies who went freelance in the biotech world after the Gulf War pork barrel emptied out."

That reply told me everything I needed to know.

Cole McAdams's security personnel had dug deep into the layers of my cover and learned that "Hank McClaine" had been discreetly released from his duties in the CIA because of a substance abuse problem, and that while no malfeasances had been allowed into his public record, he had not been allowed his complete pension.

This meant that "Hank McClaine" had just enough red on his column to keep him from a lucrative job commenting about state affairs on conservative radio and television. This meant that "Hank McClaine" was very lucky to be sent out to consult on movie sets every once in a while.

Bug did his work beautifully on this one. And that work was directly responsible for my not being tied up, stripped down, and hot-prodded in some orifice not designed for that sort of action. The life of "Hank McClaine" had been carefully designed to broadcast the message that "Hank McClaine" was eminently vulnerable to a handsome bribe.

"Okay . . . ," I said, acting like a man trying to keep his cool when he has been completely and totally made. "What's that worth to you?"

"We'll wire a hundred thousand dollars to the offshore account of your choice."

"What makes you think I'm such a cheap date?" I grumbled.

Cole McAdams looked back at the man in the three-piece suit. Nods were exchanged. Three-Piece lifted a Bang & Olufsen remote control from a bookcase as Blond Mountain roughly swiveled my chair to face a screen the size of a Buick.

The display came to life with multiple high-def and full-color security camera views of a research sciences facility that would have made DARPA drool—stainless steel and glass, all standard-issue Bond villain shit. With something absolutely god-awful as the main event.

Strapped upside-down on a shiny scaffold at the center of the lab was the once vibrant form of Amy Garfunkel.

Her body had been stripped down to two black cloth bands to preserve what these animals must have believed was her dignity. The rest of her was crisscrossed by a network of wiring, monitoring devices, and tubing, some of them carrying fluid into her body, most draining it out.

Her skin was the color of brittle newsprint and about as thin and wrinkled. Her eyes were black. All life had been leeched from her features. The monitors buzzed with flatlines.

I was looking at a corpse.

"We won't bother you with the technical details," said Three-Piece, his voice sheer with the sinister silk of an impending threat.

And you don't have to, asshole, I kept thinking—because even with a murderous rage for justice occluding my every instinct for self-preservation, what I saw before me also clarified this entire situation:

I know the technical details. Just like I now recognize your Ukrainian accent. I'm looking at a rapid-fire p21 gene therapy combined with a pluripotent stem cell harvest designed to create a transplantable suite of biocompounds that can target and heal any injury in minutes with complete regenerative efficacy.

How did I know all this?

The same way I knew fourteen hours ago at the sight of an arm with no road rash that this was a day I was gonna start some shit:

I popped a cap in your former boss's spine five years ago when he tried selling this shit to a couple of undercover North Korean MSS agents and found out that even they weren't batshit crazy enough to invest in a life-extension and tissue-regeneration treatment that required an investment in the billions . . . and the agonizing death of multiple donors per treatment.

Three-Piece finally got to his point:

"We used up our entire supply of our proprietary serum fixing Mr. McAdams's compound fracture this morning . . . and we have several local clients waiting for treatments in the next two weeks. . . ."

I guess I should have known, I thought while he threatened to do to me what they did to Amy, *that Hollywood would have an even more sociopathic narcissist than Kim Jong Un: one willing to bankroll this operation and provide a list of ultrawealthy clients motivated to pay billions to stay young and spry.*

"So you can either take the money . . . ," concluded Three-Piece while Cole McAdams nodded in agreement, "or . . . maybe . . . you will go on a bender after being seen at tonight's party with my business partner . . ."

Which one of that commie Mengele's acolytes are you, Three-Piece? Lupinsky? Vartamian? I know there's at least three more of your colleagues on the DMS's most wanted list.

Three-Piece concluded his threat with an *ain't I clever* grin:

". . . and be found a few days later, dead of an unfortunate overdose."

That's when my own thought process came to its own inevitable conclusion.

Fuck it. Dr. Hu and his pencil-necks'll figure out your identity. I'm just gonna go ahead and kill the shit out of you and every other motherfucker in this room.

When you have sent as many men to meet their Maker as I have, you develop an attuned situational appreciation for any new methods, or weapons, that come your way.

Take, for example, the People's Choice Award for Best Actor (which Cole McAdams won for his 2003 tour-de-force performance as an autistic mathematical genius in *Fermat's Last Dance*).

I bolted from my chair, picking it up in one seamless motion and heaving it into Cole McAdams's chest to stop him from reaching for the gun in the polished steel box on his desktop. As I did that, the thought crossed my mind that the People's Choice Award might *just* be the perfect cutlass with which to skewer Blond Mountain's head. From looks alone, you could have come to the same conclusion. The thing's basically a massive, bulbous arrowhead with a *very* sharp point.

So I used the momentum from the chair-throw to whip around to the trophy case and snatch the People's Choice Award from the shelf. When I jammed it mercilessly into the skin under Blond Mountain's neck, however, I quickly realized that his gouting blood was messing up my grip on the crystal surface of the trophy.

The People's Choice Award became so slippery, in fact, that I had to slam two open palm strikes into its square base. The first strike hammered it through the open space above his jaw, past the roof of his mouth, and into his sinus cavity. The second strike was necessary to find lethal purchase in Blond Mountain's frontal lobe, just behind his orbital plate.

So that slowed me down.

It also gave Cole McAdams time to hit a panic button and disappear behind the pneumatic hiss of a rapidly opening and closing wall panel.

The good news is that, being the world's biggest movie star, Cole McAdams wasn't going to be hard to find. I already had an idea where he was headed.

So, as Blond Mountain fell twitching to his knees, and then face-planted onto the hardwood floor to let out a sad little death rattle, I let Cole McAdams bitch out of the straight fight he could have had with me and turned my attention to Three-Piece.

It turns out that the Emmy Award (which Cole McAdams had won in 1997 after attaching himself as executive producer to, and narrator of, *The Silent Struggle*, an unimpeachable PBS documentary about the role of deaf-mutes in the civil rights movement) provided not only a perfect pommel as I rammed the lightning-shaped wings of the statue just above Three-Piece's jugular notch but also a profoundly satisfying *crack!* when I delivered its heavy metal base against the bottom of his skull.

I turned to the now bloodstained screen and took a final look at the corpse of Amy Garfunkel.

All she did was spill some fucking paint on the ground.

Wherever she is, I hope she knows that her broken dreams fueled the vengeance I took in her name.

I found my cell phone in Blond Mountain's breast pocket, wiped his blood and gore off the screen, removed the monitoring chip, and dialed the emergency transponder activation number. In less than an hour, this place would be crawling with DMS forensic investigation experts.

Using the remote control, I changed the channel on the display screen to Cole McAdams's security feed. I found him in the garage, angrily shouting orders at a man I can only imagine was Blond Mountain's backup—and his three-man team of gun-drawing private security thick-necks, all in black suits.

The men advanced into the house in cover formation, presumably heading up to the office to finish me off.

I reached into Blond Mountain's clothes, retrieved both his shoulder and ankle carries (Beretta 93R machine pistol on top, Glock on the bottom), and headed out to intercept the coming army. I imagine that this would have been a scintillating gun battle had the security camera feed not told me exactly where they were coming from.

Also, because I'm nice like that, I did try sparing them all by attempting to escape through the only other exit to the office: the panic button/wall panel. That turned out to be coded to Cole McAdams's thumbprint.

So yeah, I found a nearby hallway closet and closed the office doors behind me on the way out. When they got there, opened the doors, threw in a flashbanger, and then opened fire into the smoke, thinking they had fish in a barrel, I rolled out of the closet and plugged every last one of the sons of bitches in the back.

It turns out that "TMZ" is a fancy Hollywood term for "thirty-mile zone": the area around the city proper where movie companies are allowed to film without paying travel expenses, per diems, and lodging to their actors and crew. It's also the name of an annoying celebrity gossip website from which I had spent most of my life mercifully shielded.

Anyway, in an incident that TMZ would later report as an unfortunate confluence of bad weather (in Los Angeles, shyeah) and pilot error, Cole McAdams's 747-100 jumbo jet (which had been lavishly restored for his personal use) skidded off a runway at a private airport in the San Fernando Valley, fully fueled for an impromptu international flight, and exploded, killing everyone on board. The reality was a little more cinematic. Hell, it might have won me a People's Choice Award had Mr. Church not chosen to keep it off the papers.

As Cole McAdams boarded his plane, I was screaming up the Cahuenga pass on his first-off-the-assembly-line Ducati Multistrada 1200 S-Touring, trying to keep the backpack I had shanghaied from his gear locker attached to my body as I white-knuckled the heated grips.

Yeah, you read that right.

Heated grips on a motorcycle.

What an asshole.

In the cockpit of his luxury jetliner, Cole McAdams went through a seriously shortened pre-flight checklist with his co-pilot, a former Soviet fighter jockey whose silence and loyalty had been purchased with vast sums of cash and the occasional life-extension/healing treatments from McAdams's illicit operation. Meanwhile, at the front gate, I was shouting at Homeland Security officers, telling them to call the number leading straight to Mr. Church's "give this guy whatever the hell he needs and stay out of his goddamned way" red phone.

Cole McAdams's 747-100 taxied out of its hangar and onto the runway. His flight plan said nothing about how he intended to fly it to a private South Pacific island well outside of the rule of United States law.

I peeled rubber in a hairpin turn that Tokyo-drifted me right behind the jumbo jet's enormous tailplane. Now, I know what you're thinking: Is this gonna be a martial arts fight on the wing like in *Die Hard 2: Die Harder*, or a game of "land vehicle vs. airplane chicken" like in *Face/Off*?

Okay, maybe you're not thinking that, but since it was the first thing out of Dr. Hu's mouth when I told him the story, I figured I'd mention it.

Anyway, the 747 turned onto the runway.

I gunned the throttle on the Ducati and took advantage of that one last remaining moment in which I'd be faster than four Rolls-Royce jet engines tasked with lifting a half-million pounds of shining steel into the air.

I overshot the plane and kept going at top speed to the end of the runway. Before running out of blacktop, I skid-turned the bike to a near halt and let it scrape the road in a shower of sparks as I dismounted.

I could see Cole McAdams's smug, self-satisfied, grin. I caught a flash of his perfect teeth as he saw me and gunned the throttle.

The foremost of his landing gear trembled, tentatively letting go of the ground below.

I also saw the change in Cole McAdams's expression right before the forward landing gear rose to expose the plane's underbelly.

It was at that exact moment that I reached into his backpack and pulled out the prized item of his indeed massive and varied arms collection.

The hero prop rocket-powered grenade launcher from *Relentless 2*.

I don't care how famous you are. I don't care how many awards you've won. I don't care how much money you've earned. And I truly don't care how many fugitive life-extension and limb-regeneration scientists from the bowels of the Cold War you have in business with you.

No murdering son of a bitch comes back from a rocket-powered grenade to the center-wing fuel tank.

Fade to black, motherfucker.

ABOUT THE AUTHOR

Though best known as one of the Emmy Award—winning producers of *Lost*, and for creating *The Middleman* comic books and TV series, Javier Grillo-Marxuach is a prolific creator of TV, films, graphic novels, and transmedia content. In addition to his work as writer/producer on shows ranging from *The 100* and *The Shannara Chronicles* to *Medium* and *Boomtown*, Grillo-Marxuach co-hosts the *Children of Tendu* podcast, an educational series for writers, and is an avid participant of the Writers Guild mentors program. Grillo-Marxuach can be found online at www.OKBJGM.com and on Twitter @ OKBJGM, and his podcast is available free of charge on iTunes, with Stitcher, and at www.childrenoftendu.com. Javier Grillo-Marxuach was born in San Juan, Puerto Rico, and his name is pronounced "HA-VEE-AIR-GREE-JOE-MARKS-WATCH."

GANBATTE

BY KEITH R. A. DeCANDIDO

The wind whipped through Lydia Ruiz's hair as she drove her cherry-red Mercedes-Benz SL550 convertible down US Route 1, the Overseas Highway, through the Florida Keys.

When she booked her trip home with the travel office at the Department of Military Sciences, the woman there was confused as to why she was booking a flight to Miami International Airport rather than Key West International Airport.

"My car's in long-term parking at MIA," was the only answer she gave.

But that wasn't the real reason.

You didn't just fly into Key West. It was too abrupt a transition, to go from the real world to paradise.

No, it was better to fly into Miami, get into a car, and take the three hours to drive south on US 1. Made it way easier to assimilate.

And right now, Lydia needed paradise. The real world had gotten too unreal since joining the DMS.

As she took the bridge from Long Key to Marathon, she glanced down at the digital display. It was 5:30 PM on a Tuesday, so the dojo was open and Yona Congrejo would be teaching the five o'clock kids class.

When she reached 89th Street, she made a U-turn and pulled into the small shopping center on the northbound side of the Overseas Highway.

But Kaicho Bill's wasn't there. Instead, there was a clothing store.

She pulled into a parking space and leaped out of the Mercedes without opening the door.

For about ten seconds, she just stared at the clothing store and thought back to the first time she came to this shopping center.

You look up at the sign that says KAICHO BILL'S MARATHON KARATE, *then you look at Yona. "What the fuck am I supposed to be doing here?"*

"Watch your mouth, chica.*"*

Then you smile. "Don't call me chica, *bitch."*

Yona throws up her hands. "Fine, you don't want to do this, I'll go tell the Key West cops who left José Alvarez bleeding on Southard last weekend."

"Motherfucker had it comin'!"

"Funny thing about felony assault—there is no proviso in it for whether or not the person being assaulted had it coming."

"Well, there fuckin' should be."

Yona grabs you by the shoulders. "Look, Lydia, you've got two choices— karate or jail. Doesn't matter to me which it is."

"If it don't matter, then why we here?"

"Because I give a fuck."

You grin, then. "Watch your mouth, chica.*"*

And Yona grins right back. "Don't call me chica, *bitch. Now you gonna take the trial class?"*

"I guess. But do I gotta wear the pajamas?"

"It's a gi, *not pajamas."*

Yona brings you inside. There's a waiting area up front, and a tiny, wizened Asian guy standing in the middle of the wooden floor just past the waiting area. Eight kids wearing different-colored belts are facing him, performing moves while the Asian guy yells out instructions.

"That's Kaicho," Yona tells you.

Kaicho Bill Nakahara sees you and Yona walk in and he says, "Stop!"

He doesn't say it very loudly, but something in his tone makes you completely freeze.

"Turn," Kaicho says, indicating Yona with his left hand, "and face Senpai Yona. Bow, osu!"

All eight kids make fists and bend their elbows so those fists are in front of their chests, and they all bow toward Yona and cry out, "Osu!"

The thing that really strikes you is how Kaicho moves. He's like a coil about to spring. It's the coolest thing you ever have seen, and right there you decide you need to learn how to be a badass like this guy.

Lydia pulled out her cell phone and immediately called Yona's cell.

"Holy shit, Lydia, is that you?"

"Watch your mouth, *chica*," Lydia said automatically.

"Don't call me *chica*, bitch. Where are you?"

"Well, I *thought* I was at the dojo. What the hell happened?"

"Didn't you hear?" Yona's voice caught. "Lydia—Kaicho died last year."

"What!? How?"

"Heart attack, they said."

"So the dojo just closed?"

"Yeah." Yona let out a long breath. "Did you know Kaicho had three kids?"

"Uh, no."

"Neither did anyone else. I only found out 'cause some lawyer was supervising the people taking all the equipment out to put it up on eBay or something before they broke the lease. Turns out he has a kid in Seattle, a kid in San Francisco, and a kid in D.C., and none of them give a damn about the martial arts, so the dojo's dead."

"*Carajo.* So now what?"

"Now nothing. I joined up with one of Grandmaster Ken's dojos here in Miami."

"Hold up." Lydia shook her head. "You're in fuckin' Miami? You swore to me you'd die before you lived there."

"Well, that's why I shouldn't swear. My job moved up here."

"You ain't workin' for Martinez no more?"

"The congresswoman lost her seat in a hotly contested election and is now back in the private sector, so I went to work for Congressman Nieto here in Miami. And I kinda need to get back to work, I was just out for a smoke break."

"Since when do you smoke?"

"Since I started working for a lunatic. Look, how long you back home for?"

"Just a few days. We just finished an assignment that—well, it was kind of . . ." Lydia's voice trailed off.

"Crazy?"

"Nah, *chica*, it needed to get a helluva lot calmer before it was as good as crazy. I got a few days to decompress, figured we could get together and hoist a tequila or six—maybe I come by the dojo and get in a workout."

"Well, I'm still game for the tequilas. Look, tonight's no good, but what about tomorrow at the Schooner Wharf? I'll leave the office at five, should be there by nine or ten, depending on traffic?"

Grinning, Lydia jumped back into her Mercedes. "You are *on*."

She pulled out of the driveway and turned right onto US 1 until she could make a U-turn, then headed back down toward the Keys.

The Seven Mile Bridge stretched out before her as she left Marathon, and as she always did, she found herself lost in the expanse of blue water on both sides of her.

There were no vampires (*vampires!*), no terrorists, no jihadists, no nuclear bombs, none of what had become the new normal since she joined the DMS.

No, there was just the bridge, the water, and the memories.

You struggle to thrust yourself upward into a push-up position, and each one is agony, your arms simply not up to the task of raising your weight off the floor.

Expecting Kaicho to yell at you or scream at you or call you a failure, you hear him say in a gentle but firm voice, "Keep trying. Keep pushing."

And you do.

That first class has a total of thirty push-ups in sets of ten at various points in the one-hour class. You successfully do maybe eight.

You feel like a total fuckup. It's a class for beginners, but the other three adults in the class all seem to at least have an idea what they're doing. You look like a klutzy fool.

At the end of the class, after you all bow out and clean the floor as a courtesy to the next class, you expect Kaicho to tell you how badly you screwed up this trial class he let you do as a favor to Yona. You expect him to tell you to not bother showing up for the next class.

Instead he says, "Osu, Lydia, are you familiar with the Japanese word ganbatte?"

You barely remember to start your sentence with "Osu, Kaicho," before continuing: "Only Japanese I know is what you said tonight in class."

He smiles. "It is what we traditionally say before a student is about to engage in a difficult undertaking."

"So it means 'good luck'?"

"In fact, it does not. It means 'try your best.' That is all I ask of my stu-

dents, Lydia, is that they give the maximum effort. It matters less if you succeed. It matters more that you make every effort to succeed, because without the effort, the success will never come." He bows his head. "Osu, Lydia, you did well. I hope we will see you again on Thursday."

Yona drives you home to Stock Island, and you think about what Kaicho said, which encourages you, since you sucked pretty hard in that first class.

But you'll get better.

Yona finally made it to the Schooner Wharf Bar in the Old Town section of Key West at almost 10:30.

"Sorry," she said breathlessly as she joined Lydia at a table near the bar that also had a good view of the stage, where a band was playing country music. Off the beaten path of the main drag of Duval Street, the Schooner Wharf was right on the water and tended to be calmer than the other bars on the island. That was what had drawn Lydia here in the first place years ago. People went to the bars on Duval to get drunk. People came to the Schooner Wharf to drink.

Lydia had already ordered Yona's favorite so it was waiting for her when she arrived. For her part, the first thing Lydia noticed was that Yona pretty well reeked of cigarette smoke.

Holding up her strawberry margarita, Yona said, "It's *really* good to see you, Lydia."

"Likewise." Lydia held up her neat tequila. "To Kaicho."

"To Kaicho. *Osu!*"

"*Osu!*"

They clinked glasses.

After licking a bit of the salt on the rim and sipping her margarita, Yona put the big glass down and pulled out a cigarette.

"So talk to me, *chica*," Lydia said while Yona lit up. "I Googled this Grandmaster Ken *pendejo*. Didn't think he'd be your kinda teacher."

"He's kind of intense." Yona looked away and stared at her margarita. Puffing on the cigarette, she grabbed the drink. "Four of us went over to his dojo after Kaicho died. I'm up to yellow belt now, so that's good."

"Wait, you had to start over?"

Yona nodded, after licking another bit of salt and gulping down more of her drink. "It's no big deal, that's what usually happens when you switch dojos."

Lydia nodded. "So all four of you had to go back to white belt?"

"Me and Ana did. *Senpai*—Sorry, Master Phil and Master Cliff both got to keep their black belts, though they did have to go through a full black belt promotion."

Eyes widening, Lydia said, "What the *fuck*? You and Ana were the best students in that dojo!"

"Phil and Cliff have been at it longer, and Grandmaster Ken's dojo is more physical, more emphasis on fighting. That was never my strong suit." For the first time, Yona actually smiled, though she still wouldn't look directly at Lydia. "It was more yours."

Lydia snorted.

"So enough about me," Yona said, even though Lydia had about fifty more questions about Grandmaster Ken, "what are you up to?"

"I'd tell you, but then I'd have to kill you. And I wish I was kidding. Seriously, the shit I'm into is so classified, *I'm* not even allowed to know about it, and I'm in the thick of it."

"Okay." Yona still wouldn't look Lydia in the eye, but instead gulped more of her margarita, having already licked off all the salt. "It's like your SEAL days all over again."

"Hey, I owe you for that, *chica*. My life was one big assault-and-battery charge waiting to happen." Lydia then grinned. "Now I get to beat people up legally."

"Honestly, I heard some stuff in the office about the DMS. No details, but the congressman talks about you guys like you're superheroes or something."

"Yeah, they totally based the Black Widow on my ass," Lydia said with a laugh. "You said this guy's a crazy man?"

"Ah, not really. I mean, he's not as awesome as the congresswoman was. Honestly, Betty Martinez is the one you owe, not me. I just made the introductions."

"Bullshit. Look, *chica*, you don't step in, I'm doin' time in Dade. You put me in the dojo, and that put my ass on the straight and narrow."

Making a show of looking at the bar stool, Yona said, "Your ass is anything but narrow."

Lydia crumpled up a napkin and tossed it at Yona. They both laughed, but something was wrong with Yona's tone. She was barely even chuckling.

And she still had yet to look Lydia in the eyes. She was also on her third cigarette since walking into the Schooner Wharf.

"What the hell's going on, Yona? What's wrong?" She put a hand on Yona's.

She yanked the hand out from under Lydia's. "Nothing's wrong! Look, you haven't been here. You've been off with the SEALs and DMS, you got *no* idea what it's been like."

"Then *tell* me!" In Spanish, she added, "Get your head out of your ass and talk to me!"

"What?" Yona asked, frowning.

Lydia shook her head. "What, you forgot Spanish in the last six years, too?"

"I only used it with you."

"You work for a congressman in a state that's got a huge-ass Latino population."

"*He* needs to speak Spanish, I don't." Now Yona was staring at the stage.

Fed up, Lydia grabbed Yona's jaw and turned her head toward her. "*Look* at me, for fuck's sake!"

But Yona just flinched, and Lydia realized that she was in pain. "What's wrong?"

"Sore jaw is all. From sparring. Look, everything's fine, okay? I'm working my way back to black belt, I've got a good job. Everything's fine. Really! Okay? So let's cut the maudlin shit and get on to the serious drinking!"

To accentuate the point, she gulped down the rest of her margarita.

One of the perky young female servers that Key West bars seemed to have an endless supply of went by, and Yona flagged her down. "Refill, please?"

"I'm good," Lydia said when the server flashed her a look. She still had half her tequila left.

By the time a year has gone by, the day you most look forward to driving up to Marathon is on Friday, because that's the day you do kumite. *The sparring class is your favorite, because you don't have to get the details right. Doesn't matter if your chamber hand is in the right spot, doesn't matter if your fist touches your ear the right way before you do a down block, doesn't matter how you cross your hands at your ear before an inner temple strike, all you have to do is punch and kick the person you're facing while keeping them from punching and kicking you.*

By the time you reach yellow belt, Kaicho is talking about sending you to kumite *tournaments.*

But Yona—or, rather, Senpai Yona, you have to remember to call her that at least when you're in the dojo, never mind that she changed your fucking diapers—has something else in mind. She brings it up after you pound the living hell out of Senpai *Albert one Friday night. Like Yona, Albert's a Seminole, but he's also built like a brick shithouse. He's another one who gets sent to* kumite *tournaments.*

You get a side kick to his ribs, a front snap kick to his groin (thank Christ he was wearing a cup), and a solid uppercut to his solar plexus that causes him to collapse to his knees, trying and failing to catch his breath.

Kaicho stops the fight after the groin kick with a lecture on how all techniques are to be above the belt. You don't tell him that Albert's got a foot on you and it's really difficult to kick that high, but instead just are determined to make your kicks better.

After class, Kaicho addresses the students, all drenched in sweat after twenty rounds of sparring. "What is of most import," he says in his quiet yet impossible-to-ignore voice, "is respect. Remember, this is not a street fight. The purpose of kumite *is not to learn how to fight on the street. The purpose is to enrich our spirit through honorable combat. In the dojo, we are friends—we are family. We wear safety gear because the object is not to hurt each other." Then a wry smile and a look at* Senpai *Albert. "At least not much."*

Everyone chuckles, Albert more than anyone.

The smile drops. "But if you are in a position where you must fight someone outside the dojo, then your first recourse should be to get away. Because if you are forced to fight, then you have already lost."

"So Albert just talked to me," Yona tells you in the parking lot after class. "He says he told Kaicho to make sure he pairs up with you at least three times per class."

"Really? He that hot to get his ass kicked again?"

"He's that hot to make you a better fighter. You got lucky tonight, but that won't necessarily happen again—mostly because now he knows not to assume that you're just some little yellow belt girl who's just learning how to fight."

"Yeah, right." You just think he wants revenge next time. Whatever.

"Listen, what are you doing Monday morning?"

"Sleeping off my late shift at the bar Sunday night, why?"

"I want you to come up to Congresswoman Martinez's office on Simonton."

"Uh, okay. Why I wanna talk to some politician for?"

Yona smiles. "Just come to the meeting. Don't you trust me?"

You have to admit to trusting Yona. In fact, even after a year at the dojo, Yona's probably the only person you really trust.

Yona was in no shape to drive back to Miami—or anywhere else, for that matter—so they left her car parked on the street near the Schooner Wharf. Lydia double-checked to make sure it wasn't a residents-only spot—they were everywhere, and not always clearly labeled—and after determining that it was safe to stay parked there, she stumbled back to the bed-and-breakfast she was staying in.

As she poured Yona into one side of the king-size bed, she muttered, "Tha's s'm good t'quila."

"Go the fuck to sleep, Yona."

"Watcher mouth, *chica.*"

"Don't call me *chica*, bitch."

Yona was snoring a moment later.

Lydia, though, was still kind of wired. She opened her laptop and did some more research on Kenneth Coffey, aka Grandmaster Ken.

The martial arts sites were all pretty much hagiographies of the man.

A few news sources, though, and especially a couple of blogs, had some accusations, though no charges had ever been pressed.

Then she looked at the schedule for his Miami dojo. Tomorrow night was his adult color belt class, which Yona was probably going to be attending. The day after was listed as an "open sparring class." Clicking on that part of the schedule led to a page that claimed that anyone from any discipline was welcome to join in, as long as they brought their uniform and belt.

Looked like a trip to the storage unit was in order to retrieve her *gi* and yellow belt.

The next morning, she woke up around eight—which was luxury for her, since she rarely got up later than sunup since she started her SEAL training—but Yona was already gone.

Checking her phone, Lydia found a text from Yona time-stamped at a little after 5:00 AM: *Thanks for the crash space. Gotta haul ass to Miami. Really good to see you again. Love you, chica.*

Lydia stared at the phone. "I love you, too, bitch."

"Ms. Ruiz, my aide speaks very highly of you."

You're in the Key West office of Congresswoman Bettina "Betty" Martinez, the person who represents the 26th District in Florida, which covers most of south Florida, including all of the Keys. Yona's off on the side, leaning on the wall, while Martinez is at her desk, looking all prim and proper, like someone's aunt.

You sit in the leather desk chair, wondering what the fuck you're doing here.

"Well, ma'am, she's about the only one who does."

"Nonsense." She opens up a folder, and you catch a glimpse of your high school yearbook picture. *"Straight A's all the way through to high school, and a 4.0 for all your classes during the one semester you were at FKCC. Why'd you drop out?"*

"I'm gonna go back," you say defensively, just like you say it every time to Yona, who stopped believing you would ever return to Florida Keys Community College about a year ago. *"Look, even community colleges want you to actually pay the tuition. And I got this eating habit I can't kick, so that's what all my disposable income from working at three different bars is going to."*

"I also have an email from William Nakahara, who runs one of the most respected martial arts schools in south Florida. He says you have the potential to be his finest student." She smiles. *"I've known Kaicho Bill for thirty years, Ms. Ruiz. I've heard him speak that highly about maybe six students over those years. Seven, now."*

You blink in amazement at this out-of-left-field praise. Every time you step into the dojo, you expect to be unmasked as a fraud.

"I'm spearheading a new program for the navy, Ms. Ruiz. I'm trying to convince the secretary to approve an all-female SEAL fire team. I'm trying to find the best of the best from police forces and in the military, but I'm also looking for special people in martial arts schools. You have exactly what I'm looking for to fill out the team."

"Uhm—" You squirm in the guest chair, the leather making strange noises in response. *"Ma'am, with all due respect, there's much better fighters just in our dojo."*

"I'm not looking for better fighters, Ms. Ruiz, I'm looking for smarter *fighters. From what my aide tells me, and from what these transcripts tell me, and from what Kaicho tells me, that's you."*

Lydia sat in one of the folding chairs set up near the front desk at Grandmaster Ken's Martial Arts School of Miami, one of seventeen branches he had all up and down Florida from as far north as Tallahassee all the way down to a tiny one in Florida City. But the Miami one was his main headquarters—if he hadn't completely eschewed Japanese terminology, it would be called the *honbu*—so this was where he taught. The adult color belt class had thirty students. Grandmaster Ken—a burly, broad-shouldered white guy with a shaved head and a goatee—led the class, with three black belts wandering throughout to check on individual students.

Kaicho Bill's dojo had had lots of Japanese decor. There was the *shinzen*, the spiritual center, which was a tiny reproduction of a Buddhist altar. There were three flags on the wall, one American, one Japanese, and one Florida state flag. Japanese art decorated the entire place, and there was a wooden placard over the entrance to the dojo floor that had the words *nanakorobi yaoki* in *kanji* characters—it was a common saying among martial artists: "seven times fall down, eight times get up."

Grandmaster Ken had none of that. The only flag he had was the Stars and Stripes, and the only decor was a big shelf full of trophies. The grandmaster himself wore a black *gi* while all the other students wore white ones.

The students were all in a fighting stance. "I want to see left jab, left jab, right cross, right roundhouse kick, left back kick. I want the back kick to be groin height. Go!"

Together, all the students did those techniques, with varying degrees of quality.

"Stay together! Go!"

Lydia noted that the higher belts—purple, blue, and black—were moving in perfect unison. The lower belts, not so much.

Grandmaster Ken went to several of the students to yell at them for not keeping up. But he seemed to be yelling only at the women. She saw two yellow belt men whose form was awful—they had strength and speed, but they got the sequence wrong several times.

At no point did Grandmaster Ken say a word to either of those two, but the one time that Yona was a second late with the roundhouse kick or another woman with an orange belt kicked too high or too low on the back kick, or a third threw only one jab, he was all over her.

After the fighting drill, he called out techniques and pointed at a student to perform that technique.

To a male purple belt: "Right side-high kick. No, that's a regular side kick, side-high is to the side, and don't bend your knee."

To a female blue belt: "Hook block. Wrong! That's a forearm block! Ten push-ups!"

After class, a sweaty Yona went straight to the changing room. Lydia noticed that they didn't clean the floor for the next class.

Yona immediately went outside, with Lydia following, and lit up a cigarette. "Good workout," she said weakly.

"That was some *bull*shit. For the whole year I was in Kaicho's dojo, you know what word I never heard? 'Wrong.' *Carajo*, even my instructors at SQT weren't this hard-assed! This asshole is always telling people what they do wrong. Kaicho tells people how to do it right."

"Yeah, well, that was Kaicho. This is Grandmaster Ke—"

One of the black belts who'd been helping teach came out, still in his *gi*. "Hey, Yona. Grandmaster wants you to pick up his kid tomorrow at three."

"No problem, Master Ethan." Yona wouldn't make eye contact with this guy, either.

"Good. And we're still on for drinks after fighting tomorrow night, right?"

Before Yona could agree, Lydia stepped forward. "Actually, we got plans tomorrow night."

Ethan looked down on her as if she were a fly that had gotten into his soup. "Who the hell are you?"

"I'm *Senpai* Yona's friend in from out of town."

Waving a hand in front of Lydia's face, Ethan said, "Don't give me that *senpai* crap, you're in *America*. And she ain't no *senpai* or master or nothin'. And if she wants to be one, she'll go out with me tomorrow night like she said. Grandmaster Ken doesn't like people who go back on their promises."

Lydia looked at Yona, who was cowering near the wall of the dojo, taking a drag on her cigarette, and trying very hard to shrink herself into a ball.

Then Lydia turned back to Ethan. "She didn't know I was coming into town—it was a surprise. And tell you what. I'm a yellow belt in karate"—she avoided saying what discipline—"and I'm a decent fighter. I was thinking about coming to the open fighting tomorrow night."

"It's for *real* fighters, little girl, not decent ones."

"So you're scared to bet me?"

Ethan rolled his eyes. "Yeah, 'cause I'm twelve."

"You ain't that old. What I'm sayin' is, you get one solid punch or kick on me tomorrow night, then you can have drinks with Yona. If you don't, I take her out and we toast what a *pendejo* you are."

At the epithet, Ethan started to move toward her, arms raised, fists clenched.

Then Yona stepped forward. "It's okay, Master Ethan, it's fine, my friend's just a little jet-lagged from her trip."

Ethan backed off, and then stared right at Yona. "I'll see *you* tomorrow night, right after I kick *your* ass," he added with a look right at Lydia.

He walked back into the dojo, and Lydia immediately turned on Yona. "Why'd you stop him?"

At the same time, Yona cried out, "What the fuck were you *doing*?"

"He was being an asshole, Yona. They're *all* assholes, far as I can tell. And I'm gonna enjoy kicking his ass fifty ways from Sunday tomorrow night."

For the first time since she arrived in Florida, Yona looked right at Lydia. Her eyes were wild, and intense, and *scared*. "Please, Lydia, *don't*."

"Don't what?"

"Don't come tomorrow night!" Yona grabbed Lydia's arms at the shoulder in a grip that was not nearly as firm as Lydia would have expected it to be. "Just—just go back to D.C. and forget about this, all right?"

Shaking her head, Lydia asked, "What did they *do* to you, *chica*?"

Yona looked away again. "Nothing. Look, just go."

"I don't get it. You were my mentor, *chica*. The dojo, the SEALs, DMS—I don't do *none* of that without you. Shit, the first all-female fire team is 'cause of *you*. I know it was Martinez who took all the credit, but that was *your* project."

"And where the *fuck* did it get me?" Yona turned angrily back at Lydia. "Martinez lost to some Republican asshole, she went back to her law firm, and I was unemployed. Your little SEAL team fell right off the damn radar after Betty left office. Dorian got her leg blown off, you and Luci both quit, Helene transferred, and Dayana got promoted. And the SEALs don't do publicity unless they're killing bin Laden, so nobody really gave much of a shit anyhow. And then Kaicho died, and I couldn't even call you to tell you, and . . ."

Yona trailed off, the tears welling up in her eyes, and then she broke, her taller form collapsing against Lydia's chest. Lydia held her up, wrapping her arms around her, feeling Yona's body convulse with sobs.

"It's okay," Lydia whispered, letting her cry it out and hoping that, once the sobs subsided, she'd finally explain what the hell was happening.

When Yona stood upright, her cheeks were red and streaked with tears, her eyes puffy. "You don't know, Lydia, you just—"

"Then *tell* me."

"Not here. C'mon."

Lydia got into her Mercedes and followed Yona's Chevy Malibu to a bar a mile away.

Once they were seated in a corner table, tequilas in front of them, Yona finally spoke.

"I tried to fight back, y'know? Tried to get Ken to—to treat me and Ana the same as he treated Cliff and Phil. He—he kept saying they were tougher competitors, and he needed to see fire in our bellies. Not discipline, not self-improvement, but fucking *fire*. We tried, we really did, we did everything he said, but it just—it *never* got any better. And then—and then there was the Christmas party." Yona lit up a cigarette. "We—we were all drinking. A lot. I—I went to the bathroom, and Ethan . . ." She took a long drag on the cigarette.

Lydia prompted: "He followed you in?"

She nodded, looking grateful that she didn't have to actually say those words. "He—he told me that if I knew what was—what was good for me, I would stop giving Ken such a—such a hard time. And then—then he yanked up my skirt, and—"

Again, she broke. Sobs racked her again, and Lydia got up and sat next to her at the table instead of across, wrapping her arms around her mentor. "It's okay."

She wiped tears from her cheek with her palm-heel. "No, no, it's not, it's not okay, I couldn't tell *anyone* what happened, Ethan is Ken's total right hand, and they *worship* him! He gets you trophies, he makes you stronger, he's a *winner*."

"If you're a guy."

"Yeah." She dragged on her cigarette, and that seemed to stop the sobs. "That—that wasn't the—the end of it. After the party, Ken asked me and the other women to—to help clean up. Except he didn't want help, he wanted us to do it all while the guys stood around and—and drank more. And then Ken—he pulled—he—God, he pulled down his fucking pants! Said if we did a good job, he'd let us blow him."

"'Let' you?" Lydia stood up. "C'mon. We're going back to that dojo so I can kill him."

"Lydia—"

"C'mon. I'm a federal agent now, I can kill the *cabrón* and just make up a reason."

"Lydia, *stop*! Sit down, please!"

Reluctantly, Lydia did so, grabbing her tequila and slamming two-thirds of it with one gulp.

"Please don't do anything crazy. You—you don't understand the following Ken has."

Recalling her dive-bombing around the World Wide Web for stuff on the so-called grandmaster, Lydia said, "Yeah, I do. I just don't give a shit."

"Well, I have to. Fine, you go beat him up or shoot him or whatever. Then what? Even if you get your military buddies to cover it up, I'm still stuck here. Ethan and the other black belts will come after me."

"Then fight them."

"I *can't*. Not all of them."

Lydia stared at the woman who had been the source of her strength for her entire tumultuous adolescence. "Fuck, Yona, you—This can't be fucking happening! When *Mami* died and *Papi* disappeared, you were there. You got me into the dojo, you got me out of trouble, you got me in the damn SEALs! You can't be broken like this, you just—"

Yona put a hand on Lydia's and looked into her eyes again. "Just go back to your life, okay?"

"And just leave you behind? Fuck that shit, *chica*. Kaicho may have been the teacher at the dojo, but you? You were my real sensei. At the very least, I want a piece of those assholes tomorrow night."

"No, don't, you'll only make it worse. Remember what Kaicho always said? Once you get into a fight, you've already lost. Well, I tried fighting, and I lost."

"Bullshit. There's a way to win. Put his ass away."

"And how do I do that?"

"How the fuck do you think? Fill out a police report. Then get your boss to go on TV and tell the nation how one of his staffers was molested by two black belts."

"I—I can't. They'll crucify me, tell everyone that I was mad because I didn't get a black belt and made up the accusation. They've *done* this before, Lydia."

"So what? If nobody says anything, he'll keep doing it."

"He'll keep doing it anyhow." Yona looked away. "Just leave it alone, okay?"

"I can't. Because you didn't leave me alone when I beat the shit out of José Alvarez. You gave me another chance. Now it's my turn for you. Tomorrow night, when he's busy running the fighting class? Go to MPD HQ and fill out a complaint."

Yona was shaking her head. "I can't fight him."

"Alone, no. But you've got a congressman for a boss, you've got me, and you've got the Miami Police Department, if you actually give them something to work with. Maybe it won't work, but if you don't make the effort, you won't get the success."

For several seconds, Yona just stared at Lydia.

Altogether, there are twenty-seven women in Martinez's pilot program. The congresswoman is a realist: she knows that between 80 and 90 percent of the people who sign up for the grueling one-and-a-half-year SEAL training wash out. That's why she's only angling for a single fire team, which is usually four or five sailors. Eight fire teams in a squad, four squads in a troop, three troops in a team. She thinks this is realistic.

You think it's nuts, and you don't think you've got a chance.

But you also remember what Kaicho Bill said that first day at the dojo in Marathon: Without the effort, the success will never come.

So you make the effort.

A year and a half later, you've passed SQT, along with four others: Helene Lagdamen, Dorian Michaeli, Dayana Copeland, and Luci Ousmanova. The congresswoman has her fire team.

Grandmaster Ken had looked dubiously upon Lydia when she arrived at the dojo and gone straight to the changing room. Upon seeing the symbol of Kaicho Bill's dojo on her *gi*, he was even more dismissive. "This is a *fight* class, not a ballet class like what that old man taught."

"You know what else he taught? Respect."

"Respect is earned, little girl."

"Call me 'little girl' again, and I guarantee you won't earn mine."

There were an even number of students, so Ken didn't participate in the fighting, though he did put on protective gear anyhow.

At first, he paired her up with low-level fighters, white belts and lower belts who were new to sparring. They were all long on enthusiasm and short on technique, and Lydia worked with them, encouraged them to throw combinations and keep their hands up.

By the halfway point, one of the purple belts was limping and needed to stop fighting. At that point, Master Ken started joining the fights.

She overheard several people talking about what a strong, smart fighter this Lydia woman was.

So finally, Ken teamed her with Ethan.

KEITH R. A. DeCANDIDO

"Your turn to go the fuck down, cunt."

Lydia somehow managed not to laugh in his face.

She spent most of three minutes of fighting on the defensive. Ethan was fast and strong, but had no discipline, and telegraphed every move. Lydia saw every long punch, every awkwardly set-up kick, and every unimaginative combination coming a mile off.

Ethan grew more and more frustrated, because his techniques got sloppier. He also tried shin kicks and knee kicks and groin kicks, as well as punches to her head.

Nothing landed.

Ten seconds before the buzzer would signal the end of the round, Lydia finally went on the offensive.

Two seconds before the buzzer went off, Ethan was on the floor clutching his belly and trying very hard to breathe.

Ken went to check Ethan out, but after a quick glance, he bore down on Lydia. "Lucky shot."

"He was lucky he didn't try to duck. I was going for his solar plexus, and if he ducked, my kick would've cracked a rib."

Snorting derisively, Ken said, "You're fighting me next."

Lydia just smiled.

Ken was a much better fighter than Ethan. His punches were shorter and sharper, his kicks faster, his combinations more imaginative. Lydia struggled to keep pace, popping a few jabs and moving around quickly.

Then she went on the offensive.

First was the right hook punch toward his head, which he easily blocked, then she followed with a left uppercut to his solar plexus and a joint kick to his right shin.

Grandmaster Ken fell to the floor, sweat pouring from his face, teeth gritted in an obvious attempt to not scream in pain.

"She cheated!"

"How'd she do that?"

"That wasn't a fair fight, she must've done something."

"Stupid twat!"

Lydia turned to the men gathering around Ken with concern and said, "That's Chief Petty Officer Twat to you. It's the rank the navy gave me when I joined the SEALs."

"Fuck you, bitch, you ain't no SEAL."

Several of the fighters then started to move toward her.

She caught her breath, trying very hard to psych herself up. The fight with Ken was brutal, and even though these guys individually were no match for her, if they all ganged up on her, particularly as tired as she was . . .

But then the door to the dojo opened and six police officers walked in.

"Everybody hold still, don't move!" one shouted, holding up a piece of paper. "I've got a warrant for the arrest of Kenneth Coffey and Ethan Shaw."

When you pass SQT, there are four congratulatory emails waiting for you. One is from your former bunkmate, Taylor Benson, who washed out of SEAL training. One is from Kaicho Bill. One is from the congresswoman.

But the one that matters is the one from Yona. It just reads, I always knew you could do it, *chica.*

Yona came into the Schooner Wharf, where Lydia was waiting with a tequila and a strawberry margarita. To Lydia's relief, Yona did *not* reek of cigarette smoke, though she did light up when she sat at the bar.

"How you doing, *chica?*" Lydia asked.

"I had to change my cell number and get a new email address because of all the death threats. I can't even look at the Internet right now. Congressman Nieto has hired security for me."

"I saw his press conference." Lydia smiled. "Told you that would work."

"It's a nightmare. It's a fucking nightmare." She licked the salt and then gulped down a quarter of her margarita. "But I feel better than I've felt since Kaicho died. It's gonna suck, but it sucked before and nothing was getting done. Now, at least, people know just what kind of man Ken is. And maybe more women will come forward."

"I hope so." Lydia sipped her tequila. "I gotta get back to D.C. I got a call from my boss this afternoon, and they're sending a private jet to come get me at the airport."

"Fancy." Yona dragged on her cigarette, then put it out unfinished. "Thank you, Lydia."

"Just doing the same thing some fucking crazy lady did for me once upon a time."

"Watch your language, *chica.*"

"Don't call me *chica*, bitch." She raised a glass. "To Kaicho."

"*Osu.*"

They clinked their glasses and drank.

ABOUT THE AUTHOR

Keith R. A. DeCandido is a second-degree black belt in karate (he both teaches and trains) and has spent an inordinate amount of time in Key West, so this story comes from the heart. Other tales of his taking place in the Keys include "We Seceded Where Others Failed" in *Altered States of the Union*, the *Mack Bolan, Executioner* novel *Deep Recon*, "Raymond's Room" in *Doctor Who: Missing Pieces*, and a series of stories featuring Cassie Zukav, weirdness magnet, in the anthologies *Apocalypse 13*, *Bad-Ass Faeries: It's Elemental*, *A Baker's Dozen of Magic*, *Out of Tune*, *Tales from the House Band*, vols. 1 and 2, and *TV Gods: Summer Programming*, the online zines *Buzzy Mag* and *Story of the Month Club*, and the collections *Ragnarok and Roll: Tales of Cassie Zukav, Weirdness Magnet* and *Without a License: The Fantastic Worlds of Keith R. A. DeCandido*. Other recent work includes the Marvel *Tales of Asgard* trilogy, featuring Thor, Sif, and the Warriors Three; *Stargate SG-1: Kali's Wrath*; *Heroes Reborn: Save the Cheerleader, Destroy the World*; *A Furnace Sealed*; *Mermaid Precinct*; three novellas in his *Super City Cops* series; and stories in *Aliens: Bug Hunt*, *Baker Street Irregulars*, *Limbus Inc.* Book III, *Nights of the Living Dead*, *V-Wars: Night Terrors*, *The X-Files: Trust No One*, and others. Find out less at his cheerfully retro website, www.DeCandido.net.

WHITE FLAME ON A SUNDAY

A JOE LEDGER AND DEACON CHALK YARN BY JAMES R. TUCK

Yeah, I know Joe Ledger.

Intense motherfucker he is, and if *I'm* saying that you know it's the gospel truth.

Let me reel that in a bit, I don't *know* Joe Ledger. We aren't going out and doing bourbon shots to celebrate special occasions or taking long walks on the beach, but we worked together once and he more than had my back. In my line of work, that's fucking gold.

What happened?

Pull up a chair, pour a drink, and I'll tell it.

It all started in a shitty abandoned warehouse on the Southside of town outside the airport. Atlanta's a lovely city, my hometown and all, but down by the airport it goes to hell. Local politics here have left us with miles and miles of lost real estate. Empty warehouses, abandoned mills, houses falling in on themselves. We ain't Detroit, or even Memphis, but we have our bad side of town, as most cities do.

I'd picked up a tip that the White Flame had been active in Atlanta and they were targeting a shady deal happening on the Southside.

And when an ancient Sumerian blood cult that just won't die sets up in my town you best believe I'm looking into it. The White Flame are like rats, they multiply faster than you can kill them. They've been around for thousands of years doing evil shit. I don't know a lot about them. That's not my gig, I have people for that. They deal in dark magick and human sacrifice, and that's all I need to know to put a foot up the ass of whatever plans they have.

I followed that tip to a shithole place that used to make paint and now just stood on a kudzu-covered lot. Kudzu really will eat abandoned buildings. Kids here learn if you find a huge section of the shit, be careful because there's something rotting underneath. Go climbing in it and you wind up falling forty feet into a dilapidated building you couldn't even see.

So there I was, crouched in the dark behind some big mixing vat in the corner of the warehouse. It smelled like old latex and made my eyes burn, but I had a good view of the meet so I wasn't moving.

No, I am not telling you how I know what old latex smells like.

The middle of the warehouse opened to an old loading dock, a big open space in front of what once was a rolling steel door. The door had fallen, or been torn down, and hung on to one side of the steel frame like a rusted curtain. Two pickup trucks had been pulled inside, real redneck-mobiles, jacked tires, rebel-flag bumper stickers, the whole nine yards. Four shitkickers stood by them. Two of the fellas were big hunks of meat, heads gleaming in the late afternoon sun that streamed in the open bay doors. Beefy arms full of jailhouse ink hung out of their T-shirts. Red suspenders and white laces in their boots put them as white pride assholes and not ashamed of it. I hate skinheads.

Nazi fucktards.

The other two with them were older, could have been their dads, maybe uncles. Both of them wore BDUs and had full heads of hair. The one on the left's shirt had letters big enough for me to read from my vantage point.

It said WHITE MAKES RIGHT.

Goddamn idiots.

Across from them stood everything they hated.

Big Jolly and his crew.

A real piece of work, Big Jolly, selling some shit he had no business selling to some dumbasses who had no business buying it. Big Jolly wasn't jolly at all, he was a ruthless bastard with a real cruel streak, but he came by the "Big" part of his name honestly. Big Jolly was a hefty sonuvabitch. Pushing 450 pounds at well under six feet, he was nearly as wide as he was tall. Lumber as a verb, not a noun. His suit lay over him like a tarp on a pile of garbage, tucking into folds and creases his mass made against itself. His crew was international and interracial. Three hard cases from three different continents probably here on exile for crimes against humanity.

Everybody packed heat.

The rednecks had a pair of pump shotguns and three handguns amongst them. Big Jolly's crew were strapped, the Jamaican, in particular, holding a Mini-14 capable of slinging lead across the whole place if cut loose.

I was also strapped, you know I'm always strapped, but all their guns made me wish I'd put on the ballistic vest Tiff kept trying to get me to wear. But it was too hot to wear in the Georgia humidity, and most of the things I go against don't use bullets.

It was a weird thought, even for a moment, considering the possibility of dying without wanting to and going on to be with my family. It made my stomach turn sour, so I pushed it aside.

I'm good at that. Been doing it for years.

But if I caught a bullet from one of these yahoos, Tiff would be pissed.

Back to work.

I couldn't hear what was being said, I was too far for that, but I could see one of the older rednecks gesture and Big Jolly lift up the backpack he held.

It was a plain, dark gray backpack, like millions of people use every day. No markings on it, nothing to make it stand out. Generic. Damn near invisible if left in a busy area.

The best thing that could possibly be in that pack was drugs.

I had a shit feeling it wasn't drugs.

I wasn't there for that. My target was the White Flame and whatever they were going to do. I'm not law enforcement, I'm an occult bounty hunter. Fancy way of saying I hunt monsters for a living. Regular criminals I leave to the people who signed up for that.

But I'm not an asshole, I was going to take that pack out of play no matter what.

One of the skinheads pulled a duffel bag from the bed of one of the trucks and carried it over toward Big Jolly when the first creep of magick slid across the back of my neck.

One of my guns was out and in my right hand.

The magick rolled around me like a sticky fog in a shitty nightclub, that machine-generated bullshit that just coats your skin with a layer of chemicals that feel like movie popcorn butter. I couldn't get a pin-point on it, my ability is a bastard like that, all impression and slippery sensory clues, nothing specific, all of it wildly inconsistent, like spidey-sense that's drunk. Sometimes it pisses me off, but it's saved my ass more than once.

The White Flame was in the house, doing some magick shit, but I didn't know what yet.

The skinhead with the duffel bag unzipped it and held it open. It was full of crumpled money.

Big Jolly nodded and began swaying forward, holding out the backpack.

That's when the cultist tried to cut my head off.

I felt it more than saw it, the long wavy blade swinging out of the dark. I jerked away and dropped, my head hitting the vat in front of me, flashing a sharp jolt of pain across the backs of my eyes, but the flame knife missed me. I rolled, eyes watering, to find a cultist wrapped in black cloth swinging the blade back toward me.

My finger twitched three times and the .45 kicked three times, spitting lead into the center of him. He kept swinging, the flame knife dropping as he did, but it was just momentum. He was gone before he fell.

My ears buzzed inside as I turned back around, the reactionary earplugs I had in shut down from the boom of my pistol.

The meeting area had become a bloodbath.

Two dozen black-clad cultists had dropped from the shadows and began cutting people down. Already one of the skinheads lay on the floor, sliced open from throat to hip. His killer knelt beside his twitch-ing body, shoving his hands in the open wound, drawing them out covered in blood and gore, and then using that blood to write out weird symbols on the cement floor.

Two of Big Jolly's men had fallen as well, cultists beside them, paint-ing with their blood.

Every line they scrawled, the magick in the air began to close around me, tightening like a noose.

Big Jolly sat on the ground clutching the backpack, his last man standing over him and using the Mini-14 to keep the cultists off his boss. He fired in three-round bursts, but his eyes were so wide they looked as though they would pop out and he couldn't hit anything at all. Slowly the cultists closed in.

The remaining rednecks had guns out, shooting everywhere.

In the back of my skull came that twinge about not having a vest, but I was already moving and so I ignored it and concentrated on picking targets.

I dropped the cultists who were drawing symbols first, ending whatever fuck-shit spell they were conjuring. One bullet per, easy to hit because they weren't moving. The rest of them weren't standing still.

Shooting people isn't easy, especially when they are hopped up on drugs or magick or both, in service to their ancient blood cult leaders. You're flinging a few ounces of lead at them, riding a fucking explosion; just get a few degrees off target and you'll miss entirely.

Still moving forward, I took three more cultists before my slide locked back.

Thumb the magazine release, let it fall, and have another one in before it hits the ground.

Practice.

In that three seconds, the cultists took the other rednecks.

Cut them down, hit their knees, and began drawing in their blood while the rest turned toward Big Jolly and his last henchman. I hit them from behind just as they closed in, slamming my body into cultists as I fired into them at point-blank range. I was too close, didn't aim, just shoved the gun forward and pulled the trigger.

I pushed my way through as Big Jolly's henchman caught a flame knife in the gut and folded in on himself. The cultist that stabbed him pulled the blade out with a hard jerk that split the man just above his hips. A gout of blood splashed onto the cement, spattering up on Big Jolly. The cultist immediately dropped to his knees and began painting in the gore and the guts.

I kicked him in the face, making him snap back and lie flat on the ground in the puddle of blood. I spun, boots slipping on the wet cement, and found my gun locked back and empty again.

This is where Joe Ledger comes in.

He strode in through the bay door like the fucking Terminator, spine straight, shoulders locked, and holding an M4 carbine pressed to his cheek. With each step he took, he popped a cultist. Double-tap motherfuckers.

Head shots almost every one.

The cultists began falling around me like Pentecostals at a tent revival.

One came by me like liquid shadow, and I turned just in time to see him disappearing into the shadows.

Holding the backpack.

When I turned back I was face-to-face with the barrel of a semiautomatic rifle.

The man on the other side of it stood in the ring of people he had just killed, their blood drying on his boots, and kept his gun pointed at me.

"What are you going to do now, Cowboy?" I said.

The eye of his I could see opened in surprise. "What did you say?"

"You might be surprised to know that this isn't the first time I've had a gun pointed in my face."

"Who do you work for?"

I weighed my options. I could've said the OCID, but it's a shadow organization and I'm more an independent contractor than an employee. I went with, "Freelance. What about you?"

"Department of Military Sciences."

"Military? That explains the G.I. Joe vibe."

He lowered the rifle and sniffed. "Freelance explains the Dog the Bounty Hunter vibe."

"You saved my ass a minute ago, so I'll let that slide."

"Wasn't an insult, just a reference. Like yours."

Keep telling yourself that.

Behind me, Big Jolly sat crying, big chest rolling with strangely muted sobs that lifted his entire upper body with their intensity. He began to roll over to climb to his feet. The man swung his rifle that way.

"Stay on your ass until I tell you to move."

Big Jolly nodded and rolled back onto his ass. His suit squelched in the blood puddled around him.

Moving deliberately, I pulled another magazine from the row of pouches under my arm and reloaded. The man just watched me with flat eyes, not raising the rifle. Locked, cocked, and ready to rock, I slid the gun back into its holster.

"What's your name?" he asked.

"Deacon Chalk."

"Seriously?"

I get that sometimes. "Yeah, it's the South."

"I know a guy goes by Deacon."

"I don't go by it. That's my name."

"He's a prick sometimes."

"Then he's half stepping. I was born an asshole and just got bigger."

He looked up at me. "Joe Ledger."

"Pleased to meetcha."

He let go of the rifle, and it slid around his body on the strap to hang behind him. He'd be able to have it ready in a blink. He nudged one of the dead cultists with the toe of his boot. "So, Deacon, what's going on with these ninja-looking assholes?"

"White Flame," I answered.

He grunted. "I didn't know they had moved down here."

"Yep, everybody comes to the South."

"Muggy here."

I shrugged. "Be glad it's not pollen season."

His hand swept, indicating the dead bodies. "Hell of a welcome."

"Just for you," I said. "So what are *you* doing here?"

"Got wind Big Jolly here was trying to sell a suitcase nuke to the Heritage Militia, which I assume are these four examples of the laces-and-braces battalion. They planned to use it to kick off a race war. Thought I'd spoil their action."

"Fuck."

"What?"

"One of the White Flame assholes got the backpack from chubs and took off before I could stop him."

Ledger's face went dark and he stepped around me, moving with purpose toward Big Jolly. Three steps and he was on the fat man, dropping to one knee and grabbing Jolly's hanging jowl. Jolly screamed and Ledger yanked on the flesh between his fingers. "Shut the fuck up."

Jolly quit screaming as if his throat had been slit.

Ledger leaned in and growled, "Don't lie, not even a little. Is that nuke real?"

"I . . . I . . . I didn't make it!"

Ledger jerked Jolly's face hard to emphasize each word. "Is. It. Real?"

"Yes! Yes, it's real! It's real!"

Ledger pushed Jolly away and stood. "We have a fucking problem."

No shit, Sherlock.

It took longer to hike to the car than it should have because Big Jolly moved like a conversion van with two broken axles. I'd parked a few streets over from the warehouse, about a half mile away. Big Jolly was a florid color of purple and soaked through with sweat by the time we got there. Ledger had pulled some zip ties from somewhere by his belt and cinched Jolly's hands in front of him. There was no way he could have done it behind him, not as big as he was. After much huffing and puffing on his part, we turned the corner and there it was, long and lean and badass to the bone. My car. A hopped-up Mercury Comet with a motor that runs like a scalded dog.

"That's us," I said, hitting the unlock button on my key fob.

"Nice ride," Ledger said. "Sixty-nine?"

"Sixty-six."

"Nice." He nodded. "Pretty small back seat."

"Two steps ahead of you." I pushed another button on the fob that popped the trunk.

Big Jolly protested the whole way, but he went. The car sank four inches as he rolled himself into the trunk. I shut the lid.

"That's a big trunk," Ledger said.

"It's a six-body."

"Or a one-Jolly."

"Yep."

Ledger put his phone away. I don't know who he was talking to, someone at the DMS—fucking government agencies and their fucking initials—but his face was grim. I could have called Tiff or Heck over at the OCID, but Ledger wanted to avoid any interjurisdictional logistics, so he called his crew and sent them over pictures of the symbols the cultists had been painting.

"Early Mesopotamia."

"The fuck does that mean?" I asked.

"It's where the symbols are from."

"That's a real shit clue."

"Yeah, it doesn't narrow it down. My people will keep cycling through them until they get closer, but for now, four-thousand-year-old symbols are all we have."

"Four thousand?"

"Yeah."

I started the Comet with a roar and dropped it in gear. "I know a guy."

* * *

The man looked at Ledger's phone with twinkling eyes. His thin fingers reached up and adjusted the wire-framed glasses on his face.

The glasses were all he wore.

We were outside his house in a small courtyard, surrounded by a tall privacy fence. It sat on a large plot of land outside the metro area that was shared by a commune. Acheron's Grove was a vaguely Lovecraftian nudist colony run by Philben, the man in front of us.

He was a late-fifties-style English professor type with slightly stooped shoulders over a not insignificant paunch. A lot of people get uncomfortable being nude, but Philben was as unaffected as a house cat. We'd passed many of his people on our way in, all of them nude, and none of them seemed even remotely bothered by us, no matter their age, shape, or appearance. Philben fronted the money for it all, allowing the free spirits under his care the ability to be free indeed, no job or bills to worry about.

Philben claimed to be almost four thousand years old.

Probably full of shit, but there's always the off-chance.

"Very interesting," he said.

"What do they mean?" I asked. He was my referral, so I felt I should take point.

He handed the phone back to Ledger and closed his eyes. "It's been a long time since I've seen that language. Let me process it."

While we waited I studied Ledger. He was a stone-faced sonuvabitch, no betrayal of his emotions, if there were any. He could have been an android waiting for someone to turn him on. A woman came in and went to a bookshelf. She was young, late twenties, and comely. A nice figure on her and a pretty face. She adhered to the dress code of the commune and it agreed with her. Because of Tiff, I felt no pull toward her. I didn't know what Ledger's romantic situation was, hell, he could be gay, but he didn't even flick his eyes in her direction.

After she left with a stack of books under her arm, Philben finally opened his eyes. "I don't understand."

"What don't you understand?"

"These sigils are a summoning for an ancient deity named *Doar' Kun Shinnahleth*."

"English."

"Loose translation is the Crushing Eldritch."

"Don't know that one," I said.

Philben waved his fingers. "A Sumerian sect worshipped it long ago.

It's an elephantine god who will one day destroy the world by stampeding across it, using its immensity to press humanity into a sweet wine for its consumption."

"Sounds kind of fucking ridiculous," Ledger said.

Philben frowned. "The Sumerians were given to excess. They did imagine things, make them up from nothing but debauched imaginings. This deity isn't one of those, it is real, but to try a working focused on it is sheer folly."

"Why?" I asked.

"A god of this magnitude, well, it is just impossible to call. You are completely wasting your time."

"So, these assholes are spinning their wheels?"

"Yes," Philben said, "they cannot conjure this entity."

Ledger frowned. "Why do you say that?"

Philben sighed. "A thing of this size would require a matching sacrifice to call it to this plane of reality. It only responds to bloodshed and death and destruction on a massive scale."

"How many would have to be killed?" I asked.

Philben squinted away at nothing and scratched his face, then his balls, then his face again. "A half a million at least."

"Well, fuck," Ledger said.

We were back in the Comet, zipping up the highway at a high clip and driving right into a brilliant sunset of pink and orange and red. Ledger hung up his phone again.

"Apparently that's what my guys needed."

"What is?"

"That this thing revolves around death on a large scale and is an elephant."

"An elephant." I shook my head. "Cults and the shit they think."

"They still have a nuke and a shitload of belief. It doesn't matter how far afield it is after that."

"True." I'm a dyed-in-the-wool, cradle Catholic. I've seen a lot of fucked-up shit, but it always reinforces my belief instead of destroying it.

"So where can we find elephants in Atlanta?" Ledger asked. "The circus in town?"

"No, but we have a world-class zoo." Sliding my thumb across my phone, I found Jimmy the Zookeeper's contact info and hit the green call sign.

The Atlanta Zoo is a different place after hours. Trust me, I once had to hunt down a stray Nosferatu up in there, the place gets kind of weird.

Maybe it's that I'm a city guy and all the fake forestry and jungle environs just give me the heebie-jeebies in the dark.

I was hunkered down beside a display, gun out. Behind me I could hear dull splashing as the alligators and crocodiles and whatever other big-ass lizard they put in a cement holding pond swam around and crawled over each other.

Every so often one of them would make a low sound, like a grunting bellow that rumbled across the entire area, and it would crawl up in the back of my brain and live there.

The oppressive taint of magick already had my skin feeling as if I'd been rubbed down with acid, that damn noise really set my teeth on edge.

"It's me."

I didn't jump, not on the outside, but I had to clamp down on myself to keep from swinging my gun around. "You are one sneaky sonuvabitch."

Ledger grinned. "I've cleared the path, but we need to move, now."

He turned away silently.

Jimmy hadn't answered his cell, so I'd called his wife. She hadn't heard from him. This sent me and Ledger straight to the zoo. It was after hours, the park empty of patrons and employees, but the moment we turned on the road I felt the magick working that had begun. Because of Ledger we'd infiltrated our way this deep inside without detection. Left to my own devices I would have pulled the Comet up in the gate and driven to the elephant enclosure. It's my way. I'm not a soldier.

Joe Ledger is a fucking soldier.

He acts like one and has the skills of one. I'm a thug. A goddamn gorilla with a purpose. I break shit to do good.

Usually it works out, but sometimes it has consequences.

The nightclub I used to own, now burned to the ground.

Friendships.

Kat . . . fuck. It cost Kat everything.

It cost Tiff her eye.

Fuck.

Fuck.

Give me a minute.

Pour another shot.

Okay.

So, with Jimmy the Zookeeper unaccounted for, the magick so cloying thick in the air I could barely breathe, and all of that guilt I keep shoved in the back of my skull, I followed Ledger's lead and went into stealth mode.

We crept along the pathway toward the elephant enclosure. Halfway there Ledger pointed to the ground and we stepped over a black-robed cultist he'd taken out earlier. He knelt and parted the foliage and we were looking into the enclosure from across the way.

The place looked like a movie set full of extras.

How the fuck did an ancient blood cult have what looked like fifty or sixty members in this day and age?

Jimmy lay on the ground in a circle of cultists, these wearing red robes and holding weird hatchets in their hands. He was tied hand to foot. His hair still swept up and back into the massive mullet he rocked with abandon. Even in the dark I could see his eye swollen shut over the gag stuffed into his mouth.

He'd gone down swinging.

Good for him.

More cultists stood around the elephant, who had been put on its knees in front of what had to be the high priest in a white robe. The mighty beast knelt there, its massive head drooping, resting on short shorn tusks. Black eyes shone in the light, glassy. They must have doped the creature to make it so passive.

The high priest held a claymore sword, its four-foot steel blade sweeping up and over his shoulder, where he let it lie as he gestured and spoke in some weird version of language—Sumerian, I assumed. The longer he spoke the tighter the band around my skull became.

He was heading toward the finale.

A short podium stood next to him and on it a black box. Slim and sleek, it just sat there, unassuming.

"I don't see a trigger," Ledger said.

I shrugged. It wasn't my area of expertise.

"I could drop him from here, but if he has a dead man's switch or someone else has the trigger then it'll do no good."

"We don't have much time," I said.

He nodded, taking my word for it.

With a flourish, the high priest screamed out a guttural sound and swung the claymore over his head.

I was pushing through the foliage, moving toward the high priest, when I heard Ledger say: "Gotcha, motherfucker." One second before his gun went off.

I cleared a short rise of dirt and saw one of the cultists, this one in a yellow robe with a widening red stain, lying on the ground bonelessly. Six inches from his outstretched hand lay a black tube that looked like a flashlight with a button on top.

The trigger.

I wasn't going to touch it, but I wasn't going to let anyone else, either. Two long strides and it was at my feet. Then I started shooting motherfuckers in robes.

I dropped the high priest first as he ran toward me with his sword. Two quick shots in his chest turned his robe pink from the inside. He stumbled past me as the life ran out of him. The sword fell and stuck in the ground, jolting him to a stop until he slewed sideways and collapsed.

Cultists swarmed in confusion, looking for someone to hurt. I jerked my head around, watching in all directions. Any of them that started my way, I put down, so close that aiming became instinctive. Pull the trigger, pivot, acquire target, pull the trigger; pivot, acquire target, rinse and repeat; eject magazines when empty and replace them as fast as possible.

Cultists tried to circle me, but they were disrupted by Ledger coming up firing into them. Every time they would slide into formation, a formation that would easily take me down if they charged, Ledger popped another one.

I didn't know how much ammunition Ledger had left, but I was running low. You can only carry so many backup magazines. Once I was out, I would have just my backup gun from the small of my back, with its six bullets.

After that, I was going for the claymore.

The cultists had stopped trying to close in, their numbers shredded but still more than ours. They seethed on the other side of a short field of their fallen brothers. Ledger stepped beside me, scooping up the trigger as he did. One quick hand motion and he had the thing in two pieces. Lowering his head, he brought the wires inside to his mouth and bit through a yellow one, pulling it loose with a jerk of his head.

He spit the wire out and dropped the trigger into the dirt. "There. One less thing to worry about."

He holstered his gun.

"What are you doing?"

He grinned. "I'm out."

I raised my Colt. "My last clip."

He tilted his head behind me. "Save it."

I turned my head to find the elephant climbing to its feet. On its back was one rightfully pissed-off Jimmy the Zookeeper, his face twisted in rage, his hair twisted like a tornado. He gave a rebel yell and leaned forward over the elephant's forehead, pointing toward the cultists. The elephant stumbled a little, obviously groggy, but those big black eyes locked on the ones who tried to kill it, and from where we stood I could see that this mighty creature knew and it was going to deliver retribution. Even as the elephant tripped forward, it picked up speed, charging the cultists like a runaway freight train.

Robes are terrible for running away in a panic, all trippy and tangly.

Some of them made it.

Most didn't.

"This has been a really weird day," Ledger said.

I shrugged as we watched Jimmy ride the elephant across the paddock, knocking over cultists like bowling pins. "Not overly."

I pulled the Comet up to the entrance of the Atlanta airport and left it running as we got out. I didn't ask how Ledger was going to fly with the M4 he had in a bag over his shoulder. Being affiliated with a secret military organization has its benefits. We stood at the back of the car and shook hands.

"I'm sure we'll run into each other again," Ledger said.

"More than likely."

We held each other's grips for a moment. I don't do good-byes very well. I wasn't choked up or anything, they've just always been foreign to me.

We'd just let go when a noise from the trunk made us both look. Oh. Damn.

I went around and popped the lid.

The smell that rolled out was atrocious.

Big Jolly blinked up at us. He'd been in there for over ten hours.

He'd had to go to the bathroom about five hours before this.

He smelled like a chicken-processing plant on a hot summer day.

"That is *your* problem," I told Ledger.

He grimaced and hauled Jolly up and out of my car. "I'll give him to TSA to hose off."

"I'll send you a bill for cleaning my trunk," I said as he walked away, pushing Big Jolly in front of him.

"You do that."

ABOUT THE AUTHOR

James R. Tuck writes the *Deacon Chalk* series and the *Robin Hood: Demon's Bane* series (with Debbie Viguie) and edits anthologies such as *Mama Tried: Crime Fiction Inspired by Outlaw Country Music*. He also writes the *Mythos* series as Levi Black. He's on the Internet, look him up.

WET TUESDAY

BY DAVID FARLAND

THE WAREHOUSE, DEPARTMENT OF MILITARY SCIENCES FIELD OFFICE,
BALTIMORE, MARYLAND; SUNDAY, NOVEMBER 16, 2014, 7:03 AM

*Some people are too evil to live. I know because I work with them every day.
Take this case just a few days ago.*

"This had better be critical," I groused, "waking me on a *Sunday*
morning." My head throbbed dully from the aftermath of last night's
party.

Church stood at my door beneath a black umbrella. He looked past-
ier than normal, as if he'd grown five years older in the past day. His
lack of sympathy for my hangover carried in his tone. "Got a dead
Saudi prince." He handed me a photo fresh off the AP newswire.

I squinted at it.

I'd seen what was left after car bombs before. Usually a fractured
frame from a car, lots of smoke stains full of the explosive's residue,
and a charred corpse or two. What remained of the prince's stretch
limo and its passengers resembled a can of diced tomatoes that'd been
blown up over a bonfire. Too many body parts for just one person.

"Looks like the prince isn't the only one who got face time with
Allah," I said.

"Whole family," Church confirmed. "Two wives and four or five
kids. Detonated in downtown Riyadh."

The Kingdom Centre loomed in the background, a distinctive tower
with a top like a strange crown. I'd had lunch there once. I could

never see that crown without thinking that the eye of Sauron should have been gleaming from its center.

"In the heart of the city? Holy shit!"

Now, one fewer rich Saudi oil-monger in the world is no skin off my ass, but when you drag women, children, and innocent bystanders into it, that's a different story. "Sounds like somebody was being made an example of," I said. "What'd he do to torque off the local Wahhabis, give financial backing to some American porn producer?"

Church shrugged. "Here's the kicker, Captain. It was a self-driven car, no chauffeur."

He gave me a second to let it click. We hadn't seen that one before—a new death delivery system. There's an arms race that has been going on for thousands of years, from the time that man invented the first club, to spear-throwers, to . . . well, this. A new death delivery system. The thing is, I saw the potential instantly. Back in the Middle East, suicide bombs are popular. It makes a statement: *I hate you so much, I'm willing to kill myself to be rid of you.* You've got to be a true believer to be a suicide bomber—and an asshole. But for the past few years, a lot of these suicides have been committed by kids—twelve or thirteen. The jihadists fill the young boys with bloodlust, maybe inject them with a bit of heroin, and then aim them at an embassy or military compound. Half the kids don't even know how to drive, so the jihadists tape their foot to the gas.

But the kids get scared, and sometimes they try to drive the wrong way, or they get shot while trying to break through a checkpoint.

Self-driven cars would allay that problem, take out the human dynamic. And a big truck could carry massive payloads.

Church said dryly, "Looks like we've got a terrorist who's taken his childhood fascination with remote-controlled cars to a whole new level. I need you to shut him down."

Now, I don't like terrorists, but I admire them sometimes, the way you can admire a jaguar in the jungle, all full of deadly grace. I imagined my target that way.

"I'm guessing you want it done now?"

"With this kind of terrorist," Church said, "there's always a ticking bomb waiting to go off. We don't know what targets might be lined up, but I want the killing spree stopped. Now would be good." Church smiled, and I smiled in return.

This was already feeling up close and personal.

Ashley slipped me one of her *come-on* glances as she placed a folder, stamped with TOP SECRET and a couple of compartmented code words, on my desk. "Here's the latest from the CIA, Joe. I included links to a handful of videos."

Somehow, knowing that Ashley wasn't getting her Sunday off, either, made me feel better. She didn't appear sleep-deprived. A lot of top researchers are like that—half machine—but she was special.

She had platinum-blond hair that drifted like sunlit fog to her nicely rounded butt and swayed enticingly as she walked; sapphire eyes as deep as cenotes in the Yucatán, so wide they gave her a perpetual expression of mild surprise; and a wardrobe of blouses that fit like second skins, hugging in exactly the right places. Never mistake her for the stereotype blonde, however. Ashley is the Baltimore Field Office's top analytical researcher, and a deadeye with any firearm you hand her. She's outshot me on the range a couple of times, and *not* because I let her.

She also has a low purr of a voice that always sounds like a come-on. Something in my vitals stirred.

"Thanks, Ash." I returned the best smile I could muster under the circumstances. *Maybe when I wrap this up we can do something video-worthy ourselves*, I thought.

Her pursed lips and the glance over her shoulder as she sashayed away weren't exactly a turndown.

As usual, Ashley had been thorough. The fat folder she'd brought me contained maps; geo-coords; a page of photos with names, personal data, and high-value target ID numbers; and half a dozen black-and-white stills of a rambling, single-story building taken by Lockheed Martin's RQ-170 Sentinel. Developed by LM's Skunk Works specifically for the CIA and operated by the U.S. Air Force, the Sentinel collected much of the intel that had resulted in Osama bin Laden meeting his seventy-two virgins in May 2011.

Except this facility wasn't in Abbottabad, Pakistan, or Kandahar, Afghanistan. This building was identified as a technological research facility on the outskirts of the Syrian city of Al-Raqqah, capital of the northern Syrian governate, or province, of the same name. The CIA had confirmed that ISIS was using the place to create car bombs.

Conclusive proof of that came with the videos Ashley had provided. Though annoyingly jerky, they followed a trio of Middle Eastern men, middle-aged by their salt-and-pepper beards, as they sauntered along the kind of assembly line one would see in a DOD explosive ordnance plant. A great deal of gesticulating punctuated their muffled discussion.

The last video included white arrow markers and a voice-over by some spook linguist who called himself Mack. Yeah, I know, really imaginative. I kept thinking Dweeb and picturing the Napoleon character from that odd little movie made in Idaho a few years back. Nothing dynamite about this guy, however.

When the flighty camera managed to zoom in on each of the terrorists' faces for a couple seconds, Dweeb identified each man by name. None of the hot ISIS leaders one occasionally hears about in the news—when the news services actually admit that Islamist terrorism exists—but I knew who they were. I tried to adjust my monitor's focus. Or maybe my bleary eyes just needed adjusting.

Dweeb went on to explain, in a monotone as dry as a stale biscuit, that even with these state-of-the-art upgrades to their factory, the three scientists doubted they could produce sufficient car bombs in time.

In time for what?

That made my short hairs stand at attention and not just the ones on the back of my neck.

I watched eagerly as they went into a room where they had taken a mannequin and had fitted its head and arms with various gears so that it could move in a semi-realistic way. A red butch wig completed the description.

Shit, I thought. These guys weren't just rigging up cars to drive themselves, they were creating robot drivers so that they could fool any bystanders. All the better to get close to military checkpoints.

The kicker was, the mannequin was wearing a uniform: Royal Mail. I saw the joke immediately: *I've got a message for England.*

"Pay dirt," I told Church. "But these guys aren't settling for one lousy prince. Sounds like they're planning something big. Watch this." I showed him the video.

Church arched an eyebrow. "Time to deploy the fleet." Before I could ask what he meant by "the fleet," he ordered, "Contact Bug."

Jerome Taylor, known as Bug to everybody including his mother, is DMS's resident computer supergeek. He's also the undisputed nerd master of pop culture. That's actually proven useful on a few occasions.

"What did he mean by 'the fleet'?" I asked Bug via telecom a few minutes later. He's located at our headquarters based at Floyd Bennett Field in Brooklyn.

Bug grinned like a prankster about to pull off a practical joke. Obviously, *he* hadn't been out partying a few hours earlier. "Fly cams," he said.

I flashed a quizzical smile.

"Remember that hummingbird UAV our friends at DARPA announced in, what, 2011, 2012?" When I nodded, Bug said, "Well, they've taken it a step further. Several steps, including taking it operational. CIA's using them all over the Middle East, where houseflies are as thick as mosquitoes on a Louisiana bayou."

I couldn't resist. "How many of them have been swatted in the line of duty?"

"Only one so far," Bug said, "when it literally got in the face of its intended target."

That explained the random jerkiness of Dweeb's videos. I guess that was the price we'd have to pay for up-close-and-personal imagery intelligence.

THE WAREHOUSE, DEPARTMENT OF MILITARY SCIENCES FIELD OFFICE,
BALTIMORE, MARYLAND; SUNDAY, NOVEMBER 16, 2014, 5:28 PM

"Here you go, Cap," Bug said. His face filled the massive telecom screen on Church's office wall. "First feeds from Al-Raqqah Technological Research Facility."

Bug's face blinked out, to be replaced by . . . a bug's-eye view of a surprisingly modern laboratory.

"The fly's eyes are the camera's lenses," Bug said as our pest-sized drone made an initial reconnaissance loop around the spacious room. It jinked like a fighter pilot with pursuers on his six, and careened toward a turbaned man with a neatly trimmed beard.

The target absently waved our bug away with a hand bearing several heavy gold rings, and it swooped in toward a top-of-the-line, secure computer setup parked on a desk in a windowless corner.

"Indistinguishable from the real thing," Bug said from offscreen. I didn't miss the grin in his voice. "That's our lead scientist it just buzzed."

"Skip the sales pitch, Bug," I said, "and cut to the chase."

"Right." The screen blanked for a few seconds, then lit up with an over-the-shoulder view of our scientist at his computer. Metadata in the video's lower corner showed a time-hack a couple of hours after the opening recce shot. A log-in box, labeled in Arabic, glowed on the monitor, while lean, gold-ringed fingers darted across a keyboard. When one hand rose in a shooing motion near the guy's ear, the drone skated clear, maintaining its view of the hardware.

"Did you capture that?" I asked Bug when the log-in screen yielded to an austere email in-box, also in Arabic.

"Sure we got a freeze-frame," Bug said. "I gained access to our terrorist's system a few minutes after he walked away. His whole email account and the contents of his research files are now being analyzed and translated by our Arabic section. We should have results for you first thing tomorrow."

I nodded, and suddenly got a nervous feeling, as if someone were training a sniper rifle on the back of my head. I couldn't shake the feeling that . . . something was coming soon. "Get it to me sooner," I said. "Tomorrow might be too late."

THE WAREHOUSE, DEPARTMENT OF MILITARY SCIENCES FIELD OFFICE,
BALTIMORE, MARYLAND; MONDAY, NOVEMBER 17, 2014, 6:58 AM

I didn't even make it as far as my office before Church waved me into his. "Our friends lit up an embassy in Pakistan an hour ago."

"Their objective?"

Church's brows furrowed in an uncharacteristic way. "That, I'm not sure. I think it was just a field test, to see what they *can* do."

"I got a bad feeling about this," I said. "They've got a bigger game in play."

Church nodded in agreement. "First load from the translators just came in," he said. I hadn't heard that deep of a rumble in his voice or seen that hooded narrowing of his eyes since the second airliner hit the World Trade Center on 9/11.

"That bad?" I returned. I took a gulp from my coffee mug and swallowed before he said something that might prompt me to spray it all over his office.

"They've uncovered a veritable *Encyclopædia Britannica*," Church said, "but only two points matter to us. The ISIS bomb-makers are getting their driving robotics from a small company in Freiberg, Germany, and they're planning a massive attack in London."

"London?" A number of potential targets crossed my mind. Buckingham Palace, Westminster Abbey. "Do we know where?"

"The State Opening of Parliament," Church replied.

Good thing I'd swallowed my coffee.

"Are they hoping to take out the queen?"

"And as many members of the Houses of Lords and Commons, and civilians as they can. They're calling the operation Carmageddon."

"Lovely sense of humor," I growled.

Church gave a stiff nod. "They're planning to position large, self-driven trucks loaded with explosives close to Buckingham Palace and Westminster Parliament, and along the queen's route from one end to the other, and detonate them all at once."

"Holy shit!"

The State Opening usually takes place in May. I'd been in London for it once. I still remembered Londoners pressed six or seven deep against police barriers, children in front, of course, dressed in their Sunday best and waving miniature Union Jacks as the queen rolled by in her horse-drawn carriage. I had watched the parade under the keen eyes of British troops, and bobbies mounted on leggy bay horses. It looked as if the whole city had turned out.

I shook my head against horrific mental images. "Has the British government been informed?"

"Through appropriate channels," Church confirmed. "In the meantime, Captain, our jet is being prepped at BWI for a flight to Germany. Takeoff is four thirty this afternoon. You're to put a stop to this."

No guidance. Pretty much carte blanche. Church preferred it that way. If necessary he could fall back on the Sergeant Schultz defense: "I know noth-ink."

"I'll start packing," I said, "once I've called in a strike on that research facility." I considered some options. An MQ-9 Reaper carrying a couple of five-hundred-pound GBU-12s or GBU-38 JDAMs should do the job.

I'd want to hit them in the evening, light up the sky—shock-and-awe style.

DMS personnel don't use commercial airlines when we're on a mission. Ghost, my combat-trained white shepherd, dozed at my feet while I reviewed Ashley's info packet on the little company I'd be checking out in Freiberg.

Established five years ago by a former nun named Frieda Stoltz, Assistenzdienst, (Assistance Services, in English) designed and produced equipment and software apps to assist people with various disabilities, everything from blindness to quadriplegia. Sounded innocent enough. But was the company only a front? Did Fräulein Stoltz have ties to terrorism herself? Or were her products being used in ways she wasn't aware of?

In spite of the airport's spacious, modern terminal, all glass and steel with a high-speed tram, history loomed around me like the usual winter overcast as I disembarked from the jet.

Private jet or not, I still had to deal with Customs. I used my tourist passport to stay low-profile, though I'd brought my "official" one just in case. I flashed Ghost's equivalent of a passport, too, which identified him as a service dog. The chipper young official didn't ask what kind of service he provided, which was fine by me.

I could read a little German, better than I could speak it, so I picked up a map along with the keys to a brand-new, shiny black Porsche 918 Spyder. With 887 horses under its sleek hood, I couldn't help wishing I had time to put it through its paces on the autobahn.

I opened up the throttle when I found surprisingly little traffic for a dreary workday morning and just enough chilly rain to necessitate windshield wipers. The Spyder purred like a kitten and responded to my touch like an experienced dance partner.

Occasional farms dotted the terrain. Fräulein Stoltz had acquired one of them, situated on a small rise, for her assistive technologies company. Six or seven mature oaks, stripped of leaves and dripping, huddled around an old house that could've passed for a small manor.

I lowered the passenger window a few inches to let Ghost poke his nose out and he snuffled noisily at the rain.

We were halfway up the lane to the house when my secure satellite phone sounded in my duffel, which lay on the passenger-side floor. That couldn't mean anything good.

I had to stop to fumble for the bag. The phone never stopped ringing as I searched for it, which reinforced my gut feeling of "not good."

I wasn't disappointed. Well, actually, I was.

"Where are you?" Church asked.

"About a hundred yards from Sister Stoltz's Home for Disadvantaged Terrorists."

I heard a grunt before he asked, "Have you seen her?"

"Not yet, I'm on approach."

"Well," Church said, "no joy on the air strike. Drone got to the target and found the cockroaches had scuttled. Looks like they knew they were in somebody's crosshairs."

"Damn," I said. I hate terrorists, but terrorists with good intel are particularly scary. "Out here."

He didn't say, *Proceed with caution*. He didn't have to. The hair on the back of my neck was already doing that.

I left the Porsche at the side of the lane and, with Ghost trotting a few yards ahead, conducting olfactory reconnaissance, I strolled toward the house. Classic architecture, built of stone, three stories high, lots of windows. A façade displaying the company name in blocky white letters had been added to the front, and a dozen or so small cars, most of them gray or white, stood in an orderly row along the left side.

As I passed the first oak, I studied the yard. Bare branches couldn't conceal security monitors and floodlights mounted among them.

Typical for a business in a crime-ridden urban neighborhood, but it seemed like overkill in the German countryside. I furrowed my brow, wondering what she was afraid of.

Ghost ranged around the yard, nose to the ground, tail wagging with the rhythm of his trot. No indications he'd detected explosives, drugs, or anything else of concern.

I called him to heel with a hand signal before I pulled the antique doorbell chain. Soft, quick, padding footsteps reached me before the front door swung open, and a slim woman peered up at me with sky-blue eyes. About my age, I estimated, with blond hair twisted up in a braid around the back of her head. Not a knockout, but certainly she surprised me. I'd imagined more of a Mother Teresa. The eyes revealed boundless compassion veneered with caution.

"Sister Stoltz?" I queried, and hoped she spoke more than rudimentary English.

She offered a small smile that bordered on shy. "Fräulein Stoltz now. May I help you?" Her pronunciation was precise, but not accent-free.

I introduced myself, displayed my credentials.

"American government?" She sank back, one hand going to her ample breasts, and her eyes widened with concern. Not fear, I noted. "Is something wrong?"

"I hope not," I said, and genuinely meant it. Something I couldn't put a finger on touched a still-painful spot in my heart. *Grace. What is it about her that reminds me of Grace?* "I need to ask a few questions," I said. "May I come in?"

"You may, Mr. Ledger," she said. Her gaze fell on Ghost, who sat near my feet. He cocked his head in a beguiling manner and gave her his best tongue-out dog-smile. Even offered her a paw to shake. Yeah, my highly trained combat dog. But her fine brows lowered slightly. "I must, however, request that your dog remain out of doors."

I swore inwardly. I really wanted Ghost to help me check out the facilities here, but dared not push it.

"Sorry, boy," I said, and slipped him the *guard* hand signal as I stepped inside. My hackles hadn't entirely lain down even if Ghost's hadn't risen. Yet.

As Frieda Stoltz guided me through a variety of labs and assembly rooms on all three floors, giving me the nickel tour, I noted how she had preserved the old home's refinements despite converting it to a lab. I also observed unfeigned warm greetings from several researchers and mechanics as we entered each area, and their eagerness to demonstrate or explain their projects to me.

One older man stopped to shake my hand and confided, "Fräulein is the angel for people who suffer with disadvantages." The radiance in his eyes more than compensated for his uncertain English. I had no doubt he believed that to be true.

None of the workers seemed well-dressed or had driven new cars. I realized that these folks weren't out for money. They were trying to save the world. I knew that feeling.

Of all her creations, she clearly considered her self-driving auto technology to be her magnum opus. Excitement lit her features as she explained, "This will allow blind persons in Third World countries to have greater independence without the expense of human drivers. We are conducting a test program that I believe will bring about great change."

She opened the door into her office on the second floor, what appeared to have been a spacious bedroom, complete with a tall, antique armoire against the wall opposite her equally antique desk, and bay windows that overlooked the front grounds. "Please be seated, Mr. Ledger," she said, indicating a deep wing chair. She closed the door, sat opposite me, and said, "Now that you have seen my company, what questions may I answer?"

I cut to the chase. "We have reason to believe your self-driving auto technology is being used by ISIS."

Frieda transformed into a human ramrod before my eyes. She stared with mingled shock and outrage. "How dare you—"

"I'm not accusing you," I began, raising a placating hand.

"How can you believe such a thing?" she demanded. "What evidence do you have to support such an accusation?"

The demise of the Saudi prince and his family had been all over the international news since Sunday morning. While that was open source, certain details uncovered in the investigation were highly sensitive and had not been released to foreign nationals. I said only, "There's ample evidence."

She studied me for several heartbeats, her shapely jaw taut.

"Who buys your self-driving technology?" I pressed. "What countries have the highest demand for it? Do you only sell whole systems, or also parts for them? Do you handle shipping yourself?"

"This is foolishness!" she insisted. She sprang up from her chair, arms rigid at her sides, her fists clenched. "At this time the cars are going only to North Africa, where they are being tested. They are not available on the open market."

"Who conducts the tests?" I persisted. "How do the cars get to them? Do they provide you with reports? Written documents, for example, or videos of the tests?"

"Yes, yes." Frieda slipped behind her huge desk, her face a mask of determination. *Grace*, I thought again. But she had opened a drawer and produced a simple business card, which she thrust at me. "He is from Sudan," she said, "a very pleasant man who is very hopeful for my work."

The name hit my eye like a boxer's glove. One of many that the thug went by. *He's also very wanted by Interpol, for trafficking in opium, little girls, and anything that goes boom. He's playing her for all she's worth.*

I didn't tell Frieda that, at first. Instead I said, "Thank you. May I keep this?" as I slid the card into my shirt pocket. "Please, sit down now."

To my mild surprise, she did, though her sky-blue eyes still held a furious glint.

"In ancient China," I said, "it was actually considered a virtue for a military commander to be unspeakably evil." Hitler is still a sensitive topic in Germany, so I skipped the comparison. I just said, "That mentality remains to this day in some circles. The man that you're dealing with is one of them. In fact, he deals closely with China. Years ago, he used to buy machetes cheap from there and provide them to Hutu rebels. They made cheap weapons, since they only cost fifty cents each, but with them they committed genocide against more than a million Tutsis, and from there spread terror—"

"You lie!" she said, her face going pale as chalk. She began trembling and leaned back from me in revulsion.

I had a lot more to tell her—about blood diamonds and arms deals and a recent shipment of stolen uranium—but as I tried to warn her, she grew paler, more rigid, and fell into muttering denials in German. I don't think that it was that she didn't believe me, but that the thoughts I spoke about were too horrifying, too repugnant, for her mind to hold.

"Being unspeakably evil is also touted as a virtue by ISIS," I said. "Especially if that evil is used, ironically, to advance the cause of Allah, to build a world caliphate and bring down, once and for all, the

Great Satan and its allies. Because of that, they take perverse satisfaction in deliberately using the good intentions of Westerners against them. For example, in West Africa, when Christian organizations supplied wells to provide clean water for poor villages, your man poisoned them, killed thousands of children, and then said that the Christians themselves had done it."

She had to know that I was speaking the truth. Certainly, she'd heard tales of it.

"Nein!" Frieda leaped to her feet again, fists clenched once more, eyes blazing. *"Nein!"* She took two swift steps toward me, and for a couple of heartbeats I thought she was going to pound on me. I could have restrained her without hurting her, but I didn't like the thought. But she whirled and began pacing her office. "That is a complete fabrication! Terrorists are *not* using *my* technology! How could they?"

I've seen people transfixed by horror. She wasn't faking it. Her eyes widened and darted back and forth. I've seen people black out from it, rewrite thoughts, erase memories that they couldn't hold. I knew that she wasn't owning this.

I let her rant, storming back and forth across the office.

Outside, Ghost barked, whimpered, and barked twice. Bomb.

My heart began racing, and I knew that we had to get out. Frieda's unwitting ties to the ISIS cell in Syria had to be pretty tight. Enough so that they were probably spying on her.

My glance swept the room. Yep, there they were. A small protrusion like the head of a nail under the deep windowsill; a video pickup the size of a pencil eraser in one corner against the ceiling, camouflaged by the wallpaper pattern; a "chip" in the rim of the desktop. Clumsy bugs that Ghost would've detected in a wag of his tail if he'd come in with me.

But I should have spotted them as soon as I followed Frieda in here. The hair rose on my neck again, and my pulse stiffened.

"Fräulein," I said, keeping my voice absolutely casual as I pushed up from the deep chair, "let's step outside for a few minutes, take a little stroll. Looks like the rain's finally stopped." I cracked a smile. "I've probably got a wet, brown dog waiting for me by now."

I didn't expect her to come with me. I don't know if it was the smile or mentioning Ghost, but she stopped pacing, eyed me for a moment, then gave a small nod.

Ghost was damp and already exuding wet-dog odor, but not brown from testing mud puddles. He hadn't moved from his guard position. I'd known he wouldn't. He stood as we emerged into the soggy midday and wagged so hard his whole posterior swung back and forth.

"May I pat him?" Frieda asked.

"Be my guest." While she did, and Ghost squirmed like a puppy and licked her hand, I squinted up the lane. "Fräulein, have you ever seen a Porsche 918 Spyder up close?"

"No, I—"

"Come take a look." I took her by the elbow, in a totally gentlemanly manner. I didn't want to scare her. Not yet. And I forced myself, against a slow rise of adrenaline, to stroll.

I waited until we'd left the encircling trees behind, with their "security" monitors. Waited until we'd practically reached the car. Then I stopped and turned her to face me. And I told her exactly what was going on. All of it. Top-secret umpety-ump be damned.

"Get in the car and don't look back," I begged. "We can worry about nondisclosure statements later. Your life and the lives of your employees aren't worth dog crap if you stay here."

She'd resumed her human ramrod posture. She stared at me with her jaw set, then made her decision. "You Americans! You are always full of crazy imaginations and wild stories." She spun on her heels.

I made a swipe for her arm. She shrugged away from it. "Frieda, you've got to believe me," I pleaded.

She didn't reply, didn't glance back.

I didn't go after her. I didn't know if ISIS was live monitoring her office or just replaying things later. I stood by the Spyder, Ghost at my side, and watched her march back up the lane, across the tree-hemmed lawn, into the lovely old house.

I should go in and warn everyone, I thought, *get them out of there.*

The explosion's deep boom reached me a second or two after the black-and-orange billow blew out three front windows on the second floor. Frieda's office. The bomb must have been stowed in the armoire, I thought.

"Damn." I called Ghost, slid into the Porsche, and just sat, watching smoke billow, black and toxic, from the shattered windows, as ash and debris peppered my hood.

I actually jumped when my satellite phone sounded. So did Ghost, since he was sitting on it. I scooped it out from under his furry backside and muttered, "Yeah?"

"They're back, Cap."

Under other circumstances that line would've prompted a poltergeist quip. It took a moment to realize what Church meant. "Who, our little ISIS scientist shits?"

"Seems they went off for a celebratory feast. They've got an important visitor."

"Let me guess," I said, and named Frieda's contact.

He didn't ask how I knew, but there was a respectful silence at the end of the line for a moment.

"So," he said, "should we light them up now?"

"Do it now," I said. "I want to see craters where their assholes were."

Smoke from the burning house melded into the lowering sky as I wheeled the Porsche around, into a fresh wall of rain. But Frieda Stoltz's face glowed in my mind, radiant and eager as she showed me her creation.

I felt unaccountably happy. When it comes to death's delivery systems, no one is better than us. Those damned ISIS scientists probably couldn't comprehend the laser guidance system of the PAVEs we'd deployed on our GBU-38s. They wouldn't understand how our satellites made sure that the bombs kept coming, coming, to fly right up their butts.

Fuck 'em. Some people are too evil to live.

But that day I began to wonder if some people are too innocent for their own benefit. I wondered if Frieda had been too good to live.

ABOUT THE AUTHOR
David Farland is an award-winning, *New York Times* bestselling author of science fiction and fantasy, with more than fifty books in print. Currently, he is in the process of writing a thriller that deals with the dark underbelly of filmmaking in Hollywood called *The Blockbuster*.

◆

PRINCE OF PEACE

A JOE LEDGER/JACK SIGLER STORY BY JEREMY ROBINSON

1

As I stand before the window of my small but well-appointed hotel room overlooking the rich blue ocean of Micronesia, I find myself pondering a question I should have asked—more than once—before submitting myself to twenty-plus hours of travel: *What the hell am I doing?*

The answer is simple enough: An old friend needs my help. Those six words propelled me around the globe to a volcanic island that seems to be mocking fate with its name. Pohnpei. The spelling is different enough from Pompeii, I suppose, but when I say it aloud, it sounds close enough. I left my girl, Junie Flynn, my dog, Ghost, and the job three plane flights behind me. For some, that might sound like a vacation, and I suppose it *should* be, but I've learned to depend on the people in my life. They keep me alive. And sane.

Working for the Department of Military Sciences isn't exactly a low-stress job, and genuine vacations are hard to come by, thanks to the pervasive nature of the threats facing the world. I asked Mr. Church for some unstructured, unsupervised, unencumbered time off. He opened a fresh packet of vanilla wafers, selected one, tapped crumbs off it, and ate the whole thing before he answered me.

"The world is not currently on fire and there are no missiles inbound to the White House," he said slowly. "Enjoy your vacation."

I was on a plane three hours later, and back on the ground on one of the planet's wettest locations, before the day was done. And that's where things get complicated.

I came all this way, as I said, for a friend. Honestly, she was more than a friend. A lot more. But like the ruins that pock the outer fringe of this tropical Pacific island, she was ancient history. *Was* being the operative word. This morning—or is it yesterday morning now?—she leaped back into my present. Reading the morning news is a habit for many people, but I go deeper, scouring for hints that one of the DMS's adversaries might be active again. While the DMS has Mind-Reader—a globally connected supercomputer—for tasks like that, I think there are some things only the human mind can niggle out of a news report's text.

But in this case, no niggling was required. The headline said it all:

AMERICAN WOMAN, LAURA JONES, HELD ON SUSPICION OF TERRORISM

I didn't believe the woman in question was my Laura Jones until I saw the photo topping the article. She looked older, and a bit tired, but there was no questioning her identity. Laura Jones, the girl who won over the Civilized Man in me, who stole my heart for three years in high school, who volunteered to feed homeless people on weekends, who wrote letters for Amnesty International, and who collected unicorn stuffed animals. This woman had been caught planting a bomb under the bleachers of a school gymnasium. Hundreds of kids could have been killed.

My bullshit meter pinged red, and I started making calls. The story seemed to check out, but was so far outside the DMS's sphere of influence, and mission parameters, that I decided to take some personal time and step into my old detective shoes. Get to the bottom of it. Find out what really happened.

Two hours after touching down, I walked out of the Pohnpei State Police office feeling as though I'd been on the receiving end of a very elaborate prank. When I asked the receptionist about Laura Jones, I got a blank stare. When I asked about a bomb planted at a local school, the blank stare turned panicked. After assuring her I must have misread a news article, I checked in at the Ocean Breeze Hotel, confusion melting into anger.

On the far side of my third-floor window, there are palm trees, a sandy beach, the orange glow of a setting sun, and a view of the ocean that would lull most people into a relaxed state of mind. But until I can answer the question of what I'm *really* doing here, relaxation is the furthest thing from my mind.

After a quick speed-dial to the person best equipped to shed light on my situation, the voice of Jerome Taylor answers. "Hey, Joe, how's the—"

"Go secure, Bug," I say, using his call sign, which lets him know I've gone from "Detective Joe" to "the shit is about to go down, Cowboy." I wait as a series of clicks indicate our phone call is being rerouted and encrypted.

"We're secure, Cowboy," Bug says. "What's happening? Did she do it?"

"There is no she," I say.

"They didn't kill her . . ."

"I'm not sure she was ever here. Do me a favor and check on Laura Jones. From Baltimore. Married in '04. Teacher. No kids."

"Stalker much?" Bug says, trying to lighten the tone as his fingers clack over keys. "Got her. Annnd . . . you're right. Financial records show her buying laxatives on Amazon two days ago—that's embarrassing—and groceries earlier today. Probably prune juice. I can send someone to her house to confirm if you—"

A knock at the door interrupts him. I drop the phone on the bed's comforter, reach for my sidearm, and find the holster not only empty but missing entirely. I'm here as a civilian. I flew internationally, on commercial flights. I'm a long way from my guns, but I'm far from defenseless. The hallway on the far side of the door is narrow, and gun or no gun, I excel at close-quarters combat. I lift my hard-shell suitcase in front of my torso and pick up the empty instant-coffee carafe seated atop the room's minifridge. Armed like a hobo-gladiator, I give the door handle a twist and prepare to lunge.

The door creaks open and thumps to a stop against the wall. Aside from a small envelope on the floor, the hallway is empty. A quick glance in either direction confirms it. I crouch down, snatch up the envelope, and open it. It's a dumb move, but I don't think someone lured me all the way to the middle of South Pacific Nowhere to slip me an envelope laced with anthrax. There's a stark white card inside, its front gilded with elaborate calligraphy reading: *You're invited*.

Inside are two words and a set of numbers I recognize as coordinates.

I retrieve the phone from the bed. "Bug?"

"You realize I spoke to myself for like two minutes before I realized you were gone, right? What happened?"

"Send a team to Laura's house. I need confirmation. ASAP."

"On it."

"And run these coordinates for me." I read him the digits, suspecting they won't be far from my present location.

"Nan Madol," he says. "Ruins on the eastern side of the island. Capital city of the Saudeleur dynasty until 1628. Built in a lagoon. Lots of canals. Like Venice, but actually sunken. Pretty popular tourist destination. And not small. Nearly a mile from end to end."

"So lots of places to hide?"

"If Nan Madol meant 'Ambush City,' it would be an appropriate name."

"Uh-huh."

"You want backup?"

I consider the request for a moment. Even if backup left now, it would be nearly a full day before the team arrived. I'm not one for sitting around and waiting. But since I've clearly been lured here, probably for nefarious reasons, my little side mission is now official DMS business. "Fill in Deacon. It's his call."

"You got it. And Cowboy, be careful."

I hang up the phone, thinking about being careful, and I decide against it. Whoever brought me here—unless they have a very good and noble reason—is going to find themselves in a world of hurt, courtesy of my fists, or this coffee carafe.

2

During the hour-long taxi ride from Palikir to the outskirts of Nan Madol, I learned a few things about the ruins, the first of which was that Bug had taken his short breakdown of the historic site straight from Wikipedia. The actual history was much more colorful. The city was built upon one hundred man-made islets at a time before the invention of modern landscaping machinery. The massive stones used to build walls, floors, sculptures, and steps are said to have been flown in via black magic. Given the ruins' mysterious origins and otherworldly feel, it's not surprising that the city of R'lyeh, in H. P. Lovecraft's Cthulhu Mythos, was inspired by Nan Madol.

The city once housed one thousand ruling elite and local chieftains who were forced to live on the islets, where they could be watched and, if deemed untrustworthy, slain. The megalithic site's centerpiece, as with many ancient cities around the world, is its walled mortuary. I wonder how many people met their end inside the city, which had no fresh water and was incapable of growing food. Nan Madol was completely dependent on outside support. It's no wonder it was found abandoned in the early nineteenth century, by Europeans, some of whom believed they had found the lost islands of Lemuria.

Now it's a tourist trap that isn't quite a trap, because it really is stunning, though I may never confirm that with my own eyes. It's been two hours since I hung up with Bug. After visiting a hardware store, waiting twenty minutes for the taxi, and then the drive around the south end of the island, the sun is far below the horizon.

The taxi's worn brakes squeal as we roll to a stop. The driver, a man with a perpetual smile, swivels around with his elbow on the seat back. He's shirtless and slick with sweat from a day in the car without air-conditioning. Yet somehow, he doesn't smell. "Should I wait?"

"I'm fine," I tell him, handing him two $20 bills—U.S., which oddly enough is Pohnpei's official currency. I point to the dirt path beside the old mustard-yellow vehicle. "Your friend knows I'm coming?"

"Yes. Yes. I called him. He is not happy about the nighttime rental—there are sharks, you know—but for the right amount of money . . ." He shrugs and smiles.

For the right amount of money, just about anything, good or evil, can be bought. I've seen it with my own eyes.

I step out into the humid night, offer the driver a wave and a smile, and start down the narrow, muddy path. At the end of it better be a kayak rental joint, or Mr. Smiley cabdriver is going to be short a few teeth when I catch up with him. I click on the flashlight I picked up at the hardware store. I also picked up a machete, a utility knife with a three-inch blade, and a hammer. All excellent weapons in a pinch. And if I'm lucky, I won't need a single one of them.

Problem is, I'm lucky only when it comes to finding trouble.

After ten minutes of slogging through damp earth, I part with another $200 and park my ass inside a kayak. It's a two-seater . . . just in case it's Laura's husband who's constipated.

There's not a lot that creeps me out. I've seen shit that can't be unseen, forgotten, or tamped down into the subconscious through hypnosis. It's hard to get me spooked. But something about being on the water, at night, in a snack-sized boat, unnerves me. Each slap of water against the plastic hull conjures images of sharks. I turn the light on the water, but I only manage to see a few feet down. Anything could be lurking below, and I would never know. The mesmerizing number of stars above tugs my eyes upward and help me forget about the dark possibilities swirling beneath me.

As I leave civilization behind and plunge deeper into the mangroves of an ancient coastline, I do my best to put on my game face. People lured me here. Not sharks. People with unknown but likely malicious intentions. People who probably have guns. And that, I can deal with.

I put my shoulders into the paddle and surge along the coast, guided by the feeble illumination provided by my $20 flashlight. When I spot the first of a hundred islets covered in the blocky ruins of a time long forgotten, I turn off the light and coast through the darkness.

In the silence that follows, insects sing out a tinnitus-like buzz. I close my eyes and focus beyond them, listening for anything out of place, anything unnatural. A chirping, like some kind of homunculus-bird hybrid, echoes through the night. *Voices*, I think, and then I refine the realization to a singular speaker. Despite the high pitch, I can identify the speaker as a single, incredulous man.

My instinct is to leave the kayak behind and wade through the water, but I'm faster and quieter in the small vessel. I dip the paddle in the water and push closer to the voice, letting the stars and moon light my path through the maze of lush trees and the walls of gray stone. When the voice is loud enough to clearly hear, I dig the paddle into the water and let it drag me to a stop, just a few feet short of a staircase ascending out of the calm sea.

Just hours ago, the site would have been full of tourists in kayaks like mine. Whatever is going on here hasn't been happening very long.

"You will scream," the homunculus-bird man says. "If I have to fillet you one sinew at a time."

My first thought is that I've stumbled across a violent interrogation, but the man's words reveal something far more sinister. The silent person on the other end of this one-sided conversation isn't being questioned.

He, or she, is being tortured. There's no way to know why, or if it has anything to do with Laura, or if it's Laura being tortured. But the silence in response to the man's taunts, and who knows what else, speaks of a strong character.

The torturer growls something unintelligible. The muffled sound implies he's right up next to his victim, speaking into the ear, close, like a lover. He's frustrated, but he's still getting off on it.

"You think about that while I'm gone," the man says. I duck as loud footsteps plod away. A silhouette moves through the ruins beyond the staircase. The footfalls become splashes as the man enters the water. This is followed by the clunk of an oar on the side of a boat, the noise sounding more like a canoe than a kayak—perfect for transporting an unconscious victim.

Guessing the victim is now alone, but not sure, I slide out of my kayak and into the water, letting the liquid cushion absorb my bulk. I slip out of the sea, onto the stone stairs, staying low so the water dripping from my body makes no sound. I slip up to the stone wall and peek around the edge. Ten-foot walls constructed of thousands of flat gray stones surround what looks like a small courtyard, but may have actually been a building's interior a few hundred years ago. Shrubs and lush vegetation fill the open space to my left. To my right is a tree with coiling roots. And strapped to the tree is a shirtless man.

He hangs limp. Eyes closed. Blood drips from a handful of cuts on his chest and arms. What I first think is blood on his side turns out to be a large, port-wine-stain birthmark. He has the body of a man who's seen action. Chiseled, but not shaven like a bodybuilder or beach bro. His face sports a healthy dose of stubble, and his black hair hangs loose over his forehead. My guess is ex-military. A mercenary, most likely. Which means he's probably not up for any good citizenship awards. Whoever he is, I can't in good conscience let his torture continue.

I creep toward the man, still careful, still quiet. I've left all of my fear and apprehension behind. But when the man speaks, I nearly stumble and fall.

"Don't need your help," the man says without looking up.

What the fuck?

"You're tied to a tree," I point out. "Being tortured."

His eyes open, the color hidden in darkness. "Not really. Not yet."

Hand on the machete sheathed on my belt, I take a step closer, evaluating the man. Despite his situation, he's fearless. The kind of fearless that only comes from 1) having been in this situation before, and 2) knowing you've got a way out. And if he has a way out, I can't see it. His hands are cuffed to a branch high above his head. His legs are tied to roots below.

"Why are you here?" I ask.

"He'll eventually start asking questions," the man says. "And every question is an answer."

Something clicks. This man's presence, at the location to which I was given coordinates, is not a coincidence. I draw the machete and spin around, on the lookout for danger that's not coming.

"You can leave," the man says, and then he falls silent for a beat. When he speaks again, I hear a threat in the tone. "Unless you're here for a reason?"

"Same as you, would be my guess." I fish the small white card out of my pocket and hold it up, the gold *You're invited . . .* text easy to read in the moonlight. "Came here to help a friend in trouble?"

"Shit," the man says, and with a quick yank, he's free of the cuffs. They'd already been picked. He was just biding his time, allowing the homunculus-bird to cut him with the hopes of garnering information about his friend. "You military?"

I hand the man my utility knife, and he starts to work on the ropes binding his feet. "Something like that. You?"

"Something like that." After a few quick slices, he's free. He stands up, swivels the short blade around in his hand, and offers it back, handle first.

"Keep it," I say. "You'll probably need it."

He looks at the knife and smirks. "I'm used to longer."

"Thankfully," I say, "you're the first person to tell me that." I offer my hand. "For now, you can call me Cowboy."

He shakes my hand and introduces himself with a single word. "King."

3

My grip on the man's hand and the machete's handle tighten in unison. "King of what?"

Still unruffled, the man named King glances down at our hands, and then the machete. "That's a bad idea."

"King of *what*?" I ask again. If he makes me ask again, I'm going to punctuate the question by removing his hand. My previous experience with the Seven Kings has left me with a stark distrust of anyone bearing the name. King of Plagues. King of Fear. King of War. They're all dead now, but there are always unsavory people looking to claim their legacy.

Without tugging his hand away, he turns his back to me, revealing a tattoo of Elvis Presley. He wiggles his shoulder blade and the King of Rock 'n' Roll looks as if he's swaying his leg back and forth. "That and chess," King says.

I release his hand and step back.

"Good grip," he says, flexing his fingers.

I motion in the direction the homunculus-bird exited. "Did you learn anything from him?"

"Not much," King says. "He's a slight man. Aryan features. Hooked nose. Whoever he works for, he's not the brains. But he does enjoy his job. What I really want to know is—" His head twitches as though he's listening to something. Then he taps his ear and speaks. "Copy that. Thanks, Lew."

He taps his ear again, grumbles, "Damn it," and then seems to remember I'm there. "The old friend used to lure me here is missing. Looks like someone has been living in his house for a week. Collecting the mail. Making purchases. And not leaving a trace."

I dig into my pocket, retrieving my phone, which is powered off and protected by a Ziploc bag. I power it on and clench my jaw when I see several messages from Bug. I play the newest, listen to the short message, and nearly crush the device in my hand. Laura is missing. Her husband is dead. Rotting in the bathtub, while someone created the digital illusion that the couple was still safe and sound.

I don't need to confirm my situation. He can see it in my eyes.

Over the din of insect chirps rolling out of the jungle on the island's coast, my ears pick up the familiar whine of small engines. "Take cover!" I lean behind the ruins of an interior stone wall, while King remains rooted in place, making me look and feel a little like a chicken-shit. But my caution comes from experience. When most people think of drones, they picture Peeping Toms hovering the craft outside bedroom windows or over nude beaches. But they're easily modified to carry more than cameras—a fact I learned the hard way.

"It's a drone," he says, eyes on the night sky, watching the stars, any one of which could be something else. "Ten of them, actually."

This revelation pulls me out of hiding. "You can see them?"

"Their lights."

If the drones have lights on them, they blend in perfectly with the backdrop of stars.

"I've looked at the stars long enough to know which of those"—he points at the sky—"shouldn't be there. And if they wanted us dead, it would've been easy to blow up this rock when you arrived."

He's right about that. They want something from us. From what I can tell, we're similar men in similar positions. He's a little more . . . casual about his mortality, but he's got a familiar look in his eyes, as if he's already strategizing. Chess King indeed.

Several of the stars high above start shifting about, revealing themselves as drones, hundreds of feet up, where the buzz of their rotors blends with the sound of insects.

Before either of us can react, a loud buzzing brings our attention to the air just thirty feet above us. A hexa-rotor drone hovers overhead, capturing King and me within the cone of its spotlight.

"Glad to see you both made it." It's the homunculus-bird, his voice pumping from a speaker. "And thank you for not killing each other. The others bet against a civil meeting. Thought you two might tear each other apart. After all, life requires you both to sometimes shoot first and ask questions if there are survivors. But I had faith. You are two of the best candidates I've seen. Noble. Determined. Skilled. Team players. *Deadly.*"

Candidates? This is some kind of test?

A single drop of water, the faint bloop striking my ear like a Klaxon, warns me of danger. I whisper, "Incoming on my ten."

"More at my three," King says.

"This is a little elaborate for the Boy Scouts," I say to the drone. "Who are you?"

To my surprise, the man gives an answer that I suspect is honest, because it's too ridiculous to be fiction. "The Princes of Peace."

"Listen, princess . . . ," King says.

"*Princes.* Plural of prince." The man's loud retort makes the speaker crackle. King's quip has revealed just how short a temper the man has, and people with short tempers make mistakes. "We will bring peace to Earth by ending conflicts before they begin. By toppling violent despots. By—"

"Who decides?" I slowly pull the hammer from the belt loop where I tucked it. I tap King's hand with the handle and he takes it with a subtle nod. It's not much, but it will complement the three-inch blade. "Who decides who to kill, or overthrow?"

"The Princes." He enunciates more clearly this time. "We vote."

"Democratic assassins," I say. "That's new."

The drone buzzes for several seconds. When the man speaks again, it's clear he's trying to remain calm. "I'm no longer sure which of you I want to see survive this."

And here it comes. The reason why we're here, and why only one of us is supposed to leave.

"As you've no doubt already discerned, we have your friends. Whichever one of you walks out of Nan Madol will have their friend returned and be welcomed as a Prince of Peace. The other will meet the same fate as their fallen hero. And no, I don't expect you to fight each other. I'm many things, but cliché is not one of them."

"Says the man giving a monologue." King grins and it takes a concerted effort to not laugh.

"And if the survivor refuses membership?" I ask.

"There is no refusing. You are a member whether you accept it or not. Votes will be cast via text. Refusing to vote simply allows members you might disagree with to direct our course. Participation is the only way to influence the outcome."

"We could always stand directly in your way," King says.

"One of you," homunculus-bird says, "is welcome to try. The other will be buried alongside Pohnpei's ancients. Now then, the rules are simple. You—"

King lunges to the side, hammer raised. There's a shout, a *thunk*, and a splash.

"Stop!" homunculus shouts. "The rules!"

When King is thrown back into the small courtyard, rolling back to his feet, knife and hammer at the ready, I head for the men entering to my left.

"You can't start yet! I haven't—"

There's a *thunk* of metal on plastic, followed by a grinding. I glance up to see the drone wobbling, canting off to the side, two of its propellers shattered. King's hammer clangs on the stone floor between us. He's impulsive, but I think I like it.

The sound of wet feet focuses my attention on the entryway through which I came just minutes ago, unaware that I was being watched, not by sharks but by evil men with evil intentions. The first man, dressed in a black wet suit and holding a hatchet, all but walks into the machete's blade. The second man sees it happen and waits for a third man to join him. None of the men carry firearms, but they look comfortable with the assortment of blades. When one of them double-takes the machete now dripping with his comrade's blood, I realize they expected us to be unarmed. And while a machete, hammer, and short knife don't an arsenal make, they help even the odds a little.

Though his face is mostly concealed by the wet suit's hood, I see a surge of desperate confidence fill the man's eyes. I'm not sure if these men are here willingly, or somehow being cajoled, but as the first of them swings a sword toward my neck, I decide it doesn't matter. The sword comes to a stop when his wrist slaps into my raised machete hand. Gripping his shoulder with my free hand, I pull him in close and drive my forehead into his nose. Crunching bone is followed by a wet howl. There's almost no resistance when I shove the man back, toppling him into his partner and sending them both sprawling into the sea. These men might be killers, but they're also amateurs.

King handles his attackers with the same lethal force, but employs a series of knife cuts, jabs, and pressure-point strikes that appear chaotic at first, but are actually a fluid use of multiple martial arts and more modern fighting techniques. King has been fighting for a *long* time.

Who the hell is this guy?

When the last of his assailants hits the stone floor, I say, "The drones have a limited range. Two thousand feet, tops, if they have an extender on one of the islets. We'll find them on the mainland. And not far."

King gives a nod and steps toward the exit on his side, about to dive in and start swimming.

"I came in a kayak," I tell him.

He pauses, looks back, and says, "Behind you."

I sidestep the man I heard coming before King's warning and give his back a shove. He stumbles forward into King's fist and drops. He's alive, but he won't be moving anytime soon. When King doesn't put the knife in the man's back, I know I'm dealing with someone whose sense of honor resembles my own. He has no trouble killing, but only when it's necessary.

King steps over the unconscious man and pauses as orange light fills the sky above us. A softball-sized orb of fire plummets from one of the drones.

"Looks like Greek fire," I observe.

The comment snaps King's eyes wide. "Down!" he shouts, sounding worried for the first time.

The fiery sphere strikes an outcrop of angled stone and bounces like a kid's rubber ball—if kids' toys left explosive mountains of flame in their wake. The fireball ricochets off a wall, the tree, and the court-yard floor, each strike setting more foliage and vines ablaze, before zipping out the entrance beside me. There's a thud and then a high-pitched wail. The man whose face I caved in took the projectile in the chest, and he's now a walking inferno. He throws himself into the ocean, but the flames continue to eat him up as he thrashes. When his body falls still, floating out to sea, he looks like a Viking funeral pyre. The ball strikes the water and floats, flames spreading out from its core.

"They're kinetic fireball incendiaries," King says. "They're filled with jet fuel."

Before I can ask how he knows that, the night lights up around us. Ten more fiery spheres drop from the night sky. In their initial burst of orange light, I catch sight of the drones dropping them. Fucking drones. And then I don't have time to think. Most of the KFIs strike islets around us, setting fire to the ancient ruins and the surrounding water. But three plummet toward the already burning courtyard.

As fast as I am, and King appears to be, neither of us will be able to avoid being struck if one of the balls ricochets in our direction. And taking cover is a no-go. Our little fortress is about to be transformed into a volcano.

"Water!" I shout, and dive out over the stone staircase I crawled up just minutes ago. I arc out over a blazing trail of jet fuel still leaking from the first fireball and plunge into the depths.

I spin around underwater, watching through the waves, as orange trails of fire bounce around the ruins and through the water. The re-sult is a fiery maze stretching farther than I can see, much of it be-tween me and the mainland shoreline.

I see no sign of the mysterious King.

A twenty-foot gap between fiery streaks burning atop the water provides plenty of space for me to surface. I rise slowly, letting my face break the water just enough to take a breath and check things out. The air stings my nose and throat. It's choked with chemical smoke. The fire burns hot, steaming the moisture from my skin. All around, ancient ruins burn. The stone structures will survive, just as they did the city's sinking, but the vegetation will be scorched clean, along with any animal life on the islets—including myself and King if we linger much longer.

There's still no sign of the man, but my kayak floats free, overturned, but still buoyant. I can turn it back over, but will it carry me safely through the fires? I flinch back when the side of the kayak tips up and a face peers out at me and a deep voice says, "Under."

"Shit. King." I dip under the water and come up inside the kayak, treading water, just a few feet away from King.

"If you don't want rules," our adversary says, voice booming from another drone above, but muffled by the kayak's shell, "that's fine. We were going to do this in stages, but I think we'll all just embrace the chaos you two seem to prefer." A series of loud clunks sounds out. I have no idea what they could be, but I'm sure they're not good.

"Did you know that while uncommon, the occasional saltwater crocodile finds its way to Pohnpei? It's a surprise every time, but it happens. A half dozen is far less likely, but we're not making a *National Geographic* documentary, now, are we? And do you know the one thing every crocodile has in common when it reaches Pohnpei, after swimming through hundreds of miles of open ocean?"

"They're hungry," I say a moment before our host continues.

"They're hungry."

"And he said he wasn't cliché."

King grins, but the smile is wiped away when a loud *thunk* on the kayak's hull is followed by a bright yellow illumination. The yellow plastic above us starts to thin and liquefy.

"Get to shore!" I shout before ducking under the water, chased by globs of melted plastic. Under the water, King and I have the same idea. Before swimming, we shed our remaining clothes and shoes down to our boxers. King has the small knife gripped between his teeth, and I refasten my belt, with the machete, around my waist. Looking like a couple of *Men's Adventure* action heroes, we swim for shore.

Surfacing to breathe is tricky, but not impossible. The real problem is that the longer the fire burns, the more foul the air becomes. We've swum only a few hundred feet when I surface in three-foot shallows, breathe, and gag. We're between two islets, both on fire. The real problem is that I've surfaced just ten feet away from a KFI, bobbing in the water and spewing toxic fumes.

I turn to King, ready to plunge back in, when I see the ocean surging up over some kind of projectile headed for his back. Without warning, I shove King to the side, which is noble of me, but also puts me directly in the torpedo's path.

Only it's not a torpedo at all.

It's a croc. Sort of.

The front of its head is covered in electronics. Where its eyes should be are two sheets of brushed metal, riveted to flesh. I catch only a glimpse before its jaws snap open to engulf me, but there's little doubt that the predators unleashed in Nan Madol have been somehow modified. Perhaps being controlled. Living drones.

I fall back and slip under the water, letting my body arc beneath the croc. Darkness surrounds me as its massive form blocks out the fiery light above. A loud clunk reverberates through the water as its jaws snap shut, thankfully not on my head. But I'm far from safe. The behemoth starts to thrash. Its tail slams into my gut, shoving the acrid air from my lungs.

Something clamps down on my wrist. I struggle for a moment, but then see King, yanking me out from under the croc. He shoves me above the waterline and my lungs fill with poisonous air. King surfaces beside me, coughing. Despite not being sucker punched by a croc's tail, he's not faring much better. But the croc has seen better days. Its thrashing illuminates the area, as its head and then body burst into flames thanks to the KFI clutched in its jaws.

"Divide and conquer, mighty heroes," the homunculus-bird says, apparently still watching from above. "If you both die, your friends both die. And we really would prefer one of you to survive. That *is* the point of all this."

"How long can you hold your breath?" King asks.

"Three minutes," I say, not taking into account that my lungs want nothing to do with the air I'm currently breathing.

"We need to get off their radar. It's the only way."

"So we go deep," I say. It's bullshit. My body says so. But the Warrior side of my personality is firing on all cylinders, roaring louder than the Civilized Man and Cop ever could.

The familiar whir of chain guns warming up joins the chorus of insects and drones. Without another word between us, we dive into the sea once more, swimming away from the shallows between islets and diving deep. Angry bullet swarms pursue us into the depths, but the water saps their energy after just a few feet, protecting us better than any armor could.

When my ears are about to burst from the pressure, we angle toward shore and kick hard. Forty feet above us is a light show from hell. Fire burns everywhere, in the water and on every dot of surrounding ruin. Water ripples from crosshatching lines of bullets scouring the surface. The silhouettes of four large crocs shift back and forth far above, but just under the waves, seeking us out. One of the apex predators leaves a trail of blood in its wake, most likely struck by friendly fire. The icing on top of this shit-cake is a fifth silhouette gliding toward the wounded croc.

When there's blood in the ocean, it's never long before the first shark arrives. And in this part of the world, where the waters have been deemed a shark sanctuary, man-eating species are as plentiful as they are large. Luckily, neither King nor I are bleeding, so the sharks will home in on the croc, but it sure makes me a lot more eager to get out of the water. That, and I'm about to drown. And I'm not the only one. King hitches a thumb toward the surface and we angle upward, while slipping ever closer to the mainland. We surface just beyond the farthest ring of fire, still fifty feet from shore, both of us sucking air as quietly as possible.

Still recuperating from our long swim, when a loud thrashing sounds out behind us, all we can do is turn and look. A croc has been struck by a shark. Blood pools into the water, mixing with burning jet fuel. The assault attracts the remaining crocs, one of which is struck from below a moment later. Jaws snap. Bodies death roll. Sharks twitch. The feeding frenzy is mutual and bloody as predators from two different worlds clash. The absolute mindless violence disturbs me, and despite still not being fully recovered, I find myself moving away.

"We need to get the fuck out of this water."

King swims beside me, his strokes steady and smooth to not attract attention. We could swim faster, but flailing limbs look and sound a lot like struggling fish. Of course, that won't stop the swirling mass of sharks from detecting our rapid heartbeats. When I feel the soft sand of the mainland beneath my feet, I start to feel better, but we're still ten feet from shore, and anyone who's watched *Shark Week* knows that even knee-deep water isn't safe. So when we reach waist-deep water, two men who have seen their fair share of action stand and run for shore, lifting our feet high to clear the water.

Mangrove roots turn our run into a climb, but then we're clear. I turn back, expecting to feel embarrassed by my retreat from the water, but when a dorsal fin passes by and, fifteen feet behind it, the tip of a tail, I realize the fear crawling up my back wasn't cowardice. It was something closer to a sixth sense.

"Find them! Kill one of them!" homunculus-bird shouts, shouting at whoever is controlling the drones, and maybe the crocs. His amplified voice sounds smaller and distant, but also in stereo.

My head snaps to the dark jungle ahead. "They're close."

Without another word, we slip into the twisting coils of tree branches and roots. Distant voices grow louder with each step through the slick earth. There's light ahead. A camp nestled in a recently hewn clearing. All of this for us. I crouch lower when I see movement ahead. King follows my lead, ducking beside me.

"We can flank them," he says. "Come in from either side."

A chip of wood slaps my face. There's a bright white gouge in the bark just above King's head.

"Or not. Stay here," he says, and then he's on his feet and moving, running pell-mell toward the camp, like a man who thinks bullets won't hurt him.

"Stay here?" I say to myself. "*Stay here?* Not fucking likely."

I move away from King, who has done a splendid job of drawing fire. So far, the web of trees are shielding him from the barrage, but he's not going to last long if he charges out in the open.

I exit the jungle behind a trailer, but it looks and feels like a prop. I peek around the corner. The clearing is lit by a pair of floodlight stands. There's a smoldering fire pit at the center. Two wooden posts jut from the ground. Laura is bound to one, her head hanging down, unconscious. There's a man tied to the second post. King's friend.

Gunfire highlights the positions of four men. They're standing by a table, upon which are several sets of drone remotes and a series of interconnected laptops. They're controlling a dozen aerial drones and the crocs with just four men, which means the laptops must be using some kind of AI. It's a fairly sophisticated setup, and very expensive. Whoever the Princes of Peace are, they're not hurting for money.

But where they've got money, they're lacking in brains.

The machete silently slides from its sheath. Homunculus-bird reveals himself by screaming toward the jungle where King continues to evade the bullets being sprayed by the assault rifle–wielding men dressed in black BDUs. "You're breaking the rules! You should have let me tell you the rules!"

I step out from behind the trailer and cover the distance to the nearest man in ten quick steps. The sound of the man's life ending is drowned out by the roar of gunfire. Unfortunately, all three men run out of ammo just as the dead man's death groan slips from his lungs.

All three shooters turn to me, reloading quickly.

But not quick enough. I reach down, snatch up the AR-15 hanging from the dead man's shoulder, turn the barrel toward the men, and pull the trigger. The weapon's last three bullets tear through the night air and then through one of the men. While he drops, the other two take aim.

Bullets thud against the dead man's body. I drop the spent AR-15 and clutch his shirt and the machete, holding his twitching form up, knowing that eventually one of the rounds is going to slip through his flesh and into mine.

And then one does, lodging itself in my shoulder. My arm gives out, and the dead man falls.

I fall with the corpse, trying to stay behind cover, but he's falling faster than me. I see the assault rifle barrels tracking me, and then chaos arrives. King punches his three-inch blade into the neck of one man, ending his life with a quick jab. He pulls the blade out, eyes on the second man, when he's shot in the side. The blast jolts the knife from King's hand, but it doesn't slow him down. He moves in close as the soldier holds down the trigger. Bullets tear through the night. The scorching barrel hisses against King's skin as his hands reach up, one grasping the back of the man's head, the other coming up under his chin. His strong hands twist in unison, first to the right and then the left. There's a crack and then the man falls away.

King is fearless, skilled, and fast, but the third man draws a bead on him, too far away for King to reach, too close to miss.

But he's not alone, and the confidence in his eyes says he knows it.

I draw the fallen soldier's sidearm, lift it fast, and squeeze off three rounds. The second and third bullets strike the last soldier's thigh and gut, throwing off his aim. King closes the distance and ends the fight with a throat chop that drops the gasping man to the ground.

Mostly naked and unarmed, King's body glistens with water, sweat, and blood. He looks possessed, but he doesn't move. I roll to my feet, gun in hand, and see what's stopped him cold.

Homunculus-bird.

If not for the dead man's switch clutched in the man's hand, he'd look about as threatening as a toddler with a rattle. He backs away toward the jungle. "I told you there were rules. I *told* you."

"One of us has to die," King says. "We got it."

"But if one of you doesn't," the man says. "If one of you doesn't . . . if you *both* survive . . . they"—he points to the two gagged prisoners, who have been roused by the fight; Laura meets my eyes, confusion giving way to desperation—"*both* die." He cackles out a laugh. "And you'd have done it. One of you would have died to save them. I honestly don't know which, but one of you, and that's the kind of person the Princes of Peace don't want. Good riddance. We wanted the survivor. The one who valued his life. Instead, here we are, with both of you."

I aim at his chest, but don't fire. If he dies, Laura dies.

She's already dead, the Civilized Man mourns. *You killed her.*

The homunculus-bird man pauses at the jungle's edge.

"Don't," King says, coming to the same realization.

"Next time you hear from us," the man says, "listen to the rules." His thumb comes off the trigger at the same time my index finger squeezes. I lose sight of him as a fireball erupts from beneath the two prisoners. In a blazing flash of heat, the bodies are incinerated, their screams coming and going with the speed of my fired bullet.

I'm lifted off the ground and slammed into the trailer, my consciousness sinking into the depths along with my hopes of saving Laura.

I wake to find the site smoldering. A crater is all that remains of the wooden stakes and the people tied to them. Twenty feet away, King sits up holding his head. Blood seeps from a gash on his forehead, no doubt the result of metal fragments from the explosion.

We stand in silence, surveying the scene. The table has been overturned, the laptops destroyed. The drones under their control are no doubt sinking to the bottom of the sea, along with the remains of the crocs. Despite the amount of physical evidence, not to mention bodies, I suspect it won't lead anywhere. But there is one corpse I'm glad to see as I hobble across the clearing.

Homunculus-bird lies at the jungle's fringe, a look of surprise frozen on his face, a neat hole punched through his forehead.

King grunts at the man, but says nothing. His death provides little comfort for the two innocents who died here today, who died because King—because both of us—didn't listen to the rules. Rules we might have chosen to ignore. It seems equally likely that one of us would have given up his life. But we'll never know who.

A phone chimes, spinning us around. The sound comes from the overturned table. Then it's joined by a second phone. We head for the mess and find two phones, one adorned with a king chess piece, the second with a Stetson hat. The screens display identical messages.

Cast your vote.
Target: Afanas Konstantinov, Russian oil tycoon.
Tap for more details.
Operation parameters: Assassination.

The text is followed by two buttons: *Approve* and *Oppose*.

"Shit," King says.

"We have no choice," I say.

He nods. "I know."

We both tap *Oppose*, casting our vote against the assassination and confirming that we are both, like it or not, Princes of Peace.

ABOUT THE AUTHOR

Jeremy Robinson (aka Jeremy Bishop and Jeremiah Knight) is the international bestselling author of more than fifty thriller, horror, science-fiction, fantasy, and action-adventure novels and novellas, including *Apocalypse Machine*, *Hunger*, *Island 731*, *SecondWorld*, and the *Jack Sigler* thriller series, the first of which, *Pulse*, is currently in development to be released as a major motion picture. His bestselling Kaiju novels, *Project Nemesis* and *Island 731*, have been adapted as comic book series from American Gothic Press/Famous Monsters of Filmland. His novels have been translated into thirteen languages. He lives in New Hampshire with his wife and three children. For the latest news about his novels, comics, movies, and TV projects, and the *Beware of Monsters* podcast, discussing all things monstrous, visit www.bewareofmonsters.com.

ROOKIE

BY JOE McKINNEY

Takes one to know one, right?

That's what all the kids say.

Well, I used to be a Ranger, and the guy who walked into the D. B. Grocery that night, he was a Ranger.

He had Fort Benning written all over him.

"Pay attention," my close-quarters combat instructors used to say. "It don't cost nothing."

For Rangers and cops alike, that's the mantra. Pay attention. Head on a swivel. If you get surprised, it's your own damn fault.

Don't ever let it be your fault.

Good words to live by.

So I was over by the freezers, trying to figure out which TV dinner was going to keep me company that night, when I heard the door chime and saw movement out of the corner of my eye.

I pay attention.

Naturally, I turned that way.

The light from the corner lamppost poured in, framing a tall white guy in a dirty yellow halogen stain, as if he were stepping out of an old sepia photograph. He was built trim, like a swimmer. I'd guess six three, maybe 180 pounds. He had a surfer's haircut, blond and shaggy, but the rest of him looked like a killing machine. His chin looked as though it had been carved out of stone and in his icy gaze I saw the reflection of all the crap I'd seen back in my time with the teams. If he'd been dressed in BDUs and a boonie hat, his face painted green and black, rather than a T-shirt and jeans, he'd have been a ready-made recruitment poster for the Rangers.

That is, if they had recruitment posters.

And trust me, they don't.

He stopped in the doorway, made a long, slow scan of the store, skipping over Jun Kwai, the shop's owner, and then lingered for a bit on me, summing me up, before taking in the rest of the place.

Only then did he walk in.

I let out a sigh. I knew the guy was trouble. When you see someone like that, a full-boat military bad boy, in the middle of one of the rowdiest neighborhoods in West Baltimore, you just know something's wrong. I'd been a Baltimore police officer for something like seven months at that point, but even a rookie cop like me could have told you the guy didn't belong there. West Baltimore is almost all black, and a white guy with a surfer haircut and a Ranger stare just doesn't fit with the general population.

Was I racially profiling him?

Yeah, maybe.

But the guy didn't fit the neighborhood, and any cop worth his or her salt will tell you that is what the FBI calls a clue that something bad is about to happen.

Plus, the guy had a fine sheen of sweat on his face.

And he was out of breath.

Just a little.

He might have looked normal to anyone else, but like I said, I used to be an operator. I know the breathing drills they teach you. I know how they teach you to step outside of your own OODA loop, how to master it. How to stay glassy calm, no matter what you're dealing with. How to work the problem. He was pulling himself together right in front of me. Something had happened, and this guy was trying to stay on top of it.

But whatever his problem was, it was my problem now.

I put the milk down on the shelf and steadied my breathing with the same technique Grunt Boy had just used. My hand moved to my sidearm and I thumbed down the holster's hood. Nice and slow, nice and quiet. Grunt Boy was on full alert. No need to agitate him further.

Still, I wanted to be ready. If my instincts were right, and they always are, this guy had a trailer full of trouble dragging along behind him. I wasn't going to be surprised. I wasn't going to be last on the draw.

Grunt Boy glanced over his shoulder, just once, and so discreetly someone else might not have noticed it, and then headed toward the back of the store. The bathrooms were back there. I thought maybe he'd lock himself in.

Maybe, I thought, he was a junkie.

That's becoming more common these days, even in the Ranger community. All that time in the Sandbox has left a lot of guys with some serious hurt, both inside and out, and sometimes, when you come back home and find the world tells you they love you, but shows you nothing but hate and indifference, the needle and the spoon can make that hurt seem a million miles away.

For a little while, at least.

Maybe, I thought, that was this guy's deal. It would explain the furtive glance over his shoulder. The brief spark of worry that lit his eyes when he saw me. The sweat on his brow.

Maybe.

I looked at Jun Kwai. He answered me with a shrug. This shop was a regular stop for me on my way home from work. Jun Kwai had run this business for twenty years. He'd seen three riots and more robberies than most of the cops I knew, and all of it had given him a sort of Zenlike calm in the face of the weird. Not much of anything fazed him.

It was then I spotted the trucks outside.

Two FedEx trucks pulling up to the curb across the street. Like I said, I was pretty new to the Baltimore Police Department, but I'd worked this neighborhood long enough to know that FedEx rarely puts in an appearance around here, and never at two in the morning.

Much less two trucks at once.

Behind the cash register, even Jun Kwai was starting to get nervous. I saw him fidgeting out of the corner of my eye. I knew from previous experience—actually, a lot of people knew from previous experience—that he kept a Ruger Super Redhawk revolver under the counter. It was an obscenely huge handgun, way too big for him. He was reaching for it now.

I shook my head, gave him a hard look. *Don't do it. Not yet.* I had a feeling things were about to get out of hand, and I didn't want any unintended collateral damage.

Out on the street, the back end of one of the trucks rolled open and a team of soldiers in black BDUs jumped out. They moved quickly and efficiently, a well-oiled machine.

And they were armed to the teeth.

I checked out the other FedEx truck and saw the same scene repeated.

The two teams rolled out, then melted into a dark, vacant lot at the corner.

They were pros. That much was obvious. Who they were I had no way of knowing, but I had a pretty good idea of who they were looking for.

"Keep that pistol out of sight," I told Jun Kwai.

"You got it, boss. You sure you don't need any help?"

"You want to help?" I asked. "Keep your finger on the phone. Get ready to call 911."

"I'll call right now."

"No," I said. I knew my fellow cops. I also knew the kind of men recruited into special teams like the ones I'd seen off-load from the FedEx trucks. If I called in backup without knowing exactly what was going on, somebody was going to get shot, and good men would probably die. I wasn't ready to let that happen. I've been to enough funerals. "Not yet. Let me figure who the players are first."

"You got it, boss."

I went to the bathrooms at the back of the store. I drew my weapon and set up next to the men's room door. Just outside of the kill funnel that would form if the guy decided to start shooting at the door.

The door was the kind that opened outward, so I grabbed the handle and pulled it hard.

Unlocked door.

My first clue.

A junkie would have locked it while he shot up.

I quickly scanned the visible half of the bathroom, then threw my shoulder into the open door and leveled my weapon on the other half.

Empty.

Filthy, covered in graffiti, and stinking of piss, but still empty.

I repeated the drill at the women's restroom. Same thing. A busted crack pipe and some scorched Brillo pads on the floor, but otherwise empty.

I stepped into the hallway and looked to the only other place Grunt Boy could have gone.

Jun Kwai's office.

I'd watched about a million store surveillance videos on the TV in there, and I knew he kept it locked.

Always.

But the door was open by a crack. The lock had a few fresh tool marks on it, and it occurred to me that nowhere in my Ranger training had I ever been taught to pick a commercial dead-bolt lock. Blow them with det cord, sure, but not pick them.

Who, exactly, was I dealing with here?

Jun Kwai's office was tiny. It was shaped like an L, with the small part of the room wrapping around behind the coolers. He kept it packed to the gills with boxes of inventory records and old surveillance tapes and all the other odds and ends he'd accumulated from twenty years of running a busy grocery store. In the cramped little space left over he had crammed an old schoolteacher's desk and a battered chair. There was hardly enough room to breathe in there, and if I was going to have to fight an operator in a space like that, it was going to be interesting, to say the least.

But hesitating gets you killed, so I threw open the door and leveled my gun on the darkness inside the office.

My eyes adjusted to the darkness in time to see one of Grunt Boy's sneakers disappearing into the ceiling. He'd pushed back one of the sectioned tiles that hid all the plumbing, and in another five seconds, he'd have been completely out of sight.

I didn't give him the chance to slip away.

"Hey, what are you doing?" I called out to him.

The foot hung there for a second. It was all the chance I needed.

I jumped onto the desk and grabbed hold of his leg. I felt him flinch, and then start to buck and kick. His leg slipped from my hands, and when I reached back to grab him, he kicked at my face.

I was ready for him, though. I leaned right just enough to let the kick go by, and at the same time threw a block that caught him just above the ball of his ankle. I heard him grunt in unexpected pain, and that was all the encouragement I needed. I grabbed his leg again and jumped from the desk. My body weight pulled him straight through the ceiling tiles, and he came crashing down in a shower of crumbled ceiling panel dust.

He crashed down on the desk with a loud thud. Papers and old VHS cassettes slid to the floor. Grunt Boy let out a noise somewhere between surprise and pain, and for a moment, I thought I had him.

He was fast.

Before I could even climb to my feet, he'd jumped from the desk and kicked the chair out of the way.

I found myself nose to nose with him, the two of us standing in a space no bigger than a bathroom stall. He threw a quick jab with his right. I tried to move, but he was fast. He caught the side of my jaw and left me with a ringing in my ears.

I didn't let him follow up, though. Before he could pull the punch back and strike with a backhand, I snaked my right arm over his wrist and shot my hand up behind his shoulder, putting him off balance. I jammed my knee into his thigh, causing him to snarl in pain.

I raised my boot to bring it down on the back of his knee, but he was ready for that. He took all the weight off his left leg and knelt down.

It was a basic move, but it was perfectly executed, and with him gone as my support, I rolled over the top of him and landed in the chair.

He was on me before I could get up. He snapped a front kick right at my chin. I managed to deflect it with my hands. Grunt Boy followed it up with another front kick, and I blocked that one, too. When I was first learning how to fight, my sensei told me that one day my techniques would be so finely honed I could fight in a phone booth, and I learned my lessons well. Grunt Boy sure seemed surprised.

He tried the front right kick a third time, but I was ready for it. I caught his heel with my left wrist and pushed up on his calf with my right. With his leg still in the air I lunged toward his other knee with a side kick and caught him just below the joint. He fell forward, hard, and landed facedown on the desk.

When we stood up to face each other again, his lip was busted up and leaking blood all down his chin.

"I bet that hurt," I said.

That got him mad, but rather than try to hit me again, he just wiped away the blood. "You need to let me go," he said.

"Yeah, the chances of that happening are hovering right about zero," I said. "How about you turn around and put your hands behind your back. That way I won't have to bust that other lip."

He glanced down at my nameplate. "Look, Officer Ledger, you have no idea what's going on here."

"You just described most of my life, buddy. Why don't you explain it to me after we put these cuffs on you?"

"There's no time for that."

"Oh we got—"

I didn't get the rest of the sentence out. Before I knew it, he'd kicked a broom leaning up against the wall, making it flip in midair. He caught it and swept at my knees the next instant, leaving my calf muscles screaming from the sudden pain. I staggered a bit and lurched forward—right into the business end of the broom. He brought it up under my chin and shoved upward, causing me to rock back on my heels. The last place I wanted to be.

Grunt Boy could have slapped my temples and laid me out, but he didn't follow through. Instead, he backed off. I heard boots hitting the floor outside the office door, and then the sounds of men barking fast, clipped commands.

So they weren't worried about us hearing them.

Not a good sign.

"There's no time to explain," he said. "I have to get out of here. You should, too. You don't want to be here when those guys come through that door."

"Who are they?"

"Sorry," he said, and tossed the broom aside. "That's classified."

He put his hands on the table and was about to jump onto it when the door burst open. He was caught in a bad spot, but Grunt Boy moved fast, I had to give him that. He spun around and kicked the door back into the soldier's face.

"You're gonna want to move," he said, and grabbed the front of my uniform. He pulled me toward the wall next to the door and threw his arm across my chest, as if I were some kid in the front seat and he was my mom trying to keep me from going through the windshield.

The next instant I heard the rattle of a fully automatic rifle and the door exploded into splinters.

Grunt Boy stayed frosty.

Two of the soldiers came running through the door. Grunt Boy kicked the second one in the back, just below his body armor. The man crumpled to the floor. The lead man turned, and even through his gas mask, I could see the surprise in his eyes. He tried to bring his rifle up, but Grunt Boy was on him. He knocked the rifle to one side and got in close enough to throw one arm around his neck. He snaked his other hand under the man's chin, and kept up steady pressure until the man's neck snapped like a twig.

Grunt Boy had the pistol out of the dead man's holster even before the body hit the ground.

He kicked the second man's helmet, exposing a portion of the back of his head, then shot him twice.

"Whoa!" I said.

I looked down at the dead man. His gear was state of the art, but there wasn't a single piece of insignia on it. It didn't look like American gear, though. Russian, maybe. Maybe even Israeli.

"Who are these guys?" I demanded.

"I told you," he said as he scooped up the rifle. "That's classified."

"You just shot a man in front of a Baltimore police officer. You're gonna need to do a whole hell of a lot better than that."

"Look," he said. "All you need to know is that these guys are part of a team, and here in about five seconds, all their friends are going to come running through that front door."

He walked out the office door and into the bright lights of the store.

I keyed my lapel-mic and said, "Bravo 16-20."

Nothing.

Grunt Boy glanced at me over his shoulder. "That's not gonna work."

"Bravo 16-20," I said again.

Still nothing.

I hit the red emergency button on the top of my radio. It should have given me dedicated access to the airwaves. Hit that tone and nobody hears anything but you.

"Bravo 16-20," I said. "Bravo 16-20."

But I got silence.

"What the hell's going on?" I asked him.

"They're jamming us. You won't be able to talk with anyone until this is all over. That is, if you're still alive."

Before I could answer, gas canisters came flying through the windows, spewing OC. It spread across the ceiling and then started to seep its way down between the rows of shelves. I felt the familiar bite in my nostrils and the fullness in the back of my throat, but I held back the coughing. At Fort Benning I spent more time in the gashouse than most soldiers spent in the latrine. OC and I were old friends.

"Better get ready," Grunt Boy said. He crouched down near one of the endcaps, his stolen rifle at the ready.

Hesitation kills, but I hesitated anyway. That man had saved my life back in the office, but I still had no idea who he was. I didn't know who the men he'd killed were, either. They were wearing foreign-made gear, but that didn't mean they weren't U.S. military. Back in my time in the Sandbox, at one time or another, I wore everything from a burka to a fine Italian suit to full-on BDUs and body armor. It just depended on the mission.

"Get down!" Grunt Boy barked at me. "They're coming through the door."

I crouched down just as a team came crashing through the windows. Grunt Boy returned fire, dropping two of the soldiers before they even cleared the rack of girlie mags next to the door.

I pulled my pistol and peered around the opposite end of the shelf.

One of the soldiers fired at me, hitting the bags of chips on the end-cap and showering me in Pringles and Lay's.

I ducked back behind the row. "Damn it."

"Hey!"

It was Grunt Boy. He was nodding toward Jun Kwai over at the register. The poor man's normal glassy calm was gone. He looked like a deer in headlights. He just stood there, staring at the men chewing his store up with bullets. He was holding his Ruger Super Redhawk, though.

"What's wrong with your friend?" Grunt Boy said. "He's gonna get himself killed."

I had to hand it to Grunt Boy. No hesitation. He laid down a steady line of fire as he ran from cover over to the register. I saw him grab Jun Kwai by the shoulders and turn him around, away from the door. It looked as if he were smoothing the man's shirt. With more of the soldiers charging through the door, Grunt Boy pulled Jun Kwai from behind the registers and pushed him toward the office.

I watched Jun Kwai stumble by me, looking like a sleepwalker. There was snot running out his nose and he was crying like a baby, but he hardly seemed to notice. He just made his way to the office in a haze.

"Behind you!" Grunt Boy said.

I spun around just as one of the soldiers came around the corner. His face was lost behind a gas mask, but I knew he saw my uniform. He saw my police uniform and raised his rifle to kill me anyway.

Before the soldier could fire, Grunt Boy got the jump on him. He came around from behind the man and hit him in the back of the head with the butt of his rifle.

Once the man was down, Grunt Boy shot him.

"What the hell's wrong with you?" he said to me. "Pay attention."

By way of an answer I raised my pistol and fired at the two soldiers who had come up behind him.

Both dropped like a bag of rocks.

Grunt Boy's eyes went wide. He stared at the business end of my pistol for just a second, then glanced over his shoulder at the two dead soldiers.

"Pay attention," I said. "It don't cost nothing."

His eyes went even wider. "Fort Benning?"

"You guessed it."

"I should've known."

"Shoulda but didna."

He reached down to the corpse at his feet and relieved it of its machine gun. He slid it over to me.

"I guess you know how to use that, then?"

It was a Heckler & Koch MP5, 9 mm. Fantastic weapon. Not my preferred platform, but still a beauty. I scooped it up, ejected the magazine to make sure it was functional, and then slammed it back home.

"I've seen the training films," I said.

He chuckled, then turned back to the front door. Two of the remaining soldiers were moving to the register counter for better cover.

He smoked them both.

I had no idea how many men they had left, but I could tell, at that moment, that we had them scared. They weren't popping their heads up, and they weren't putting down suppression fire. When you stop taking the fight to your enemy, you know you pretty much have given up.

Knowing that, I actually cracked a smile. I'd gone from wondering what in the hell was going on to actually feeling like I had a handle on this thing.

Crazy how that happens.

I made hand signals to him that I was going around the other way so we could put channel fire their way.

He nodded, and I moved out. I went down to the end of the row, near the coolers, nearly all of which were shot to hell, with waterfalls of beer and soda and milk running into lakes on the floor. There was a little bit of glass still hanging from a corner of the store's front window, and in it I could see the reflection of one of the soldiers. I could tell at a glance how scared the man was, and it occurred to me at that moment that we weren't dealing with soldiers at all, but mercenaries.

Well-equipped mercenaries, but still mercenaries.

A man who fights for money has no cause, and a man who fights without a cause can never win.

I genuinely believe that.

You either believe in what you do, or you fail.

And when you play the kind of game we were playing, that means you die.

Still, it made me wonder what Grunt Boy was fighting for.

I took a deep breath and got ready to charge the man. He was armed with a full-auto MP5, but so was I, and I knew at that moment that I could take him. This would be over in four seconds.

But just as I was tensing to strike, I heard a familiar noise.

Helicopters.

I stopped and picked apart the noise in my head. Two of them. Sounded like Black Hawks. As they got closer, I could feel the thropping of their rotors beating against my chest, and the Warrior part of my mind hardened and took over.

How well I remembered that sound, that feeling.

At first I thought it was more mercenaries, but one look in the broken window dispelled that. The mercenary was frantically trying to call into the mic built into his wrist-comm system and obviously getting nothing.

His backup must have abandoned him.

Outside the window, a dozen or more ropes hit the street.

Within seconds, U.S. Army troops were fast-roping down to the pavement. They moved toward the store with guns blazing, mowing down the mercenary I'd been watching, plus four more I hadn't seen.

I stood up just as one of them came around the corner.

He leveled his machine gun at my chest as a reflex when he saw me, paused for a second, then lowered it.

I did the same with my MP5.

He took off his gas mask, and I was shocked to see my old friend Mark Roberts. We'd served in the Rangers together, and from the looks of things, he was still with the teams.

Only now, judging from the insignia on his chest, he was a command sergeant major.

"Joe?" he said. "What the hell?"

"Command Sergeant Major?" I countered. "They just giving that rank away now?"

"Screw you."

"Yeah? Only if you kiss me first."

"In your dreams, you skanky little whore." He threw his arms wide. "Come to papa."

We man-hugged.

"You guys really tore this place a new one," he said.

I looked around. He was right. Grunt Boy and I had pretty much leveled Jun Kwai's shop. There wasn't a shelf, a drink display, a magazine rack, a cooler door, or a wall of cigarettes that didn't have a bullet hole in it. The flood of spilled soft drinks and beer and milk and orange juice was an inch deep on my boots.

Not to mention the spilled ice.

And the Skittles and the M&M's all over the place.

And, of course, the dead mercenaries.

"The cleaners are going to have a bitch of a time with this place," Mark said.

"You're using cleaners?" Cleaners were our support staff, the guys who came in and erased all evidence that the team had been there. They weren't used that often, but when they were, they were a wonder to watch. They could make evidence of a firefight disappear in a moment's notice.

"Actually," Mark said, "that's classified."

"I've heard that word a lot tonight," I said. "What gives?"

"What gives is it's classified."

"Seriously?"

"Yeah," he said. "Seriously. You really stepped into the shit tonight, Joe. You gotta stop doing that."

Seriously, I thought. I used to be one of these guys. I hold a top-secret clearance, even now. I looked around and realized that, at one point or another, I had been to a school with every single one of the guys in Mark Roberts's team. They couldn't tell me what was going on?

But of course they couldn't.

I knew that.

I was once part of the team. I was on the outside now.

I was what the guys affectionately called a FAG. A former action guy. A friend of the team, but no longer one of the team.

"Let me take you outside, okay?" he said.

I knew the drill. Mark and I were friends. Had been for a long time. But he had a job to do, and part of that job was evacuating those who had no business knowing what his job was.

That meant me.

"Sure," I said.

I followed him out to the street. As I stepped onto the sidewalk I heard glass crunching behind me. I turned and saw Grunt Boy walk up to a team member who had Jun Kwai firmly in tow. He put his hands on Jun Kwai's shoulders, just as he'd done when he'd saved the man's life earlier in the evening, and seemed to straighten his shirt. Only this time I saw him remove a long blue vial, about the size of a cigar, from Jun Kwai's inner pocket. He checked it, I guess to make sure it was still intact, then caught me looking at him.

He held up the vial. "Trust me," he said. "This right here. Everything that happened here. This was worth it."

With that, Mark led me away from the building.

We headed over to an unmarked ambulance and he asked me if I needed anything.

I told him I was good.

"Cool," he said. Then he looked me in the eye. "In just a bit we're going to release your radio so you can call in the fire. Cool?"

"What fire?"

"Cleaners, remember?"

"Oh," I said. "Yeah, right."

"And this is classified."

My turn to look him in the eye. "Screw you, Command Sergeant Major."

And we both laughed.

Nick Stewart carried the vial back into the store. It'd been a hell of a week, but they had the formula at last.

He found Mr. Church standing in front of the cookie aisle. The man was tearing into a bag of Oreos.

"Here it is," Nick said, and put it on the shelf in front of Mr. Church.

"That's excellent," the older man said, though how much older Nick could never tell. The man could have been forty-five or maybe sixty-five. There was just no way of telling. He was one of those people who defied description.

"Anything else?" Nick asked.

"You had help, I see."

"That cop, yeah. Former Ranger, I'm pretty sure of it."

"He handled himself well?"

"Very well."

"Oh. That's excellent." Mr. Church twisted open an Oreo cookie and ate the filling first. "Someone we should keep an eye on, perhaps?"

"I think so, yeah."

Mr. Church finished off the rest of his Oreo, apparently lost in thought.

Nick knew better than to fill up the silence with small talk. With nothing more to say, he quietly bled back into the night.

ABOUT THE AUTHOR

Joe McKinney has his feet in several different worlds. In his day job, he has worked as a patrol officer for the San Antonio Police Department, a DWI enforcement officer, a disaster mitigation specialist, a homicide detective, the director of the city of San Antonio's 911 call center, and a patrol supervisor. He played college baseball for Trinity University, where he graduated with a bachelor's degree in American history, and went on to earn a master's degree in English literature from the University of Texas at San Antonio. He was the manager of a Barnes & Noble for a while, where he indulged a lifelong obsession with books. He published his first novel, *Dead City*, in 2006, a book that has since been recognized as a seminal work in the zombie genre. Since then, he has gone on to win two Bram Stoker Awards and expanded his oeuvre to cover everything from true crime and writings on police procedure to science fiction to cooking to Texas history. The author of more than twenty books, he is a frequent guest at horror and mystery conventions. Joe and his wife, Tina, have two lovely daughters and make their home in a little town just outside of San Antonio, where he pursues his passion for cooking and makes what some consider to be the finest batch of chili in Texas. You can keep up with all of Joe's latest releases by friending him on Facebook.

THREE TIMES

BY JENNIFER CAMPBELL-HICKS

Emily Grant's assignment that day: cover the historic unveiling of the Freedom Bell. She walked from the newsroom, only a few blocks away. Hundreds of people had gathered outside the Liberty Bell Center in the muggy summer heat, waiting for the July Fourth festivities to begin. Emily wove her way through the crowd to the building's entrance.

A uniformed guard eyed her. "What's the name, sweetheart?"

Sweetheart? She cringed.

"Emily Grant. *Philadelphia Inquirer.*"

"Credentials?"

She flashed her work ID, which he checked against a list.

"Over there with the others."

The others were reporters, photographers, television camera operators, and TV talking heads—local and national—crushed along one wall, roped off like dangerous animals.

"Good idea," Emily said. "Wouldn't want us mingling with the First Lady and the Washington bigwigs. You never know, we might bite."

"Next," the guard said.

Scowling, Emily walked through the metal detectors and inside.

She spotted the *Inquirer*'s photographer Craig and joined him against the rope line. The toll from decades of chasing down news was etched into his weathered face. He nodded to her while he fiddled with his camera's buttons and dials.

Emily looked around the open, airy hall. She'd meant to bring her daughter, Mia, here but hadn't found the time. They'd moved to Philly only a few months ago, after Mia's father left them. Not that Emily blamed him. Doug wanted stable, and she'd been anything but. As always when she thought about Doug, her fingers sought out the small silver medallion hooked to her purse zipper. Three months sober, it said.

Across the hall stood the Liberty Bell, encased in glass, Independence Hall visible through floor-to-ceiling windows behind it. The bell radiated history, more than its copper and tin, the very soul of its era. Everyone felt it. Visitors, journalists, dignitaries, guards, they all kept glancing its way.

A second, similar platform stood draped in a tent decorated in stars and stripes. That could only be the new Freedom Bell, a replica of the Liberty Bell but without the crack.

People packed the hall, first the city's movers and shakers, then a few dozen lucky members of the public, all under the watch of grim-faced government agents—tough-looking men and women, some in suits, some in civilian clothes. They looked ready for trouble, as though they expected it.

One agent in particular caught Emily's attention. Short brown hair and a fit body. She moved with confidence and poise, a woman whom men respected instead of objectified, who didn't take shit from anyone. If someone called her "sweetheart," she would kick their ass.

"Who is she?" Emily asked, mostly to herself, but Craig answered.

"Homeland Security or FBI. She looks tough. I heard someone call her 'Major.'"

"Is that a rank? Call sign?"

He shrugged. "All I know is I wouldn't want to cross her."

"I don't want to cross her. I want to be her," Emily said—instead of a recovering alcoholic single mother who hadn't been to the gym in ages.

"We'll never be like her," Craig said. "We eat cornflakes for breakfast. She eats bullets."

Emily laughed. "Bullets? Are you serious?"

"Hey, it sounded good."

"It sounds like bad 1950s noir. And I hate cornflakes."

"Me too," Craig said.

When the hall was packed tighter than a bar during an Eagles game, and the stink of too many bodies bordered on intolerable, the First Lady stepped onto a podium and tapped her microphone.

"Cue the boring speech," Craig said.

"You think?"

"Bet you a dollar."

Emily didn't take the bet and was glad she didn't. The First Lady launched into a recitation of the Liberty Bell's history. Emily took notes on her reporter's pad and recorded audio on her phone to play back later in the newsroom. Not that she planned to include a history lesson in her article.

The crowd shifted, restless. No one wanted to see the First Lady. Not really. They wanted the grand finale, still draped in patriotic red, white, and blue. The First Lady gestured to another woman on the podium wearing a yellow pantsuit—Andrea Lester, maker of the Freedom Bell, as grim-faced as the federal agents who prowled the hall.

That was strange. Andrea Lester was the reason for this pomp. Every newspaper in the country would centerpiece her work on 1A, an artist's dream come true. Shouldn't she be glowing?

"Something isn't right," Emily said.

"What's that?" Craig asked.

Before she could explain, the First Lady finished her speech with a triumphant wave. The red, white, and blue covering fell away to reveal the Freedom Bell. The audience gasped and applauded. The crowd outside the windows roared. Craig and the other photographers snapped photos.

A scream. A shout.

Emily looked for the source.

A yell from the podium. It was the artist, Andrea Lester. In her hand she held a knife.

Emily froze. She couldn't move. Couldn't breathe. Couldn't look away as Andrea Lester lunged toward the First Lady.

This isn't happening.

Gunshots. Red blossomed across Andrea Lester's yellow pantsuit, and she fell away from the First Lady. Panic crashed down like a tsunami, immediate, total, inescapable. It swept up Emily, too. An attack on the First Lady!

At the rope line, Craig snapped photos.

More gunshots. Suddenly every agent in the room held a weapon.

Bullets flew. Emily ducked down. Why were they shooting at each other? Weren't they all on the same side? What the hell was going on? The pop-pop of shots mixed with the screaming.

"Seal the room!" a man yelled.

On the podium, the First Lady had vanished under a pile of Secret Service agents.

I have to get out, Emily thought with the dead certainty that she could never manage it. Too many people stood between her and the exit. And if agents had sealed the exits, no one was going anywhere.

Agents bellowed orders.

One yelled, "No!"

The yell was desperate. Terrified.

Something triggered in Emily. An instinct. Without knowing why, she dropped to the floor.

The Freedom Bell exploded.

It broke apart with a loud bang. Bits blew outward in all directions. Shards hit Congress members, dignitaries, ambassadors, children.

By sheer chance, Craig stood between Emily and the bell. He dropped his camera as he reached to where a shard had punctured his neck. Emily snatched the camera and set it aside.

Craig swayed. She helped him to sit on the floor. The room descended further in chaos. Now Emily silently thanked whoever had put the media pen where they had, because she and Craig weren't in the middle of it. She pulled the shard from his neck. Glass, hollow with a pointed tip.

"It's a dart," she said.

"What the hell?" Craig said, and pulled another dart from his leg. "Why? What's it for?"

"Don't know. Keep still."

"Are you hit?"

She checked herself. "No."

"My camera—"

"I caught it."

"Give it to me."

"Are you crazy? We have to keep down. We're in the middle of a terrorist attack."

Even as she said the words, she couldn't believe them. Of course the United States had been hit before, but these things happened to other people, in other places.

"My camera," Craig repeated firmly. His face had a pallid, sickly sheen.

He was right. They were journalists. People looked to them to make sense of the nonsensical. They had to do their jobs.

Emily set the camera in his hands. He struggled to his feet. The shutter clicked. Legs shaking, Emily stood beside him and started taking notes again.

Later, she would look at her notebook and not remember a single thing she had written there. She would recall only bits and pieces, like fitting together fragments of a broken mirror.

Like when Craig dropped to his knees, eyes feverish and skin clammy. Others were also falling sick. Agents separated them out, though Craig still lay beside Emily, moaning.

The agent in charge was the woman Emily had spotted before everything had gone to hell, the one Craig said was called Major. Blood splattered her clothing and skin. While others whimpered and shook, she kept her back straight and her voice steady.

"Listen to me!" she said, and talked about a highly contagious disease. Emily caught only some of it. She couldn't stop thinking about her daughter. What would happen to Mia if she died here? And what about Craig? Would he live? She clutched his camera to her chest.

Craig stood with a strange, glassy expression. He moaned. The sound was inhuman. Emily gasped and tried to back away. Craig lunged at her, mouth wide-open, canines bared, so fast she could only scream.

Then he was on her, his weight bearing her down. But no teeth broke her skin. Craig didn't move. He lay on top of her, limp, a dead weight. His head lolled. Blood from a hole near his left ear dripped onto Emily's dress.

Above them stood Major, gun aimed at Craig, mouth pressed in a thin line, her eyes two bright, precise points.

"Did he bite you?"

"No."

"Stay there. Play dead. Don't move."

She pivoted, aimed, fired.

Emily flinched at each shot, squeezed her eyes shut, kept quiet, and followed the agent's orders exactly.

Emily returned to work. She didn't want to, but rent was due, and the bills didn't care if you'd been in a terrorist attack. One morning in the newsroom, her head pounded from the bottle she'd emptied the night before, and her mouth tasted evil. There was only one way to fix that. She was pouring bourbon into her coffee when she looked up.

Her editor, Chuck, stood over her desk, bald head gleaming under harsh fluorescent lights.

"Come with me," he said.

Damn it.

Chuck did most of his work in the newsroom with the reporters, but he also had a closet-sized office with bare walls, a desk, and two chairs, which was where he led Emily. He squeezed his considerable bulk behind the desk, sat, and gestured for Emily to do the same. She couldn't meet his gaze. She focused on his tie, blue with pinpoint yellow dots.

He rubbed his thick brown beard. "How much have you had?"

She shook her head.

"Are you drunk?"

Not drunk enough. Guilt tore at her, for the sobriety medallion gone from her purse zipper, for what she was doing to Mia. Such a sweet, trusting girl, she deserved better.

But only drinking made Emily forget the weight of Craig's dead body, blood from the hole in his head dripping onto her cheek.

Play dead. Don't move.

That woman had saved Emily's life.

Emily didn't even know her name.

"We have a zero-tolerance policy," Chuck said. "You can do what you want at home, but there are no drugs or alcohol when you're on the clock."

"I know."

He waited. "That's it? That's all you're going to give me? All right. You don't leave me a choice. I have to suspend you for a week."

That surprised her. "You can't. It was just a little kick in my coffee."

"Doesn't matter."

"But my investigation. I'm so close. I'll have the story by Thursday. You can publish Sunday. No one else has this. It'll be the scoop of the year!"

This time Chuck rubbed his bushy eyebrows, as if he had a headache. As if she were *giving* him one. "We've talked about this. You said you'd drop it. I know what you think happened on July Fourth, that a biological agent turned people into some kind of zombies—"

"Craig is not just *people*."

"It's not true. FBI, DEA, NSA, they all say the same thing. It was a hallucinogen."

"It was real."

"You imagined it, Emily."

"They're lying."

"Why would they do that?"

"I don't know. You heard the audio I recorded."

"It proved nothing. It was mostly screams and static. If we had Craig's photos . . ."

"I don't."

"Then there's no story."

Not for the first time, Emily wished she had grabbed the camera when she'd been ushered from the center, but the bodies had terrified her. Her only thought had been to get to Mia and hug her daughter, and then get drunk. Just the one time.

"I don't need the photos," Emily said. "I have twenty interviews, at least, maybe more."

"Let it go."

"I can't."

"Why not?"

"I have to find her!"

Emily jumped to her feet and yelled at her editor. Chuck also stood, not anger in his expression, but pity.

"Who?" he asked.

Emily's voice was small. "The woman who saved my life. I've gone through all the agency files—the public ones, anyway—and checked with every government contact I have. I've talked to every survivor I can find. No one knows who she is, but I'm close to finding her. I know it."

More beard rubbing. "Go home," Chuck said.

Emily sank into her chair. The false story of the hallucinogen did a disservice to all who had died and survived that day. But part of her wondered: What if the story wasn't false? What if she was wrong?

No, she couldn't accept that. Because if Chuck was right, then she was losing her mind. "I'll show you," she said.

"Not this week. As of right now, you're suspended. Use the time to get some help, all right? For your daughter's sake, if nothing else. We'll talk when you get back."

Emily left to pick up Mia at day care. She pulled her old Ford Escort onto Market Street, headed out of Center City, and slammed down her hands on the steering wheel in anger.

"Damn it!" she yelled.

A week's suspension. Really, it was a final warning. Zero-tolerance policy? Sure. Zero tolerance for the post-traumatic stress from living through a terrorist attack. Zero tolerance for survivor's guilt. Why had she walked out while so many had not?

As she had stumbled from the Liberty Center that day, she had fixated on the shattered glass case around the Liberty Bell, what was left of it splattered with red.

Happy July Fourth, America. Here's your freedom, drenched in blood.

A black SUV pulled in front of her just before a red light. She didn't think anything of it until an identical one pulled in behind her. The light turned green, and the SUV in front didn't move.

She laid into her horn.

The SUV still didn't move. The one behind her had stopped so close, she couldn't pull out and go around.

What was this?

Other drivers honked, drove around, flipped the bird.

A door opened on the back SUV. A hulking man in a T-shirt, jeans, and sunglasses walked to her Escort, a gun in a shoulder holster. He didn't even try to hide that he was packing.

"Oh, God," Emily said.

She fumbled in her purse for the mace she had taken to carrying since the attack, then thought better of it. She could spray him and run, but she couldn't spray every person in two SUVs. She stuffed the canister into her pocket.

The man pressed a badge to her window. National Security Agency.

"Get out of the car, ma'am."

The badge might be real, or not. She shut off her engine and cracked the window.

"Is something wrong?"

"Out of the car, please."

His gun hung at her eye level, an implicit threat. She opened the door and got out.

"What's this about?" she asked.

"Someone wants to talk to you."

"Who?"

"Just come with me, ma'am."

She went, and tried to not hyperventilate.

The SUV's back seat was dark behind tinted windows. Emily slid onto the brown leather. A person sat beside her. Emily could make out only a silhouette.

"Hello, Ms. Grant."

Emily gasped. She knew that voice.

Stay there. Play dead. Don't move.

It was the Major.

"Buckle up," the Major said.

Emily's breath came quicker. Her heart jackhammered. She clicked her seat belt. The Major rapped the glass between the front and back seats, and the SUV moved.

"My car—"

"Will be fine until you get back."

"I'm going back?"

"That depends on you."

"You're not NSA."

A faint smile. "What makes you say that?"

"Your accent is British."

"Let's say I'm on loan."

The SUV made a right turn. A blur of coffee shops, restaurants, stores, streetlights, trees, and pedestrians passed outside the tinted windows. A clink of metal drew Emily's gaze to the Major's lap, where she gripped a gun in a familiar way. As if she had been born holding it.

Emily shivered. "Why am I here?"

Suddenly, the Major was in Emily's face. One second she had been across the seat; the next she forced Emily back until the door handle jabbed into her spine. The gun pressed into Emily's side, colder than she had thought possible. Her muscles tensed so hard they hurt. She felt for the mace in her pocket, but who was she kidding? "We eat cornflakes for breakfast," Craig had said. "She eats bullets." Then she killed zombies for lunch. In a fight, Emily didn't stand a chance.

"You're asking questions," the Major said.

"How do you know about that?"

"That doesn't matter. Here's what does: You need to stop your investigation."

Or what? Emily almost asked, but she feared the answer had to do with the gun, so she said nothing.

Her investigation had drawn these agents to her. They hadn't started this. She had. And her decision alone would determine how it ended. That gave her leverage.

Or it might get her killed.

"This is about national security," the Major said. "I'm not asking you to drop it. I'm ordering you. Do you understand?"

"I hate guns," Emily said, voice trembling. "The attack. Please."

The gun pressed harder into her side.

"Understand?"

"On one condition."

A scowl. "What condition?"

"Tell me what happened on July Fourth. Not for print. Say it's off the record, if you like. It's for me alone. I need the truth."

The Major searched her eyes. Emily met her gaze unflinching, one of the hardest things she had ever done. Finally, the Major nodded.

"I see you do."

"I'll drop my investigation, I swear. I won't print it."

"I believe you," she said, as though she knew something about Emily's ethical code. How much did she know? She must have one hell of an information source. "You have until the SUV stops."

The Major set the gun on her lap.

Emily dove in.

"Was there a hallucinogen?"

"No."

Despite herself, Emily smiled, relieved. She wasn't crazy. "Was there a pathogen in the darts, a bioweapon that turned people into—" She stopped.

"Zombies? Yes, there was."

Holy crap.

"Was it contagious?"

The Major took a shuddering breath. "Very. Those who were infected were driven to infect others by any means."

"Like a bite," she said, thinking of Craig.

"Especially a bite."

"That's why you killed them."

"They were already dead." Her voice was steady but sad. "It was over the moment the pathogen entered their bodies. Our only option was to eliminate all the carriers right then. Otherwise, the pathogen would have spread, uncontrolled, across the Earth."

That sank in. The human species would have been wiped out. But it hadn't been, thanks to this woman and her fellow agents, while Emily had only cowered under Craig's body and then drowned herself in a bottle of bourbon.

She had been weak.

Her face heated with shame.

"Who are you?" Emily asked. "What's your name?"

The Major stared. Her expression softened.

The SUV stopped.

The door opened, letting in fresh air. An agent stood there. Emily blinked at the sudden invasion of sunlight.

"She's free to go," the Major said to the agent, then added to Emily, "Remember your promise. I'll be watching."

Emily didn't doubt it.

The SUV had parked behind her Escort. They had gone around the block. As soon as Emily got out, blinking in the bright sun, both SUVs pulled out and drove off down the street. Gone. As though she had dreamed it. Except Emily knew the truth now and couldn't tell a soul. She slid into her driver's seat and imagined what devastation the pathogen would have caused had it spread. On this street alone: wrecked cars, broken windows, looting, gunfire, screams, and moans.

Then she imagined herself as one of the agents who had prevented that apocalypse, wrapped in Kevlar, a gun in each hand, picking off the infected with perfect shots like targets in a carnival game.

That just wasn't her.

A pickup honked.

"Come on, lady, go!"

She wanted to yell back, *Shut up, you're lucky to be alive!* Instead she flipped him off, turned on the ignition, and drove. Two blocks later, she made the vow. No more wallowing. No more drink. No more suspensions. She should have died on July Fourth, but she hadn't. This was another chance to not screw up her life, and she wouldn't waste it.

Only when she parked outside Mia's day care did she remember that Major hadn't said her name.

A month later, Emily listened to the police scanner in the newsroom while hunting through social media feeds for news. A murder or car wreck. She'd settle for a cat up a tree.

On one of the newsroom's many televisions, set to CNN on mute, the words *BREAKING NEWS* and *TERRORIST ATTACK FOILED* blared across the screen in capital letters, bright red. The pretty blond anchor looked solemn as she talked into the camera.

"Hey, John," Emily yelled. "Turn that up."

John, who sat next to the TV, thumbed the volume.

". . . not giving details on the attack," the anchor said. "Again, here's what we know at this time. The intended attack was global in nature, but halted at the last minute by an American strike team . . ."

Emily listened intently.

She didn't jump at every car backfire anymore, not since she had learned the truth about the Liberty Center attack. She had feared she would never sleep soundly again, but that night, her insomnia had melted away and she had slept better than in weeks. She'd called her AA sponsor and attended meetings. She spent more time with Mia. She had even started yoga classes three mornings a week. Life got better.

But she still paid attention to any terrorist action anywhere in the world. "It's an obsession," Chuck said, and he was right.

No one could blame her, considering.

The CNN anchor put a hand to her earpiece. "We're getting new information. I'm told the Defense Department is confirming a death. A British agent. This is the first we've heard about any nationality besides American involved in the action. The DOD has released a photo and a name."

The photo flashed on the screen.

She wore a uniform, her hair pulled back.

Smiling. Happy.

Emily had never seen her happy.

She doubled over her trash can and vomited up the coffee and bagel she'd had for breakfast.

"Are you all right?" John asked.

"Fine," she said.

"Not pregnant, are you?"

"Are you?" she snapped back.

That shut him up. She wiped off her mouth and walked to Chuck's desk. Today's tie sported stripes of deep green and silver—Philadelphia Eagles colors. He was typing an email.

"In a minute," he said.

"It's important."

"So is this. We're trying to find out if there's any local connection to that." He pointed at another TV, also tuned to coverage of the attack.

"There is," Emily said.

He stopped typing. "Go on."

"The British agent who died was at the Liberty Center. She was in charge of the agents who brought down the attackers."

"You're shitting me."

"I'm not."

"You're not having a relapse, are you? Because if this is another one of your delusions—"

Emily bristled. "Every survivor I interviewed talked about her. No one knew her name, but they all described a female British agent that the other agents called Major. That's her. She was there."

Chuck swiveled his chair to face her. "She's the one who saved your life."

"Yes."

"Do you need to go home? Take the day off?"

That sounded attractive.

She couldn't.

"I need to write this story, Chuck."

"You're too close to it."

"That's why it has to be me. I can't bear the thought of anyone else doing it. I already have the contacts and interviews from before."

"You're sure?"

She nodded.

"Then it's yours. This isn't the hard news. The wires will have that covered. You write the reaction from local survivors. That woman is a hero, twice over. That's the story. I want you to do your best to answer one question."

"What's that?"

"Who is she?"

"The DOD isn't going to release that information—"

He waved her off. "I don't care about the DOD. I want to know who she is to the *survivors*. Think you can do that?"

Oh, yes, she could.

"Absolutely, boss."

"Then get to it."

Emily returned to her desk, pulled up her file of survivors' phone numbers, picked one, and dialed.

"Hello?"

"Hello, Tim Weiss?"

"Yes."

"This is Emily Grant at the *Inquirer*. Have you seen the news?"

A pause. "I thought I might hear from you."

Emily worked the story hard, well into the afternoon. This was her zone, what she did best. She left out what the Major had told her. That promise she would never break. Instead, she wove in her memories with the other survivors' stories. Their hero was dead. No one could bring her back. But Emily could bring her to life on the page, help people to know her as more than a name and photograph, and make certain she finally received the recognition she deserved.

Details on the attack leaked over the next few days. The Extinction Wave. Cyrus Jakoby. And the woman who stopped them.

The influence of Emily's article in setting the public conversation was huge and immediate. Media across the United States and as far away as Russia and Australia picked up the story. Emily did interviews with CNN, BBC. Some of her co-workers joked about her sudden fame, but in every interview, Emily deflected attention from herself. She wasn't the hero, and she made sure everyone knew it.

The world needed real heroes.

Now more than ever.

The funeral was six days later in Baltimore. The procession past the coffin took hours. Thousands of people came, but only a few hundred attended the private service. Those seats went to the president and First Lady, members of Congress, heads of state, ambassadors.

Because of her article, Emily received the honor of an invitation— not as a reporter but as a mourner. That was the deal. She couldn't write about the funeral because no press was allowed.

She sat in the back and cried.

In this chapel were the people who kept the world safe. They asked for no recognition, but they had Emily's total respect. She had never fired a gun. She couldn't stop a terrorist attack. But she could bring sense to the nonsensical. Her tools were phones and computers, and her bullets were words. Her work wasn't flashy, but it was just as important, in its own way.

It was enough.

Emily walked past the coffin, which was closed. She appreciated that. She didn't want her last memories to be of a body. She brushed her fingertips over the American and British flags draped over the top and moved away.

Three blocks from the chapel, in a green, leafy park, an impromptu memorial had sprung up, the kind where people left flowers and Hallmark cards. Someone had donated a pink teddy bear. The fur was matted and one eye was missing, perhaps a child's cherished friend and the biggest way that child could say thank you.

Traffic roared in the distance. A squirrel chattered and scurried up a tree while a young woman in military blues walked up, set down a single red rose, snapped a salute, and walked away.

Emily knelt by the memorial, took a folded paper from her pants pocket, and laid it beside the teddy bear. She didn't have to unfold the paper to know what she had written.

"The first time, you saved my life. The second time, you saved my sanity. The third time, you saved the world. Thank you, Major Grace Courtland."

ABOUT THE AUTHOR
Jennifer Campbell-Hicks's work has appeared in *Clarkesworld*, *Nature: Futures*, *Raygun Chronicles: Space Opera for a New Age*, and many other anthologies and magazines. She is a journalist who was on the Pulitzer Prize–winning staff of the *Denver Post* and lives in Colorado with her husband, her two children, and her dog. Visit her blog at www.jennifercampbellhicks .blogspot.com.

PSYCH EVAL

BY LARRY CORREIA

"Why am I being interrogated?" she snapped as soon as Rudy walked through the door.

"Relax. It's just an interview."

"Then why does the sign say INTERROGATION ROOM?"

Rudy pulled out a chair and sat down across the metal table from one of the survivors of Bowie Team. She was obviously suspicious and frightened, but his goal was to help, not make this adversarial. Lieutenant Carver had been through enough already. Rudy's plan was to be his normal, good-humored self, and help this brave soldier through the aftermath of her ordeal.

Unless Mr. Church's suspicion was right, and she was a murderous traitor, because then her fate was out of his hands.

"This room is what the army had available on short notice. Believe me, I'd much rather be having this conversation in a nice office." As usual, he wanted to make his patient feel safe and comfortable. Only it was summer in Texas, the building's air conditioner was dying, and it was muggy enough in these stuffy, windowless rooms that sweat rings were already forming on his shirt. So comfort was out, but Rudy could still try to make her feel safe.

"We've not spoken before, Lieutenant Carver. I'm Dr. Sanchez. You can call me Rudy."

"The Department of Military Sciences' number one shrink. I know who you are, so I know why you're here. But I'm not crazy."

"Nobody said you were."

"I'm not a liar. I know what I saw. I gave my report."

She was clearly agitated. Rudy had read her file on the way over. The DMS mission was so sensitive that every team member's background had been gone over with a fine-tooth comb. Her record wasn't just clean, it was spotless. Her service record was exemplary. Carver's previous psych evaluation had made her sound as a rock, solid under pressure, but the poor young woman in front of him today had been reduced to an emotional wreck.

He'd watched her through the one-way glass before coming in. She'd spent the whole time staring off into space and occasionally muttering something incomprehensible to herself. Now that there was another person for her to focus on, she was demonstrating bad tremors in her hands. Her eyes kept flicking nervously from side to side. By all accounts Carver had been fine before leaving on this mission, but she'd developed several severe nervous tics in the last forty-eight hours.

"I've read your report, Lieutenant. Do you mind if I call you Olivia?" She didn't respond, so he went with it. "Believe me, Olivia, I'm on your side. After some of the things I've heard from other teams over the years, I never assume anybody in this outfit is lying, regardless of what they say they ran into."

"Do you believe in the Devil, Rudy?"

Considering what she'd just been through, with most of her team murdered and the only other survivors in critical condition, it wasn't such an odd question. "I believe in good and evil. My small part in that struggle is helping good people deal with traumatic events and the horrors they've faced. I'm just here to help you."

Carver stared at him for a long time. It was the first time her tremors had stopped. She responded as though she hadn't even heard his words. "I believe in him now."

"You hungry? Want some coffee or something?"

The survivor lifted her arm to show that her wrist was handcuffed to the metal table.

"Yeah, well. Sorry. That's not my call," Rudy explained.

"No. It's his." She looked over at the mirrored wall and raised her voice. "Hello, Mr. Church."

Rudy just shook his head, but he didn't deny who was on the other side of the glass. He'd asked about the necessity of the restraints already—it was hard to make somebody feel safe enough to open up while they were chained like a prisoner—but he had been shot down. Apparently it wasn't clear yet who had done *all* of the killing. Lieutenant Carver could be the survivor of some kind of new chemical hallucinatory attack, or the victim of an unknown terrorist bioweapon, or she could have just had a psychotic break, or even be a traitor who had simply murdered her teammates in cold blood and lied to cover it up. The fact was they didn't even yet know what they didn't know.

Say what you will about working for the DMS, it was never predictable.

"Let's just talk. Tell me about the mission. Tell me about what happened in Mexico."

This part of Sonora looked a lot like Arizona. She was born and raised in Phoenix, so it seemed weird to be rolling hot in an area of operation that looked suspiciously like her hometown. Only back home she hadn't been worried about car bombs or cartel gunfights growing up, common threats the poor folks stuck here had to deal with on a daily basis.

Their convoy moved fast. The black government Suburbans barely slowed as they left the paved road and hit gravel. Carver was at the wheel of the second vehicle in line. The view out the window was creosote bushes and sun-baked rocks as far as the eye could see, just as it had been for the last hour. The only difference was now the ride got bumpier, and she began to taste dust in the air-conditioning.

Captain Quinn got on the radio. He said something in Spanish, and the last three vehicles in their convoy broke off. Those were white-and-green pickups filled with *Federales*. They would be setting up a roadblock to keep anyone from getting in or out of the AO. From here on in, the DMS was on its own. The Mexican government and the U.S. State Department had come to an agreement that all parties were cool with. This was the DMS's show. Everybody official was just going to deny that this op ever happened anyway.

Their commanding officer was in the vehicle behind them. Satisfied that they were now speeding toward the target by themselves, the captain switched to the encrypted DMS channels and addressed Bowie Team.

"We're ten minutes out. You know the drill."

There would be silence between their vehicles the rest of the way in.

Intercepting even garbled radio transmissions could warn the bad guys something was up. Carver just concentrated on driving. The loose gravel turned to washboard, which threatened to rattle their armored vehicle to death. These pigs didn't have the smoothest ride in the best situations.

Sandbag was riding shotgun. Gator and Corvus were in the back seat. Louie was serving as trunk monkey, ready to pop open the back window and open fire with a SAW.

"You really think there's something to this intel, LT?" Sandbag asked.

"We know Hezbollah has an exchange program going with the cartels for years," she answered. "One side has expertise, the other has more money than it knows what to do with. Smuggling people and weapons across the border is a piece of cake to the cartel, and terrorists get an easy way into the U.S. It's a match made in heaven."

"Yeah, nothing like sharing your cultural traditions with others, like beheading, or car bombings," Gator interjected.

"Well, now DMS thinks they're sharing something else. Word is a few days ago an unknown weapon was shipped from an undisclosed location in the Middle East to this little town. Once it is ready, they'll send it north. We just don't know what it is yet. Which is why we're going to nab these bastards and find out," Carver stated. She was trying to stay right behind the truck ahead of her without rear-ending it while blinded by its plume of dust. At least the dust was obscuring the view of cactus and endless nothing. "It's one thing to look at this area on the map, another to see it in person. They picked a village so isolated that it's making me worried they're playing with something really nasty."

Her teammates readied their weapons. They were pumped. They'd done this sort of thing many times before, but it was always exhilarating. When they were only a few minutes out, Carver hit play on the sound system. This song was pre-raid tradition for them. Captain Quinn was a proud Texan, so when the DMS had set up a team out of Fort Hood, he had christened it Bowie Team. Of course, his boys had immediately decided that meant David rather than Jim.

"I'm Afraid of Americans" began playing over the Suburban's speakers.

Carver grinned. *Good.* The terrorist assholes they were hunting should be.

The Suburban ahead of them was slowing down. That didn't make any sense—the village was still a mile away—but she slammed on the brakes fast enough to keep from rear-ending them.

"Get ready." Something was up. It could be an ambush. It could be a barricade. Regardless, speed was their ally. Getting bogged down out here meant the cartel was more likely to see them coming and get ready. "What the hell, Zeke?" she muttered. He was driving the lead vehicle and wasn't the type to hesitate.

But nothing happened. The point vehicle maintained radio silence, lollygagged for only a few seconds, before speeding up again.

"Yo, LT. Check it out." It was Sandbag who first saw what had caused the point vehicle to hesitate. He tapped the bulletproof glass of the passenger-side window. "There's a—Good Lord . . ."

There were telephone lines running alongside the road. The poles were the tallest thing for miles, and so constant, flashing by every couple hundred feet, that she'd begun to tune them out. Only this one was different. Somebody had been *nailed* to it.

There wasn't much time to assess. Hanging ten feet up . . . adult male, Mexican, mid-thirties, jeans and a flannel shirt, coated in dried blood. Arms extended above his head, dangling with multiple nails— no, spikes—through his hands and wrists.

Then it flashed by. She looked in her mirror, but the body was already obscured by the dust.

Since Louie was in back he'd gotten the best look. "I know the cartel leaves some brutal warnings, but crucifixion? Damn. Fucking barbarians."

Then they passed another pole, and there was another body stuck to it. Female. Twenties. Vultures were perched on the crossbeam above her. There was more swearing and muttering. And then she, too, was swallowed by the dust.

The next telephone pole had another body hung on it. This one was elderly. Had she been somebody's *abuelita*? And the next. And the next. Every couple hundred feet the spectacle repeated. Men, women, children. The soldiers quit talking. This wasn't a warning. This was a massacre.

Numb, Carver concentrated on the road.

"All the way to the village?" Rudy asked.

"All the way," she confirmed. "Every single pole."

He swallowed hard. "That wasn't in your initial report."

Carver shook her head. "Considering what else we saw, it wasn't that noteworthy."

Bowie Team rolled into the village ready for a fight.

It was dead.

She'd been ready for the sound of gunfire, but there was nothing. There should have at least been a dog barking. There was no movement, no sound other than the wind. There were a few dozen small houses and other assorted buildings, but not so much as a curtain parted for the locals to spy on them. No matter how scared they were, nobody kept their heads down that well.

Ten seconds after dismounting, they stacked up on the little grocery market that their intel had said housed their targets, tossed bangs through the windows, breached the doors, and rushed inside.

"Clear!" Carver shouted after she swept through the back storage room. The smell of death assaulted her nostrils. There were dried blood puddles on the uneven wooden floor, big enough that it looked as if they'd butchered a cow in here, but no bodies, and certainly no living terrorists or cartel members.

Somebody had set up a shrine inside the storeroom. She'd seen the painted skull faces in the briefings, *Santa Muerte*, popular with the cartel assassins. Corvus walked over to the shrine and started shoving around the flowers, papers, and dolls with the muzzle of his SCAR, checking if there was anything interesting. All of the crucifixes had been turned upside-down. He found a plastic dog bowl. Corvus gagged and backed away from the shrine. There was a pile of glistening white spheres inside.

"I think those are human eyeballs, LT."

A bunch of little devotional candles were still lit around the shrine. So the occupants couldn't have been gone long.

"They must have bolted," Sandbag said. "Did they see us coming?"

She shook her head. There was only one road out, and nobody had passed them. The terrain was rugged enough that they could have escaped on foot, horseback, or four-wheelers, but she wasn't getting that vibe at all. "My gut's telling me nobody got out of this place."

"Yo, LT. I've got something weird here. It looks really old." Gator had picked up an odd-looking silver amulet. He was scowling at it. "Is that Arabic?"

She looked at the antique. It was the head of a goat, with ruby eyes. An unconscious shiver of revulsion went through her and she had no idea why. "Greek? Maybe. I don't know what language that is."

Gator was holding it in his glove. Suddenly, red droplets of blood appeared on the silver. She looked up to see that it was coming from Gator's nose. He was just staring at it, and didn't seem to notice the rivulet of blood running down his chin. It was as if he were in a daze.

"Gator, you're bleeding."

It took him a long second to focus. He slowly looked up from the amulet. "Huh?"

"Did you hit your head or something?"

Gator seemed to snap out of it. He wiped the blood away with a sleeve and looked at it in surprise. "Naw. Damned dry heat."

Captain Quinn came over the radio. "Target's in the wind. We're splitting into teams and searching the town. Zeke, take the cantina. Carver, you've got the church."

"Roger that. We're on the church." She let go of the transmit button. "Bag that necklace and let's go."

"What did you find in the church?" Rudy asked softly.

"He found us." The lieutenant's trembling had gotten worse. He was inclined to give her a sedative, but Mr. Church had been adamant they needed answers now.

"Who is *he?*"

Rudy waited for her to elaborate, but this interview was like pulling teeth. "Tell me about what happened in the church, Olivia."

Abruptly her trembling stopped. The change in manner was so complete, so chilling, that it brought to mind patients he'd worked with suffering from dissociative identity disorder. In the blink of an eye, there was a different person sitting across from him. Only this one was utterly calm.

"Are you okay, Olivia?"

Seemingly curious, Carver tilted her head to the side, a bit too far. "I like eyes. Your eyes are broken, Rudy. I can only see through one of them."

The shift was so sudden, and the topic so unexpected, that it put him off his game. "I was injured. I have a glass eye."

Carver nodded slowly. "Your world is flat."

"You mean I have no depth perception. Correct."

She stared at him for a long time. "It makes me sad you're broken."

Despite being summer in Texas, Rudy felt a sudden chill. There was a knock on the other side of the glass. It made him jump.

He tried to hide his relief at having an interruption. "Excuse me a minute." Rudy got up and went to the door. He had to wait for them to unlock it.

There were four MPs waiting in the hall. Mr. Church was by himself in the observation room. He was simply standing there in the dark, watching Lieutenant Carver through the one-way glass, inscrutable as ever.

"What do you think, Doctor?"

"It's too early to tell. She's a severely traumatized young woman who has been through a lot, but beyond that I'm going to need more time to reach her."

"I've received a call from another agency. They are sending a specialist. He'll be here soon."

"What kind of specialist?" Rudy asked suspiciously. "From what agency?"

"The kind you don't ask questions about. His name is Franks. I've worked with him before." Considering how broad and mysterious Church's background was, that was incredibly unhelpful. "Agent Franks is a thoroughly unpleasant individual, but very good at what he does. You'll want to stay out of his way. He's not big on conversation."

"It's unlike you to turn over DMS jurisdiction to someone else. Carver is one of us."

"Is she?"

"What do you mean by that?"

Church glanced at the wall clock. "He should arrive in an hour."

"Then let me keep talking to her until this specialist shows up."

"I wouldn't advise that. . . . However, I will admit I'm curious to hear what she has to say. Carry on."

"Okay, then." Rudy started walking away.

Church called after him, "By the way, Doctor, we got the preliminary results back on her dead teammates. No toxins, drugs, or biological agents were present in their systems. The causes of death were all straightforward—gunshot wounds, stabbings, strangulation, blunt-force trauma, that sort of thing."

"Okay. Anything else?"

"It might be a sticky subject, but I would suggest asking her about the cannibalism."

"*What?*"

"Human tissue was found in some of their stomachs. We have not had the time to get the DNA results yet, but considering some of the bite patterns on the survivors, it probably came from their teammates."

Rudy blanched.

"Do you still want to continue?"

As he'd told Carver, his small part was helping put the good people back together. Until proven otherwise, he was going to assume good whenever possible. "Yeah, I've got this."

"Very well. Can I help you with anything else, Doctor?"

"Sure, tell the army to turn down the air conditioner. It's freezing in that little room."

"Really? They were just apologizing to me for the accommodations. According to the thermometer it is over eighty degrees in here."

"Shit." Rudy put his head down, plowed through the hall, past the MPs, and back into the oddest psych eval he'd done in quite some time.

Carver had gone back to shaking and mumbling. It was sad, but that sign of human frailty made him far more comfortable than the creepy mood swing from a few minutes before. Rudy sat back down. She gave him a weak smile.

"Okay, Olivia. Tell me about what happened inside that church."

Corvus kicked the door open and her men swept inside. They had trained so constantly that their movement was like clockwork. Each one covered a sector.

"Clear!"

A minute later the small Catholic church was secured. There was still no sign of the tangos, or any of the locals, for that matter. There should have been something.

The church was old, and humble. The wooden walls had been painted white a long time ago, but they were faded and chipped now. Heavily lacquered wooden saints looked down on them. The pews were polished smooth from decades of use.

"Where is everybody?" Louie wondered aloud.

"Nailed to the telephone poles," Sandbag muttered.

"No, this town held more people than that." But that didn't mean she had a clue where they'd gone. Carver had her men take up defensive positions on the doors and got on her radio to contact Captain Quinn. She got nothing but static. *Weird.* "This place is giving me a bad vibe."

Carver turned around and nearly jumped out of her skin when she saw a little Mexican boy sitting on the altar. Sensing her reaction, her men spun around, lifting their weapons.

"Hold on!" she shouted before fingers could reach the triggers. "It's just a kid." He was probably only seven or eight years old, barefoot and wearing a T-shirt and shorts. "Whose section was that? Damn it, Corvus! Why didn't you clear that?"

"I did, LT. He wasn't there a second ago."

It didn't matter now. They'd found *somebody.* Carver swung her carbine around behind her back and let it dangle by the sling. She lifted both hands to show they were empty. *"Hola."* She spoke three languages fluently, but Spanish wasn't among them. Sandbag was fluent, though. "Tell him we're friends."

Sandbag started talking. He was a big, scary dude, but he kept his voice nice and soothing. Only the little boy kept staring at her instead. She found it odd that he was sitting cross-legged on the altar. She wasn't religious, but that seemed really disrespectful. "Ask him what's going on."

Sandbag did. The boy smirked as he answered.

"He says he just got up from a long nap."

"Huh? Where?"

"In the ground, I think. No. A tomb." Sandbag shrugged. "He's not making a lot of sense, LT."

"Ask him where everybody is."

The little boy finally looked at Sandbag and rattled off a dismissive answer. Sandbag seemed really confused by it.

"He says that he forced them to walk across the desert."

"Who did?"

"Him." Sandbag nodded at the kid. "He's talking about himself. He said he did it."

The little boy had an annoyed expression on his face. He said something else, as if he were correcting the translator. He spoke for a long time. Sandbag's eyes kept getting wide.

"He says he made them take their shoes off so their feet would bleed on the rocks and thorns, and to not stop until they fell. They're probably dead from thirst by now." Sandbag was distressed. He'd never struck Carver as the religious type, so when he unconsciously crossed himself, it unnerved her. "That was only for the ones who pray. The rest he nailed to the poles."

"Little fucker would need a ladder," Corvus muttered. "He's gone mental."

"He says they brought him here, but they didn't understand what they dug up. He's insulted they thought he was just some mere weapon."

The kid smiled at them.

Then he began weeping blood.

That was when everything went horribly wrong.

Rudy realized he was gripping the edge of the table so hard that his knuckles had turned white.

"What's wrong, Rudy?" Lieutenant Carver asked him with unnerving calm. "You seem frightened."

"I'm fine."

"No. You are broken. You are an unworthy vessel."

All the hair on his arms stood up. "You mean my eye?"

"Among other things." She smiled, but it wasn't a real smile. It was more as if something were wearing Carver's face as a mask, and pulled the strings to make the face muscles perform the motions it assumed were appropriate. "I've been hidden away so long. The world above has changed. I do not understand it anymore. I was supposed to rest until the final days. Only the Canaanites opened my tomb. By the time I was fully awake, they had brought me to the hot lands below."

"Canaanites?"

"I don't care what you name them now. I was weak, without purpose. I have found one again. I will seek out my old enemy, and begin our war anew."

Rudy didn't know where his next question came from. "Why did you come *here*?"

"I heard this one's song. I had to come and see for myself if it was true. Is my enemy here?"

"Who?" It was now so cold his breath came out as steam.

She leaned close and whispered to him.

Rudy bolted upright and headed for the door. He pounded on it.

Thankfully the MPs opened it right away. "Keep that locked. Nobody else goes in or out." He didn't have the authority to order them around, but it wasn't a suggestion.

Church was waiting for him in the observation area. "She really seems to be opening up to you, Doctor."

Rudy raised one hand to stop Church. He wasn't in the mood. He was silent for a long time, breathing hard, staring through the glass at the woman on the other side. She'd gone back to trembling, knees nervously bouncing, just a poor, traumatized woman who had seen her squad turn on each other and rip themselves to pieces.

"Clinically, on the record, I'd say she's severely delusional."

"And off the record?"

"I'm not going back in there without a priest."

Then the lights went out.

"Stay calm." Church's voice was flat.

The logical part of his mind immediately rationalized the power outage. The overworked air conditioner had caused the building to blow a fuse. But the part of him that had just been laid bare, and terrified by an alien presence that should not be, knew that wasn't the case.

The lights came back on.

She had left two bloody red handprints on the other side of the glass for them.

"Carver's gone."

The interrogation room was empty. The handcuffs were on the table, still closed, as if she'd just torn her hands right out of them. The door was closed.

Church moved to the hall. The MPs were still there, oblivious but unharmed. He threw open the door, and despite Rudy's admonition to the contrary, they knew not to mess with Mr. Church. He came back out. "Sound the alarm. Find her, but do not engage." The soldiers rushed off. Church returned a moment later, glowering. "She's escaped."

Nothing ever seemed to shake Church, but Rudy was sick to his stomach. "That specialist who's on the way . . . he's an exorcist, isn't he?"

"I don't know if Agent Franks puts that on his business cards, but I suppose that might be among his many qualifications," Church replied. "This is important, Doctor. I couldn't make it out over the speaker, but the last thing she said to you, when you asked her about this old enemy, about why she'd come here, what did she say to you?"

"The song said '*God Is an American*.'"

ABOUT THE AUTHOR

Larry Correia is the *New York Times* bestselling, award-winning author of the *Monster Hunter International* series, the *Grimnoir Chronicles*, the *Dead Six* trilogy, and *Son of the Black Sword*. He has also written dozens of short stories and two novels set in the Warmachine universe, is actually the basis of a G.I. Joe character, and wrote the audiobook *The Adventures of Tom Stranger, Interdimensional Insurance Agent*. Before becoming a full-time writer, Larry was an accountant, a machine gun dealer, a firearms instructor, and a military contractor. He lives in the mountains of northern Utah.

CRASH COURSE

BY DANA FREDSTI

"Why are we doing this again?"

"Because Colonel Paxton owes someone a favor."

Nathan held out a hand to me as I climbed out of the helicopter on unsteady legs, one hand clutching my *katana*. My legs weren't the only shaky thing about me. My stomach turned one or two more gentle somersaults even after my feet hit the tarmac, and the *whupwhupwhup* of the rotors throbbed unpleasantly through my head. Helicopter travel has been on my shit list ever since a copter I was on was sabotaged and went down in zombie-infested San Francisco.

"So we're paying Paxton's debt? Hardly seems fair."

"It's not," Nathan agreed. "But it's SOP in corporations and the military."

"Huh?"

"Standard operating procedure."

"Evidently so are acronyms," I muttered.

Nathan grinned. "Why do you think I went off the grid for so long?"

Nathan's one of those rough-hewn but handsome types who could be anywhere between forty and sixty. When he smiles it knocks at least ten years off his age, and I can almost see why my mentor, Simone, likes him.

"Now stop bitching and let's get going. We have people to meet."

Almost.

Our mission? Fly to a little island off Costa Rica to pick up Brock, the son of some Very Important gajillionaire industrialist or arms dealer or whatever. The kid was bitten when zombies breached the family compound and left for dead by the faithful family retainers during the subsequent evacuation. Only the kid didn't die.

Can you say very wealthy wild card?

When the dad—who'd been stateside doing business when the shit went down—found out his son and heir was alive and well, he immediately started pulling strings to get him out of Costa Rica. Those had to be some hefty strings to let him commandeer people from two of what were formerly top-secret security organizations—the Dolofónoi tou Zontanoús Nekroús and the Department of Military Sciences— to be what sounded like glorified babysitters.

Nathan and I were supposed to be meeting two operatives from the DMS. Colonel Paxton had told us they were hot shit. Okay, my words, not his, but honestly, he'd practically gone all fanboy when he'd talked about them. Not something I'd ever expected—or wanted—to see from our boss.

We walked across a reassuringly bustling airfield on NAS North Island, located on the far end of the Coronado Peninsula in San Diego. Thanks to quick thinking on someone's part, Coronado had been turned into a relatively safe zone by blowing up a section of the Coronado Bridge and putting up an effective blockade on the strip of land leading to Imperial Beach. The beaches were patrolled 24/7 to make sure no one infected with Walker's made it to shore.

"And there's our ride."

I followed the direction of Nathan's pointing finger and stopped short.

"You said there'd be a plane." I didn't bother to hide the accusation in my voice.

"That is a plane," Nathan replied calmly. "Oh. And the thing we flew in on? That was a helicopter."

Amazing how much sarcasm the man can impart without changing his inflection. You'd think I'd be used to it by now. Of course, you'd also think I'd be used to traveling via helicopter, as I'd had to do it at least a dozen times since the zombocalypse had started.

"I meant a real plane. Not a . . . a . . . a Tinkertoy." I gestured at the little plane sitting on the tarmac at the far end of North Island's military base. It looked like one of the toy planes my dad collected, not much longer than the copter we'd flown in on, and sure as hell *didn't* look sturdy enough for a trip to Costa Rica and back.

"Did I just hear her call my Porter a Tinkertoy?"

I looked up to see a burly black man wearing worn jeans and a green-and-black-checked flannel shirt walking toward us and giving me one hell of a hairy eyeball. He was flanked by two other men, one in his late twenties or so and the other somewhere in his thirties or early forties.

Both men toted an impressive amount of high-tech-looking weaponry, and both wore the type of camo meant to blend into forests and jungles, same as Nathan and me. They were also both blond, but that was the only physical attribute they had in common. The younger guy had to be at least six and a half feet, maybe taller. The very definition of corn-fed.

Assuming a metric shit-ton of corn was involved.

The other man wasn't as physically overwhelming, but he carried himself in a way that I'd learned to associate with people who could probably kick the shit out of 99 percent of the population. Kind of like Nathan. Same look in the back of the eyes that hinted of dark things that, once seen, couldn't be unseen.

Nathan shook hands with the black man. "Jack, good to see you. Ash, you'll be glad to know that Jack is one of the best pilots around."

"Damn straight I am," Jack growled, still giving me stink-eye.

Nathan turned to the shorter of the two blond men. "You must be Joe Ledger."

The man nodded. "And you're Nathan Smith."

They shook hands, one of those manly-men handshakes that had the potential to degenerate into an arm-wrestling match unless the men involved were both secure in their masculinity. No arm wrestling ensued and the testosterone levels in the atmosphere remained tolerable.

Ledger and his companion exchanged a brief look and I got the sense Nathan had just passed some sort of unspoken test.

"I'm Ash," I said brightly. Both men looked at me.

"You're Ashley Parker, huh?" Ledger's tone was neutral.

"Um. Yeah."

"Huh."

Another brief silent exchange between the two men.

Maybe I was feeling insecure, but I got the feeling I was not what he'd expected. Maybe someone taller?

Whatever, I didn't need to be a mind reader to know I'd most likely failed whatever exam Nathan had just aced.

"Statistics prove you're safer in a plane than driving in traffic," Corn-fed said. "You're a lot more likely to be roadkill than ground jam."

I stared without love at Mr. Corn-Fed-on-Steroids. His full name, if it was to be believed, was Harvey Rabbit, but Ledger called him Bunny.

"Aren't you supposed to be invisible?"

Bunny just grinned at me. He and Ledger sat across from me and Nathan in two of the plane's four passenger rows. Jack had modified the interior so the front and third rows were reversed to face the second and fourth rows, making conversation easier. It also made it a lot harder to ignore one's fellow passengers.

Thanks a lot, Jack.

To be fair, once Jack realized how deeply I hated flying, he had done his best to reassure me how safe I'd be in his beloved Porter by inundating me with statistics. Factoids involving takeoff and landing performance, payloads, airfoil, and other stuff that rattled around in my head like marbles in an empty can. I paid as much attention as I could, especially in regard to the location of a very tiny bathroom at the back of the plane.

At this point, all I cared about was that the Porter would get us safely from San Diego to Costa Rica and then back again ASAP. The shorter my in-flight incarceration with Joe Ledger and his man-mountain sidekick, the better. They made me feel totally incompetent—and kind of girly—just by their existence.

"So," I said, desperate to talk about something other than road jam, "other than friends in nose-bleedingly high places, is there a good reason this kid rates such kick-ass escorts?"

"The dad already sent a team to extract him," Nathan said. "They didn't come back and both the team and the kid have gone radio silent."

"Yeah," said Ledger. "If we're lucky, it just means communications went down. Some mechanical failure. Rust in the machine. Whatever. If we're unlucky, we're looking at the possibility that hostiles have taken over the compound and are holding the kid for ransom."

"What about zombies?" I asked. "I mean, if they overran the place once, no reason they couldn't do it again. And I personally would rather deal with zombies. They don't shoot back."

"What little intel we could get showed zombie activity in the jungles outside the walls," Nathan replied. "But none inside the compound itself."

The plane gave a sudden lurch. So did my stomach.

"Excuse me." I unbuckled my seat belt and made my way to the bathroom.

When I opened the bathroom door five minutes or so later, I was less queasy but still defensive. So when I heard Ledger say my name, I stopped and eavesdropped.

"Does Ash know how to use those fancy blades of hers?"

"She's not bad with them," was Nathan's neutral response.

Gee, thanks a lot.

"She spent much time in the field?"

"If by 'field' you mean zombie-infested streets," Nathan said, "then a couple of months."

Ledger gave a noncommittal grunt that managed to convey how unimpressed he was with my credentials. "I'm just a little surprised she was chosen for this particular mission," he said. "I get me and Bunny. And you're an obvious choice. But I'm not quite seeing what she brings to the table, other than a weak stomach."

That was it.

I stomped over and stood next to his seat, glaring down at him.

"Are you one of those MRA types who thinks I should be cooking and all pregnant and shit?"

"Here we go," Nathan muttered.

Ledger raised an eyebrow. "Did I say that?"

"You implied it," I snapped. "I get it. You're a real manly man, built the Eiffel Tower with brawn and steel, and all your furniture is rich mahogany."

"You forgot all of my leather-bound books."

I glared at him. I hate being one-upped on my pop-cultural Tourette's. "Oh, come on," I snapped. "You don't think I can do my job because I'm a woman."

"Actually," Ledger said with infuriating calm, "some of the best combatants I've known have been women. Women who've trained for years and, in some cases, been through hell to achieve their skills. You've been training for a couple of months."

Even though I'd been through my own version of hell, I couldn't argue with him and Nathan didn't seem inclined to say anything else in my defense. So I did a modified Jan Brady, turning and stomping two feet to the row of seats behind Ledger and Bunny, where they couldn't see me.

Nathan dropped his voice, but I still heard him. Wild-card hearing and all. "One of the reasons Ash was chosen was because Brock's supposed to be difficult and his father thought he might respond better to an attractive woman. Ash is good with people." He paused. "Usually."

I didn't have to be a wild card to hear Ledger's snort, followed by, "Well, this mission is screwed."

You're a poo, Ron Burgundy, I thought.

"Trust me," Nathan said. "She handles herself well under fire."

Semimollified, I huddled back into the semicomfortable seat, popped two Dramamine, and did my best Hicks impression, falling sound asleep within minutes.

"Ash, wake up."

"I'm fine," I mumbled. "Don't need to stretch my legs."

This was the second time someone had tried to wake me out of my Dramamine-induced sleep. The first was when we'd made our first stop to refuel somewhere in Mexico. I'd ignored them then and tried to do the same now.

"Ash. You have to wake up."

Someone shook me by the shoulders.

"We have to jump."

My eyelids flew open and all cobwebby sleepy thoughts vanished. Ledger's face was inches from mine.

"You've got to be kidding," I said. "Tell me you're kidding."

He gave a small shake of his head.

Shit.

I scanned the plane. No Nathan, no Bunny.

Instead there was a man in black holding a nasty-looking firearm, business end pointed at me and Ledger.

He grinned at me. A really smug, ugly grin. I'd have wiped it off his face if not for the aforementioned firearm.

Well, shit.

"Where's Nathan and Bunny?"

"Last time I saw them was when we stopped to refuel. I left the plane for five minutes. When I came back, they'd been replaced with our friend here."

My heart stopped.

"Are they alive?"

Ledger nodded. "For now. But if we don't do what this asshole says, that could change at any time."

I had a million questions, but enough common sense to not ask any of them other than, "What about Jack?"

The man with the gun sneered at me. "There's been a change of pilots, too, hon. Now get up." He jerked the barrel of his gun at me.

I looked longingly at my *katana* and M4, both propped against the seat next to me, and the man shook his head. "Don't even think about it, sweetheart. Besides, you don't wanna be lugging all that shit when you jump."

"C'mon, Ash." Ledger helped me to my feet. For the first time I noticed he had a parachute strapped to his back.

"You've got to be kidding me." I looked at Ledger, hoping against hope this was some really over-the-top macho fraternity-type hazing.

He shook his head again. "He's not joking."

"But I've never skydived before," I said, as though that would make a difference.

Asshat laughed and said, "Time for a crash course, hon. And you'd better hurry 'cause you crazy kids are running out of time. You jump in the next minute and you've still got a thousand feet of airspace to deploy. Every minute you waste, you lose a hundred feet. Wait five minutes and I figure you two'll be lawn darts when you hit the ground."

This had to be a nightmare.

"Where's my chute?"

Ledger said, "We've only got one chute."

My heart raced, the sound pounding in my ears like bongos played by a meth-head. "No, really."

"Hey, if you've never done this before, you're better off this way." Asshat smirked at me. "You guys get a chance to get all close and personal right off the bat."

Both Ledger and I shot the man the bird simultaneously. First thing we'd agreed on since we'd met.

Asshat gestured us to the side with the gun. "You've just lost a hundred feet."

Fuck fuck fuck.

I looked up at Ledger. "You've done this before, right?"

"Yeah. Not a big fan, but I'll do my best."

"Hey, I'll try not to barf on you on the way down if you get us there safely." I tried to keep my voice from shaking, but failed miserably.

Ledger put a hand on my shoulder. "Okay. This is a BA-18 parachute. It sacrifices comfort for quick opening. In other words, there's gonna be a jolt. You need to be ready for that."

"I really don't wanna die," I whispered.

"You won't. Wrap your arms around me and hook them through the harness. Hold on as tight as you can."

I did as he said, looping my hands and wrists around the chute harness as tightly as possible. My stomach lurched.

"Eight hundred feet."

Oh, for the chance to wipe the grin off the bastard's face . . . with an extra-strong Brillo pad.

"You're gonna have to jump with me." Ledger's tone was quiet yet urgent. "When it's time to jump, don't make me drag you. We're gonna need to get the chute open ASAP, which means we need to work together. Hold on tight, try not to panic, and we'll make it okay."

"Promise?"

"As much as I can."

The asshat with the gun gestured at Ledger. "Open the door."

"What? You're not gonna give us valet service?"

"Funny guy. Oh, yeah. Here. You'll need this." He tossed what looked like a small black cell phone at Ledger, who caught it easily and pocketed it after a brief glance.

The pounding of my heart almost drowned the sound of the wind when Ledger opened the door. The plane bounced as wind flooded the cabin, increasing the turbulence. I tried not to look at the carpet of greenery some eight hundred feet below.

"Seven hundred."

Fine. Seven hundred feet below. But I couldn't help looking. Trees, lots of them, interspersed with splashes of aqua and brown.

DANA FREDSTI

"God, I don't want to do this."

I didn't realize I'd spoken out loud until Ledger gave me a reassuring squeeze with one arm.

"Look at the bright side," he said into my ear so only I could hear him.

"There's a bright side?"

"He's not making us use a raft."

I gave a choked laugh. I hated *Temple of Doom*. "If you call me Willie, I will kill you."

Joe looked at me. "You ready?"

"No fucking way." I took a deep breath, then exhaled. "Let's go."

"Good."

"Six hundred feet." Asshat tapped his wrist in a *time's a-wasting* gesture.

Ledger tossed a salute toward Asshat and shouted, "Nice try, Lao Che!"

My laugh turned into a scream of terror as we jumped.

Ever been on one of those rides at an amusement park where you wait in line for an hour and then are basically hurtling to the ground in free fall?

This was so much worse.

At least I didn't pay money for it, though, right?

I kept my eyes squeezed shut and held on for all I was worth, which, considering my wild-card strength, was worth quite a bit. Even so, when the chute deployed, the jolt nearly dislodged my grip. I managed to keep hold of the harness as we resumed our drop at a somewhat more leisurely pace.

Maybe we'll live through this after all, I thought, clinging to Ledger like a baby koala with separation anxiety.

Then we hit the canopy of trees. Branches whipped against my back, legs, and arms. It stung even through the fabric of my shirt and pants. I kept my face buried against Ledger's chest to avoid getting an eye poked out.

Then our descent stopped with a bone-rattling suddenness. Something wrenched my right arm with white-hot pain and the back of my head collided with something hard—

And the lights went out.

* * *

I woke up to a throbbing pain in my right arm, a headache, and the all-too-familiar sound of moaning as something pawed at my feet.

If it's Tuesday, it must be zombies.

I opened my eyes slowly, waiting for the initial wave of dizziness to subside before checking out my surroundings.

I was sprawled over a branch, my right arm still wrapped around Joe, who dangled from the parachute canopy spread out in the tree limbs above us. My wrist was still entwined in the harness and the weight of Joe's inert form threatened to dislocate my shoulder.

I carefully extricated myself and took stock of my situation.

Head. Aching, but no double vision or residual dizziness.

Arm. Sore, but nothing that would slow me down if I needed to use it.

Attitude. In dire need of an adjustment.

Sense of humor. MIA.

I looked toward the ground, where a half dozen extra-gooey and rapidly decaying zombies gathered beneath us, flesh oozing off the bones in the tropical heat.

One of the zoms, a tall, skinny one wearing nothing but the tattered remains of blue board shorts, kept batting at my dangling feet. Thankfully it fell short an inch or so from being able to get a good grip and pull either of us down.

"No lunch for you," I growled, and pulled my feet up.

Sweat trickled down my forehead and in between my breasts under the Kevlar. The humidity was through the roof, and the temperature, even in the shade, had to be in the upper nineties. My ears buzzed and at first I thought it was a side effect from the fall. Then I recognized the sound of insects.

Lots of them.

"And people pay to come here on holiday?"

"Most people stay in nice villas or hotels by the beach."

I turned back to Joe, who was now awake and evidently nonplussed at being treed above a bunch of zombies. He rubbed the back of his head.

"You okay?" I asked.

"I'll live," he said. "You?"

"I am profoundly grateful to not be a red smear on the ground about now," I replied. I paused and then added, "Thank you."

He grinned. "Thanks for not barfing on me."

DANA FREDSTI

Something chirped in one of his pockets. He pulled out the little black rectangle Asshat had tossed him before we'd jumped.

"Is it a phone?" I asked hopefully.

Joe shook his head. "Looks like some kind of a GPS device. A little more high-tech than your typical geocaching gadget."

"That's the adult version of a treasure hunt, right?"

"Yup. And it looks like someone's sending us on one." He pointed to two black dots on the screen. "This is us." His finger indicated a set of coordinates. "And that's whatever we're supposed to find. Looks to be in the general vicinity.

"Gotta get down from here and past this bunch first."

I smiled and patted the *tanto*, still sheathed across my chest. "Allow me to show you what I learned in my two months in the field."

It didn't take me long to clear out the zombies. They were in pretty crappy shape, what with the hot and humid climate, and they stank to hell and back.

Joe let me do my job without argument. When I'd finished the last zombie, he climbed down from the tree. He looked around and gave a nod. "Good job."

I shrugged, trying to hide my pleasure at his approval.

He looked at the GPS and set off on a rough trail of sorts through the overgrowth. I followed, still holding my *tanto* while keeping my eyes on the ground and my ears open for the moans of the walking dead. For the time being, though, all I heard was a gentle chorus of frogs mixed with the ever-present buzzing of insects, punctuated by the occasional bird and monkey call. A black-and-yellow snake slithered across the path and a line of leaf-cutter ants scurried back and forth on a branch, carrying sections of leaves four or five times their size. Large flowers splashed vibrant colors against the green-and-brown background of the jungle.

The whole effect was kind of cool and even pretty, but the heat and humidity were soul-crushing, and there was no shortage of mosquitoes and flies attracted to the sweat now streaming down my face, neck, chest, and back.

"It's like the Tiki Room at Disneyland," I commented as we walked. "Except in hell."

Joe snorted, then gave a satisfied grunt. "Here we are."

A tangle of colorful flowering vines mostly covered a large white sealed bucket. Upon closer inspection, it proved to be a detergent container, probably purchased at Costco.

Joe studied it for a minute, then reached into the tangle of vines and pulled it out by its metal handle. He popped the top off to reveal two bottled waters, two protein bars. Joe held up the bars with a disgusted look. "Atkins?"

"Well, yay for our waistlines."

He checked the bottles, then tossed me one. The seal was still intact. I twisted the lid off and sniffed the contents, then took a sip.

Pure, sweet bottled water.

Joe raised a dubious eyebrow as I munched happily on one of the peanut-butter chocolate bars. "You like this shit?"

I shrugged. "I went through the whole no-carbs phase when my ex told me I needed to lose twenty pounds. I kind of developed a taste for these."

"Your ex is an asshole."

"I won't argue that point."

The GPS starting beeping again.

"Another set of coordinates," Joe said.

"Maybe this time it'll be pizza and Coke."

We walked for another hour or so without talking, the effort of forging through the thick foliage and uneven terrain using most of our spare oxygen. The ground was covered with roots, ferns, and all sorts of plant life, some of which were equipped with sharp thorns. I tried not to think of snakes and spiders hanging from the ever-present tree limbs.

Honestly, this is a vacation destination?

I guess if one could toss out the crocs, mosquitoes, and such and just focus on the admittedly gorgeous butterflies and assorted birds and mammals, it was kind of understandable. But the heat alone was enough to make it a no-go for me. Give me fog and redwoods any day.

Sweat dripped down my forehead, my back, and in between my breasts. The heat was brutal, and even though I tried to make my bottled water last I found myself down to the last inch in what seemed like no time.

"You should save some of that," Joe cautioned.

I knew he was right, but I was so damn thirsty I didn't care. Still, I capped the bottle, leaving that last precious inch inside.

The GPS beeped. Joe studied the coordinates and led us through an impossibly thick grove of large-leafed trees that brought to mind dinosaurs. The smell was thick and vegetal, with an underlying tang of decay wafting from the ground. Our feet crunched on mulched leaves, dying flowers, and—

My right foot punched through something, the impact releasing an odor I was way too familiar with.

Ah yes, dead zombie.

"That's just nasty," Joe said.

I pulled my foot out of a female zombie's abdomen, the flesh falling off my boot like pulled pork after a day in a slow cooker. It wore the remains of a peasant skirt and tank top. Its eyes were still open, milky corneas sunken into yellowed, blood-streaked whites. One of the signatures of Walker's. A single gunshot wound punctured its forehead.

I wondered who'd shot it way out here in the middle of Cannibal Holocaust territory. Before I could say anything, the GPS got mouthy again and Joe pointed toward a tree a few feet behind me, where another white bucket hung suspended from a low-hanging branch.

"I'll get this one."

I stepped toward the bucket, feeling something brush against my ankle.

Three things happened at once.

Joe yelled my name.

A rotted hand clutched my shin and I slammed down hard on my hands and knees. My *tanto* skittered off a few feet away.

Something swept over me with a *whoosh*ing sound and slammed into the tree in front of me, where it stuck.

The owner of the rotted hand gave a plaintive moan. I looked down and saw another gooey zombie, a female, in the remnants of what was once probably a very expensive white linen dress. Maggots wriggled happily inside three large puncture wounds in its chest. It reached for me, gaping mouth releasing several buzzing flies.

Just when I thought things couldn't get any grosser or more stinky.

I used my free leg and shoved the thing away with one kick of my booted foot, retrieved my *tanto*, and put it out of my misery.

The cache itself looked harmless enough. It sat in the middle of a clearing on top of a log. Just a wooden crate latched shut.

Further investigation showed no trip wires and no Rube Goldberg–type booby traps. I still didn't trust it.

"What do you think?" I asked Joe.

He gave the crate a sharp rap on the top with his knuckles and was answered by a muffled moan.

We looked at each other, and then Joe kicked the crate off the log with enough force to splinter the lid and disengage the latch. The crate landed on its side, the lid bouncing open to disgorge the contents.

A head rolled out onto the ground along with a few oblong objects wrapped in plastic. Several large, disgruntled tarantulas scurried out as well. I swear one of them hissed at us before skittering into the undergrowth.

The head came to a stop, facing us. Impossible to tell if it had been a man or a woman when alive, it had a half-eaten tarantula in its mouth, several hairy legs drooping over the zombie head's chin.

No wonder the others had been so pissed off.

I put a blade through the head's brainpan and picked up one of the plastic-wrapped items.

"Twinkies?"

Joe and I looked at each other.

"Oh, come on." He shook his head. "Think someone's seen *Zombieland* a few times?"

"I hate Twinkies," I said glumly.

"Cool. I'll be Tennessee and you can be Cleveland. 'Cause, y'know, I like Twinkies and I'm sensing you can be a bit of a bitch."

I was about to retort but noticed something sticking out of the crate. "Hey, there's something else in there."

Joe took a look and gave a little whoop. "Now we're talking!" He reached down and plucked the object from the crate.

"What is it?"

"A KA-BAR." He held up a leather-sheathed knife that had to be more than a foot long, including the handle. "This'll come in handy."

Thunder cracked and suddenly the skies opened up to release a torrential downpour. The kind of rain that fell in sheets rather than drops and made it impossible to see more than a few feet in front of you. I held my water bottle out for a free refill and enjoyed the feel of the rain sluicing the sweat and dirt from my hair and body. Joe did the same, but only after retrieving the Twinkies and squirreling them away in his pockets.

The rain stopped as suddenly as it had started. Joe and I trekked through more jungle in what was now an oddly companionable silence, listening to the ever-present sounds of birds, monkeys, and frogs, along with the occasional zombie moan and the now familiar beeping of the GPS.

It was only about fifteen minutes before the beeping sped up.

"I think we're close," Joe observed.

"You think?"

"That's sarcasm, right?"

I grinned. "Ya think?"

The beeping sped up, like R2-D2 on speed.

"Definitely hot."

I followed Joe as he followed the GPS into a grove of what I thought were banyan trees, with big arched roots that vanished into brackish, brown water. A river.

Joe knelt on a patch of damp earth and examined a dark burrow at the base of a large banyan. The roots looked like some Cthulhian nightmare, wood tentacles intertwined and frozen in midwrithe.

"You really gonna stick your hand in there?" I peered dubiously into the dark hole, visions of Peter Jackson's version of the insect life on Skull Island dancing in my head.

Joe must have had similar visions because he pulled out his KA-BAR.

After unsheathing it, he poked the business end of the blade into the hole, immediately rewarded with a sharp metallic sound. Nothing squealed, hissed, or moaned. This was a good thing.

Joe poked around a little more. Nothing came scurrying, crawling, or slithering out of the burrow, so Joe reached into the hole, pulling out an olive-drab metal container about the size of two lunch boxes.

"It's an ammo case," he said.

"Ammo doesn't usually slosh, right?"

He set the box down on semidry ground next to the root and flipped the latch up with the knife, opening the case the same way. Miracle of miracles, nothing exploded, and no poisonous snakes, spiders, or frogs slithered, crawled, or hopped out.

Joe dumped the contents on the ground.

Two more bottled waters, more energy bars, and a party-sized bag of potato chips, which Joe snatched up before I could touch it.

"You're gonna share, right?"

He ripped the bag open, grabbed a handful of chips, and then held the bag out to me.

Junk food had never tasted so good.

"Seems to me," he said in between bites of salty, greasy goodness, "that whoever set up this gaming board doesn't want us dying too quickly."

"Gaming board?"

Joe nodded. "Haven't you noticed? This whole setup is like one big *Dungeons and Dragons* game. You find treasure in one room, and traps in another, and—"

The water in front of us exploded in a geyser of brown-and-white foam. Joe threw himself into me, knocking me to the ground as a reptilian nightmare snapped huge jaws shut in the spot where I'd been kneeling seconds before.

A scale-plated tail thrashed, spraying mud and water all around, and what had to be at least a ten-foot crocodile twisted around faster than anything that size had the right to move. I just knew it was looking for me. I lay on my back in shock, stunned at the impact of Ledger and the jungle floor, not to mention the sight of this thing bearing down on me.

Before its jaws could close on my leg, Joe grabbed it around what passed for its neck, looking like something on the cover of an old *Men's Adventure* magazine. All torn shirt, muscles, and . . . well, crocodile wrestling. Croc and Joe rolled over in the mud several times before Joe managed to shove the point of the KA-BAR in one of the thing's eyes.

It thrashed for a few seconds, churning up mud with its tail and feet in its death throes before finally subsiding into stillness. Joe lay sprawled with the croc across his thighs and hips, one arm still looped around the croc's neck, the other hand still holding the handle of the KA-BAR. When the croc didn't move after a good five minutes, Joe finally unclenched his grip, still half-pinned by one very heavy dead reptile.

"You really did build the Eiffel Tower out of brawn and steel, didn't you?" I observed.

Joe shot me the bird without bothering to look at me.

I heard the moan before I saw the zombie dragging itself on its stomach out of the water. It had been a well-built man, the sodden remains of khakis and a black T-shirt still clinging to its body. Its degloved fingers grabbed Joe's ankle, using it to haul itself out of the mud and water with a squelching sound. One of its legs was missing below the knee, deep gouges in the thigh where some nasty-ass teeth had dug in.

Joe gave a surprised and disgusted yelp and tried to pull his leg free from Swamp Zombie's grasp, but couldn't manage it what with being pinned by however many pounds of dead croc. It would be difficult for the zombie to bite through the leather and khaki covering Joe's lower parts, but there was plenty of exposed meat on his arms and torso, and I had a feeling the zom smelled blood. Joe tried to pull his KA-BAR from the croc's eye socket, but it was wedged in too tightly for him to extract from his position.

My turn to save *his* ass.

I rolled to my feet in what I'd like to say was one smooth movement, but what was in reality an awkward, painful lurch. Just as the thing opened its mouth to sink green moss–covered teeth into Joe's shoulder, I jammed my forearm into its mouth, giving a yelp of pain as it chomped down right above the Kevlar guard into my wrist. I grabbed my *tanto* and jammed the point into one rotting ear before the zombie managed to tear out a piece of flesh.

"Son of a bitch," I muttered as it flopped down across Joe and the croc.

I shoved it off to one side, then lifted up the tail end of Mister Croc so Joe could extract himself. He then grabbed the hilt of his knife, braced one foot against the zom's body, and pulled the blade free.

"You've been bit."

I shrugged. "Occupational hazard."

"You've been bit!"

The *we're truly fucked* tone in Joe's voice made me look up. The knife in his hand and regretful expression on his face made me step back.

"You're not planning on using that on me, right?"

"I've seen what this shit does to people, Ash. It's almost as bad as being eaten alive. Do you really want to go through that?"

"Wild card, remember?" I peeled back the sleeve of my right arm and held it out for Joe's inspection. The scars of my original bite mark were still clearly visible.

"A small percentage of the population is immune to this shit," I added. "A very small percentage."

Joe shook his head. "I guess I thought it was too good to be true."

"Well, I wouldn't call anything about the process 'good' other than the not dying part. It hurt like hell."

I retrieved the water bottles and held one out to Joe. He ignored it in favor of checking out the corpse. He flipped it onto its back, the movement accompanied by a slight jingling. Then he yanked the dog tags off Swamp Zombie's neck, studied them up close, and then looked at me.

"Well, shit. Say hello to a member of the last team."

This was not a good thing.

"How did he die?"

Joe shrugged. "Far as I can tell, a croc got him. No bullet or knife wounds."

"And his teammates?"

"Either zombies or croc chow about now, I'm guessing."

"Do you think this"—I gestured at the croc—"is part of the game?"

"Given the placement of the cache?" Joe gestured toward the estuary. "I'd say it's the equivalent of rolling the dice and either getting lucky or getting eaten."

"But why?"

Something glinted in a beam of sunlight that had managed to sneak through the trees. It was a very small video camera hooked up to a branch.

Somewhere, someone was watching us.

Joe shook his head. "Just when you thought reality TV couldn't get any worse."

I stared at him in disbelief. "This kid's parents have influence with the DZN and DMS. So this rescue mission has to be a legit one, right? I mean . . ."

My voice trailed off as Joe shook his head. "It may have started out that way, but it doesn't mean someone else hasn't stepped in."

"One of your enemies or one of mine?"

He shrugged. "You tell me. I have a few."

"I thought I'd killed mine," I said.

Joe gave a laugh that held little amusement. "Don't you hate it when they keep coming back?" He dug in his pocket and then groaned.

"What?"

Silently he held out the GPS, which looked as though it'd been stomped. Or possibly rolled on by a very heavy crocodile. I stared at it.

"Well, shit."

"Yup."

"So what now?" I asked.

"Find the kid and get the hell out of the jungle before it gets dark. And if we see any more cameras?" He took out his knife, reached up, and shattered the lens with one solid blow. He smiled grimly and finished, "Smash the shit out of them."

Joe's plan seemed simple enough, but it turned out to be one of those "easier said than done" types of things. The jungle seemed endless and both Joe and I suspected we were, if not going in circles, at the very least retracing our steps. Our worst fears were confirmed when we found ourselves at the edge of the banyan grove. Several of the dead croc's buddies had dragged its corpse down to the water and were chowing down on it.

"Let's keep going," Joe said in an undertone.

I nodded silently, blinking back tears of frustration. Then I froze as I heard the unmistakable sound of footsteps somewhere close by. Not the shambling, staggering gait of a zombie, either. These footsteps were even and purposeful, and headed in our direction.

I grabbed Joe by the arm, pointed in the direction of the footsteps, and then pulled him behind a clump of trees where we'd be hidden from view but could see anyone or anything approaching. To his credit, he didn't argue or question my actions, and by the time we'd taken cover, the footsteps were clearly audible.

Two tough-looking men in jungle camo and combat boots strode into view, both armed with rifles. They stopped midstride and cursed in Spanish when they saw the crocodile convention at the edge of the water.

One of the men pointed to the broken camera up in the tree and cursed again. I recognized the words *hijo de puta* and nudged Joe in the ribs.

"That's you," I mouthed.

The other man pulled what looked like a replacement camera out of a canvas bag slung across his shoulder and tried to hand it to his buddy, who shook his head vehemently. I didn't blame him—the old camera was mounted in a tree uncomfortably close to the feeding crocs.

They argued for a few minutes until the second man reluctantly set his rifle against a log, took the camera, and cautiously approached the tree, his attention on the reptiles. Meanwhile, his pal trained his own firearm on the crocodiles.

Which meant neither of them was paying attention when Joe quietly snuck out from cover and snagged the discarded rifle.

"*¡Hola, amigos!*"

Both men whirled around, the first raising his rifle to shoot. Joe beat him to the punch, however, firing two shots in rapid succession that hit the man in the chest and sent him staggering backward straight into the crocodile buffet. He screamed amid the grunts and roars of at least a half dozen crocs fighting to get the best bits while their food was still alive.

Joe trained the rifle at the man with the camera, who stood frozen in place.

"You're gonna take us back to your boss now," Joe said in a deceptively casual tone.

The man evidently understood English because he snarled something along the lines of "Go fuck your mother." I was pleased I'd retained something from my high school Spanish classes.

Joe smiled. It was the kind of smile that made smart people run in the opposite direction. This guy was not smart.

He spit something else that hadn't been covered in Spanish 101. Joe responded by putting a round about an inch above his head.

"Try again."

"He'll have me killed!"

"Maybe," Joe said calmly. "Maybe not. But I'll shoot you in the kneecaps and leave you here with your friend." He pointed at what remained of the man's partner.

The man blanched, his skin growing pale under his tan.

"So," Joe said. "You wanna take us to your leader?"

Less than a half hour later we stood outside of a ten-foot wall, hidden in the deepening shadows of twilight as our new buddy unlocked an iron gate. There was a driveway and a motorized gateway big enough for vehicles, but we wanted a less conspicuous entrance.

As soon as the gate was unlocked, Joe gave our friend a sharp rap on the back of the skull with the butt of his rifle and left his unconscious body outside the wall. I raised an eyebrow at that and Joe shrugged.

"He'll either wake up before a zombie finds him or he won't. It's more of a shot than he would have given either of us."

"Works for me."

Joe locked the gate after us. We found ourselves on the edge of a large courtyard with a large-roofed carport across the way. At least a dozen guards patrolled the area.

"How do we get past these guys?" I whispered.

Joe grinned. "Allow me to show you what I've learned during *my* time in the field."

"Nicely done," I said. I wondered briefly if any of the guards Joe had put down would be getting up again, and then decided I didn't give a shit.

Joe gave a small nod. "Whoever planned all this may be smart, but he or she didn't make allowances for his game pieces to break the rules."

"That sounds oddly profound," I commented.

"I know." Joe looked pleased with himself. "Next I'll be opening up my own line of fortune cookies." He pointed toward a doorway in the carport. "This way."

With one last admiring glance at the trail of devastation Joe had left behind us, I dashed after him through the door. Sometimes it's nice to not be the only badass in the village.

I guess I was expecting all sorts of James Bondian villain traps, like sensor-activated laser-beam death rays and stuff, so the inside of the compound was bit of a letdown. Lots of high-beamed ceilings and tiled floors in a classic Spanish-style square, with a courtyard in the center, the better to keep the structure cool in the oppressive Central American heat.

We found what—and who—we were looking for at the back of the square. Two more armed guards stood on either side of double doors, looking all serious and tough and like something out of *Commando*, but thankfully without the tacky leather and chain-mail getup the villain had worn.

I hate tacky villains.

I didn't bother offering assistance, instead hanging back and watching Joe make yet more flunky hash out of the poor suckers standing guard. Once again, he made it look like no big deal, like Bob Ross painting happy little trees in seconds. Except kicking butt instead of painting.

Okay, analogies are not my strongpoint.

Once the two guards were made happy little unconscious guards, Joe and I snagged their M4s. Joe made an *after you* gesture at the doors. I grinned and went inside in my best *I'm a stealthy ninja* imitation.

I was expecting a roomful of more armed guards, but the room appeared to be empty except for a bank of security monitors, each showing a different jungle location.

Joe held up a finger in front of his mouth and then pointed across the room.

Seated in a replica of Kirk's captain's chair on the *Enterprise* was a kid in his midteens who looked as if he were going through a particularly awkward adolescence. Shock of dark hair falling over an acne-studded forehead. Slightly overweight in a doughy way, with an unhealthy pastiness that screamed too many video games and too much junk food.

Like the Twinkie he held in one hand.

It could only be Brock.

Oh, that little motherfucker. . . .

Brock frowned as he stared at one of the screens . . . which was conspicuously blank. He hit a button and the screen went from blank to a close-up of Joe and the butt end of his knife. It re-rewound farther to show an unpleasantly familiar location—the tree and estuary where Joe and I had nearly been snacks for Crocozombie. The entire fight for our lives played out in high-speed reverse as we watched. Then, with a push of a button, the speed slowed to real time and we watched the whole thing from beginning to end.

"Totally awesome," the kid said, giggling.

Can you say psychopath?

He frowned as the tape went blank again.

"That should be up again by now. Stupid assholes. Dad was right. Can't trust these stupid natives to do anything right. Oh well." Brock shrugged and went back to viewing the screens, stuffing another Twinkie in his mouth.

"Come on, I know you're out there, Ledger," he muttered, pushing buttons on the console in front of him, the video feeds changing with each push. "And where's that tasty ass of yours, Ash?"

Tasty ass?

Oh, this little fucker was *so* going down.

"I'll handle this," I told Joe.

"Be my guest."

I marched over to the console behind Brock and spun the chair around so he faced me. I yanked the headphones off his ears, leaned in close, and growled, "I'm right here, you little shit."

Brock gave a yelp and fell out of his chair, landing hard on his out-of-shape, not-so-tasty ass. He stared at us in outraged disbelief. "How did you get in here? You're not supposed to be in here! I'm totally gonna fire all my stupid guards."

I grabbed him by his shirtfront and yanked him to his feet. "And you're not supposed to try and kill the people sent to rescue you."

He smacked my hands away and glared at me. "I didn't ask to be rescued. I like it here. Besides, Dad only wants me back because I'm a stupid wild card."

I grabbed him by his shirtfront again and shook him. "Did you kill Nathan and Bunny?"

"No," he said with a note of petulance only an entitled teenager could summon. "They're locked up until it's their turn to play."

"Play? You've killed people!"

The little creep had the nerve to shrug as if his little half-assed Hunger Games were no big deal. "You guys are supposed to be good. You're supposed to be the best. That's why my father sent you, right? Because you're the best. The last ones he sent weren't that good. So they died."

My eyes narrowed. "You're gonna show us where Nathan and Bunny are. Then we're gonna get a plane here to take you back to California. Although I'd rather leave you here with the crocs."

"How about you stay here with me?" Brock looked me up and down in a way that made me long for a steaming hot shower. "You. Me. That tasty ass of yours. We could—"

I coldcocked the kid with a right cross that knocked him out and back into his captain's chair. He'd be out for a while.

Joe gave me a thumbs-up and grinned. "What do you know, Ash. You really *are* good with people."

ABOUT THE AUTHOR

Dana Fredsti is an ex-B-movie actress with a background in theatrical combat (a skill she utilized in *Army of Darkness* as a sword-fighting Deadite and fight captain). She is the author of the *Ashley Parker* series, touted as *Buffy* meets *The Walking Dead*, as well as what might be the first example of zombie noir, *A Man's Gotta Eat What a Man's Gotta Eat*, first published in *Mondo Zombie* and edited by John Skipp, and more recently published as an e-book by Titan Books. She also wrote the cozy noir mystery *Murder for Hire: The Peruvian Pigeon*, is coauthor of *What Women Really Want in Bed*, and has written several spicy genre romances under the pen name Inara LaVey. Additionally, Dana has a new urban fantasy series, *Spawn of Lilith*, with Titan Books, the first coming out in 2017. She also has a story in *V-Wars 4: Shockwaves*.

ATOLL

BY JONATHAN MABERRY

THE PIER

DEPARTMENT OF MILITARY SCIENCES SPECIAL PROJECTS OFFICE
PACIFIC BEACH
SAN DIEGO, CALIFORNIA
SATURDAY, DECEMBER 5, 2:11 PM

"Something has crashed on an island south of Hawaii," said Mr. Church, frowning at me from the videoconference screen in my office.

I was not dressed for a teleconference. I was wearing ancient, ragged board shorts and a Hawaiian shirt with images of old fifties roadside diners on it. My feet were bare and propped on the edge of my desk next to an open take-out box of Wahoo's fish tacos. Five empty bottles of Gift of the Magi golden ale I'd brought back to the Pier with loving care from the Confessional in Cardiff-by-the-Sea, just up the road. The Magi has spicy hops balanced with moderate malt sweetness and an aroma like nuts and honey. It also has 12 percent alcohol and I was on my sixth.

It's entirely possible that Church did not have my full and undivided attention.

Two teams of enthusiastic and talented college women were playing volleyball outside of my office window and I had Art Pepper blowing cool jazz from the four Bose speakers in my office. The Pier was nearly deserted except for me, my big white shepherd, Ghost, and a few disgruntled employees who had to man the battlements on a gloriously warm Saturday in December. Quite frankly I couldn't care less if Air Force One had crashed in my own parking lot.

"As I recall," I said, "we have a field team in Honolulu. They love playing with boats. Send those guys."

"I did," said Church.

"And . . . ?"

"We've lost all contact with them."

I sat up. "What?"

"They are the third investigating group to have visited the island since the crash," he said. "Following the crash, the Coast Guard tried to contact members of a small Nature Conservancy research team on the island, but they were unable to make contact via radio or satellite. A Coast Guard cutter was dispatched and they launched a drone for flyover. The live feed from the drone terminated as the aircraft crossed into island airspace. Contact with the cutter was lost within minutes. A navy ship, the USS *Michael Murphy*, an Arleigh Burke–class destroyer, was within three hundred miles and it sent in a Seahawk helicopter, which has since vanished along with its crew of six. This occurred four hours and ten minutes ago. The *Michael Murphy* was ordered to maintain station fifty nautical miles from the island until the DMS can send a team."

"What do we know?" I asked. "Do we have an eye in the sky on this yet?"

"Yes," said Church after the slightest pause. "And that's why this has been handed over to us."

The screen split into two windows and the second showed a good-quality satellite black-and-white image of Palmyra. Church explained that it was one of the Northern Line Islands, and was about a thousand miles due south of the Hawaiian Islands and about a third of the way between Hawaii and American Samoa. The nearest continent was thirty-three hundred miles away. Nicely remote.

Palmyra Atoll is in the middle of nowhere. Seriously. Nowhere. The whole thing was a bit over four square miles, with sand and forested land wrapped around a seawater bay. It might have once been pretty, and parts of it still were, but it was scarred by a long trench that started from the southeast tip and drove inland for half a mile. Sand had been pushed up on either side of the trench, speaking to the force of the impact, and there was evidence of a forest fire that destroyed a lot of palm trees. The trench was shaped like a big spoon, with the bowl part of the spoon being the final impact point.

In the center of the bowl was an object.

Big. Triangular. And definitely not a chunk of space rock.

I recognized that shape and it immediately turned me cold frigging sober and dropped the temperature of my blood to that of ice water.

"Holy shit," I breathed.

"Yes," said Church.

"It's a T-craft."

"Yes," he said. "But it's not one of ours."

"Whose?" I demanded. "The Russians? The Chinese?"

Several of the world's superpowers had been conducting a very quiet arms race to launch triangular-shaped craft like this, based on technologies recovered from places you might have heard of. Kecksburg, Rendlesham, Roswell. Like that.

Yeah.

Exactly like that.

Church said, "I don't believe this craft is of local manufacture."

An hour later I was on my private jet, heading to Hawaii. My two most experienced and reliable shooters, Top and Bunny, were with me. And Ghost. All of us rushing headlong to a place where no one seemed to come out.

I hate my job.

-2-

ABOARD THE USS *MICHAEL MURPHY*
FIFTY NAUTICAL MILES NORTH OF PALMYRA ATOLL
SATURDAY, DECEMBER 5, 6:01 AM

The captain of the destroyer was a friend of a friend of a friend, but that didn't make him a friend of mine. In fact, he was pretty frigging unhappy to have me and my team delivered like an unwanted pizza onto his aft deck in the middle of a bad night. The fact that we were pretty damned unhappy to be there made it a real party. At least we'd changed into attire more appropriate to one of Uncle Sam's clandestine Special Ops gunslingers—black BDUs without any trace of unit patch or rank insignia. I offered no credentials to the deck officer and was not asked for any by Captain Tanaka. We shook hands, but there was no warmth in it.

He studied us for a long, silent time. First Sergeant Bradley "Top" Sims was a forty-something stern-faced black combat veteran who looked as if he could eat live crocodiles. He smiled exactly as often as he wanted to, which wasn't all that often. Master Sergeant Harvey Rabbit—known as "Bunny" by everyone including his parents—was a six-and-a-half-foot-tall white kid who looked like an Iowa farmhand but was really a surfer and volleyball player from Orange County. They had joined the DMS with me and we had walked through all kinds of hell together. And I use the word *hell* a lot less metaphorically than I'd like to. Our after-action reports could qualify as horror short stories, or so we've been told. Ghost was 105 pounds of combat-trained attitude, and after losing six teeth in a battle in Iran, he'd been gifted with titanium replacements. He loved showing those gleaming fangs to anyone he doesn't like, and there are a lot of people he doesn't like. He wasn't overly fond of Captain Tanaka.

We stood in a cluster and endured the officer's inspection, allowing him to draw whatever conclusions he wanted from our appearance, our lack of credentials, and our presence. Tanaka's only comment was, "Well, this should be interesting."

Not said with a smile.

He knew our combat call signs and addressed me as "Cowboy," which meant that he had been briefed. The DMS does not have any official rank in the U.S. military command structure. We operate on a very special and highly secret executive order that gives us extraordinary powers and freedom of action. The captain had been contacted and told to offer us every assistance and cooperation. He did that. He hadn't been ordered to be warm or fuzzy, so we got none of that. And for the record, experienced captains of ultrasophisticated guided missile destroyers do not, as a rule, like having someone else come in to solve their problems. Particularly where their own crew members are involved. His ship carried everything from Tomahawk missiles to Harpoons and lots of other goodies, and the crew of three hundred enlisted men and twenty-three officers were among the finest in the service, which made them easily world-class. In almost any other circumstance, Echo Team would have been, at best, a mildly annoying bit of extra baggage or, at worst, a useless pain in the ass. A good case could have been built either way.

This was not one of those other circumstances.

And in every way that mattered this was my case anyway. There was a standing order that all incidents involving T-craft or even *suspected* T-craft were to be handed over without pause or interference to the Special Projects Office of the Department of Military Sciences.

To me.

That order had been put in effect following the Extinction Machine case, in which a rogue group of DARPA called Majestic Three had built a small fleet of T-craft using taxpayer dollars but for very private purposes. The man behind all of that was Howard Shelton, and that fucking maniac had wanted to use the craft to start, and win, World War III. You see, Shelton had discovered a fact that eluded the other superpowers involved in the recovered-technologies part of the arms race. While their experimental T-craft kept exploding every time one of the engines was fired, Shelton figured out how to stabilize the ships. Doesn't sound like too big a thing until you step back and look at what's happened when T-craft have exploded over the last thirty years or so.

The engines were typically built in remote spots, far away from prying eyes and in areas where large amounts of hydroelectric, nuclear, or geothermal power was available. The energetic discharge from an exploding engine delivered a blast several orders of magnitude larger than the apparent fuel. It was a kind of zero-point energy that has resulted in some of the world's biggest natural disasters. Mount St. Helens. The tsunami that slammed into Japan. The massive earthquakes in China. Like that.

Shelton figured it out. The trick was to play a long game and breed pilots who had a small percentage of DNA from "other sources."

Yeah, E.T. phone home. You get the point.

The biomechanical connection allowed the ships' engines to stabilize. Shelton then rigged his ships to kill the pilot as soon as a T-craft was over a target city. Like Beijing or Moscow. He launched his ships to force a confrontation that began with the demonstration of a weapon so powerful that the other nations could not risk fighting a war like that. A fully powered T-craft could stroll past any fighter jet in existence because it used alloys based on what was learned from stripping the wreckage of alien craft. Fiber optics, microminiaturization, and other sciences in common use have quietly benefited from those same technologies. Even Velcro.

Sure, some urban legends are true.

The DMS went after Shelton and took him all the way down. However, the ship he sent to destroy Beijing was destroyed by someone else. We never met them and I'm very, very cool with that. An eloquent message had been conveyed to us to turn over all materials related to the development of T-craft. Or else.

The "or else" part was scary as shit. We did, and E.T. went home. No good-byes, no wet, sloppy kisses with our friends from wherever.

Actually, we never really found out where they were from. I had a theory, but I was pretty badly concussed when I came up with that theory, so no one has leaped up to say that I solved one of the great mysteries of the ages.

That was all years ago. Since then things have been very quiet. UFO sightings around the world have dropped considerably, except in cases where people are seeing drones, actual weather balloons, airplanes, the Goodyear Blimp, or other ordinary things.

Side note, I fucking *hate* drones, but that's beside the point. What matters is that reliable sightings of saucers, T-craft, mother ships, the Death Star, *Firefly*-class space freighters, X-wing fighters, and the starship *Enterprise* have dwindled to a precious few. Which has made everyone in the know sleep a little more soundly.

Past tense.

Now we had a T-craft crashed onto an island in the middle of the South Pacific.

"We've had no contact with anyone since the object crashed," said Captain Tanaka. "And except for the one image that was sent to you, we've had nothing from the satellite."

"No images?"

"No telemetry, no feed, no signal. If it's up there we can't find it."

Bunny murmured, "Oh, shit."

"Yes," Tanaka agreed dryly. "Though I was hoping for a bit more than that from you fellows."

Tanaka was a middle-aged man who looked fit enough to run a marathon while carrying me on his shoulders. One of those guys you can't even imagine with a hangover, love handles, or a hair out of place. Steely eyes and a hero jaw. Made me feel like a grubby beach bum with indifferent hygiene.

"Was there any evidence that your chopper crashed?" asked Top.

"No. Same goes for the Coast Guard drone. There is apparently some kind of line out there near the beach, and once something has crossed it all transmission ends. I sent a drone in to circle and photograph the island at a distance, standing half a mile beyond the surf line. We have lots of pictures of burned trees and mounds of dirt, but we can't get a good angle on the object from that distance. We don't know how firm the dead zone is, or even if it is still active, because orders came down to wait for you."

I met his stare and said, "And that wasted almost a full day where you don't know if your people are injured and in need of assistance. I get it, and I'm sorry, but this situation is complicated and sensitive."

"And clearly above my pay grade," he said, barely hiding his contempt of any policy that did not allow him to protect his people.

"Yes," I said, "it is. I'm sorry for the inconvenience and the obfuscation but—"

"But you're not really sorry."

"Frankly, Captain, I'm sorry any of us have to be out here, but this is how it is."

Top and Bunny both muttered, "Hooah," under their breath. Ghost *whuffed*.

Tanaka took a moment and I could see the muscles bunch and flex in the corners of his jaw. He had a lot of control and knew enough to think and compose his thoughts before he opened his mouth.

"Let me know what you need from me and I'll make it happen. Weapons, equipment, people . . ."

"Thanks," I said. "We brought our own toys. What we need is a boat and a whole lot of rope."

"How much rope?"

"Enough to run a line from a second boat out in the water to the one I'm going to take all the way in. This might be a stable or repeated null field."

Tanaka frowned. "Wait . . . like what was used two years ago?"

I nodded. A rogue CIA agent had gotten his hands on a man-portable device capable of canceling electronic power within a certain range. Unlike the EMP cannons DARPA was developing, this did not destroy electronics but merely interrupted them.

"You think someone on the island has Kill Switch technology?" he asked.

"That," I said, "would be best-case scenario."

He gave me a funny look. "What exactly do you *do* in the DMS?"

"Mostly?" I asked. "We get the shit scared out of us on a regular basis. Better than a high-fiber diet, but my blood pressure could pop rivets on a submarine hull."

-3-

The *Michael Murphy* carried two RHIBs, or rigid-hull inflatable boats, that could zip across the water with great speed and surprising grace. Bunny was good with boats, but not as good as the chief running the second RHIB. Top and I had our rifles ready and we studied the shoreline through sniper scopes. Saw a few seabirds and a turtle, but nothing else.

Bunny asked, "If I say that it looks quiet, will one of you cats say, 'Yeah, *too* quiet'?"

"If I wrap an anchor chain around you and drop you in the water, will the cap'n cry the blues?" was Top's reply.

Bunny grinned.

When we were five hundred yards from the beach, the chief cut his engine and stopped, but we kept going, spooling hundreds of yards of thin line behind us as Bunny drove toward the beach at reduced speed. The counter on the spool on the chief's boat would record how much line had paid out before we hit whatever electronic barrier was present. I was surprised that we made it all the way to the mouth of the lagoon before the engine died. There was no sputter, no spark trying to catch inside the motor. One second the engine was running normally at fifty knots and then it wasn't. Just like that.

"Now we know where the fun and games start," muttered Top.

"Just like with the Kill Switch," observed Bunny.

The day became very quiet very fast.

Bunny had to wrestle for steerageway and used a passive rudder to angle us in toward the shore. There was just enough impetus to allow him to beach the nose of the boat; Top and I jumped out and dragged it onto the sand. Ghost bounded out past us and ran up and down the beach like a silent gust of white smoke, then he returned to me and sat. It meant that he detected no immediate threat. Not sure if that was a good thing or not. We all moved toward the shelter of a stand of palms.

Top tapped his earbud and shook his head. Mine was just as dead, not even the white noise of an empty channel. Nothing. We checked all of our electronic gear and it was all down.

Bunny made a rude noise, then said, "If some ISIL dickheads are out here with one of those Kill Switch machines, I'm going to get cranky."

"You'll have to wait your turn," I said.

Even my flashlight didn't work, which wasn't much of a problem because the sun was up. I looked out to sea and saw the other boat about half a mile beyond the farthest point of the island. The faint thrum of its idling engine drifted to me on the humid morning air. They would keep the engine on to allow them to maintain a safe distance. There was a quick two-pulse flash of light as a signal. I stood up and waved my arms three times to indicate that I was safe. Then I turned and moved into the dense foliage, vanishing from their sight. Not, I hoped, from history.

The island was not big enough to get lost on, which meant it was small enough to get found on. So, I was very damn careful as I made my way along the southern reach of it, staying inside the trees, pausing to listen. Hearing nothing. Not a bird, not a bug. Nothing but the sway and hiss of palm fronds moving in the sluggish breeze. Ten minutes in, I heard a sharper hiss and looked up to see a flare rise in an arc from the direction of the other RHIB. It popped high above me and stained the sky with green smoke. It was intended to both signal any survivors on the island and draw the eye away from the beach—away from us.

Without saying a word, we moved, spreading out, weapons up and ready, eyes and gun barrels moving in unison, fingers laid along the outside of the trigger guards, going fast but no faster than good caution allowed. Ghost ranged ahead but not too far, and if there was something to see, he didn't see it. That was comforting, but only if you didn't look too closely at it. Just because a dog didn't see, smell, or hear something did not mean it wasn't there.

We swept along the strip of jungle fifty feet in from the sand, using the slanting rays of morning light to pick our way.

Top was on point and he stopped with a raised fist. Bunny and I immediately knelt, alert and ready. Top pointed to something ahead and off to our right, then gestured for us to approach. We came up on it quickly.

It was the Coast Guard RHIB, a seventeen-foot Zodiac Hurricane with a 100-horsepower diesel engine and M240B machine guns mounted fore and aft. Very fast and fierce.

It sat on the sand. Empty, abandoned, undamaged.

There was no one there. Not even footprints in the sand. No sign at all of what happened except for something Ghost found. He jumped into the craft and stood growling at something I couldn't see until I climbed in. Top and Bunny provided cover in case it was someone or something nasty hiding there. It wasn't.

On the back of the pilot's seat was a muddy handprint. Full palm and fingers.

Only here's the thing. The fingers were way too long and each finger ended in wickedly sharp points.

And there were four of them.

I'm not talking about a hand with a missing finger. What we saw was a handprint of something that had a thumb and three fingers. Three clawed fingers. Like a bird's, except that's not what it was.

All the hairs on Ghost's back stood up in a stiff row. The hairs on the back of my neck did the same thing. Ghost growled at the handprint and took a slow, fearful step backward.

I looked from the print to Bunny and then to Top, and then we all slowly turned and looked at the thick wall of shadow-filled forest.

"Fuck me," whispered Bunny.

"Don't touch that shit," warned Top.

I almost laughed. "There is not one chance in ten trillion that I was going to do that."

We backed away and then climbed out of the boat. We all wanted to talk about that print, maybe we *needed* to. We didn't. Instead we moved off down the beach and then edged back toward the trees. The jungle seemed a lot less inviting now than before. Instead of seeming to offer cover it had a feeling of occupation to it, a vague presence that was impossible to define. Could have been my imagination running hot after seeing that print on the boat. Just as easily could have been my rational mind wondering why in the wide blue fuck I was on this island and in this line of work. I used to be a cop in Baltimore. Not once in all those years on the force did I encounter a four-fingered monster handprint. It's not the sort of thing you tend to encounter, even in Baltimore. Made me long for a boring life of being shot at by gangbangers and cartel *pistoleros*.

I was on the island right now, though, and tough as they were, my men looked to me for guidance, for leadership, for the kind of stoic toughness that makes great copy in speeches about Special Operations. So I kept my poker face in place and shifted to take point. Top yielded that position without argument.

Inside the wall of the forest the ground was a soft mixture of sand and soil, with many palm fronds knocked loose by the crash. As we moved, we began to smell the stink of burned foliage and torn earth. There is a distinctive smell to land that has been torn by cataclysm, be it a bomb, an earthquake, or a plane crash. The richer soil is ripped up and exposed to the air, releasing microparticles of nutrients and rotting plant matter, and infused with it are the smells conjured by great heat. Of silica sand fused into glass and wood burned to charcoal.

We did not find a single human footprint. Nothing to indicate what had happened to the sailors from the boat we'd found. No prints, no shell casings to indicate a fight. Nothing, and that was very spooky.

I stopped the team because Ghost suddenly crouched low and bared his teeth. Thirty feet in front of us was a thick tangle of vines draped between a stand of pines and an ancient overgrown aloe plant. I couldn't see anything, but Ghost did. His titanium fangs gleamed with reflected sunlight, making it look as if he had bitten down on raw fire. His eyes were fixed, unblinking as he stared at a spot just behind the stiff, serrated aloe leaves.

I felt it then.

That strange, unnerving sensation of being watched. Not suspecting that you are. *Knowing* it. I snugged my rifle stock into my shoulder and aimed at the aloe plant. At what was behind it.

It's such a strange feeling, and your conscious evolved mind wars with the instincts of the lizard brain as to whether to believe it or not. Good soldiers don't ignore those kinds of feelings. I may fail at a lot of important things in my life, but I am a good soldier.

We shifted around and found cover, each of us kneeling, aiming, waiting, straining with our senses to justify what we *knew* was there. The jungle was unnaturally still and even the soft slosh of the waves on the sand was muted. The breeze died as if the world held its breath, silencing the whisk of palm leaves and the creak of tree trunks. It was a silence so complete that you become unnaturally aware of your own shallow breathing, certain that it is far too loud, that it can be heard all the way across the forest floor, that it draws the ear, the eye, and the aim of whatever weapon is seeking you from the shadows.

There was no good play here. If we fired, we could hit someone hiding in fear, and that could be a sailor from the navy or Coast Guard, or one of the scientists from the nature research team. Or maybe we'd be firing at a bunch of plants and trees and accomplish nothing more than revealing our location and our numbers. Or we could hit one of *them*. Whatever they were.

I signaled my guys and sent Top cutting left in a wide circle, indicating that Bunny should go right down to the sand and circle around behind the trees. I'd wait for them to get into position and then go up the pipe. They moved off, though I could see from their expressions that they didn't like the plan for the same reasons I didn't like it. But there was no better way to play this.

Cold sweat trickled down my back between my shoulder blades and zigzagged over the knobs of my spine. Ghost was still crouched low, still caught in that animal zone where fear and anger are the same thing. I could relate.

Top and Bunny reached their points and gave me nods.

I moved first, went in with my own zigzag, cutting left and right to make use of natural cover and spoil aim. Ghost was right at my side because I did not want him to rush into a blind spot like that without my eyes on him.

"Cowboy!"

I heard Top yell out my combat call sign, but it came one-half second too late. The whole front of the forest seemed to move, to pulse outward toward me as if it were a door someone was kicking open. The huge aloe plant crashed into me before I could even think about stopping. There was no time to evade, no time to brace. There was only time to feel it.

It was hard.

It hurt.

It was like a tidal wave of plant matter and it struck me with enough force to knock all the light out of the world.

-4-

I was nowhere.

It was the strangest feeling.

I had a body and I was aware of it. Breath wheezing in and out of my bruised chest. The gunfire rattle of my terrified heartbeat. The pain of shocked and abused skin. The ache of muscles.

But there was something missing.

There was no downward pull. It's something you never take notice of day to day. The pull of gravity. You feel lead-footed when you're tired, but otherwise it's normal to be tied to the earth, to be pulled into standing, sitting, falling, lying down.

Not now.

There was no actual sensation of gravity, not in any specific direction.

I've never been in space, but I've been in a reduced-gravity aircraft. A vomit comet, they call them. They're fixed-wing aircraft that provide a brief near weightless environment for astronaut training. Hollywood uses them for making movies about space travel.

It was like that.

But not like that.

In reduced-gravity aircraft you feel your skin become rubbery, your hair and clothing tend to float on you. I could feel my clothes hanging normally on me, as if gravity applied to that but not to me. Which made no sense at all.

It was absolutely pitch black. So dark I had to blink to make sure my eyes were even open.

No sound. I was neither hot nor cold. No sensation of air passing my skin, no wind. Nothing like that.

A smell, though, and a taste to go with it. Metallic, like copper. And a bit of ozone, like after a lightning strike.

"Hey!" I yelled, and my voice was strangely distant, the way it sounds when you're in a wide-open place and there's no wall to bounce or trap your noise.

Yelling did not help, but it gave me something to do. I could hear my own voice, so I kept yelling. It was a long, long time before I heard another sound. I think it was a long time because time itself had no meaning for me.

A voice spoke. Male. Heavily accented, but it was a kind of American accent I'd never quite heard before. New England, but not. A rough voice, used to yelling in order to be heard.

"Captain, there's a reef two points off the port bow," called the voice. "A mile or less. God's love and we'd have struck 'em if we hadn't dropped anchor last night."

I listened for more, but that was it. There and gone.

"Hello!" I yelled, then as I replayed what the man had said, I tried, "Hello the boat."

Nothing.

"Ahoy the ship."

I'm not a sailor, but I hoped that was the right thing to say.

Nothing.

I drifted in nowhere.

Maybe I fell asleep. Maybe I just stopped thinking. No way to know, but I was jarred to awareness by the unmistakable sound of something heavy and wooden smashing into something immovable. Men screamed. Many men. I could hear the pop and snap of cloth. Sails? People cursing and calling orders out to shorten this and belay that and plug something else. Lots of nautical terms that I barely understood, and the gushing sound of water rushing in where it wasn't supposed to be. Even a landlubber like me could figure it out. A ship had hit the reef of the island.

Right?

I remembered seeing the reef on the chart, but the RHIB had hydroplaned over it and Bunny had steered us around the fangs of rock that had jutted out of the water. The destroyer was steel and I doubted they had any wooden boats aboard. Why would they? This was the age of metal, of plastic and rubber.

So what was I hearing?

The men screamed and called out for help, yelled orders, cried out to God and their mothers, and gradually, gradually, the voices faded as if drowned by the sea. But it wasn't the sea that took the voices away. It was the nothingness in which I floated.

I tried to make sense of it.

Was I dead?

Was I in a coma? Or dreaming? Or, had I finally gone mad? All of those were real possibilities with me.

Sounds came and went. The creak of oars and the splash of the oar blades in the water. Men slogging through surf. Laughing, joking, telling stories. None of it made sense, though. They talked about whales. They talked about the brown-skinned girls of Hawaii, but they spoke of them in the rude exaggerations of simple men to whom such things were rare and magical. Some of the voices were American, though crude and strange; and some were clearly British. One of the men said something about making a legal claim for Queen Victoria, and that made no goddamn sense at all.

Queen Victoria?

Jesus H. Christ.

I slept again.

And woke when someone kicked me in the ribs.

-5-

"Aufstehen!"

The voice growled it as he kicked me again. Harder.

I twisted away and sand shifted under me and all at once there was light. Not much of it. Moonlight spilling down and painting everything around me in silver. I saw two figures standing above me, silhouetted against the moon. Men. Big, young, broad-shouldered. Wearing black skin-diving outfits. Fins and old-fashioned tanks lay on the wet sand.

"We bist du?" said one of them, and all at once I realized two very strange things.

The first problem was that they were speaking German in a tense, secretive whisper. The man who'd told me to get up and asked who I was. I understood it; I'm good with languages.

I was less good with the second thing I realized.

Their equipment was wrong. Very wrong. The one who kicked me held a Gustloff Volkssturmgewehr semiautomatic rifle. It was a classic example of a weapon known as a *Volkssturm* rifle, a "people's assault" rifle, a cheap last-ditch kind of gun used in combat in the final months of World War II. The other guy held a Luger. Not the modern P38 used in Germany nowadays. No, that might have made a fraction of sense. This was the older model, the one collectors prized and hundreds of U.S. soldiers smuggled home after the fall of Berlin. A P04 or maybe the P08. Hard to tell because it was dark, I was scared, and there was a cheap-looking silencer screwed into the barrel.

So, here we are. A couple of big blond guys with new-looking antique gear. The wrong moon in the sky. What the actual fuck? At that moment I was pretty sure the world had fallen off its hinges and that I was in deep shit. The two men weren't tourists. These weren't gun nuts that got lost at sea. And they weren't amused to find me.

Crazy as it sounds, crazy as it *felt*, I was absolutely certain I was a lot more lost than I thought. This may have been Palmyra Atoll, but I was lost.

They were Nazis.

-6-

PALMYRA ATOLL
TIME AND DATE UNKNOWN

I smiled my very best *I'm not your enemy and the world isn't bug-fuck nuts* smile. They seemed to expect me to raise my hands, so I obliged.

"Wer bist du und was machst du denn hier?" demanded the man

with the Luger. He had the officer look, expecting to be answered at once.

Who are you and what are you doing here?

The rifleman gave me an evil look and said, *"Amerikanisch."*

They were not happy at all with the thought that I was an American. Although I could speak German, I was pretty sure there was going to be some kind of need for a code word, which I did not have. On the upside I wore no insignia or other markings. Nothing in my pockets other than a folding knife clipped to my inner right-hand trouser pocket, some nonfunctioning electronic doodads, and the SIG Sauer P226 Combat TB snugged into my shoulder rig.

The moment was surreal.

The moon was full and bright, and when all this insanity started it was bright morning. Last night's moon had been a sickle slash of a crescent. So there was that. The island—what I could see of it in the moonlight—was different. I was on the same part of the beach where we'd stopped by the aloe plant and knot of palm trees. There were plenty of aloe plants, but none of them were the right size or in the right place. The trees looked strange, none of them squaring with my memory of the landscape I'd traversed with Top, Bunny, and Ghost.

The officer ticked his head toward me and barked an order to his companion: *"Suchen seine kleidung."* Search his clothes.

The rifleman stepped forward to pat me down. He paused for a moment, staring at the handgun I wore. Even in bad light he had to know it was a model he'd never seen. There wasn't much I could say that would turn this situation in my favor. These cats were up to no good, and if I played it wrong I was going to die on this beach.

I kept my hands up and tried to look dumber, shorter, and slower than I am. The rifleman switched his gun to his left and reached out to take the SIG while his boss kept the Luger trained on me.

That's where they made a mistake.

As soon as the rifleman grabbed the polymer grips of the handgun, I pivoted my body real damn fast, clamping his hand to the gun with my left and shoving him hard with my right. It put his body between me and the Luger and I ducked and drove, using his center-mass as both shield and battering ram. The Luger barked twice and I could feel the impact of the bullets punching into the rifleman, knocking wet coughs from him. I rammed the dying man into the officer and they went down hard onto the sand. Unfortunately, I caught a glimpse of my SIG Sauer flying from the rifleman's hand, turning over and over as it spun through the air and then landing barrel first in the wet sand. Shit.

No time to worry about it, though, because the officer was quick and much stronger than I thought. He shoved the rifleman to one side and came up off the ground with a disheartening degree of rubbery agility, the Luger still in his grip. There was a fragment of a fragment of a moment open to me and I took the long reach and knuckle-punched the back of his hand. The Luger fired and the bullet tugged at the loose fabric of my upper inner left thigh. Half an inch more and I'd have been singing castrato in the celestial choir. His gun vanished, but the German did not gape or hesitate. Instead he punched me in the face with a pair of rapid-fire jabs that loosened the light bulbs inside my brain. I staggered back and tripped over the rifleman's outstretched ankle. I went down just as something silver whipped past my face. I turned the fall into a backroll and came up on fingers and toes, spitting blood from my mouth, and saw the knife in his hand. It was another relic of a war that ended decades before I was born. A brass-handled German navy diver's knife. Twelve and a quarter inches overall, with a wickedly sharp seven-and-five-eighths-inch blade. Sturdy and lethal. He came at me, moving well and low, nicely angled and well-balanced, with the blade shielded by the other hand, doing it all the right way, very smooth and professional and deadly.

I pushed off the ground and danced sideways as I reached for my own knife. The Wilson Tactical Combat Rapid Response folder sprang out of its holster and thudded into my palm and I flicked the blade open with a snap of my wrist. The German saw the knife and smiled. My blade was only three and a half inches long.

I smiled, too. There's a reason I prefer the shorter, lighter weapon. It's so light that it puts no drag on my hand speed. He darted in, trying to close the deal with a fake lunge and high short-slash across my throat. He was good and the tip of that knife nicked the point of my chin as I lunged back, but I caught him, too. The key to good fighting is never purely attack or purely defend. There needs to be elements of both in play, otherwise the fight is too long and too fair. As I slipped his cut, I whipped my blade in a very tight slap down across his forearm. The speed and force of his own attack added cutting length and depth to my counter.

A stupid fighter pauses to admire his work. In the movies there's an exchange of witty taunts, or there's banter. In the real world, it's all about killing the other guy as quickly and efficiently as possible. I had a moment, so I took it. His lacerated nerve endings tricked him into recoiling from my cut, and I followed that reflex movement with an attack, elbow-checking his injured arm, cupping my hand around the back of his neck, stepping my right leg in around the back of his leg, and leg-wheeling him down to the ground while my blade chased his throat down and cut him from ear to ear.

Very quick, very messy. His heart stopped beating and the arterial spray hissed down to nothing. I pivoted toward the rifleman, saw a dark bubble form between his parted lips as he struggled to breathe. I clamped a hand over his mouth and corkscrewed my knife into his heart, felt him settle back, removed my hand as he let out a last wet breath against my palm.

The whole fight took about two seconds. From when the rifleman had tried to frisk me, call it five. Fights should be short or you're one of the dead ones on the ground.

I cleaned my blade on the rifleman's clothes and my hands in the surf. My SIG's barrel was choked with sand but I holstered it anyway. Something caught my eye and I peered out to sea and saw moonlight glinting on the conning tower of a submarine. A U-boat? Probably.

I think that's when the shakes hit me.

I'd survived the moment, but this wasn't *my* moment.

There was no reason to stay where I was, so I moved along the beach, running fast in the cold moonlight, trying to find my way out of here.

It took only a few minutes to run to the end of the atoll and then I skidded to a stop. That end of the island was mostly flat and sandy, with trees rising up from the middle of the arms that reached around a kind of small bay. I expected to find nothing but empty sand and dark trees.

That's not what I found. I stood staring at something that continued to shove the world toward a steep drop-off into the impossible.

The T-craft was there.

It lay in a bowl of ruptured earth at the end of the long impact trench, with burned and shriveled trees on either side of it. But that couldn't be. The moon was wrong. There was a German U-boat in the water and I'd killed two Nazi frogmen. It was night instead of day.

Then I heard a sound behind me, and as I turned, I knew whatever it was could not be good. It wasn't.

A ship rose up on night-black waters and then slammed into the hungry teeth of the line of sharp volcanic rocks. Not a World War II submarine. Not a modern navy destroyer. This was an old wooden ship. A brig, I think, though I'm no expert in sailing ships of the nineteenth goddamn century, and I'm pretty fucking sure I was watching one tear its guts out on the rocks. The impact jerked the hull to a stop with such force that several masts snapped, dragging rigging and sails down. I saw men fall, heard them scream as they hit water or stone or debris.

Then behind me a dog barked.

I whirled.

And there was Ghost, running from the exploding forest wall, chased by bits of torn aloe and palm. Top and Bunny dove for cover and I stood there like a goddamn idiot, too shocked to move, or speak.

Or duck.

A big piece of tree trunk slammed into me and I was gone.

-7-

PALMYRA ATOLL
TIME AND DATE UNKNOWN

It was the sound of metal clanking on metal that woke me.

I opened my eyes and realized that I wasn't stretched out on the ground or hanging in zero gravity. I was on my feet. Daylight was warm on my face and there were insects buzzing in the humid tropical air. The greens of the surrounding forest were very green. Intensely so. Unnaturally bright, as if lit from within each leaf. The same with the blue water I glimpsed through the trees, and the sky above was eye-hurtingly vivid.

The metal clank sounded again and I turned. My body was strangely leaden, as if I were sleepwalking. I saw Top and Bunny. I saw Coast Guard and navy. A couple of marines, probably from the *Michael Murphy*. But there were other people, too. Men dressed in clothes from some weird mix of History Channel wardrobe department. Heavy coats with embroidered cuffs and fringe epaulets, barefoot bearded men in ragged shorts and simple shirts, Germans in the uniforms of the Kriegsmarine, people dressed in lab coats and others in casual sailing clothes from throughout the last century. There were at least three hundred of them.

They each held a tool of some kind. Some of the tools looked vaguely like wrenches or drivers or hammers, but many were so strange that I could not even guess at their purpose. Everyone who held a tool, though, seemed to know what to do with it. All across the bowl of the impact point, all around where the T-craft lay, men worked. Some carried pieces of metal or plastic, but most were hard at work doing repairs on machines. And again, I had no idea what any of the machines were. Some were of metal, but most seemed to be blends of metal, plastic, cloth, and something else, something that pulsed and throbbed and looked as if it were alive. Maybe it was alive.

The T-craft was propped up on some kind of hydraulic struts, and as I watched, Top and Bunny helped two German U-boat sailors lift a glowing device into place and hold it there while a navy helicopter pilot, still wearing his helmet, set to work with a kind of spot welder.

It was then that I realized I was not standing still. I looked down at my legs and saw them moving, walking. And I saw my hands. There were tools in them. A long, flat device with curling wires sticking out of one end, and a pair of something that looked like pliers but had bright blue glowing pads on it. I watched myself walk over to where a piece of machinery lay on a plastic pad near one of the hydraulic jacks; I felt myself kneel; I stared as my hands went to work on the device, using the tools with a precision and efficiency that did not belong to me.

I was aware, somehow, of being watched, but not by the other men. Or by Ghost. Or, in fact, by anyone I could see. It was as if the watcher were inside, looking out through my eyes. Watching me work but also studying me. There was some dried blood on the back of my wrist, a few drops I'd missed when I'd washed in the seawater. I raised my arm—or, *it* raised my arm—and I felt my nostrils flare as I sniffed. As *it* sniffed. My mouth spoke a single word.

I can't spell it or repeat it because the word did not fit into my mouth. It was too awkward, too strange, better suited for the construction of some other kind of throat. And even though it was a word in a language I had never heard before, I knew what it meant.

Savages.

I knew as surely as I know anything.

My hands returned to their work.

The day passed. Seconds into minutes into hours.

I don't remember when I fell asleep. I don't remember when the lights went out. I don't remember floating away.

-8-

PALMYRA ATOLL

SATURDAY, DECEMBER 5, 7:19 AM

Ghost woke me up.

He nudged my face with his muzzle, whined. Licked my nose and mouth. Barked once. He did everything short of bite me.

I woke up.

It was still daylight. I blinked and looked at the sun. Low on the horizon. Sunset? No, that was impossible. We were on the wrong side of the atoll for that.

We . . .

I realized that I was in the RHIB with Top and Bunny. In the water of the entrance to the lagoon. Drifting, turning slowly in the sluggish current. Ghost stood over me, staring at me with frightened brown eyes. He barked again, loud and sharp, and it chipped away a big chunk of my stupor. I sat up.

Top and Bunny were groaning softly, turning over as they moved upward from sleep to that pre-wakefulness where dreams and reality have no perceptible difference. I looked at my hands, my arms, expecting them to be badly sunburned, or covered with cuts from the debris from when the aloe plant and trees exploded. I looked at my palms, expecting to see calluses and blisters from using those tools for so many hours.

But, no.

"*. . . to Cowboy . . .*"

A fragment of sound in my ear made me jump, and I looked around.

The second RHIB was out there five hundred yards from the beach. The line snaked over the edge of our boat and vanished inside the seawater until it reappeared over their gunnels. Another sound made me jerk and suddenly a helicopter rose from behind the trees. A big

Seahawk painted with navy colors. It wobbled in the air, then it rose and moved away from the island.

I heard the call again. It was Captain Tanaka calling me from the USS *Michael Murphy*. Top sat up slowly and held his head in his hands. I looked at my watch. It was running again. The last time I'd checked it was right before we crossed the dead zone. It had been 7:19. I watched the digital timer go to 7:20. At first I thought that it was simply starting up again, but when we compared our watches to those of the chief on the RHIB and the chronometer on the ship, they matched perfectly. As if no time had passed.

On the beach, I saw a handful of people come out of the jungle. Coast Guard and scientists from the conservancy station. Wandering a little as if dazed, but finding their footing. They stopped when they saw me. We all looked up at the helicopter, and then one by one we turned and looked toward the southeast end of the island. We could not see the burned trees or the torn ground. Not from that angle. But I knew what we would find there.

Nothing.

Not a goddamn thing.

Only the scar on the atoll. Only the memory in our minds.

I stood up in the boat and ran trembling fingers through my hair, trying to understand it. Trying to convince myself that it had been a dream. I knew—absolutely knew—that we would not find sailors from any antique ships. No. Not anymore. I glanced over to the spot where I'd fought and killed the two Nazi agents. The sand was smooth and undisturbed, as if no foot had stepped there in many, many years.

So it was what? A dream? Some kind of shared fantasy? A hallucination brought on by forces as yet to be understood? Magic mushrooms blooming? Some kind of virus? Some freaky weather thing that affected our brain chemistry?

Somehow all of those implausible theories would find their way into reports filed by the different agencies and branches of service involved.

I knew different, though. We all did, though as the day wore on and the debriefings began, most of the people on the island said that they couldn't remember. None of them were willing to say so while hooked up to a lie detector, though; and no one made them.

The thing that bugs me, though, and the item that anchors me to that little spit of land a thousand miles south of Hawaii is this: There are three dots of blood on the sleeve of my shirt. I had them tested. They're not mine.

I knew they wouldn't be.

We flew back to San Diego without saying much of anything.

I mean, what was there to say?

Back home Church asked us a thousand questions. So did Rudy. So did the navy. So did everyone. Everyone had questions.

But we did not have the answers.

Not then. Not ever.

POSTSCRIPT

The navy has since sealed off Palmyra Island. Access has been revoked for the Nature Conservancy and all other research organizations. Maybe that's an overreaction. Maybe there's nothing left. No threat, no weirdness, no nothing.

Maybe.

But, really, would you want to take that risk?

ABOUT THE AUTHOR

Jonathan Maberry is a *New York Times* bestselling novelist, five-time Bram Stoker Award winner, and comic book writer. He writes the *Joe Ledger* thrillers, the *Rot & Ruin* series, the *Nightsiders* series, the *Dead of Night* series, and numerous stand-alone novels in multiple genres. His recent novels include *Dogs of War*, the ninth in his bestselling *Joe Ledger* thriller series, and *Mars One*, a stand-alone teen space travel novel. He is the editor of many anthologies, including *The X-Files*, *Scary Out There*, *Out of Tune*, and *V-Wars*. His comic book works include, among others, *Captain America*, the Bram Stoker Award–winning *Bad Blood*, *Rot & Ruin*, *V-Wars*, the *New York Times* bestselling *Marvel Zombies Return*, and others. His books *Extinction Machine*, *V-Wars*, and *Mars One* are in development for TV/film. A board game version of *V-Wars* was released in early 2016. He is the founder of the Writers Coffeehouse and the co-founder of the Philadelphia Liars Club. Prior to becoming a full-time novelist, Jonathan spent twenty-five years as a magazine feature writer, martial arts instructor, and playwright. He was a featured expert on the History Channel documentary *Zombies: A Living History* and a regular expert on the TV series *True Monsters*. He is one-third of the very popular and mildly weird *Three Guys with Beards* pop-culture podcast. Jonathan lives in Del Mar, California, with his wife, Sara Jo. For more information, visit his website, www.jonathanmaberry.com.